"What—what are you doing?"

He smiled, his eyes hooded, the light in their depths provocative, sensual. "Making love to you, *cherie*."

There were many things she could have done: screamed, struck out at him, torn herself free from his arms and run. Instead she thought of the wedding night that was soon to come, of the man who would lie in her bed then, of that heartfelt vow made in silent anguish so short a time ago—that she would rather give herself to any other man. Any man at all. . . .

SURRENDER IN MOONLIGHT

Jennifer Blake

FAWCETT GOLD MEDAL • NEW YORK

A Fawcett Gold Medal Book
Published by Ballantine Books
Copyright © 1984 by Patricia Maxwell

Library of Congress Catalog Card Number: 84-90889

ISBN 0-449-12900-4

Manufactured in the United States of America

First Trade Edition: May 1984
First Mass Market Edition: October 1988

For my agent, Donald MacCampbell,
a Civil War buff who pointed out the
importance of the Nassau connection.

Chapter 1

The quick tread of Lorna Forrester's riding boots was muffled by the thick Kirman carpet runner as she moved along the wide hall. Without pausing in her stride, she slipped the loop that caught up the flowing fullness of the skirt of her blue-gray poplin habit over her left wrist, tucked her crop under her arm, and began to tug on calfskin gloves. There was a mutinous set to the finely molded curves of her mouth, and in her gray eyes a look of grim determination. She would not rest before dinner, would not lie in genteel fatigue upon her bed with warm milk punch at her elbow and a maid in attendance.

The passageway was dim with the failing light of late afternoon, a condition unimproved by the dark maroon brocade that hung on the walls or the peculiar green light of an April storm that threatened beyond the end windows. After the heavy meal at noon, the cool dampness and early twilight had driven everyone else to their bedchambers, or so it seemed. Lorna was not tired, not even after the long steamboat trip upriver the day before. In truth, she was too overwrought to rest. If she did not escape from Beau Repose and the people the great plantation house held, including her uncle and aunt, she might well succumb to the urge to scream and throw things. That would not be conduct at all becoming to a happy bride-to-be.

An inane giggling, high-pitched yet masculine, drifted on the still air. It came from an open doorway a few yards ahead of

1

her. Lorna recognized the sound. A spasm of what might have been dismay or disgust crossed her pale face, but her footsteps did not falter.

As she drew near the bedchamber from which came that grating laughter, a low moaning blended with it. Rich, female, the soft, panting moans took on a higher note. "Wait, Maste' Frank, that hurts now! Don't do that, Maste' Frank, just be nice. Please, I—oh, don't, don't!"

The import of the sounds, the words, did not immediately reach Lorna. It was only as she came even with the doorway that they took on meaning. In that instant, she glanced inside, and the breath was driven from her lungs in a startled gasp. She checked herself.

On the rumpled surface of the four-poster bed within the room, a man and a woman strained and heaved in a tangle of white and black limbs. It was Franklin Bacon, the man she was to marry, with one of the housemaids. That he was hurting the girl, digging his fingers into her hips and forcing her to take his hard, bestial thrusts, was immediately plain.

The soft sound Lorna made drew the attention of the pair on the mattress. Franklin reared up, staring, his pale blue eyes bulging in stunned, vacuous surprise. His reaction was slow; then with a strangled cry, he floundered, pushing from his partner, kicking her away. He scuttled sideways on the bed in obscene and hairy nakedness that showed too well his barrel chest and swollen belly above the short, powerful legs and the wet and strutted jut of his manhood.

"Lorna," he croaked, his voice rising behind her as she swung sharply away. "Come back! I ain't doing nothing. It's all right. You shouldn't have seen me, you shouldn't. You should have been laid down resting, like everybody else! Lorna? What'll Papa say? Lorna!"

She did not look back, though she heard him plunge out into the hall behind her. With her chin tilted and her face set in lines of tight control, she moved on along the hallway and down the great staircase. Her footsteps might have been a trifle fast, the hold on her crop a threat to her glove seams, but there was nothing else to reveal the agitation that gripped her.

As she neared the bottom of the stairs, a man emerged from a room that opened to the left, the paneled library with its rows of books. He stood frowning, watching her descent, a folded newssheet in one hand as if he had been interrupted at his reading.

"My dear girl," he said as she neared the bottom step. "What can be the matter? What is the shouting about?"

His voice was soothing, unctuous, indicating that he had guessed well enough. A man of medium height with heavy features and a compact frame, Nathaniel Bacon was of early middle age. He wore his hair, a nondescript brown streaked with silver, swept straight back in a pomaded pompadour style left just a trifle long to blend with his muttonchop whiskers in the manner of an elder statesman.

Lorna sent him a harried glance from clear gray eyes. "I must speak to you—" she began.

"Yes, perhaps you had better come inside," he interrupted as Franklin, still unclothed, appeared above them, whining excuses. A short, hard gesture silenced his son's protests and sent him scurrying back out of sight. Turning with a smooth smile, he ushered Lorna into the library.

"You appear to have inadvertently seen my son in a, shall we say, less than complimentary light. Regrettable, regrettable, but I can assure you that you need not fear it's happening again."

"That is, of course, a great comfort," Lorna answered, turning to face the man who would be her father-in-law, with her hand on the back of a leather armchair, scarcely aware of what she said.

"It is no more than the truth. Franklin will be faithful to his marriage vows. I swear it."

"I would as soon he—you—found another to take my place."

"That would be impossible at this late date; you know that as well as I," Bacon returned, moving past her to where a great walnut desk held pride of place in the room.

She might have known her plea would be ignored. Clenching her teeth in an effort to hold back another just as useless, she looked around her. The soft crimson, gold, and brown of the library, with its atmosphere of quiet erudition, did not suit Nathaniel Bacon. As if to point up the fact, he had been perusing a newssheet noted for its heavy humor and application to business concerns, rather than one of the new and expensive calf-bound volumes that lined the shelves of his retreat. Cigar smoke hung in a thick cloud, and the fumes from a brandy glass vied with the smell of the fine leather book bindings. In build much like his son, Nathaniel Bacon—Nate to his close acquaintances—showed the same results of rich living in his rotund, short-legged body and the veining that made a telltale tracery on his thick nose.

Pulling out a desk drawer, he rummaged inside, then moved to face her, holding out a box covered in midnight-blue velvet. "I had meant to present this to you tonight at dinner, or rather have Franklin make you the gift of it, but I think now is as appropriate a time as any."

When Lorna made no move to take the box, he snapped the catch, revealing the glitter of sapphires and diamonds. It was a bracelet, symbol of betrothal in this society along the Mississippi River where the customs of the French-speaking population had come to the fore. Lorna's eyes widened at the magnificence of the jewels, the sheer ostentation of their size and brilliance. At the same time, she was acutely aware of the satisfied smile of the man who faced her as he noted her reaction.

"Do you think," she said distinctly, "that this trinket will be sufficient to persuade me to forget what I witnessed just now?"

"No, no," Nate Bacon protested, his smile disappearing as calm reassurance coated his tone. "I realize such a thing must be impossible for a lady of sensitivity, one as carefully reared as yourself. I only hoped you would consider, try to understand the depth of my son's gratitude for your sacrifice, and his awe at the coming union. If he were not so fearful of being wed to such a beautiful and gracious female, he would not be forced to seek bolstering for his low self-esteem as the wedding day draws near."

"You speak eloquently for your son, sir, but I cannot be impressed by sentiments I have not observed in Franklin."

Between Lorna and her fiancé's father lay the knowledge that it was Nathaniel Bacon, and not his son, who had initiated what might be called, by those with a sardonic bent, the courtship of herself. She was, in cold fact and despite the pretense otherwise, being given in marriage to the half-witted son of this man as partial payment of a debt contracted to the owner of Beau Repose by her Uncle Sylvester. The elaborate charade of normality that her future father-in-law insisted on bringing to the arrangement was abhorrent to Lorna, and somehow sordid.

Nate Bacon seemed to divine something of her feelings from the tight expression on her classical features and the stiffness of her carriage. "Come, it will not be so bad. Franklin can be quite engaging on occasion. With your intelligence, you should be able to manage him easily. That is the main reason I selected you above your cousins, your uncle's own daughters. Charming creatures, all of them, but none, I venture to say, over-endowed with either wit or strength of will.''

''You flatter me, sir,'' she answered, lowering her gaze to hide her contempt for this blatant appeal to her vanity.

''Not at all.'' He tilted his head, trying to catch a glimpse of her features under the rolled brim of the shallow-crowned hat drawn low on her forehead, perched above the smooth figure-eight coil of hair the color of wild silk on the back of her head. ''No, indeed, you were the pick of the bunch. You will be able to attract and hold my son by your beauty, and control him by your superior understanding of his needs and appetites. He is a perfectly normal man, despite the accident that robbed him of a portion of his mental powers.''

She knew precisely what was meant; it had been carefully, if delicately, explained to her by her aunt. At the same time, it had been impressed upon her that she could not refuse the flattering suit by proxy pressed by the man who held her uncle's note-of-hand, one of the richest men among the wealthy planters along the great river.

''Yes,'' she said, allowing her gaze to move to the windows of the room that overlooked the river, framing the stretch of flowing water before the white-pillared mansion, and also the gray afternoon. ''I am aware.''

He reached to take her hand, placing the velvet box in her nerveless grasp. ''Accept this token of my esteem, then, and of my son's recognition of his proper duty toward you. Regard it, if you will, as a surety of his future conduct. I promise you that his behavior will, from this day, be all you would wish in respect and honor, and that from your wedding day tomorrow you will have no cause for complaint, nor reason to regret the bargain you have made.''

From the tenor of his words, Lorna thought Franklin's father entertained some notion that she feared her husband-to-be might forsake her bed for that of his brown mistress. How wrong he was! He should know better for it had been he, just the night before, who had interrupted when Franklin had cornered her on the gallery after dinner, only hours after their arrival. Her fiancé had pushed her against one of the great, soaring columns, attempting to capture her lips with his wet, open mouth; pawing, squeezing her breasts with hurtful, clumsy hands. Her shuddering distaste must have been obvious to any man not willfully blind. But reluctance to acknowledge the engagement was not the only reason she hesitated to accept the bracelet being thrust upon her.

"I cannot, must not, take it," she said.

"Come, I insist."

"It wouldn't be right, not at this time," she insisted in a low tone, "not while women all over the South are giving their jewelry, even their wedding bands, to aid the Confederate cause and bring an end to this war."

"Such matters should not concern a pretty thing like you."

"No, really, I couldn't bring myself to wear it."

"Then you must keep it until your tender conscience dictates otherwise."

"That will only be when this conflict is at an end and our men can come home—if I still have it then."

An opaque expression seeped into Nate Bacon's light blue eyes, so like those of his son. "Is there just maybe a special young man you are waiting for now?"

"No, nothing like that," she answered without hesitation.

"Good," he said, smiling once more. "Good."

She grew aware that he still held her fingers in his warm, damp grasp. She pulled them back slightly but could not free herself. "If you will excuse me now, I had meant to ride."

He released her, and, though he appeared reluctant to break his hold, he retained his grasp on the jewel box, taking it back into his possession. "As you will, though it looks as if we may be in for a storm. If you will be guided by me, you will reconsider."

"I . . . would rather take my chances."

He looked for a moment as if he might insist. Lorna stared at him with a shading of defiance in her level gray gaze. Finally, he shrugged.

"I will send to the stables to have a mount saddled and a groom ready to accompany you." His thick, formless lips lifted in an indulgent smile. "I expect you will be glad enough to scurry back to shelter at the first thunderclap."

She had been fearful that he meant to come with her; there had been a hint of calculation in his pale eyes, as if he were weighing the pleasure of her company against the effort required to venture forth. The comforts of his study, the newssheet, the cigar and glass of brandy that awaited him won, and Lorna made good her escape.

There was no such thing as true escape, however. She was just as much a hostage to her uncle's failure as a businessman outside the house as within it. If keeping to the bridle path that was carved through the fields and woodlands of Beau Repose, while perched upon the proper and uncomfortable dignity of a sidesaddle with a groom trailing ten paces behind her, did not satisfy her yearning for freedom, the fault lay within herself; for a female there was nothing closer to be had. She would have to make the best of it, just as she must learn to endure the marriage that awaited her on the morrow. Escape from that, and all its attendant duties, was also impossible, though she would rather give herself to any man other than the mindless and vicious creature to whom she would be joined. Any man at all.

Catching one side of her bottom lip between her teeth, Lorna considered going to her uncle and pleading to be released from this betrothal. Even as the idea came, it was banished by the image of her aunt: stern, overbearing, with deep etchings of disappointment along either side of her long nose. Uncle Sylvester would listen to Aunt Madelyn, would do as she said, and it was her aunt's contention that women were born to sorrow and shrinking from their wifely obligations, regardless of the man they married. Her aunt thought it reason for congratulations that she was not marrying a poor man, that it would not be necessary for her to scrimp and be eternally saving in order to feed and clothe her children, and any other unfortunate waif who might be foisted upon her.

The last was a reference to Lorna herself, who had come to live with her aunt and uncle some ten years before. She, with her mother and father, had traveled from Georgia to Louisiana at her Uncle Sylvester's, her father's brother's, invitation. The plan had been for the two men to go into partnership in a new plantation of some three thousand acres that Sylvester Forrester had already bought. Their method of transportation had been by ship to New Orleans, where they had intended to put their household furnishings on a steamboat going upriver. But as they were in the city, the largest in the South, they decided to spend a few days shopping and attending the theater. It was then that Lorna's parents had succumbed to cholera in one of those sudden deadly epidemics that sweep through seaport towns. In the confusion of that terrible time, with the hospitals, houses, and even the streets filled with the dead and dying, their money, the gold brought for investment, had disappeared. Whether it had been taken by the servants at their lodgings, the men who loaded the bodies onto the wagons for the trip to the cemetery, or merely by some of the scum who risked the ravaging disease to rob the stricken, was never discovered.

Instead of fresh capital to put his plantation on its feet, Uncle Sylvester had acquired funeral expenses and another mouth to feed, Lorna. The accusation of being an added burden had, from repetition, lost its power to wound, however. The most disturbing thing that had come from the conversation with her aunt had been the recognition that she must bear Franklin Bacon's children, that, indeed, an heir for Beau Repose was one of the most important reasons for a bride's being found for him. Unfit as he was to manage the large estate Nate Bacon had built, he could still sire a son to do the job. There was no other choice; Franklin was without brothers or sisters. His mother, Nate's wife, had been in ill health since he was born. Prostrated by the incident in her son's childhood when he had been kicked in the side of the head by his pony as he sought to beat it into submission, the accident that resulted in the loss of his mental powers, she had taken to her bed and not left it since.

Even knowing, as Lorna did, that Franklin's lack of intelligence was not an inherited condition, she could not conquer her revulsion at the thought of carrying his child inside her body. If the mere idea made her feel unwell, what would the reality be like?

"Mis' Lorna! Could you slow down, Mis' Lorna? I got to stop a minute!"

She reined in, looking back as her horse sidled, and drew up to where the Beau Repose groom had dismounted and was running his hand along the foreleg of his mount. The roan gelding whinnied, throwing up his head, his mane and tail streaming in the rising wind.

"What is it?" she called.

"Fool horse shied at a rabbit just now, kicked a log on the side of the trail. I think he's gone and hurt himself."

Though not one of the family mounts, the horse was a good riding hack kept for guests and was stablemate to the mare Lorna rode. There could be no chances taken with his welfare.

"Is he limping?"

"Yes ma'am, just a bit," the elderly groom admitted, shaking his grizzled head.

Lorna hesitated, her brows, which were like dark brown wings, much darker than the pale gold of her hair, drawing together over her eyes. "You must return with the horse, I know, but I believe I will go on."

"I couldn't leave you, Mis' Lorna; it would be as much as my hide's worth, if I did. 'Sides, it's goin' to storm soon."

"I don't mind a little rain. And surely Mr. Bacon would not blame you if I go on alone?" The wind caught her words, flattening their sound.

"You don't know that man. He's not like the old master, M'sieur Cazenave. Maste' Bacon, he don't laugh. He's a hard man, mighty hard."

With a sigh, Lorna nodded. She could do nothing that would bring punishment down on the groom. That concern, allied to the convention that said she must not ride alone, was too much to combat. Still she sat her horse with the trailing length of her riding skirt lifting and fluttering in the wind and her eyes narrowed against its growing force. The groom turned and began to lead the limping gelding back the way they had come. She looked beyond, down the bridle path that led back to Beau Repose, then swung to stare at the winding trail that lay ahead. As she glanced back, the groom paused, waiting.

"You go on," she called. "I'll ride just a little farther before I catch up to you."

"Don't go far, will you, Mis' Lorna? I tell you, it's goin' to rain!"

As if to add emphasis to his warning, there came a distant rumble of thunder. "Yes, yes," she cried over her shoulder as she set her heel to her mount's side. "I know!"

It was a useless impulse, of course. What could be gained by a few brief moments without supervision, without companions, without the somber knowledge of what awaited her? Regardless, pleasure in this solitude—broken only by the shrill call of a bird blown by the increasing wind, by the thrashing of branches overhead and the echoing thuds of her own mount's hoofbeats—ran with exhilaration in her veins. The wind whipped color into her cheeks and tossed the curling feather that lay along the brim of her hat. The gathering darkness had no power to alarm her; nor did the momentary flicker of lightning overhead. She wanted to ride on and on, to leave both her past and ugly, uncertain future behind and never return. Never, never, never.

Cold raindrops striking her face jerked her back to reality from that brief exultation. She drew rein, and her mare's effortless canter dropped to a walk. In a lull in the oncoming storm, she could hear the spatter of scattered rain against the crown of her hat and its quiet clatter among the leaves of the arching trees. She was not sure how far she had come, how long it had been since she had left the groom. She should be turning back. She would, definitely, in just a moment.

Lightning flashed, a silver stitching across the sky. Hard upon it came the shattering concussion of thunder almost directly above her. The wind rose in a keening surge. Her mount tried to rear, neighing in fright. As she fought for control, she heard the ominous splintering of wood; then behind her there came the gathering crackle, the rattling, whistling roar of a falling tree.

It hit the ground with a mighty crash only yards away. The wafted air of its fall was filled with bits of bark that stung as they struck, and the smell of scorched leaves caught in her throat. Her horse bolted, surging forward along the path. Jerked backward, she was nearly unseated. Her riding crop flew from her hand as she grabbed for the saddle horn. Leaning forward against the wind of their swift passage, she gathered up the reins once more, but the mare did not respond. She had the bit in her teeth, and was running as if she would outdistance her terror, carrying Lorna farther away from Beau Repose.

It was only a few seconds before she was able to control the mare, but in that short span of time the bridle path came to an end, emerging onto a wagon track that, in turn, joined the river road. That great, winding stretch of water, swollen to near-flood level, lay before her as she pulled the mare in at last. Screened by the willows and the great oaks that overhung the road, the river was a gray and forbidding expanse in the gloom.

Then, as she scanned the open sky above the surging, rain-speckled flow, she saw it, the dragging curtain of the storm, sweeping toward her. It pounded the surface of the water to froth, set the trees to swaying wildly with its slashing onslaught, and took the last light from the sky. With a cold rush, the storm caught up with her, a wind-driven, icy torrent that carried the tiny, sharp blows of falling hail. The balls of ice peppered down, bouncing on the road, growing larger as they tore through the leaves of the branches around Lorna and pummeled her shoulders.

She had to find shelter. Her mount, already nervous, would not stand such punishment for long; nor could she. The trees that lined the road were little protection, but if she could push her way among them, deeper into the woods, they might serve.

It was then that she saw the house. It sat back from the road at the end of a drive lined with dark, thrashing sentinels of live oaks from which hung swaying tatters of Spanish moss. A gray ghost of a house, it showed no light but sat four-square and solid, a mansion in what was called the West Indies style, two stories in height with a wide-hipped roof covering deep galleries that were supported by square brick columns on the lower floor, and white, turned colonettes on the upper. The design of the building was that favored by the Creole aristocracy along the river, those Louisiana descendants of French and Spanish colonists. Comfortable, built to make the best of a hot and damp climate, it was in sharp contrast to the Greek Revival splendor of such houses as Beau Repose, built by members of the English-speaking community. The Creoles were known for their hospitality; and, though it did not appear that the family was home, they would not mind, perhaps, if their servants took her in for a short time, until the storm passed.

As she dismounted before the front entrance, she saw what she would have recognized sooner in better light. The family would not be returning; the house was empty. The fan-lighted front door of the main living quarters, on the second floor, stood open. Shutters hung ajar at the windows, and the whitewashed plaster that covered the soft, handmade bricks was falling away in great mossy patches. Weeds and vines grew right up to the brick floor of the lower gallery, sprouting in the cracks, winding around the balusters of the outside stairs that mounted at an angle from under the gallery up to the second floor. The first floor, used as a raided basement for servants' quarters and the safekeeping of foodstuffs, had been taken over as a storage area for baled cotton.

There was not time for a closer inspection. Leading her mount, she stepped onto the dirty brick floor of the lower gallery. The rotted upper gallery would at least provide some protection from the driving hail, and there was little damage the animal could do that had not already been done. Looking around her, she saw a rusty iron loop set into the wall, once the support for a torch to light the entryway. It would serve admirably as a hitching ring.

When she had secured the mare's reins, Lorna stood quietly rubbing the horse's soft muzzle, watching the hail and rain. She thought of the groom somewhere back on the bridle path, and hoped that he had not been caught in the open. Soon she would have to start back; she certainly did not want to get the man in trouble. But perhaps he would wait for her if he were truly as frightened of Nate Bacon as he seemed.

What had the man meant when he spoke of the old master, M'sieur Cazenave? It had been a casual reference, as if he thought she should understand. Maybe she would have if hers had been a normal betrothal, though it seemed unlikely a couple happy in their coming nuptials would spend their time speaking of the past owner of an elderly groom.

The hail slackened, stopped, but the rain still fell, splashing down from the leaden sky, falling in streams from the high roof, and spattering onto the floor of the lower gallery. It was wetting the hem of her habit, and the gusting wind made her shiver in the dampness. She glanced around in search of more shelter.

She pushed wider the door to the lower rooms of the house, peering inside, stepping gingerly over the threshold. Cotton bales, compressed cotton wrapped in gunnysacking, greeted her gaze. There was cotton everywhere, stacked to the low ceiling, bulwarks of white and brown that formed tunnel-like walkways leading into other rooms where more cotton was packed bale upon bale, with a passage to a window left here and there for light. There was also an open space around a narrow closet door that concealed the sneak stair leading to the main floor.

What was it about an empty house that invited exploring? Was it the sense of the lingering imprint of other lives, the opportunity of satisfying the eternal human curiosity about the places where other people have lived and died, or merely the possibility of discarded treasure? Lorna did not know, but she could not resist the urge to climb the stairs. Though she placed her weight on each tread with care, they seemed sound enough.

The upper rooms were large and well-proportioned. Perhaps because of the time and effort it must have taken to bring any load up the outside stairway, they were only partially filled with cotton. There were plaster medallions of exquisite workmanship on the ceilings, and carved friezework and moldings around the walls. Delicately colored wall hangings were still in place, faded but serviceable. Though the rooms were empty of furniture, draperies heavy with dust hung at the windows, and on one door there remained an unbroken china knob painted with faded roses and violets, as perfectly executed as any piece of art.

Thunder rumbled overhead and lightning flickered beyond the windows. Absorbed in the examination of her surroundings, Lorna scarcely noticed. She discovered a few spots of mildew, great swags of spider webs, the hard mud nests of dirtdobbers, and the yellow-brown circles of damp where the roof was leaking in the rain, and yet there seemed to be nothing particularly wrong with the house. Why, then, had it been deserted? Who would use such a fine home for the storing of cotton, when any barn or shed would have done just as well? It didn't make sense. Unless, perhaps, there had been a tragedy. It could happen sometimes, the death of whole families from some disease or malignant fever. With no heirs, no tenants, the vacant houses fell victims to decay and the relentless encroachment of nature, the ferns and weeds that grew on the wood-shingled roofs, the vines that strangled the galleries, the birds that found their way inside to build their nests in the elaborate ceiling medallions, or the raccoons and opossums who had their young behind the doors.

She was standing in what must have once been the ladies parlor, judging from its plasterwork of roses and ferns set in flowing scrolls, when she heard the sound of the guitar. The piece being played was unfamiliar, something softly melodic with a hint of passionate melancholy in its slow, complicated phrasing. The music seemed to blend with the drumming of the rain overhead, forming a counterpoint to it. Also mingling with these was the quiet crackle of a fire, a contained noise, not the rush of a conflagration.

A frisson that might have been fear or excitement ran along her nerves. The impulse to retreat touched her; then she dismissed it with a shake of her head. She was not a coward, and she would not be discovered fleeing like one. Perhaps the person in occupation was one who was due her thanks for the protection from the elements she had claimed; and if not, the presence of someone in the house might be something that should be reported when she returned to Beau Repose.

The music seemed to be coming from one of what must, at one time, have been the back bedchambers. Listening intently, beguiled against her will by the sound, she made her way in that direction.

She saw the light, a flickering orange glow, first. It danced in the dimness of the room, beckoning. It was madness to go closer, she knew; any kind of thief or murderer could have taken up residence in the vacant house. Still she could not prevent herself, did not even try.

Her first sight of him was with the blue-white play of lightning—cold, jagged fire—behind his head. He sat before the fire on a cotton bale, one of several strewn about the room. One knee was drawn up, with his ankle crossed over his other knee, while on it he rested the neck of his guitar as he played. He glanced up, alert, as she passed through the doorway, though there was something in his manner that suggested he had been aware of her presence in the house for some time. He wore a double-breasted jacket of oak-leaf twill with a brown velvet collar over trousers of fawn brown. The jacket hung open, showing his vest of silk woven with stripes of buff and white. His cravat was of cinnamon silk, contrasting pleasantly with the fine linen of his shirt: all evidence of his status of a gentleman. Imperceptibly, Lorna relaxed, allowing her gaze to touch his face.

She drew in a quick breath. This man had the intense features and dark coloring found in Louisiana in those of Creole heritage. He was possibly in his early thirties. His hair grew in rigorously brushed waves over his head, though a wayward curl fell forward onto his forehead. His face had the bronze hue of one no stranger to the sun; his nose was straight, classically Roman, with chiseled definition about the mouth and the flaring nostrils. His lips were firm, though with a sensuous fullness to the lower one; and at the corners, cutting into the planes of his face, were the curving indentations of a quick and easy good-humor. He was not smiling now, however. His black eyes behind their barricade of thick brows and lashes were hard and predatory, narrowed in recognition.

Lorna made a small, convulsive movement, as if she would turn away.

"Don't go."

His voice was arresting, strong, deep, and warmly cordial; nothing more. He stopped playing, and the last, singing note died away. As she hesitated, he rose to his feet. "Come to the fire. You look chilled and wet."

It was annoying, the instant leap of concern for her appearance instead of the danger. And yet he made no move toward her, and so open and friendly was his gaze, so polite his manner, that her misgivings might have been caused by a trick of the firelight or of her own imagination.

"I could not intrude," she managed, retreating a step.

"There is no possibility of that."

"Oh?" she said, her interest piqued. "The house doesn't belong to you then?"

His answer was accompanied by a slight movement of the shoulders. "I lived here once."

It seemed he watched her from under his thick, dark lashes as if waiting for some reaction, some response to the knowing glint that lighted his eyes, eyes like a deep bayou in moonlight, black and opaque and still. He spoke English with ease, as if it had been his primary language for some time, though there was the faintest trace of an accent in his intonation. She swallowed, aware of the tightness in her throat. "Such a pity for a place like this to stand empty—or to be used for storage like a warehouse."

"Yes," he agreed, his dark gaze flicking over the bales of cotton around him. "The stuff has its uses, however. Here, let me pull up a seat for you."

Lorna watched as, with lithe, muscular control, he rose to set the guitar beside the mantel under which the fire burned, then leaned to grasp the gunnysacking of a cotton bale, drawing it nearer the fire. A second bale was pulled behind the first, and a third thrown with ease on top of it for a backrest. Before she could stop him, before she realized what he intended, he had stripped off his jacket and spread it over the burlap for her comfort. With a shallow bow and a graceful gesture, he indicated that she should sit.

Her footsteps were slow as she moved toward him. Taking the place he had arranged for her, she said, "I can only stay a moment. I was forced to take shelter from the storm. My . . . my groom will wonder what has become of me."

"So you were not riding alone? For someone who looks as you do, that would have been most unwise. Your servant is downstairs?"

His compliment had been so offhand, so quickly passed over for the next question, that she had not time to resent it. She shook her head, giving him a less than complete version of what had happened.

As she spoke, he reached for a flask that sat to one side. Of silver, it had a small cap that unscrewed to form a cup the size of a demitasse. Removing it, he poured a dark liquid into the cup and, as she finished speaking, handed it to her.

With a sympathetic comment for her tale, he asked. "Would you care for coffee? I'm afraid it's laced with brandy, but that should help to warm you."

The gesture was merely courteous, his smile wry. The coffee smelled delicious; brandy was used even by her Aunt Madelyn as a restorative. She reached out to accept the cup. Her fingers brushed his, and the leap of her nerves was such that she might have touched a hot coal. Her hand jerked a bit and she sent a startled glance at the man standing over her, but recovered without spilling the coffee as it was transferred to her hand.

The concoction was hot and sweet. She sipped at it with care and was grateful for the immediate, spreading warmth it brought. She was happy, also, when her benefactor stepped back, standing before the fire with his hands behind his back. At the same time, she was acutely aware of the intentness of his gaze upon her. She moistened her lips.

"You must live nearby now, to have brought such refreshment with you."

He gave an amused shake of his head at her transparent effort to discover something about him. "I have been visiting in the neighborhood but left my hostess this afternoon, returning . . . home."

"I see." His hesitation before the last word seemed peculiar. "You are seeking cover from the rain, too, then, I suppose. But I would not deprive you of your provisions for the journey."

As she held out the flask cup, still half full of coffee, he smiled. "Don't let it trouble you. I deem it an honor, and my great good fortune, to be able to contribute to the comfort of a lady."

It was mere politeness, of course; still there was something in his manner, in the inflection of his words, that disturbed her. Despite her subtle inquiry, he had made no attempt to identify himself. She proffered the cup once more. "I really should be going."

"I understand your need to be away," he said, moving to take the cup, turning it so that, deliberately or accidentally, when he raised it to his lips to drain the contents, his lips met the same place her own had touched. He smiled into her eyes, his face taking on a devastating charm, as he lowered it once more. "But it would be folly to go while the rain still falls, would it not?

And you are soaked. Surely it would be best to stay here, to remove your jacket to dry, or at least take off your hat? I'm sure that creation on your head was once most becoming, but the feather is dripping dye onto your shoulder.''

With an exclamation of dismay, she reached up to feel the sopping feather. Lifting her hands, she drew out the jet-tipped hat pin that held her small hat and whipped it off. The feather, once so fine and of a delicate shade of robin's-egg blue, was undoubtedly bedraggled. As he had said, it had been dripping down the back of her neck, though he had been kind enough not to put it in just that way. At the thought of how she must have looked in her half-drowned dignity, a chuckle escaped her. She glanced up at him with rare laughter lighting her gray eyes.

He watched her, an arrested look on his strong, bronzed features. His black eyes were fathomless, filled with dangerous, shifting currents. An instant later, his lashes came down, and a smile tugged the corners of his mouth. Reaching out, he took the hat from her hand and returned to the fireplace, where he placed both it and the cup upon the mantelpiece.

Swinging back to face her, he said, ''Now the jacket?''

''I will keep it on,'' she returned.

''Why?''

''Because I prefer it. Must there be another reason?''

He shook his head, as if in disbelief. ''You can't really want to wear anything so cold and clammy. Think of your health.''

''If you must know, it isn't made to be removed, not—''

''Not in mixed company, or in public? A peculiar vanity, isn't it? You do have on a shirtwaist?''

''A mere sham, only a front and back,'' she said through set teeth, aware of her amazement at the turn their conversation had taken. But if she expected him to be discomfited, she was soon disabused of the idea.

''Ah, modesty prevents you. Which is more important, its preservation or your comfort and well-being? Come, don't be prudish. I will turn my back.''

He did exactly that, pivoting, moving to a cotton bale on the opposite side of the fire. The close-packed bale had been torn open so that the fluffy white cotton spilled out like the stuffing from a pillow. He leaned over, with the smooth, animal-like coordination of an outdoorsman, to grasp great handfuls of the white mass. Dropping puffs along the way, he swung to toss it onto the fire. So close-fitting were his trousers of fawn broadcloth that she could see plainly the flex of the muscles in his thighs and narrow hips as he moved. She looked quickly away, aware of an odd heat in the pit of her stomach. Her gaze focused on what he was doing.

"You . . . you're burning cotton," she said wonderingly. Until that moment, she had not noticed that the flames in the fireplace did not come from wood.

"It won't be missed."

"But think of the money! Cotton is like white gold."

"The money, " he said, throwing another double handful onto the yellow-orange flames, "will not be missed either."

She frowned in an effort to understand his cryptic comment. "Because there's little market for it now, with the blockade? But when the war is over—"

"When the war is over will be the time to worry about it. For the moment, there are things more important."

She followed his movements as he returned to stand before her, then, with controlled grace, went to one knee. He raised his hands and began to unfasten the buttons of gray mother-of-pearl that closed her jacket, his fingers sure at their task. His voice was soft as he asked, "Shall I help you, *ma chère*?"

With a quick exclamation, she brought her hands up to catch his wrist. The warmth of his body, the clean male and starched-linen smell of him, the corded strength of the tendons and muscles under her fingers, the overpowering presence of the man himself assaulted her senses, and the sharp reprimand on her tongue died unspoken. A heated flush rose to her hairline for the omission, increasing as she found herself rationalizing that the soft French endearment he had spoken meant only "My dear" and was used often to address children, relatives, and friends. As she spoke, she heard with shame the huskiness of her own tone.

"I can manage."

He allowed his gaze to rise to her face, his mouth faintly curving as his dark eyes probed the gray of hers. "I'm sure you can, but will you?"

"It . . . seems the wisest course." The double entendre was spoken before she could bite it back.

"You are wise, I think, if nothing else."

There was no time to wonder at the abrupt coolness in his face or the flatness of his tone. As she set her fingers to her own buttons and began to work at them, he lifted his hands to probe the intricate coil of hair at the back of her head, quickly drawing out the pins. She jerked away, and the heavy weight slid, spilling down her back. He pushed his fingers through the long damp strands, spreading them, drawing their silken length over her shoulders where they hung shining like aged satin in the firelight.

"It was wet," he said in answer to the startled disbelief, the mute question in her eyes. "And you must be cold still, I think, you're shivering."

A moment later, he was seated beside her, drawing her against the warm strength of his chest, pushing the jacket from her and flinging it aside. She was cold, yes, but that was not the reason for the convulsive tremors that ran over her as she felt the intense furnace heat of his arms, knew their tenuous safety. Bemused by his daring, so unthinkable in a gentleman of his class toward a gently bred female, she was still for a frozen instant. His dark gaze swept her face, and he lifted a hand to touch her cheek. Another convulsive tremor ran over her as his warm fingers trailed downward over the smooth and delicate turn of her jawline to the arch of her neck and the pulse that throbbed there. For a long moment they were still, suspended in time, then, almost as if he would not prevent the impulse, he touched his mouth to hers.

Lightning crackled, flaring white and fiery into the room. Its vibrant tension invaded Lorna's senses, banishing her chill even as it paralyzed her will. Under the fierce, searching fire of the kiss, her cool lips warmed, clung. He teased their moist and tender corners, first one, then the other, brushing their sensitive surfaces with unhurried enjoyment. She murmured in protest, going rigid, but he paid no heed, only drawing her closer still, deepening his kiss. His fingers trailed a tingling path along her jawline and downward to the swell of her breasts beneath the thin, tucked lawn of her shirtwaist. He cupped that taut fullness, gently brushing his thumb over the peak.

Never had she been treated in such a fashion, never had she felt so intimate a caress. Lorna clenched her hand that lay against his chest into a fist, pushing at him, dragging her mouth from his with a strangled gasp. Recovering her breath, she demanded, "What—what are you doing?"

He smiled, his eyes hooded, the light in their depths provocative, sensual, yet shadowed with tension. "Making love to you, *chérie*."

"You can't!" The words that should have been a cry came out as a whisper. *Darling*, he had said.

"Can't I?"

There were many things she could have done: screamed, struck out at him, torn herself from his arms and run. Instead, she only stared at him in bemused distress, the unbidden thought striking deep into her mind of the wedding night that was soon to come, of the man who would lie in her bed then, of her heartfelt vow made in silent anguish so short a time ago—that she would rather give herself to any other man. Any man at all.

"This is madness," she managed. The press of his fingers into her arm was warm, light, yet with such tensile strength that she knew instinctively it would be near impossible to break his hold.

"Yes," he agreed, his voice deep.

"Then let me go."

His dark gaze searched her face, coming to rest on the vulnerable rose-pink softness of her mouth. "That I can't—won't—do. Not even it you wanted it, which, in all truth, I don't think you do."

A heated flush swept again to her hairline and she opened her mouth to refute the charge. The words died unspoken. Lorna had never lied to herself, and, even for the sake of self-preservation, she could not begin now. A stricken expression seeped into her gray eyes, darkening their color, mingling with the reckless despair that was mirrored there.

"Dieu m'en garde," he whispered, his voice hoarse as he pulled her against him. Her lashes fluttered down as his lips sought hers and, sighing, she abandoned resistance, pressing closer. The probing gentleness of his mouth tasted of brandied coffee, heady, bittersweet. His lips were firm, bringing throbbing heat to her own as he traced their finely molded edges and contours, tasting their sweetness, teasing them apart to explore the moist inner surfaces. She touched his tongue with her own, shyly at first, then with rash acceptance. His hands upon her, seeking, tantalizing, brought beguilement. She could feel the restrained power of his body as he cradled her against him, sense the deep pounding of his heart. It was as if they were compelled by desperate needs and desires, by a fine inevitability that disregarded human wishes, either his or her own.

The constraint of embarrassment ebbed, to be replaced by the flickering rise of excitement. Warmth flowed through her veins. The anticipation of pleasure uncoiled in the pit of her stomach, flowing outward, tingling through her body. With an urgency that was frightening, shocking, she wanted his touch upon her bare skin.

He pressed her back, shouldering aside the bale of cotton behind them so that it thudded to the floor, leaving the spreading surface of the other two there before the fire. The lace-edged jabot at her throat loosened under his deft touch. Untying the ends, he drew them aside, exposing the slender column of her neck and the delicate hollow at its base. He pressed his lips to that depression, testing its sweet fragility, touching his tongue to the pulse beat that fluttered there as he freed the buttons of her shirtwaist. As he drew the folds of lawn aside, he trailed burning fire downward to the gentle curves of her breasts above her lace-edged camisole. He raised his head then, unhooking her skirt, drawing the bottom of her camisole upward and stripping it off with her shirtwaist, dropping them to the floor. The heavy poplin of her habit skirt made a quiet, slithering sound as it was pushed from her to join the other clothing on the floor.

Lorna had no need of a corset beneath her habit, so slender was her form. In an incoherent corner of her mind, she was glad as she lay with only her tucked and lace-edged pantaloons left to her, waiting in languorous apprehension, watching from under lowered lashes, for what would come next.

His own waistcoat and shirt were shrugged away, revealing the bronze planes of his chest with its dark hair, the wide shoulders tapering to the narrowness of his waist. The sheathing of muscle that stood out in the firelight indicated hard effort, belying his look of the indolent gentleman. He unfastened his trousers, moving to discard them. She allowed her gaze to follow his movements, directed by curiosity. An instant later, she brought it swiftly back up to his navel, disconcerted by the virile beauty of his male body, a conviction in her mind that it was impossible for it to be joined to her, impossible.

He turned to her, gathering her close once more. His face absorbed, with twin points of firelight dancing in the depths of his eyes, he spread his hand over her abdomen, sliding it upward to cup first one white, blue-veined breast, then the other, taking each straining rosy peak into the wet heat of his mouth as the firm mounds swelled to fill his hand. She caught her breath in a ragged sound as his hand moved, smoothing in slow circles, sliding downward to slip beneath the waistband of her pantaloons. He spread his fingers wide over the velvet skin of her belly, kneading, easing lower still until he could reach the apex of her thighs.

Her muscles tensed at his first, unbearably intimate touch. She shut her eyes tightly and tried in reflex action to close her thighs, but he would not permit it. Then came that first stirring of purest sensation. By infinite degrees, she relaxed. The pleasure grew, a boundless thing that erased doubt and fear. For a brief space of time, she was acutely aware of the firm resilience of his arms, the race of the blood in her veins, the feel of the silk lining of his jacket underneath her back, the rasp of the hair on his chest against the curve of her waist, the tantalizing track of his tongue as he circled the peaks of her breasts before capturing them once more with the heated passion of his mouth. She was alive in a way she had never been before, drowning in the rising clamor of her senses. Awareness receded then, replaced by the molten flow of desire. There was nothing except the two of them and the echoing emptiness of the old house, the sound of the rain and the infinite dimness of the evening.

She touched his hair, twining her fingers in its vital crispness, sliding them down the strong column of his neck to the taut muscles of his shoulders. She spread her palms, feeling the powerful rippling beneath them with joyous wonder and pure, sensual pleasure. Her lips parted, trembling. She felt as if her blood was on fire, that her skin was aflame with a heat that was internal, consuming. There was a sense of fullness in her loins, and the ache of hollowness deep inside her that might never be assuaged, never filled. With a low sound in her throat, she turned, arching toward the man who held her.

He grasped her waist, sliding his hand over the slender curve of one hip, drawing her against the unyielding shaft of his manhood as he stretched out beside her. She did not shrink from it but, with trembling joy, moved to accommodate the burning, pulsating entry.

The piercing pain stopped her breath. She went rigid with the sudden wetness of tears in her eyes. A shudder ran over her as he stopped at the sudden, unbreached threshold, but she could not make a sound. She clung to him, her nails sinking into his arms in her extreme disappointment. The rustle of his quiet curse disturbed the hair at her temple; his hold tightened. Then with a quick twist of his hips, he thrust into her, pressing deep, breaking through that tight circle of agony into beatitude.

He was still for a long moment, then slowly, sweetly, he moved against her so that the tension receded and prickling enjoyment took its place. It was done, and the delight of it rose inside her, blending with the warm, liquid glide of ecstasy. As he raised himself above her, turning her to her back, she lifted her lashes to stare up at him.

Bathed in fireglow, burnished by its golden light, he had the look of a pagan god, self-contained and powerful. She lowered her hands to slide them over his chest, trailing her fingertips through the triangle of soft hair that led downward over the hard surface of his belly. She met his dark gaze, seeing herself in miniature reflected doubly in the mirror-like surfaces of his eyes.

"Who are you?" she whispered.

A twisted shadow crossed his face and was gone. He lowered his mouth until it was less than a hair's breadth above her own. "Does it matter, *ma chère*?"

"No," she murmured, lifting her hands to cradle his head, drawing his lips down to hers. "No," she said again as he sank into her, taking her plunging with him deep into passion's blood-red heart.

Chapter 2

The fire had died to smouldering ash. The storm had rumbled away into the distance, leaving only the softly falling rain beyond the windows. Still they lay, their limbs intertwined, their chests rising and falling with their breathing, which was even at last. Lorna's hair had dried. It lay fanned over the cotton bale, cascading down the side, shimmering taupe-gold in the firelit dimness. Her cheek was pillowed against his chest, while his lips brushed the top of her head. In the aftermath of intolerable pleasure they held each other, staring wide-eyed, as if stunned, into the gathering darkness.

Abruptly he stiffened, lifting his head. Lorna stirred. She struggled to one elbow. "What is it?"

"Listen."

Faintly there came the sound of a horse whinnying in the distance. It was answered by her mare below; then the thud of hoofbeats echoed on the drive.

He uttered a soft imprecation. Rolling from her, he leaped to his feet. He scooped up her clothing, thrusting it toward her, then stooped to find his trousers. Stepping into them, he looked around for his shirt, and Lorna, discovering it among her own things, mutely held it out.

"Lorna?"

"Uncle Sylvester—" she gasped.

The call had come from below, channeling upward through

the still house. With a muffled cry, she dived into her camisole, pulling it down in trembling haste, searching for the waist of her riding skirt. The wide circle of cloth was snatched from her hand, righted, and thrown over her head. With no more than a wan smile for the man who had helped her, she stood up, settling the folds into place and, at the same time, looking for her stockings and boots.

She had found her shirtwaist, turned wrong side out and smeared with mud, when she heard heavy footsteps on the stairs. They sounded like an army; her uncle was not alone then. A glance showed her that the man pushing his shirt into his trousers beside her was also aware of the import of so large a party. His face was grim and, as he caught her anxious gaze, the smile he gave her was tinged with self-mockery.

"I suggest," he said softly, "that you scream rape."

Hard on the words came the thud of booted feet in the outer room. Lorna's uncle appeared in the doorway, only to be shouldered aside by Nate Bacon. Behind the two men crowded a half dozen field hands, one of whom carried a lantern.

Lorna swung to face them with the shirtwaist she had just righted clutched to her breasts. Moments before, she had felt no self-consciousness in being half-dressed. Now shame rose in a hot red wave as she stood with her hair swirling like a pale golden curtain around her, through which could be glimpsed the pearl-like sheen of her skin. Even if she had wanted to take the advice so quietly given, she could not have forced the words past the tight knot in her throat.

"Son of a bitch!" Nate Bacon's voice was choked with rage as he stared past Lorna. "Son of a bitch. Cazenave!"

"Lorna!" her uncle exclaimed at the same time in tones of relief and gladness as he moved around his host, coming a few steps into the room. Then as the circle of lantern light edged forward revealing the disheveled state of his niece and the man behind her, he stopped short.

"Ramon Charles Darcourt Cazenave, at your service, M'sieur Bacon." The man who had held her in his arms so short a time before gave his name, stepping forward to sketch a bow that was far from deferential. He inclined his head also toward her uncle. "Sir."

"Cazenave," Nate said again, the word freighted with loathing.

"I am surprised that you recognize me."

"I would have to be blind not to see your old man in you."

"I am happy to think so."

"A proud man, and an honorable one, your father. Do you think he would be happy to see his son now, a rapist?"

Ramon allowed his gaze to brush over Lorna where she stood rigid near the fireplace. A darker tone seeped under the the bronze of his skin, but his features were unreadable as he answered. "He is dead."

Nate followed the direction of his glance, his protuberant eyes moving with hard greed over Lorna's soft white shoulders veiled by her hair, and the tender curves of her breasts above the neckline of her camisole. He gave a tight grunt. "It's a good thing. For what you've done to my son's future bride, I mean to see you pay the full price. Take him, boys!"

With a savage gesture toward Ramon, he stepped back. The field hands waiting in the doorway surged forward, the man with the lantern setting it on the floor before he joined the others. They fell on Ramon, reaching to pinion his arms. He stepped back, swinging a hard blow at their leader that rocked him on his heels, then ducked under a punch, driving his elbow into the man's solar plexus even as he spun to meet an attack from behind. The field hands closed in, grappling, grunting, cursing, while Nate Bacon shouted encouragement.

Ramon fought like a demon, but, outnumbered, with no room to maneuver, he could not hope to fight free. A moment later, he went down in a flailing blur of fists and kicking feet.

"No," Lorna whispered, then cried louder, "No!" She swung toward her uncle, reaching his side with swift steps, clutching his arm. "Stop them, Uncle Sylvester. He didn't hurt me, he didn't!"

Sylvester Forrester frowned, dragging his gaze from the melee. "You mean he didn't . . . harm you?"

"I mean it wasn't . . . he didn't . . . there was no . . . " The sternness in her uncle's face, the condemnation in his eyes, allied to her own embarrassment and fear of what might happen to Ramon Cazenave, robbed her of coherent speech for precious seconds. She drew a deep breath. "What I mean to say is, he didn't—"

"She means he didn't force her," Nate said, his voice harsh as he interrupted.

"But my dear Lorna, I don't understand," her uncle said, the hardness of his voice indicating far otherwise.

"She means there was no rape, because there was no need, don't you, Lorna, my dear future daughter-in-law?"

Lorna stared from Nate to her uncle. It seemed such an ugly thing, an animalistic joining tainted by sin, when seen through the eyes of the two men who waited for her answer. It hadn't been like that at all.

There came the sudden thud of flesh on flesh behind them; then all was quiet. As they turned, they saw Ramon Cazenave being hauled to his feet. He stood swaying with blood trickling from the corner of his mouth and one eye slowly swelling shut. His shirt was torn, falling open, stripped of its studs, which littered the floor. His breathing was ragged, as if every rise and fall of his chest caused him pain. The men who held so grimly to his arms had not escaped punishment. Only four of the six who had jumped him were left standing around him. The fifth nursed a broken hand, while the last man sat on a cotton bale, spitting out loosened teeth.

Nate walked slowly up to Ramon until his face was within inches of the dark-haired man's. "Is that right, what she says, Cazenave? Did she let you—"

The term he used was offensive in its crudeness, but descriptive. Though Lorna had never heard it before, she grasped the meaning immediately. She lifted her chin as Ramon turned his head by slow degrees to meet her gray gaze. There was blank surprise in the depths of his dark eyes, and also a flicker of what might have been regret.

He looked back to Nate, his bruised mouth curving into a deliberate smile. "She feels sorry for me, it seems. Isn't that flattering? But all the same, if she says she was willing, she's lying."

"Quite the gentleman, aren't you," Nate said, "but I don't see any sign of her having been manhandled."

Lorna stepped forward. "Because I wasn't, no matter what he says."

The penalty for the crime Ramon was claiming so nonchalantly to have committed was death by hanging. It was possible that the sentence might be carried out at once, given the vicious and arrogant temper of Nate Bacon. Under the circumstances, there were few who would blame him.

"What do you say, Cazenave?" the owner of Beau Repose inquired. "Will you tell us what we want to know, or shall we look into the matter more thoroughly? Maybe a better way of getting at the truth would be if we put the girl on her back on a cotton bale and threw her skirts over her head for a closer look at the evidence?''

Ramon tried to strike out at Nate but was wrestled to stillness once more. "You wouldn't do it; her uncle wouldn't let you."

Nate flung a glance over his shoulder at Sylvester Forrester. "Oh, I don't think he will object, all in the name of justice's being done, of course."

Lorna looked at her uncle, but he would not meet her eyes. It was true, she thought in dazed disbelief. So afraid of Bacon was he, so much in the man's debt, that he did not dare protest, even if he were not in agreement. But he was; she could sense it in the stiffness of his manner. It was painful to think that such a thing as this could be more important than years of knowing her as a person, more important than kinship and affection, and yet it was so.

"You would enjoy that, wouldn't you?" Ramon flung at Nate. "You can't wait."

The master of Beau Repose licked his lips before he mustered a frown. "I would not hesitate to do my duty."

"Don't you see that would be more of an assault than anything I might have done?"

"So you admit it; she did give it to you!"

Ramon stared at him. "Think what you like. You will anyway."

His words were not an admission, but their pensive quietness could be taken as such if a man desired. Nate Bacon did.

"It strikes me this meeting is a little odd," Nate said, satisfaction oozing from is tone. "Maybe it isn't the first time, maybe I bought soiled goods for by son's bride."

"No, I only saw her once before, for a moment, on the *Biloxi Belle* that brought us both upriver."

"You expect me to believe that the minute she saw you, she fell into your arms?" Nate said, his formless mouth twisting in a sneer.

Ramon smiled. "Considering who, or should I say what, she is marrying tomorrow, can you really blame her?"

Nate's hands knotted into fists. He flung a quick look at Lorna, seeing the confirmation stamped on the pale oval of her face. His mouth twisted, and an expression of malicious calculation rose into his light-colored eyes. Swinging back to Ramon, he said, "She may have let you do it to her, but you seduced her in cold blood, knowing she was Franklin's promised wife. You took her, slipped under her skirts with a lot of sweet talk for no other reason except revenge, revenge against me and mine. That's the truth, isn't it, Cazenave? That's all there was to it!''

The purpose of the charge was to humiliate her, to degrade her for her disloyalty to his son by showing her what kind of man she had presented with her first tender kisses, her virginity. Lorna felt the curling pain of sickness in the center of her being as she waited for the answer that must come.

Ramon swayed, his dark eyes bright and his cut lip curling in a sardonic smile. ''For that,'' he said softly, ''and because she offered such untouched sweetness, so lovely and irresistible a surrender—''

Nate struck out a him then, a blow with all of his boar-like strength behind it. Held by his captors, Ramon could not avoid it. It landed where it was aimed, directly upon the blue shadow and puffed swelling beneath his heart that indicated a damaged rib.

Ramon gave a choked gasp. His knees buckled so that he sagged in the arms of the men who held him, his dark head falling forward. Lorna cried out, starting toward him, but her uncle caught her arm and dragged her to a halt.

Nate stepped back, rubbing his knuckles with his other hand. ''Take him to Beau Repose and lock him up,'' he grunted. ''I'll attend to him later.''

The rain that had soaked them during that cold, strained ride back to Beau Repose was still falling the following afternoon. Lorna stood at the window of her bedchamber watching it sift relentlessly from the gray sky, streaking the window like unceasing tears of grief. A bad omen for a wedding day, the maid who had brought her coffee and rolls a short while ago had said, crossing herself. To Lorna, it seemed only fitting.

They had found Ramon's horse tied at the back of the old house the evening before. He had recovered enough to sit his saddle, reeling, but with his back straight as he was led away. They had not returned his jacket to him, however, or his broad-brimmed hat. Lorna, chilled in her still damp habit jacket, could not prevent herself from thinking of how wet and wretched Ramon must be in the rags of his shirt.

She and her uncle, along with her future father-in-law, had not ridden with the others but followed at some distance behind.

Still, they had reached Beau Repose, coming upon it from a back road, in time to see the field hands push Ramon into the plantation jail and lock the door upon him. He had staggered, falling inside, and it had been all she could do not to protest, to demand medical treatment be provided for him. But so forbidding were the attitudes of the two men with her that it seemed any intervention on her part might only make matters worse, if such a thing were possible.

She had half expected some further inquisition once they reached the great house, but none had been forthcoming. Her uncle had ordered her to her room, and together he and their host had watched her ascend the stairs toward the second floor. As she had moved down the hallway, she thought she had heard their voices, her uncle's apologetic, Nate Bacon's jeering. She had been too exhausted from the upheaval of the evening to care.

She had rung for a hot bath and, trying to be sensible, had even drunk the hot milk laced with brandy offered by the maid who had brought the bath water. One or the other had stilled the trembling inside her, but neither had been effective in helping her to sleep.

Lying wide-eyed in the dark, she had gone over and over the events that had taken place, from the moment she had left her bedchamber to go riding, until the time she had arrived back at Beau Repose. She had writhed inwardly, aghast at her conduct, unable to reconcile what had happened, the desire and intense sense of communication she had shared with a strange man, with the way in which she had had been brought up and the ideas she held of proper behavior. Finally, near dawn, she had slept then awakened far into the day with heavy, red-rimmed eyes and weighted spirits. With her still had been the same sense of disbelief.

It haunted her now, as she stared at the rain. After a life of dutiful obedience, how had she dared defy convention and go riding off alone? What had possessed her that she had allowed a man, one she had never seen before, to take her in his arms, to kiss her, and more, much more? And yet, if there had been no consequences, if no one had found them, if she could have donned her clothing again and ridden away, even without discovering the name of the man who had seduced her, she did not think she would have felt regret. That was the most shocking thing of all.

Behind her, the door swung open. She knew without turning

that it was her Aunt Madelyn. The maid who had brought her coffee had given her the message that her aunt would be with her shortly to help her dress for the wedding. In addition, her aunt had never believed in privacy for either her offspring or her niece, and so never knocked.

"Have you bathed?"

The words were without preamble, the tone of voice without warmth or basic courtesy. Her aunt knew.

Lorna turned, her expression deliberately calm. "Good morning, Aunt Madelyn. Yes, I have bathed."

"Then why are you standing about in your dressing gown? The minister is here. The guests are already beginning to arrive, and you would not believe the mud on the front steps, or the sopping rain capes in the entrance hall. The men are downstairs already, demanding juleps on the galley. I myself have been in my gown for two hours."

"I thought . . . I thought it might be called off."

Her aunt's lips, naturally thin, almost disappeared as she pressed them together. Her head, with its cap of muslin edged with Valenciennes, shot up. Moving with jerky steps that made her three-year-old gown of plum-colored silk dip and sway on her hoop, she went toward the bed where the wedding gown had been laid out along with the necessary undergarments. Over her shoulder, she said, "It would be no more than you deserve. Thankfully, Mr. Forrester was able to persuade Mr. Bacon that you must have lost your head and were only very little to blame. If you are wise, you will endeavor to prove that it is a fact. It would not be a bad thing, also, if you were to show yourself grateful for the forbearance of your groom and his father."

"Franklin has been told?" Why the idea should be so disturbing, she could not have said.

"I cannot be certain, but so I would imagine. It is not something to be kept from one's future husband." Taking up the corset of plain cambric threaded with whalebone stays, she turned, holding it out to Lorna.

"It is doubtful he would know the difference," Lorna pointed out, her tone shaded with bitterness.

"You have always been secretive, Lorna. It was not an attractive habit in you as a child and will be even less so in a wife. You will soon be made one with Franklin and will, of course, strive to make his happiness your sole object. That means you will have no thought that is not his also."

It was an unfortunate reference. ''And suppose,'' Lorna inquired dryly, ''that dear Franklin never has a thought of his own the rest of his life?''

''Do not be impertinent! I am speaking to you for your own good. Another thing, it is a mark of respect, and a most becoming one, to use your husband's surname. I have done so for twenty years, and I'm certain that Mr. Forrester appreciates it.'' Once more, she proffered the corset.

Privately, Lorna was doubtful, but it would do no good to try her aunt further. Releasing the satin bow that held her dressing gown closed in the front, she let the cotton wrapper fall from her shoulders before placing it over a chair at the dressing table. Taking the corset, she stretched the strings laced back and forth in their eyelets, stepped into it, pulling it upward over the camisole and pantaloons she had already put on. Holding it to her, she turned her back, then fastened her hands around the bedpost.

Her aunt tugged vindictively at the corset strings, pulling them tight. Lorna had felt little appetite in some time, however; it was not difficult to close the gap that gave her the eighteen-inch waist decreed by fashion. Knotting the strings, Aunt Madelyn reached for the hoops and petticoats that came next. When they floated like the layered petals of a great white flower around Lorna, the woman took up the wedding gown of Swiss muslin with its pleated ruffles at the neckline and sleeves, its trimming of white silk bows, and the deep pleated flounce around the hem. As she threw it into the air so that it settled lightly over Lorna's head, her face mirrored impatience, and she pulled at the fine muslin, placing the fullness of the skirt with sharp tugs.

''You need not have done this,'' Lorna said. ''One of the upstairs maids could have helped me dress.''

''I hope I know my duty as your nearest female relative.''

If her aunt had owned a woman trained as a ladies' maid, then it might have been she who had dressed Lorna while her aunt merely looked on; or the same might have been true if Lorna herself had been provided with a female servant. There had been no money for that sort of thing in her uncle's household. They had felt lucky to be able to keep a cook and general housemaid, plus a butler and yardman who also tended the stables. This was felt as a hardship by Lorna's cousins, the four daughters of Aunt Madelyn and Uncle Sylvester. They had learned to put up each other's hair, however, and to become adept at wielding a curling iron. There was always someone, too, to do up buttons. In fits of pique, they were apt to declare that it was their mother's parsimony that kept them from having personal attention.

Certainly it was for reasons of economy that they had not been permitted to attend the wedding. The four girls, ranging in age from nine to sixteen, had outgrown their best dresses, and materials suitable for the occasion were dear now, with the war going on, since they had to come to New Orleans through the blockade. Lorna's gown had been procured, heaven alone knew how, by Nate Bacon, but he had not seen fit to furnish apparel for her cousins. It was just as well. The girls would be much better off at school, a select academy run by a lady in Baton Rouge, than preening at Beau Repose, or so their mother said. Lorna's only attendant would be her aunt, since someone must be there to hold her bouquet as she received her ring.

Lorna turned so that her aunt could reach the hooks that closed her gown. She hesitated, then spoke the thought that had been lingering for hours in the back of her mind. "I don't suppose you have heard what has happened to Ramon Cazenave, what will be done to him?"

"That is no concern of yours." Her aunt's fingers pinched as she fastened a hook with vehemence.

Lorna flinched a little but made no sound, so intent was she on what she was saying. "He needs a doctor, I think. More than that, Mr. Bacon has no right to hold him. He has done nothing wrong."

"Nothing wrong?" her aunt gasped. "He has shamed and defiled you, used you as a harlot for his pleasure, and you say he has done nothing wrong?"

"That is only a moral view."

"Only!"

"Yes, Aunt Madelyn! He is not a criminal, he . . . he didn't hurt me. I'm afraid of what will be done to him."

"Whatever it is, it will be no more than he deserves," her aunt said in scathing tones.

"It will be petty vengeance!"

Her aunt finished the last hook, then moved to the pull-knob set into the side of the fireplace mantel and gave it a yank, summoning the hairdresser brought by Bacon from New Orleans at great expense for the occasion. That done, she returned to stand before Lorna. "If you will take my advice, something I am aware you have seldom done, my dear niece, you will put this entire episode from your mind. You will think no more of Ramon Cazenave, considering him as one dead to you.''

The coldness of the words sent a tremor of apprehension along her nerves. She stared at her aunt, her gray eyes silvery with distress. ''Dead?'' she whispered.

A knock fell on the door. Her aunt swung without answering to let the French hairdresser into the room.

Lorna's hair was drawn back in soft waves from her face and coaxed into a cascade of loose curls falling from the crown of her head. Small nosegays of white rosebuds were set among the waves, and beneath them were pinned the forward edges of a veil of sheer blonde.

Aunt Madelyn's lips were tightly pressed as she attached that symbol of purity, but she said nothing in front of the hairdresser. From the pocket of her voluminous skirts, she drew forth a velvet jewel case. Opening it, she brought out the bracelet of sapphires and diamonds that Nate Bacon had tried to present to Lorna the day before.

''Mr. Bacon asked me to see that you had this to wear for the ceremony. It is a fine gift, one you should be proud to have.'' She caught Lorna's wrist and fastened the bracelet around it with quick movements. It felt cold and heavy, like a shackle.

''But, yes,'' the hairdresser exclaimed, her eyes growing wide at the richness of the stones. She whisked away the combing cape that had protected Lorna's gown during the arrangement of her hair, and handed her the bouquet of orange blossoms and white rosebuds that lay on the corner of the dressing table. ''Stand up now, *ma chère*, that we may see you.''

Obediently, Lorna rose to her feet. Moving to the center of the room so that the enormous width of her gown would not be encumbered, she turned slowly, her skirts belling around her, their pleated flounce softly sweeping the Turkish carpet. In grudging tones, her aunt said, ''Very nice.''

''Très magnifique!'' the Frenchwoman corrected, clasping her hands together before her. She tilted her head to one side. ''Though is she not a little pale? One small moment!''

Diving to where her box containing combs and pins and pomade sat, she removed the lid from a compartment to reveal tiny, silver-lidded pots of rice powder and rouge. She chose a hare's foot, dipped it into the rouge pot, and, ignoring Aunt Madelyn's scandalized exclamation, brushed it with extreme care across Lorna's cheekbones. She stepped back with a sigh of satisfaction. "There, now. Smile for the love of *le bon Dieu*! It is not a tragedy, this!"

Lorna tried, but her lips were trembling. In distress, she looked to her aunt, who stood with such uncompromising stiffness before her. "Aunt Madelyn—"

"Yes, in a minute, Lorna. Madame Hélène, my niece and I are grateful for your services. You have done a fine job, but I'm sure that you would like to find a place to view the ceremony now."

"But of course," the hairdresser said, accepting her dismissal with a shrug. At the door, she gave Lorna a wink. "Good luck, *ma petite*."

When the panel had closed behind the woman, her aunt turned back to Lorna. "Now, you wish to say something?"

"I . . . I can't go through with it. I can't, not now!" Her voice was low and husky, with a note of desperation.

"I expected some such melodrama; that's why I sent that woman away. I suppose you would have made her a gift of this piece of folly, something to gossip about all over New Orleans, had I not!"

"What would it matter? Everyone will know, soon enough."

"That they will not!" her aunt stated, her voice hard. "Oh, I know. You are thinking of your own embarrassment when you have to face the man you are to marry, or else the whispers that may go on behind your back in spite of Mr. Bacon's efforts to stop them. It's typical of you to consider your own comfort instead of your uncle's well-being."

"No, it isn't that. Have you spoken to Franklin at all since we have been here, Aunt Madelyn? He's . . . he's an imbecile, with no more intelligence than a child. Yet two nights ago on the gallery he tried to—he put his hands . . ."

An expression of distaste pursed her aunt's mouth. "The passions of men are unaccountable. You must accept them as one of the many obligations of being a wife."

"He wasn't my husband then!"

"He was your affianced husband, which is much the same thing. But no matter. You will be able to rule Franklin absolutely, if you use your head. You will have wealth and position far beyond your deserts, and regardless of the stupid way you have behaved. You should thank your lucky stars that Franklin has some small weakness of the intellect, my girl, or you might have found yourself returned to your uncle as unfit merchandise.''

"I would much prefer that to this marriage. I haven't told you everything. Yesterday afternoon, I saw Franklin with one of the maids. They were in bed, and—''

"Stop! I forbid you to speak of such things to me. It is not a fit subject for a bride and, indeed, none of your concern.''

"Not my concern?'' she echoed in amazement.

"Enough, Lorna. You will go downstairs and pledge yourself to Franklin Bacon as arranged. You will smile and do your best to look the virginal bride. Any other course is unthinkable.''

"But I can't!''

"You can, and you will, for if you do not, you will be the cause of the ruin of your uncle and your cousins, not to speak of myself. Nathaniel Bacon has the power to take our land, our slaves, the roof from over our heads, even the clothes from our backs and the food from our mouths. He has been extraordinarily forgiving; why, I can't imagine. But if you try him further, I have no doubt that he will act to destroy all your uncle has worked to accomplish these last years. I do not think you would like to be the cause of that destruction.''

"It would not be my fault!'' Lorna protested. "If Uncle Sylvester had not borrowed from him in the first place—''

"Or the cotton crop to be used for repayment had not burned? Wishing will not help. Come. It is time to go.''

"If I were your daughter, you would not be so unfeeling,'' Lorna cried, her gray eyes dark.

"If you were my daughter, you would have no cause for such ferment of the mind, since you would never have left my side to be alone with your fiancé on the gallery, never have left the safety of your room when you were supposed to be resting, and certainly never have allowed a strange man to take liberties. If you think me unfeeling now, then hear this: If you disgrace your uncle and myself by further scenes and misbehavior, then you will never again be welcome in our home. I mean it. Quite literally, my dear niece, there is no place for you now other than Beau Repose.''

Lorna stared at the older woman for long moments. There was no escape; she should have known. Holding her head high in unconscious dignity that also prevented the spill of tears over her lashes, she turned without speaking, moving toward the door.

"One thing more," Aunt Madelyn said. "Mr. Bacon has agreed to turn the mortgage papers over to your uncle following the ceremony. Mr. Forrester and I will stay long enough after that to drink a toast to your happiness, but word has come of a steamboat on its way downriver, one behind schedule due to this dreadful conflict, and we intend to have it flagged to take us on board. Needless to say, we have put forward our return home because of the unpleasantness last evening and the possible repercussions that may arise over the imprisonment of your . . . assailant. The reason given to the other guests for our failure to stay for the wedding dinner will be my anxiety as a mother to get home to my children."

"I understand." Lorna pulled open the door, compressing her skirts with one hand as she passed through and out into the hall. From there she could hear plainly the strains of the wedding march from Wagner's *Lohengrin*.

The ceremony, in deference to the limited time Franklin could be expected to lend his attention to the dry formalities, was short. Lorna went through it in a daze, staring straight in front of her, scarcely noticing her fidgeting groom at her side. Nor did she pay much attention to Nate Bacon, serving as his son's best man and, by no coincidence, to compel his responses at the proper time.

At last it was over. Her father-in-law embraced her, placing a hard kiss on her lips. She forced the semblance of a smile, standing rigid as she shook hands and received congratulations. When someone thrust a glass of champagne into her hand, she drank thirstily, then another glass appeared to replace the first. With that aid to detachment, she was able to survive the round of toasts that followed, the endless introductions, the sly glances and arch looks that came her way.

From her vantage point at the end of the room, she was able to watch the white-coated menservants moving in and out of the butler's pantry in a constant stream. In that small serving room were set the great wooden tubs of ice where the sparkling, golden wine had been plunged to chill. The ice had been brought down the river from St. Louis and the northern states months before, to be put down in sawdust in a special cellar. It was a bit of foresight for which Nate enjoyed much congratulations during the course of the afternoon; the sort of expansive gesture, careless of expense, that had been common only a year ago but was now rare. Doubtless, everyone said, it would be the last ice they would see for awhile, the last champagne until the war was over.

The great silver urns of tea and coffee were much commented upon also; likewise the sides of beef and roast pork sliced before the guests' eyes and served on small rolls, the glazed meats in pastry shells, the sugared almonds and molded nougats and meringues and, of course, the towering wedding cake filled with the richness of nuts and dates and candied fruits. Of late the blockade had made such things scarce, and incredibly dear.

They had laughed at first at Lincoln's "paper blockade," as it was popularly called in the newssheets. With hardly more than one hundred and fifty vessels in the federal navy, fewer than two-thirds of which were serviceable, it appeared impossible for an effective watch to be kept over the three thousand miles of Confederate coastline, from Virginia to the Rio Grande, that was pocked with more than a dozen major ports. It was no longer a matter for amusement. In the months since the war had begun, the northerners had bought and outfitted double the original number of ships, snapping up every kind of fishing sloop and ferry and riverboat. Rumor said they had also rushed to build more than fifty ironclads and gunboats with which to restrict the trade of the South.

It was working. Fewer and fewer blockage-running steamers made it up the river to New Orleans with each passing month. Many were sunk, many turned back. Those that arrived showed increasing damage from their dash through the federal fleet that was stationed beyond the mouth of the Mississippi River, steaming slowly up and down like hungry cats at a mouse hole. In the past weeks, fewer than two dozen had made it: those captained by the most daring of men or those with the most urgent business in the city. It was being said of late that the businessmen who financed most of the blockade runners had not felt that the dangers of running into such a tightly guarded port justified the risks; a packet sent to the bottom of the gulf made no profit for its owners.

The war was coming closer to Louisiana as it entered its second year. Men from the state had died at Bull Run, at Fort Henry and Fort Donelson, and at Shiloh only weeks before. There was more than one woman in black in the room. Most of the men in attendance were young, scarcely more than boys, though already with the square set of heavy responsibility about their shoulders; or else they were older men, grandfathers. There were a few who, like Nate and Franklin, had paid other men to go in their places, pleading family responsibilities. They had about them a defensive air, or so Lorna thought.

Still, everyone drank the wine and ate the rich food with apparent pleasure, enjoying the viands bought dearly with the lives of men, the blockade runners who, if they had to die, should have done so for the sake of much needed arms and ammunition for the confederacy, instead of luxuries for the rich.

Lorna felt a trifle giddy. She moved to one of the long, food-laden tables set up in the dining room, intending to find a bite to eat. Nate stood near its head in close conversation with another man, but she ignored him. She wasn't really hungry. She was standing with a plate in her hand, trying to decide what to put on it, when her attention was caught.

"That's what I heard," her father-in-law's companion was saying. "The federals are supposed to have more than one of their new ironclads at the mouth of the river, some say even over the bar. It was young Cazenave who brought the news when he made his last run from Nassau."

"It would certainly pay the federals to gather their forces for a try at gaining the river, coming in on the South's backside," Nate answered, his tone expansive, indulgent, "but you and I both know they can't hope to win past Forts Jackson and St. Philip at the mouth of the river. Their intelligence must tell them the same thing. I refuse, sir, to place credence in such an unreliable source."

"Unreliable? Why Cazenave has the name of being the best of the blockade runners operating out of Nassau. You don't get that by being anything except fast, smart, and as good as your word."

"And lucky. Don't forget that," Nate said with a snort. "Who knows? Someday young Cazenave's luck may run out."

With her back to the two men, Lorna heard the sound of heavy, retreating footsteps, as her father-in-law moved on to other guests; then came the rustle of skirts as if a woman had joined the man left alone.

"My dear," came the quiet voice of an older woman, "was it wise to mention Cazenave to Mr. Bacon? You know how he is."

"I had forgotten for a moment," came the first man's voice with a tired sigh. "It's been ten years, at least."

"Regardless, he is still touchy on the subject."

"You would think it was the Cazenaves, father and son, who had done him an injury, instead of the other way around."

"Discretion, my dear," the woman, doubtless the man's wife, said. "They say his servants are paid to bring the tales they hear to him."

Their voices receded. Lorna turned to stare after the couple, her winged brows forming troubled lines over her eyes. There had been an undercurrent she did not understand in the words she had overheard. A hint of the same had also been evident in the brief exchange between Nate and Ramon. That it was connected in some way with the manner in which Ramon had behaved toward her had been made plain. That being so, the need to know more was a sudden ache inside her, a compulsion that would not be denied.

Glancing around, she saw Franklin in the front parlor, beyond the portieres that, with the massive sliding doors now set back in their slots, divided the two rooms. He was laughing raucously, talking to a group of boys younger than he and spilling cake crumbs down the front of his tailed coat. She wondered if he knew the reason for the enmity between his father and the Cazenaves or, knowing, if he could be persuaded to attend to her long enough to impart the information. Taking a deep breath, she summoned a smile and walked toward him.

He sent her a sidelong look as she approached, and a sullen expression came over his face. In answer to her carefully phrased request to speak to him, he only grunted.

"It will be for no more than a moment," she said and, with a great effort of will, forced herself to put her hands on his arm, drawing him away.

"What do you want?" he demanded. "I was having fun."

"I want to speak to you," she said soothingly.

"I don't want to talk, and I don't have to have anything to do with you until bedtime. That's what Papa said."

Lorna's face stiffened, but she did not draw back. "Yes, and not then, if it doesn't suit you, but for now—"

"Yes, I do. Papa said I have to sleep with you, at least until I make a baby in you. Then I can go back to Lizzie."

Lizzie was without doubt the housemaid with whom she had seen him. "Will you lower your voice?" she whispered sharply.

"Don't tell me what to do! I'm your husband. I can do what I like to you, even if I'm not the first, like Papa said."

The passing of a waiter with a tray filled with goblets of

champagne was a relief. Sweeping a glass up as the man paused before them, she snatched the cake plate Franklin held from his hand and pushed the glass into it. Setting the plate on the man-servant's tray, she sent him away again.

"I am not trying to tell you what to do," she said hastily as he drank. "I only want you to explain to me about Beau Repose. How did it come about that your father gained possession of land here in the heart of the French Creole section? And why should there be hard feelings between him and . . . and the previous owners?"

"You mean the Cazenaves?" An echo of his father's sneer, with the underside of his thick lips showing, crossed Franklin's porcine features. "I know what you did with Ramon. Lizzie told me, and she knows, 'cause her brother was there. You should be punished for what you did. I asked Papa, and he said it would be all right, because you would be my wife, and I could to anything I like to you."

"Yes, yes," she said hastily, paying little heed to his ram-blings, mentally castigating herself for embarking on this inter-rogation, especially as a pair of turbaned dowagers seated in chairs in a corner turned to stare at them as they passed, then looked at each other with raised brows. A militant look came into her gray eyes, despite the flush on her cheeks, as she went doggedly on, searching for the simplest way to phrase what she wanted to know. "But why is it that Ramon dislikes your papa?"

"He thinks Papa did him out of Beau Repose. It was gam-bling debt, see. Old man Cazenave lost the house and land in a game of poker." He giggled. "A while after that, he turned up his toes and died."

It was not an uncommon story. Great fortunes had been won and lost in the gambling dens of New Orleans and abroad the steamboats that had plied up and down the Mississippi River for more than a half a century. Men played their last card, shrugged, and walked away. Easy come, easy go, in the rich delta land where a gentleman was dishonored if he did not settle such affairs in the least possible amount of time, where a man with a small amount of capital and the spirit of daring had been able, in the early years, to recoup his losses by clearing and cultivating another plantation property. Some men had gained and lost sev-eral fortunes. Some plantations had been won and lost several times over. In each case, it was the women who cried and packed their belongings for the move.

"If that's the way it happened." she said, frowning, "it was unfortunate, but I don't see how your father can be blamed."

"That's right, he can't."

"But wasn't he surprised when Ramon did blame him?"

The blast of a steam whistle ripped the air, slicing across any reply Franklin might have made. His face lit up, and he swung around with a jerky, shuffling run, heading for the front door. Following more slowly, along with the majority of the other guests, Lorna saw the great white boat whose whistle had sounded. It rounded the bend in the wide river before the house, riding the current with its snub-nosed bow angling toward the landing of Beau Repose, where a Negro man stood waving a large white signal flag as a sign that there were passengers to be taken on board.

Stacked three stories high, it was iced with lace-like wooden filigree, like a wedding cake. Its great smokestacks, fluted on top in the shape of crowns, threw back plumes of dark smoke that mingled with the mist rising off the river. Because of the way the levee was constructed, an earthen dam winding with the river, rising twelve feet and more above the flat surface of the surrounding land, the boat riding the flood was on a level with the great house on its man-made elevation.

As the steam packet glided into the landing, it set the plantation skiff, a long, narrow boat with a stepped mast of the sort kept ready by most places along the river for quick visits up and down, to rocking on its rope tied to the pilings. The Negro roustabout aboard the packet jumped to the landing to loop the bigger boat's hawser over the same piling stump to which the skiff was tied, before running out the gangplank.

It had stopped raining for the time being. The pale and watery light of early evening touched the white railings of the *General Jackson* with tints of reflected gray-pink and green, glimmered on the gilded eagle strung on a cable between her smokestacks, and searched out the stirring depiction of the Battle of New Orleans painted in vivid colors on her paddle box.

Her aunt and uncle were not the only ones to take advantage of the late-running steamboat. A number of the other guests were embarking also, the men still waving julep glasses and the women clutching fluttering handkerchiefs, while young girls hugged pieces of wedding cake to be placed underneath their pillows so they might dream of their future husbands. Uncle

Sylvester and Aunt Madelyn waved once from the upper deck, their smiles taut, before turning aside to enter their stateroom.

The steamboat's bell rang three times, a melodious clanging that rang over the water and echoed from the tree line of the distant shore. The whistle blew a long blast, and then a second and a third. Gay cries of farewell filled the air. The boat began to back up, its great side wheels churning the yellow-brown waters of the Mississippi into a mud bath.

"Too thick to navigate and too thin to cultivate," Nate Bacon said from where he had moved to stand at Lorna's side.

It was an old saying, but she smiled politely. Her gray gaze lingered on the boat as it pulled out into the current.

"Shall we return to the house?" he asked.

She sent him a quick glance to find him offering his arm in ironic gallantry. Around them, the others who had come to see departing acquaintances off were straggling back across the sloping green lawn that led up to the white-pillared mansion. It would be ungracious to refuse his support over the wet grass. Signifying her agreement by placing her fingers on his sleeve, she said, "I trust my aunt and uncle's journey downriver will not be delayed unduly by the weather."

"Yes," he agreed, his tone absent as he glanced around at the leaden skies. His footsteps were dawdling, and his light blue regard swung back to her averted face. "I haven't told you how lovely you look. It's a pity you must leave the party. You're aware that you are to dine with Franklin, alone?"

"I had not been told," she answered in stifled tones.

"An oversight, I'm sure. I understood your aunt was to mention it to you, as well as the suite of rooms that have been furnished for your use as man and wife—where you will now find your belongings. At any rate, that is the arrangement. I expect you will wish to retire soon to prepare for the arrival of your groom."

"Yes." There was something about the way he watched her, the way he had fallen behind the others, that sent a wave of unease over her. It was as if, without speaking of it, he meant for her to remember the situation in which he had found her at near the same time the day before.

"I fear," he said deliberately, "that you may be disappointed in what transpires tonight."

She sent him a cool look, though her heartbeat seemed to

have stopped. "I beg your pardon, but I can't have heard you correctly."

He laughed. "Charming. It should prove amusing to have you around for the next few weeks. I was speaking of Franklin's capacity in bed. He particularly enjoys virgins, you see. Not knowing what to expect, they cannot be disappointed. He is, therefore, free to be as selfish as he pleases. Women of experience, as I discovered on the one occasion when I took him to a brothel, unman him—except for the Negro maids, of course, whose opinion of his prowess he need not consider."

"I would rather not speak of it!"

"Don't turn prudish, it doesn't become you." Nate grunted, his voice sharp with annoyance. "I am trying to warn you of what you may encounter."

"If you expect me to be grateful," she said in a flash of anger, "then I'm afraid you are the one who must be disappointed."

"I thought you might make use of the information. It could help matters if you were to pretend to a maidenly modesty at the least, to show a little reluctance, even some sign of fear. I'm sure it would do wonders."

A shudder ran over her, and she looked away, setting her teeth in her bottom lip to prevent herself from saying something she might regret. She would have liked to snatch her hand from his arm and run, but there was no one to run to, no place to go. Finally, since he seemed to expect some reply, she answered, "You need not concern yourself. I am certain it will be all right."

Nate stopped at the foot of the steps. He looked around him and, there being no one near enough to overhear, said quietly, "If it isn't, you can always come to me."

"Come to you?" she repeated, swinging her head to stare at him. Was it possible she had misjudged him? The thought drew her brows together over her eyes.

"I think I can guarantee to make up for Franklin's deficiencies as a husband. If there are any children as a result, it can always be arranged that Franklin be recognized as the father."

"Children?" She snatched her hand away from him, retreating a step.

"You needn't look so surprised at the idea. I am not more than middle-aged, you know, barely forty-six. Older men than that have sired new families. It's by no means impossible."

She clenched her hands on her skirts, lifting them to take a step. "You are mistaken," she said in a voice that shook with the disgust that gripped her. "It is impossible because you—because I will never accept your offer. The relationship we share at this moment is all there will ever be between us!"

He gave her a slow smile, his light blue gaze bright and his formless mouth twisted with derision. "We'll see. A woman like you who has had experience will expect more in bed than you are likely to get with Franklin. Pretty soon, a week, a month, you'll be bored senseless. Then we'll see!"

Chapter 3

Her new husband's ankle-length dressing gown was of blue satin strewn with life-size appliqués of Scots terrier dogs in black velvet. As they sat at the small table placed before the fireplace, Lorna tried not to look at the man across from her. She gazed instead at the fire roaring beneath the mantel, overheating the room on this night that was cool and humid from the rain, but not cold; at the pattern of the Spode china banded in pink that graced the table, at the sputtering brass gaslight overhead with its ornate scrolled arms and leaded crystal globes. She carefully avoided even glancing in the direction of the great four-poster bed, however.

It was not merely Franklin's taste in dressing gowns that offended her. His table manners were crude beyond belief. She had not noticed them particularly before, perhaps because on the one occasion when she had taken a meal in his company Nate had been there to correct him, to admonish with a stern glance. Released from that restraint, Franklin tore the roast chicken apart with his bare hands, sucked his fingers, spilled wine down his black velvet lapels, and chewed with his mouth open, dribbling at the corners.

Lorna felt unwell. The heat of the fire, the smell of the food, the sounds Franklin made as he masticated the chicken, the closeness of the room, plus the virulence of her own fears, combined to give her an almost uncontrollable urge to escape. She tried to combat it by sipping at her glass of wine and thinking, deliberately, of nothing.

Franklin's jaws slowed. He stared at her with a slab of apple pie halfway to his mouth. "Ain't you hungry?"

"I suppose I ate too much cake," she answered with a shake of her head.

"I didn't see you eat any." He took a bite of the pie and a swallow of wine. As he spoke, his words were muffled, slurred.

She had the feeling he could be extremely stubborn, inclined to cling to an idea, once he got it. Evading the issue, she said. "It was delicious."

"It sure was. But I ate all the chicken they brought for our supper. You didn't eat any of it."

"No, I . . . I'm not fond of chicken." It was an untruth, but perhaps it would serve.

"You didn't eat any of the ham."

"No."

"None of the boiled potatoes."

"No."

"Nor the bread and butter."

She shook her head.

"Nor the pickled cabbage relish."

There were several items to go before he got to the dessert. In an effort to deflect him, she said, "But I am drinking my wine."

"I've drunk more than you have."

There could be little doubt of that. If she was any judge of the matter, he had been drinking without stopping since the wedding, even while he changed. He had been assisted into his attire for a supper à deux by his valet, using the dressing room of their suite, which included also the bedchamber and a small sitting room. Lorna herself had changed earlier, removing her wedding gown and, reluctantly, dressing in the expected dishabille in the most frantic haste in the bedchamber. There had been a maid waiting to aid her. The woman had said she was sent by the master of the house, but Lorna recognized her as Franklin's Lizzie. The most disturbing thing about having the maid there had been the woman's attitude. She had shown no sign of jealousy or resentment, only a quiet, unspoken sympathy.

"I did, didn't I?" Franklin demanded.

"What?" She stared at him, at a loss for a moment. "Oh, yes, you did drink more wine."

"I'm going to have some brandy, too." He watched her, his lips pushed out in a belligerent pout, his hands clutching his wineglass and the remains of his pie.

"As you like," she murmured.

"You can't stop me. You're just my wife, not my papa."

The glance he gave her, probing the layers of muslin that covered her breasts, made her aware of how inadequate a covering was her wrapper and nightgown. She said in simple truth, "I have no wish to stop you."

"You better not. You don't tell me what to do, I tell you. Ring the bell."

The expression in his eyes was cunning, as if he were testing her. She felt instinctively that it would be unwise for him to have more to drink, but she had been given no instructions about what he was allowed to do and what he was not. Without them, it did not seem her place to interfere in his pleasures, and if he drank himself senseless this night, so much the better.

"Now!" he bellowed, raising his fists and slamming them down so hard that the stem of the wineglass shattered. He threw the pieces on the floor, along with the crumbs of his piecrust, and snatched his hand to his lips where he began to suck at the small place where he had been cut.

It wasn't his fault he was like this, she reminded herself; she must not allow him to provoke her. Giving him a cool stare, she rose and moved to pull the bell-knob on the end of the mantel. As she returned to her seat, she picked up her napkin and reached to press one corner to the tiny slash on his hand.

It was Lizzie who answered the summons. When she heard his order, she cocked her head to one side. "You know, Maste' Franklin, that they ain't goin' to bring you no brandy, even if I was to tell them what you want."

"You can get it for me," he wheedled.

"Who, me? I ain't got no key to the wine closet."

"It's not locked up. I saw a bottle in the library."

"I can't go down there! You trying to get me whipped?" The girl's tone was indignant.

"Nobody'll see you. They're all in the dining room. It wouldn't take more than a minute to shag your ass down there and back again. Damn it, I want some brandy!"

"Don't get all lathered up, Maste' Franklin. I don't like to see you that way.'' There was a wary look on the maid's face as she edged toward the door, but no surprise at his vulgar language.

''Then do what I say!''

''All right, all right, I'm going. I just hope nobody sees me, 'cause your papa's goin' to be mad if he finds out what you're up to up here.''

''He won't find out if you stop talking and start moving.''

The maid bobbed a nod and slid out the door. When she had gone, Franklin flung a smirk of satisfaction in Lorna's direction. ''I'm goin' to have brandy.''

''So it would seem,'' she said dryly.

''I bet Cazenave's not having any.''

Her head came up and she studied his vacuous face, searching for meaning. ''Won't he?''

''No wine either. No supper.''

''I see. He'll go hungry to bed then,'' she said after a moment.

''Last night, too.'' The idea seemed to give him immense satisfaction.

''He wasn't given food last night, either?''

He gave a quick shake of his head in answer to her question. ''Nor this morning, nor at noon.''

''That's barbaric! You must be mistaken.''

''Not mistaken. Went to see him before the wedding. He asked me for water. Didn't give it to him.''

Lizzie, returning with a cut-glass decanter of brandy and a glass on a tray, drew his attention. He watched as she poured out two inches of the golden brown liquor. Before the maid had left the room, taking the supper dishes with her, he had swallowed half of it. ''No brandy, no wine, no water,'' he muttered.

''Why?'' Simple questions seemed best for Franklin.

His answer was a grunt as he finished the brandy and reached out at the same time for her to pour him more.

''Is it because someone gave the order he was not to be fed?'' she persisted. ''Or is it just that no one has been told to provide his meals?''

Nothing to eat or drink, no attention for his injuries, no fire to dry his clothing, and no covering against the cool dankness of the night, just a damp dirt floor in a cell that no one came near. Ramon must have heard the faint sounds during the day of music and people coming and going. What must he have felt, knowing that if he called out it would be thought he was just a recalcitrant slave shut away for punishment, knowing that a feast was being enjoyed close at hand, being able, possible, to smell it, while he was brought nothing.

"You worried?" Franklin asked, cocking his head, his pale blue eyes malicious.

"No more than for any living creature being made to suffer."

That was the way it should be, considering the way the man had used her for his own ends. It was not pleasant to know he would have taken her regardless of her own attraction for him, or lack of it. And yet, hadn't she used him in much the same way, reaching out for forgetfulness, an experience of passion with which to comfort herself in the long, barren years ahead, without more than surface consideration for him as a person?

"You're a liar," Franklin said, the words almost unintelligible as he tried to get them out around his thickening tongue while hiccuping in the middle of them. "I bet you'd like to know what else—what's goin' to happen to your . . . to your lover?"

She did not quibble with the description. And he was quite right; she did want to know. Still, staring at Franklin's flushed face twisted by a sneer, it seemed that saying so would be the least likely way to gain the information.

She shrugged with elaborate unconcern. "Your father will decide what is to become of him, I'm sure."

"He's already 'cided."

"How enterprising of him, when he's had so much else on his mind, such as seeing to his guests and the arrangements for the wedding without the help of a hostess. Speaking of which, how is your mother? I was disappointed that she did not attend."

"She doesn't . . . doesn't leave her room."

"So I understand. I hope I will be allowed to meet her soon."

Franklin scowled, distracted by her chatter. "You were supposed to last night, but you wasn't well enough."

"No," she agreed graciously, "perhaps tomorrow. I'm sure I'll have time while your father is busy with his prisoner."

"And me. I'm goin' to watch."

"Are you?" She forced herself to smile as if at a child speaking of a treat in store.

"I bet he'll holler and squeal. The young boars always do, and the stallions, and the bull calves. They use a special tool sometimes, did you know? Or maybe just a knife. They hold 'em down and cut their—"

Sickness rose into Lorna's throat at his description, vile and artlessly vivid. A plantation was a large, self-sufficient farm, and she had seen and heard enough as she grew up on her uncle's acres to know that male animals were often castrated to prevent their urges toward procreation from interfering with their usefulness. There were names for such animals so treated; barrows, geldings, steers. Was there a name for a man? There must be, only she had never been allowed to hear it.

She got to her feet so quickly that she brushed the table, nearly upsetting the brandy decanter before Franklin could grab for it. With her hand pressed to her mouth, she turned away.

"That bother you, what I said? You don't like that?" he jeered behind her.

Exerting a great effort of will, she lowered her hand, speaking without turning. "Ramon Cazenave struck me as the kind of man who would kill anyone who dared do such a thing. He . . . will be dangerous when he is well again."

"If he gets well, maybe."

"What do you mean?"

"Can't do much when he's at the bottom of the river."

She swung around, staring at him. His words had been so garbled she was not certain she had heard him right. "What?"

"When we get through with him, we'll put him in a boat, set him loose."

"On the river? You can't do that! It would be murder!"

"He's got to be punished. You were promised to me; you ought to be punished, too." He pushed himself to his feet, moving toward her. "I can do that. I can do anything I like to you now."

She took an involuntary step backward before she halted. Her head came up. "This is ridiculous, even speaking of such things. This . . . this is our wedding night."

"But you didn't wait for me. You didn't wait." His hands were working, clenching and unclenching, and in his eyes was a feral, joyful gleam.

"Touch me, and I'll scream for help."

"Nobody will hear. They're all out front, listening to the banjos. Don't you hear?"

He was right. It was a favorite after-dinner entertainment, bringing musicians from the quarters to serenade the guests as they sat on the gallery. Besides the banjos, there would be home-made base fiddles and rattles of dried gourds. It was all too possible she would not be heard.

"Anyway, Papa won't care; he said you needed your ass blistered. And everybody else knows I'm your husband."

He was shrewd in his own way. That was the frightening thing. But she would not submit to his chastisement. She had not recognized anyone's right to correct her physically since the death of her parents; she had fought her aunt for possession of the switches and paddles used against her as she was growing up, much to that lady's rage and chagrin. To meekly allow her husband the privilege was more than she could stomach, no matter what society said about his rights.

She moistened her lips, searching for something that might distract him, aware of his bulk between her and the door, of his undoubtedly superior weight and strength. "If you did that, would it make you feel more like a man?"

It was the wrong thing to say. His face turned purple and he lunged, grabbing for her forearm, fastening his fingers upon it with a biting grip. She smelled the fetid stench of his breath and the sourness of spilled food from his clothing. She jerked her arm up, breaking his grasp, whirling away, but his fingers caught in the muslin of her sleeve. It tore with a soft rasping but did not part from her wrapper. She was dragged back toward him, stumbling.

Even as she came, however, she reached up to jerk free the satin bow cutting into her neck. She gasped for air as it came loose, then ducked, struggling, wriggling to draw her arms from the wide sleeve. As the loose garment fell from her, she evaded Franklin's ponderous lunge and, sidestepping, whirled away from him.

She skipped backward with the curtain of her hair whipping around her. Warily, she watched as he threw down her wrapper and stamped on it, then spread his arms, coming at her in a bull-like rush. At the last minute, she darted aside, twisting to avoid his clutching grasp. Her arm caught a chair with bruising force, sending it flying to crash against the wall. Thrown off balance, she stumbled to one knee. He flung himself at her, grabbing her around the hips as they fell. Lorna's shoulder struck the carpeted floor for a breathless instant sending pain through her. She felt Franklin's fingers digging into her, sinking into her flesh, pinching as he tried to drag her under him. She kicked out, catching him in the belly so that the air left him in a whistling groan.

She kicked him again and, as his hold loosened, scrambled from him, crawling, hampered by the length of her gown. There was a door in front of her, leading into the sitting room. Pulling herself to her feet, she threw herself toward it and fell into the other room.

There was no outside door into the hall. The only entrance or exit was the way she had come. She jerked around to see Franklin pulling himself to his feet in the door opening, holding to the jam. She sidestepped behind a settee covered in wine brocatelle.

In that small room filled to overflowing with tables and chests, with urns and cuspidors and marble busts on pedestals and spindly Louis XIV chairs, all dominated by a towering black walnut étagère holding tier upon tier of china bric-a-brac, there was little room to evade the man who was her husband.

"You hurt me," he growled. "I'm goin' to hurt you bad. I'll make you cry. I know how, I do. Lizzie don't like it when I do it to her that way. She begs. I'll make you beg, but I'm goin' to do it anyway."

"You're mad," she said, her voice tight.

"I ain't," he shouted, shoving away from the door. "I ain't!"

The black walnut monstrosity of a china closet stood behind her. She stepped back without looking, closing her hand on a sharp-edged figurine. As Franklin staggered toward her, she threw the minature shepherdess with all her strength.

He tried to duck but was too late. It caught him above the eye, and a red line of blood oozed, tracking downward. He was more nimble the next time, and the next, dodging as he advanced.

She turned over tables and chairs as she retreated, circling the room, heading for the door into the bedchamber. She had almost reached it when suddenly Franklin swooped, catching up a footstool. Paying her back in her own coin, he brought it around in a backhand throw.

It hit her in the ribs and she staggered. The edge of the settee caught the back of her legs and she sprawled backward upon it, landing in a tangle of skirts. It rocked, steadied, then rocked again as he threw himself upon her. Before she could move, he had straddled her waist, dragging her under him, grinding the hard swelling at his crotch against her and letting her see he wore nothing under the blue satin dressing gown. A vicious grin

stretched his lips over his teeth, and the blood trickling through
his bushy brows into his eyes gave him a wild, animalistic look.

She flailed at him, gasping as his weight compressed her
lungs. He caught her wrists, turning them, squeezing until she
gave a stifled gasp at the pain and was still. Taking one of her
hands, he pushed it under him, sitting on it. He drew back and
slapped her in the face, first one cheek, then bringing the back
of his hand across the other.

Tears sprang into her eyes, shimmering in a mist of pain and
humiliation, flowing slowing into her hair. Helpless rage glittered with sudden, uncontrollable hate in her gray eyes. Seeing
it, he laughed.

He kept a careful watch then as he tried to unbutton the top
of her nightgown. When he could not do it, he curled his fingers
into the fabric, pulling at it so that it cut into her neck, ripping
the bits of mother-of-pearl that held it closed from their holes.
Ignoring her arching attempts to unseat him, he placed his hand
on the soft white mound of her breast he had exposed and slowly
closed his fingers, tighter and tighter, his thumb and forefinger
grasping the peak, pinching. She gave a strangled cry, and an
excited, high-pitched giggle shook him.

Was it her pain or his perverted pleasure in it that brought
cold reason rushing to her head? She did not know, but abruptly
it was there. Ignoring the cruelties he was inflicting, she forced
a sarcastic smile.

"I thought," she said, "that you were afraid of women like
me."

"Me? I'm not afraid of nobody," he boasted, releasing her
breast, reaching for the other one.

"No? Prove it. Make love to me, make me feel something
no other man has. Let me see how you stand up against the
lovemaking of Ramon Cazenave. Let's see if you are any better."

Uneasiness crossed his face. "I don't have to."

"What are you afraid of?" she taunted. "That I'll find out
what a disappointment you are in bed? Your papa warned me
you might be. Maybe hurting women is the most you can do!"

Did she imagine it, or was he less tumescent beneath the
hiked-up hem of his dressing gown?

He cursed, backing down like a crab, positioning himself
over her thighs. He snatched at the voluminous hem of her night-

gown, shoving it out of his way. He grabbed at himself, pushing a fist between her trapped legs, trying to force an entry.

"Be still," he muttered as she writhed, digging in her heels.

"Why?" The answer was short as she caught her breath in unfeigned disgust. "All you are doing is fumbling. Even gelded, Ramon would be a better lover than you!"

He pushed himself from her, shoving away so violently that the settee went over backward. A leg splintered with a rending crack. The carved back slammed against the heart pine of the floor. Lorna was jolted from the seat, rolling with her nightgown about her waist. She smacked into the corner of a blanket chest, relic of some bride's long-faded trousseau, and lay there, stunned at her deliverance.

She heard Franklin's foot steps receding, crossing the adjoining bedchamber, moving into the dressing room. In the instant that she though about it at all, she supposed that he was looking for something to use to clean the blood from his face. Slowly she sat up, pushing down her nightgown. She got to her feet and, holding to the arm of the overturned settee, came fully erect by degrees. Moving to a chair, she lowered herself into it. With one shaking hand, she smoothed the hair from her face, pushing it behind her shoulders. She felt coolness against her chest. Looking down, she saw her bodice hanging open. With painstaking care, she began to push the buttons back into their torn holes.

At a scuffling sound, she looked up. Franklin stood in the doorway. He had left his dressing gown untied so that the edges fell away, revealing the corpulence of his body with its thick chest, full belly, and short legs. He was covered in a thick pelt of hair, a coarse growth that, as it tapered under his belly, did not disguise his flaccid condition. His legs were spread, set, and his face was congealed in virulent anticipation. In his hands he held a razor strap, the broad strip of thick leather used to hone a straight-edged razor before shaving.

His stomach muscles knotted as he began to swagger toward her. She could not remove her gaze from the strap that he slapped again and again across one hand, holding it by its hanging hook. She ran her tongue over her lips, rising to her feet. When he stopped before her, she faced him squarely and lifted her chin. Her voice shook as she spoke; still she forced the words through the constriction in her throat.

"Touch me with that thing," she said, "and I will kill you."

He laughed, a high squeal of pleasure. "I'll touch you. I'll give it to you, you'll see!"

The strap whistled as he raised it high and brought it slashing down toward her hips. It did not strike. Like a dancer, she whirled, leaping away from him.

He cursed, stumbling after her, whipping the air with the strap, his lunges wild and uncontrolled. As she eluded him again and again, his frustration grew and he screamed foul names at her.

She was tiring. The muscles of her legs quivered with the effort to keep beyond his reach, to avoid the obstacle course of overturned furniture and prevent herself from being trapped in the corners of the room. Once or twice she tripped, felt the rush of air as the strap fanned past her skin.

It happened so quickly there was not time to prevent it. She stepped on the pieces of a broken china dog and lurched into the étagère. The jar of her body striking it sent glass and porcelain cascading to the floor with the clatter of fragile, breaking ornaments. Franklin, close upon her, grabbed her hair, yanking her toward him. She fell, twisting in midair, catching herself on her forearms as she hit the floor. He leaned over her, a shout of triumph in his throat. The strap came whining down, striking, biting into her skin, and agony tore through her. He dropped to the floor beside her, hoisting one knee, pushing it into her back. Grunting, he brought the strap down again and again.

She went mad. Wrenching, turning her arm backward, she clawed at him, finding his vulnerable crotch. As her nails dug into him, he howled and shifted. In that moment, she dragged herself a part of the way from under him propping herself on one knee. In retaliation, he lashed her again.

The burning pain that surged across her shoulders raced to her brain. She leaped up, throwing him off balance. He beat at her, unable to swing the leather strap but catching her a glancing blow along the jaw that made her head ring. She raised herself higher, reaching with her left hand for the strap. Her right hand touched a cold and knobby object on the floor and closed around it in a desperate reflex. Heaving upward, coming to her knees in spite of his trying to press her back down, she brought her right hand around in a wide swing, striking at his face with a strength born of outrage.

The thing she held in her hand was a small bust of Parian marble on a brass base. The corner of the base struck his temple, sinking in. He made a peculiar sound, something between a growl and a sigh, and toppled backward to fall thudding to the floor. The strap fell from his lax fingers. His muscles twitched convulsively; then he was still.

Lorna sat with her head down, her chest heaving as she fought for breath. She was shivering, the tremors running over her in waves. She ached in every fiber, while the places on her body where his blows with the strap had struck seemed on fire. Her knee was stinging, and she saw with dull surprise that she was lying in broken glass.

Slowly, she grew aware of the quiet. Brushing the hair from her eyes, she looked at Franklin. He lay unmoving. Naked, with his dressing gown crumpled under him, he was not an attractive sight, yet she could not tear her gaze away. Unconsciously, her panting breaths grew more shallow as she strained to hear. There was no sound. She watched his chest. The barrel of his body did not stir.

It was an effort to move, to force herself to crawl toward him. On her knees at his side, she placed her hand gingerly on the wiry fur that covered his chest, pressing down to find the heartbeat. She could feel nothing. Only then did she glance at his face. His eyes were wide open, sightless and glazed like those of a kitten she had once seen run over by a carriage.

He was dead.

Chapter 4

Lorna got to her feet. She moved away a few steps, then stood staring at the wall. Moments passed before, abruptly, she shook her head, as if the action would banish a measure of the numbness that gripped her. She had to think, she had to.

She should call for help, tell someone what had happened. It was too late to help Franklin, however. She was a murderess. She could explain that it had been an accident, that she had not meant it, had only wanted to stop him from hurting her. But would they believe her? Might they not say that he had the lawful right to mete out punishment, to beat her if he chose; and she none to prevent him? Perhaps they were right? Perhaps after the liberties she had permitted Ramon Cazenave, she deserved it? Could it be that those few minutes of depravity the afternoon before had been but an indication of the crimes she was capable of committing?

No. She raised her hands to her temples, turning her head violently from side to side. That was the way her Aunt Madelyn would think, the way she would talk if she were here. She was not here. She and Uncle Sylvester had gone. She was alone.

What would Nate Bacon say when he knew she had killed his only son? He had loved Franklin in his way; she was certain of it. He had indulged him, made excuses for him, foisted him on the public, arranged a marriage in an attempt to steady him and provide guidance. Nate might well be responsible for the brutal, undisciplined conduct of his son. On the other hand, it might have been that he had been unable to accept what Franklin had become after the accident, and so had tried out of pride to treat him as though nothing had changed.

It did not matter. His concern for Franklin had not prevented him from making lewd suggestions to his bride. Even if Nate were able to forgive her Franklin's death, her position at Beau Repose would not be a safe one. If her father-in-law expected to enjoy the favors of his son's new wife, how much more would he not insist on intimacies with his widow?

He could not force her, could he?

She lowered her hands, clenching them before her. Her gray eyes wide, she considered the question. It was not inconceivable, given his idea of her lack of virtue. He might well use the thing she had just done as a hold upon her, forcing her compliance to prevent her being accused and prosecuted as a wanton killer. Why should it not be so? Had he not used much the same tactic to ensure her marriage to Franklin in the first place? Even if he did not try that method, his importunings, his sly glances and excuses to touch her would make life unbearable.

She could not endure it. She would not. That being the case, she could not stay at Beau Repose. She would have to leave, at once, before Franklin's death was discovered. She would have to go tonight, this moment.

She took three quick steps toward the bedchamber, then stopped. Where would she go? Her aunt had warned her that, if she brought more disgrace to the Forrester name, she would not be welcome in her home. What did that leave? She had no money, nothing of value to sell to gain funds to travel with or with which to keep herself until she could decide what to do.

Her head suddenly rose and her gray eyes widened. Wait. That wasn't true. There was the betrothal bracelet. Did she dare? Did she?

She must; there was no other way. The decision taken, she moved with quick steps into the bedchamber. Being careful not to glance at the body in the sitting room, she caught the door and pulled it to behind her. Turning then, she took a deep breath and moved to the armoire where she flung open the door.

Her gowns, for all their fullness, took up little space in the commodius wardrobe. They were few in number, and most of the space was given over to her petticoats, with the collapsed hoop of her crinoline standing in a great circle behind them. To think of making an escape in so unwieldly a costume would be foolhardy. She reached at once for her riding habit, freshly cleaned and pressed that morning, which hung on its brass hook.

She threw the garment on the bed and stripped off her own nightgown with feverish haste. Searching out pantaloons and a camisole, she drew them on, then reached for the long poplin skirt. It was only as she was hooking the waistband that she remembered.

Ramon Cazenave. She could not leave him behind at the mercy of Nate Bacon's revenge. As a prisoner, he was too vulnerable, too near, when Nate's terrible rage over the death of his son would be loosed. She would have to do something. But what?

She worried over the problem as she finished dressing and put up her hair. Franklin had gone to see Ramon at some time during the day; he had been at pains to tell her that. She did not think, from the way he had spoken, that his father had been aware of the visit. Did that mean that the key to the plantation jail was not kept by Nate himself?

Where, then, could it be? That the guards set to watch the prisoner might have it she rejected at once. The only servant trusted with keys was usually the butler, or majordomo, and then only the keys to the wine closet, smokehouse, storerooms, and the cabinets where the silver was kept. Her own aunt had carried those same keys herself on a silver chatelaine at her waist, along with the keys to the spice chest, the tea caddy, and the knife boxes. It had been her uncle who had retained the key to the jail. The padlock it opened being a heavy one, and the key, therefore, of some size, he had not liked carrying it on his person. It had hung on a peg inside a cabinet in his study. No one had dared disturb it.

There was still music coming from the front lawn when she opened the bedchamber door. The strains of ''Jeanie with the Light Brown Hair'' echoed up the stairwell and along the softly lighted hallway. It did not seem possible that so much had taken place with no change in that peaceful gathering in the encroaching darkness on the gallery.

There was no one in sight. She stepped out into the hall and, with the utmost care, closed the door behind her. Keeping close to one wall, she eased toward the stairs. Descending a single slow step at a time, she paused often to listen. The house rang with a myriad of muffled noises—the far-off clink of dishes, the low hum of conversation among the guests outside, the music. She felt exposed there on the staircase with no where to run, no place to hide if anyone decided to step into the front hall. It required an effort of will to force herself to go lower, and lower still. Then near the foot, she caught the sound of voices in the dining room; it was the servants clearing away the remains of dinner. Losing her nerve suddenly, she took the last treads with quick steps and slipped into the study. She stood for a moment with her back against the door and her heart pounding, then flung herself with nervous haste into the search.

The key was not in the book cabinet with its glass doors; nor was it in the shallow drawer of the desk. She found it finally by chance. Turning from the desk, she had stumbled against the chair behind it. The man's coat that hung over the back had fallen to the floor with a dull, clanking sound. She had pounced on it with a smothered cry. Pushing her hand into a pocket, she brought out the key on its iron ring.

The dining room across the hall was quiet when she emerged. The door stood ajar. Through the opening, she could see the cleared table, denuded on its cloth. Beyond it stood a sideboard still laden with cakes and pies on tall silver and crystal footed stands. The smell of food lingered on the air, a ripe and rich fruitiness that was nauseating. It reminded her, however, of what Franklin had said; that Ramon had been given nothing to eat since he had been taken. The ghost of an idea flitted across her mind. Before she could grasp it fully, she had slid into the room. She moved lightly to the sideboard and snatched up a silver stand holding three-quarters of a dewberry pie.''

''Why, Mis' Lorna, what are you doing there?''

She whirled at the sound of the question voiced behind her, and came face to face with a manservant in a white jacket. She remembered him as one of the men who attended to guests, bringing in their trunks and boxes, and who sometimes served at the table. His face, she saw at once, was creased with concern, not accusation.

When she did not speak, he went on. ''You should have rung for somebody to bring that pie to you.''

She glanced from the juicy dessert she held back to his liquid brown eyes, then tilted her head toward the side door that opened from the house onto a covered ramp leading to the outdoor kitchen behind the house. ''I . . . did ring. I suppose you were all out there.''

He gave her a puzzled look. "The bells are on the back gallery; somebody should have heard. Anyway, shall I carry that up for you now, and maybe bring some fresh coffee to go with it?"

"No! No, you . . . might wake Franklin. Don't worry, I'll just take it along myself."

It was a moment before he answered, a moment in which his brown gaze rested on the side of her face where the shadow of a bruise lay. In it was a flicker of something that might have been understanding, even conspiracy. He lowered his lashes. His voice was a shade softer as he spoke. "As you like, Mis' Lorna."

Had the servants overhead something of her struggle with Franklin? It did not matter, so long as they did not guess the outcome. And how could they? Just because she felt as if the brand of a murderess must be imprinted on her forehead in letters of fire did not mean that anyone else could see it.

"Good night," she said and, giving a small nod, walked away.

"Good night," came the reply.

Still, the manservant stood looking after her, and it was necessary to turn toward the stairs once she was through the door, and even to ascend them for a short distance. As soon as she heard his retreating footsteps, she tiptoed down again. Swinging around the newel post, she hurried toward the back of the house and the French doors surrounded by glass-paned transom and side-lights that stood open to the night.

Her relief at being out of the house, safe in the covering of the velvet-black night, was so great that she paused to draw air into her lungs, not even aware until she felt its sweet rush that she had been holding her breath. She could smell the heady drenched scent of roses and the sharper perfume of honeysuckle. It was a cool spring night, so gentle and filled with growing things after the rain, too gentle for the cruel things that could happen under its benign darkness. There was no sign of the moon or stars, for the sky was still overcast. For that, she was grateful.

A small shiver ran over her as had happened on and off at odd moments throughout the past half hour, but now she made a determined effort at control. Holding her head high, with the skirt of her habit caught up above the wet grass and puddles of rainwater in one hand, and the pie clutched firmly in the other, she started toward the path that led to the stables, the cooperage, and the plantation jail.

The guards, a pair of them, were squatting on their haunches near the door of the small building, leaning against the trunk of the great oak that sheltered it. They came erect, one picking up a musket as she approached, the other reaching for a stout hickory staff. There was a lantern hanging on a crosspiece tacked to the tree. Its light revealed an overseer and one of the field hands, both of their faces blank as they tried to hide their amazement at seeing her there at that hour.

She had not met either of them, but their bobbing nods as she wished them good evening indicated they were aware of her identity. The overseer held his gun loosely, seeing no threat in her presence. His gaze, as he studied her in the flickering light, held a shading of insolence that made her think briefly of Franklin's mention of gossip among the slaves. The overseer, living in close contact with them, must have heard it. A thin man with close-set eyes, he was one of a breed she had seen since childhood and accepted for what they were; men who preferred to take another's wages than endure the hard work of carving out their own acreage. Why this one was not in the army, she did not know. Most had gone, marching off as though on a hunting trip.

"It has come to my attention," she said in as calm a tone as she could muster, "that the man inside has not been given food or water. I have brought him something to eat."

The two glanced at each other, then back at her. The overseer asked, "Did Mister Bacon say it was all right?"

"Would I be here otherwise?" She stepped forward, letting fall her skirts and drawing out the key from where she had slipped it into the pocket of her habit.

They could step aside or bar her way; the choice was theirs. The overseer took a quick step toward her, reaching for her hand even as she tried to push the key into the padlock. She jerked back from him, but he only took the key and fitted it into the lock, saying, "Allow me."

As the door swung wide, she hesitated, then stepped inside. It was dark in that single cell. The gleam of the lantern light, falling in through the opening, cast her elongated shadow across the dirt floor but did not reach into the black corners. It showed faintly the outline of a wooden bunk without sheeting or mattress, and the square of a barred window. That was all.

"M'sieur Cazenave?"

There came a whisper of sound, the quiet rustle of clothing from close by. He spoke at her left ear, so near she felt the warm fan of his breath. "Isn't that a little formal, considering the closeness of our acquaintance?"

She controlled a start, conscious of the fact that the silhouettes of the two guards, plainly showing the long barrel of the overseer's musket, had joined hers on the floor as they closed in behind her. "I have brought you something to eat."

"Have you? It's early for you to be playing lady of the manor."

Stung by the sarcasm that weighted his words, irritated by the strains of the night and a sudden reluctance to have him think her actions stemmed from any personal feeling, she snapped at him. "I would think your position too hazardous for it to matter!"

"Now that," he drawled as though it had not, heretofore, occurred to him, "is very true."

She moved farther into the cramped cell. Her voice was no more than a thread of sound as she spoke. "You won't quibble then, I hope, if I have come to set you free?"

There was complete silence for the time it took the overseer to take a scuffling step across the threshold. "Mrs. Bacon—"

Ramon sprang with the coiled strength of a panther, grabbing the barrel of the musket, dragging the overseer into the cell. At the same time, he swung a hard fist with iron muscle behind it, catching the man behind the ear. Lorna stepped hastily aside as the man plunged full-length, his musket clattering to the earthen floor. The second guard yelled, charging in with his staff raised. Ramon shirled to meet him, catching the hickory rod with both hands, wrenching it free, bringing the lower end around in a solid blow that sent the man careening into the wall. He fell limply and lay still.

Behind Ramon, Lorna saw the overseer shake his head and reach for his musket, coming to his knees. There was not time to sound a warning. As he brought the weapon to his shoulder, she half-threw, half-shoved the pie on its heavy silver stand at the man. It struck the side of his face, smearing his features with dewberry syrup, which ran into his eyes as he pulled the trigger.

Orange fire belched toward the ceiling. The concussion of the shot exploded in the small room, filling it with the blue-gray and acrid smoke of burning gunpowder. The ball stuck with a solid thud, and splinters like tiny stinging arrows filled the air.

Cursing, the overseer staggered to his feet, swiping with his arm at the juice running down his face. Ramon swung to wrench the useless musket from his hands. He brought the weapon around in a swing that connected with the man's jaw, sending him sprawling.

Ramon did not wait to see if he would stay down. He reached to clamp fingers of steel around Lorna's wrist, then dived for the door, dragging her with him. Outside, he skidded to a halt long enough to douse the lantern. In that brief moment, there could be heard the sound of men, alerted by the shot, calling; of dogs barking and women chattering. Then they were running, plunging headlong into the darkness.

Where they were going Lorna did not know. She had no time to look, no time to think. It was all she could do to keep her skirt from under her feet, to try to match the pace Ramon set. The ground was soggy, splashing water up as they ran, but was also fairly level and smooth. She thought they were skirting the lawn, keeping well away from the main house, but she could not be sure.

The hem of her habit grew wet, dragging at her feet. She felt as if she were running blind into danger, pulled by a force she could not withstand, unable to control her own movements because of the hard grip on her arm that hindered her balance even as it aided her flying steps. She tried to match his long stride, but it was impossible for any length of time. Her breathing came in gasps. The blood pounded in her head. She strained her eyes but could see nothing ahead and was only dimly aware of the bulk of the great house behind and to their right as they continued.

"Wait," she gasped, pulling back her hand. "I can't keep up."

"We can't wait." He did not release her, nor did he slow his pace.

"You go on."

"And leave you to Franklin? Is that what you want?"

"No. No, he's dead," she panted. "I . . . I killed him."

"Mon Dieu," he breathed, "Then you can't be left behind, not at any cost."

The grim certainty of the words sent a flutter of terror through her, such as she had not felt before. She redoubled her efforts. Through the pounding in her ears and the thudding of their footsteps, she could hear the shouts as Ramon's escape was discovered, the first yells of organized pursuit.

"They . . . they'll have horses," she said, "and dogs."

"It doesn't matter."

She was glad *he* thought so, she told herself in a flash of anger. She thought it was going to matter a great deal in a few short minutes.

Abruptly he jerked to a halt and stood staring back the way they had come. Following his glance, she saw the big house with light flooding from the hanging lantern over the front doorway and streaming from the windows. The gallery was deserted now. Every door of the mansion was closed and window shut, however, as if the guests who had crowded inside feared the escaped man might try to break in.

On the drive before the house stood a carriage, apparently ordered by someone who had decided to make a late departure. The horses were restive, disturbed by the noise around them, flinging up their heads and jostling in the traces. A stout woman was being helped into the vehicle by a man presumably her husband, while the driver on the box held the team. Almost before the woman had dropped into the seat, her husband leaped in after her and yelled up the order to start. The driver loosened the reins and the horses lunged down the drive. The lighted lanterns on either side of the carriage body sent shafts of light splaying into the darkness.

Ramon whirled Lorna around, like a child swinging another in a game of flying statues. She needed no urging to seek the cover of an arching row of damask roses. She went to her knees behind them, choking on their rich scent, feeling the sting of their thorns and the wetness of the ground under her knees as she burrowed under the overhanging canes.

The carriage bore down upon them, sounding as if it must grind them beneath its wheels. She half expected Ramon to try and stop it for use in helping them get away, but he let it pass. Lithe, heedless of the thorns, he swung immediately from their hiding place and held back drooping roses as she scrambled to her feet. He took her hand then, and once more they fled.

There had been a time when, as a child, she had been able to run without stopping for long distances, rejoicing in the effortless ease of it, enjoying a sense of boundless endurance. When had it ended? When had she become so stifled and housebound that she had lost the ability, that capacity for hardiness? She could not go much farther. Every breath was a knife in her chest. Hearing the distant sound of the dogs being turned loose on their trail, she thought it possible she would not have to continue the footrace much longer. It would not take long for the dogs to catch up to them, not long at all.

They had crossed the open road and were heading straight for the river. The first gentle rise of the levee was beneath their feet; then it quickly grew more steep. Ramon forged on, pulling her behind him as she faltered, urging her up the slope.

"It's not far now," he said, his voice low, hampered by his own rough breathing.

She knew. It came to her full-blown then, so right that she wondered she had not seen it from the beginning. The skiff. The skiff at the landing. The skiff, on the near-flood-stage of the Mississippi River.

She dragged to a stop, gasping, "Can we do it?"

"We have to."

They did indeed. There was no other way. On foot, they could not hope to outdistance mounted pursuers. They might hide in the woods and swamps beyond the cultivated areas of the fields, but it was unlikely they would be able to elude the dogs for long. Even if they did, there were long miles to be covered before they could hope to find help or transportation, long miles of inhospitable land teeming with snakes and alligators and mosquitos, with panthers and wildcats and the occasional black bear. Even if they reached civilization, they would be fugitives with, most likely, a price on their heads. Nate would see to that; they need have no illusions on that score.

A yell split the night. Swinging her head, Lorna saw the floating glow of torches, like orange eyes in pitch-black. The baying of the hounds was becoming louder. She could see their dark, running shapes pouring from the direction of the jail. Behind them came the men on horseback, holding the torches in their hands as they rode. She heard the sharp cries of the younger men, the cracked shouts of the graybeards.

She thought she recognized Nate Bacon in the forefront, spurring the others on. What had he told them? Who did they think they were chasing, those wedding guests stuffed with contraband food and reeling with the fumes of contraband wine? Some runaway slave? Did they know that they were on the trail of a murderess? If Franklin had been found, it would be easy for Ramon to be implicated; his earlier imprisonment would no longer matter. If not, Nate could still be depended on to find some reason for taking his vengeance on the spot.

Her distress must have communicated itself to Ramon, for he pulled her around, giving her a small shake. His voice hard, he said, "Don't look back. Not now. Not ever."

There was strength in his grasp and assurance in his tall form, so close beside her in the darkness. In answer, she felt the stir of her own confidence returning, the lessening of the tight grip of fear. Her voice had regained something of its normal, quiet firmness as she replied. "No."

"Come then."

Their pounding footfalls were loud on the planking of the landing. The rungs of a ladder led down to where the skiff floated on the water, a gray-black shape swinging with the river's current, bumping with a hollow, rhythmic sound against the piling. Ramon jumped down first, then turned to hold to the landing, steadying the craft, reaching with his other hand to help her descend.

The river ran swift here and was deep in flood stage. There was no time to waste on dread, however. Behind her, she could hear the sound of hoofbeats and the baying of the hounds on a warm scent. She placed her hand in that of Ramon Cazenave and climbed down into the boat.

He shoved off at once, flipping the rope free that held the skiff, pushing with the long oar against the piling, using main strength to thrust them into the current. Lorna hastily sat down on a thwart, gripping the gunwale, craning around to look back. She caught a glimpse of their pursuers just before they were hidden from view by the height and width of the levee. Ramon went to one knee and began to use the oar like a paddle, pulling away from the landing, striving to take them into the drag of the river's main crest, to put distance between them and the bank. The river sucked and gurgled around them and, as Lorna's chest heaved with the attempt to catch her breath, she drew in the blessed dampness and the dank fish-and-mud smell of the Mississippi that, rushing, swirling, would carry them away from Beau Repose.

"There they are! I see 'em! In the boat!"

The shout rang over the water with sharp clarity. It was followed by the explosion of a shot.

"Get down!" Ramon said, a command in spite of the low tone of his voice.

Hard on his words came a whining sound, then a skipping splash behind the boat and to their left. Lorna slipped to her knees, crouching in the bottom of the boat. Another musket roared. She looked up to see Ramon duck as the ball whined past the prow, but he did not seek shelter, nor did the steady beat of his paddle falter.

"You get down!" she shouted in a sudden rush of concern. She thought he sent her a tight grin, but he made no reply, nor did he leave his position.

On the wide breast of the levee could be seen the flare of the torches as the men gathered. Their curses and shouts thinned as the gap between them widened. The crash of a volley of musket fire seemed to hold no threat, though it splattered the waves around them. Once they were farther away from shore, the wind pushed them forward, aiding Ramon's hard strokes and the surge of the current. There was no time to raise the sail and, in any case, the gusting wind on the water made it unwise.

The river noises grew louder, surrounding, enfolding them in a curious urgent intimacy. A single musket ball thudded into the side of the boat, but it was so spent that it did little more than dent the wood. Still, Nate and his followers, firing, shouting abuse, galloped along the levee after them for miles. At the landing of a neighboring plantation, they found another boat. It appeared that too many of the party tried to pile into it, for in a flurry of yells and oaths, the small craft disappeared beneath the waves, leaving men in the water calling for help.

The skiff bearing Ramon and Lorna swept on. The night closed in, cool and damp and quiet. They were alone on the river.

Time ceased to have meaning. She sat cramped on the boat seat, scarcely daring to move for fear that the shift of her weight would overturn them in the rushing, swirling water. Ramon seemed tireless as he plied the paddle, keeping them abreast of the current, warding off floating logs and crates and barrels borne on the flood waters. A whole tree, with the wind soughing through its branches held above the water, kept pace with them for long yards, until it was snagged on a sandbar. Another time, an opossum tried to scramble on board. Lorna knew a brief regret when it failed and sank beneath the waves behind them.

The wind grew stronger, lapping the surface of the river into waves that slapped against the boat, sending a fine spray blowing backward. The poplin of her habit grew damp and heavy, clinging to her skin. She did not complain. In his more exposed position, Ramon must be wetter than she. It almost seemed that, in his driven determination, Ramon had a goal toward which he was traveling. It could not be, of course, and yet it was a comforting impression. She would have liked to spell him, to take her turn with the oar, but she was not certain her strength would be equal to the task of keeping them on course and free of the debris caught in the millrace around them.

The first sign of the returning rain was a flash of lightning. The blue-white glow pulsed behind them again and again. Then came the thunder, a low rumble. The lightning once more was a silver tracery just above the treetops. In its brief light, she saw the chiseled outline of Ramon's face as he swung to look and listen. It glittered in his dark eyes but illuminated only intent calculation without a hint of apprehension. She recognized in some unaccountable corner of her mind that, though she was cold and wet, cut adrift from everything she had ever known, she was not afraid now.

The storm rolled down upon them with crashing thunder, buffeting them with wind that held the taste of rain in its breath, while lightning was a constant shimmer overhead. In the storm's cold white sheen, Ramon directed the skiff toward the more slowly moving waters on the west side. Rounding a bend, they saw a thicket of half-submerged willows growing in the levee. He steered toward it. Reaching out as they glided down upon it, he caught one slender trunk. The skiff swung as on a pivot. As he strained to hold the craft against the pull of the river, Lorna caught up the rope that had been thrown into the bottom of the boat, lying tangled around the foot of the mast. She shifted forward, stretching to place the end in his hand. He flashed her a glance of surprise and gratitude, almost as if he had forgotten she was there, before turning to make the line fast.

"It seems best to take shelter until this is over," he said, nodding toward the furor overhead. "If it rains as I think it's going to, we'll be even less able to tell where the devil we're heading than we are now."

She indicated her understanding. "You need to stop before you are exhausted."

"I'm not tired," he said with a quick smile, "but it is a shame about the pie."

She met his gaze then in the bright flash of the lightning and felt her own mouth curve in answering amusement. That she could feel such a thing after all that had happened was startling, even cause for dismay.

He reached out, brushing his fingers gently across her bruised cheek. "Don't torture yourself; there are plenty who will do that for you. You are alive, and for now that's all that matters. Come, let's get under cover."

What cover was there? None that she could see. But Ramon found it. He unrolled the canvas sail from the stubby mast and dragged it free, spreading it over the bottom of the boat. Holding it, fighting the wind, he pressed her down upon it. He joined her then, lying full-length as he pulled the sail over them, tucking it in, leaving an air space so that the canvas was not against them. The first raindrops spattered down as he was still making their shelter tight. They hit the canvas with dull thuds, scattered at first, then increasing in number until they became a muted roar. The boat swung, nudging deeper under the overhanging branches of the willows. It bobbed and rocked so that Lorna was thrown from side to side. For long moments, Ramon lay alert, listening. Then with a sigh, he settled beside her.

Room was at a premium in that enclosed space to one side of the mast. There was no place for him to put his arm except above his head. She thought he winced as she was thrown against his chest.

"You . . . you're hurt," she said, her mouth near his ear. "Is it your rib where you were hit the other day?"

His grunt might have been taken for affirmation. "It's just cracked a bit, nothing serious."

"All that paddling tonight can't have helped it."

"It's nothing I can't live with."

His tone did not encourage further inquiry. He seemed to be lying on his side, without the room to stretch full-length. She tried to shift to accommodate him. He reached out then, gathering her close, sliding his arm beneath her head. Facing him, she lay stiff at first, then by slow degrees, she relaxed.

He was warm, so warm, from his strenuous activity. The heat of his body seemed to seep into her. She accepted it with pure physical pleasure. She could feel the strong pulsing of his heart through the veins of his arm under her cheek. His chest rose and fell with the steady rhythm of his breathing. She was molded against the long, muscular length of his body. As the boat rocked, they were jarred closer, and the corded muscle of his arm that encircled the narrow turn of her waist contracted to hold her there.

He spread his hand over her back, moving the palm gently over her shoulder blades. His voice threaded with amusement, he said, "It seems that every time I touch you, you're wet."

"Yes, I suppose so," she agreed, her voice not quite steady.

"It's very obliging of you."

She drew back a little, trying to see his face in the darkness of their canvas shroud. It was impossible. "Why?"

"Because," he murmured, his warm breath caressing her lips, "it gives me such a fine excuse to undress you."

For an instant, the memory of that first time to which he alluded stood vivid in her mind, along with the accusation that had followed. It was drowned, washed away by the race of the blood through her veins, by a need to be held, to blot out the events of the night, a need so intense it was like an ache inside her.

"You are wet too," she whispered.

"So I am. If I rid you of your wet things, seeing faithfully to your comfort, will you act as my valet?"

Chapter 5

Her answer was unspoken, a gesture with fingers that trembled. She slid her hand that was trapped between them across his chest, and slipped it inside the open front of his shirt where only a pair of studs remained near the beltline. With unsteady care, she worked those studs free. She heard his deep-drawn breath, felt the brush of his lips across her brow. His mouth trailed gentle fire down her temple. It teased her ear and paused as he nipped the lobe with barely closed teeth, then dropped lower to explore the tender curve of her neck.

He shifted then, allowing her access to the front of his trousers. His hand smoothed around her rib cage, cupping the firm swell of her breasts before settling into the hollow between those twin mounds straining against the cloth covering them. She felt the easing of the taut material as he worked his way down the row of buttons there. By the time he had peeled away the habit jacket, shirtwaist, and camisole underneath, she was shivering in anticipation of the first warm touch upon her bared breasts.

It came, and as she inhaled softly with parted lips, he claimed her mouth with his own. It was a sweet and welcome invasion that sent excitement spiraling to her brain. With the tip of his tongue, he tasted the moist and sensitive inner surfaces of her mouth, his movements concentrated, unhurried. He probed the sweet depths of her acquiescence, teasing her to a response with sensuous, swirling play of tongue and mingled, sighing breaths.

It was the rise of her own desire that reminded her of the

buttons beneath her fingers. They were stiff, yielding slowly to her inexperienced ministrations. She tugged the tail of his shirt from his loosened waistband and reached to push it from his shoulders, smoothing her hand over the hard, muscled expanse and down his forearms. He shrugged from one sleeve, then the other, freeing his hands, then did the same for her, leaving her unclothed above the waist. Their lips met and clung once more. She permitted her fingers to wander back to the last buttons of his trousers, while he tried with one hand to unhook the band of her skirt.

A soft sound between a chuckle and an imprecation escaped him. He drew back, making short work of ridding himself of his remaining clothing and boots. Lorna did the same, unfastening the band of her full skirt, sliding it down over her hips, wriggling free of its heavy folds and the pantaloons underneath before kicking off her riding boots.

The surface of their skin seemed to burn, fusing as they came together again. Exhilaration ran along Lorna's veins, coupled with a fine, heedless rapture. The thrumming of the rain over them merged with the pounding of her heart in her ears. She wanted to be a part of this man, to make him a part of her. The depth of her need, when placed against the short time she had known him, was shaming; she was glad of the dark that enfolded them, concealing their faces, leaving them anonymous in their fervid desire.

His knee slipped between her thighs. His hand traveled lightly over the slender curve of her hip and along the length of her leg, following the smooth turnings as if he would commit them to memory. Drawing her slender leg higher upon the lean hardness of his flank, he sought closer, more intimate contact. His fingertips trailed upward then, lingering on the velvet tautness of her abdomen, drifting downward again to smooth the silken inner surfaces of her thighs, finding the delicately moist and intricate recess of her body. The gentle and soothing caress he began there was one she felt in every nerve. It was an exquisite sensation, bordering on pain, and she lay still, scarcely breathing, her hands opening and closing upon the rigid muscles of his shoulders. He bent his head, and she felt the searing adhesion of his mouth as he captured the peak of a breast.

She was awash in sensation, in tingling perception, suffused by the flowing heat of the sensual joy that ran in her blood, and by the full and aching vulnerability at the center of her being. The wonder expanded beyond her control. A low moan gathered in her throat. Against her thigh, she could feel the rigid fierceness of his need, held firmly in check. That was not where it should be.

"Please," she whispered.

He straightened, brushing her lips, drawing her closer against him. He eased into her with care for her tight, unstretched state. In her heated, liquid readiness, there was no pain, but infinite pleasure. She moved against him, urging him deeper, wanting, needing the surge of his strength, done with gentleness.

"Lorna, *chérie*," came his hoarse whisper.

He answered her movements, turning her to her back, rising above her, unleashing the driving urgency of his passion. She took him into her, encompassing, holding, absorbing the shocks of his drive toward release that fueled and fashioned her own.

It was an uncontrollable thing, as elemental and ageless as the river that flowed around them, and as impossible to hold. Borne on its flood, they were buoyed up, tossed in the swift current, driven by its power and grace to the edge of a swift and shining cataract. Limbs entwined, striving together with the rush and roar of water around them that sang in their veins, they were caught, pulled headlong into turbulent and near unbearable pleasure.

The boat swung on its rope. The rain died away with a last growl of thunder. Still they lay unmoving, drifting in a half-world between unconsciousness and rational thought. Lorna's face was buried in the hollow of his throat. The hairs that curled there tickled her lips, but she could not bring herself to mind. His mouth was against her temple, and she thought she felt him press a kiss to the soft wave that lay there. His weight was not upon her but rested on his elbow and forearm.

At length, he stirred. His tone was both amused and puzzled as he murmured, "What is it about you that destroys my common sense?"

"I don't know."

"Nor do I, *ma chère*, but I think it would be a good thing if I found out. This was a brainless thing to do."

"You wish you . . . we had not?" she inquired, her tone constrained. Shifting her hand that lay upon his shoulder, she used the tip of one finger to carefully press aside the hairs at the hollow of his throat that tickled her.

"*Mon Dieu*, no! But neither do I want to wind up stark naked in a rowboat floating among the ships of the federal blockade fleet in the gulf!"

The image brought a chuckle. "I don't think I would enjoy that either."

"No, but the men of the fleet would be delighted. To have the captain of a blockade runner fall into their clutches would be one thing, but, if they saw you, I would never be asked for my credentials."

"If that's a compliment," she said, "I accept it."

He raised himself up, then leaned to press a quick kiss on her lips before he spoke. "It is, and also another piece of foolishness, when I should be attending to getting us under way again."

They pushed aside their canvas covering and sat up. The cold wind off the water and the raindrops dripping from the willow overhead brought gooseflesh as they struggled into their crumpled and wet clothing. Every vestige of warmth was soon dissipated in the damp chill of the night. Ramon tried to insist that she lie down and cover herself with the sail once more; she compromised by drawing it around her as a windbreak. Even so, she had to clench her jaws to keep her teeth from chattering and, as she brushed against Ramon, she felt the shiver that ran over him before he could control it. They would have to have shelter soon, permanent, solid shelter, and a fire to warm them. She did not think they would die of exposure, as cool as it was on this spring night in late April, but they might well develop congestion of the lungs.

The lull in the rain was temporary. By the time they had reached the river's channel, a light mist was falling of the kind that might last for hours or turn to a solid downpour at any moment. It flew in their faces with maddening persistence, fine, cold drops that beaded on the skin and hair, running into their eyes. Lorna narrowed her vision, trying to see, recognizing that Ramon, in the front of the boat, was blocking much of the rain from her with his body. How he was guiding them she could not imagine, but he plied the paddle with a steady and unceasing stroke, focusing to the exclusion of all else on the stretch of water just in front of the skiff.

Some time later, they negotiated a wide horseshoe bend. Ahead of them appeared a pinpoint of light. It grew larger, separating into several squares, evolving by slow degrees into the shape of a steam packet. They were gaining on it, which could mean only one thing: the boat was tied up for the night to avoid those same dangers in the dark and swollen river that they had been dodging these past hours.

Ramon stopped paddling. A glance told her that he was

watching the packet also. His alert stillness sent alarm coursing through her. Rising to her knees, she inched forward to kneel at his shoulder. She raised her voice above the rush and gurgle of the river to ask, "Is it the *General Jackson*?"

"No, it's isn't large enough."

Without stopping to examine the relief she felt that it was not the steamboat taken by her aunt and uncle, she spoke again. "Would it be safe to board her, do you think?"

"Maybe, maybe not, but we have no choice. We both need to get to New Orleans as quickly as possible. That boat will take us faster and more safely than any other means."

As they were swept nearer, the packet's name, painted on her wheel housing, leaped out at them. She was the *Rose of Sharon*, a familiar name, that of a small riverboat that plied between Natchitoches, up the Red River, and the city of New Orleans on a regular run. Doubtless it had passed Beau Repose earlier in the evening, perhaps while she had been changing from her wedding gown. Once a fine boat, it had been overshadowed by the larger crafts that had earned the name of floating palaces in the past decade. The *Rose* was known as a "lucky" boat, however, since it was still making its regular run while dozens of the fancier, faster boats had burned to the waterline or had their bottoms torn out on half-submerged sawyers, trees floating just under the surface of the water. Of late, the larger boats, too, were being commandeered by the Confederate government, leaving only the smaller river packets to serve the people along the river. Much of the reputation for luck enjoyed by the boat was due to the captain, who was known for his caution, making it a practice, as now, to tie up at night and during severe weather.

"What if there is someone aboard who knows us?"

"That's a chance we will have to take," he answered, his tone deep. "Either way, we had better decide on the story we are going to tell. I have a couple of gold pieces in my boot that the guards back at Beau Repose missed when they took my purse. They should cover the fare but not, I think, in more than one stateroom."

"I . . . I have the bracelet Franklin gave me. If the captain will take it, I can pay my own way."

"Offer him a bauble like that, and it will be certain to set him wondering."

"It seems likely," she pointed out, a shade of tartness in her voice, "that if we are picked up before dawn in the middle of nowhere, looking like drowned rats that he will be uncommonly slow if he doesn't wonder a bit anyway.''

"In that case, what does it matter whether we are in one stateroom or two?''He turned to look at her. The light streaming from the packet gleamed orange across one side of his face, leaving the other in shadow. It illuminated the concern in the depths of his dark eyes.

Seeing it, Lorna was forced to acknowledge what he must have seen from the beginning; that their escape together, and their connection with Franklin's death, could not be hidden for long. Soon the news would be spread up and down the river and, when that happened, it would make little difference whether the two of them had observed the conventions while traveling on the *Rose of Sharon*.

"True,'' she answered.

"If you will allow me, then, I will undertake to concoct a tale that will satisfy the captain temporarily. All you need do is smile, and look . . . woebegone.''

Aware of the rain plastering her hair to her head and trickling down the back of her neck, and of the sadly rumpled and stained state of her clothing, no small amount of which was due to the man beside her, she sent him a flashing glance. Her voice flat with sudden weariness, she said, "That should be no problem.''

What exactly Ramon told the steamboat captain, Lorna did not know, though she overhead some mention of an elopement, and a guardian who did not want his charge to marry a soldier, home these past weeks on sick leave but scheduled to rejoin his regiment. She was ushered into a stateroom with "Missouri'' painted above the door in scrolled letters surrounded by sunflowers. Promising to send a can of hot water at once, the young officer who had been detailed to escort her went away.

She moved to the small, marble-topped washstand and peered into the mirror that was speckled with damp. With a quick grimace for what she saw, she turned away, lifting her hands to release the pins that held the rain-soaked knot of her hair.

A double bed with massive, turned posts took up much of the space in the cramped room. It sat upon a carpet woven in a pattern of blue and red diamonds, leaving scarcely room at the footboard for the door leading onto the deck to swing open. A brass lantern with a bulging base to hold coal oil hung from the ceiling, its brass shade narrowing the light to a small spot over the foot of the bed, leaving the corners in shadow. Still, even as small and dark as it was, the room was nicer than the common chamber she had shared with her aunt and three other women passengers on the trip upriver to her wedding.

A knock on the door heralded the arrival of a Negro maid bearing the promised can of steaming water. Directly behind her came Ramon, who held the door for a steward carrying a napkin covered tray. He had, apparently, paid their passage and received some few coins in change, for he pressed one into the hand of each servant before he saw them out.

"That was generous of you." Lorna turned away as she spoke. Her hair had uncoiled to lie in a shining rope over her shoulder and down upon one breast. Suddenly ill at ease, she made no attempt to release it further, but carefully placed her hairpins on the washstand, keeping her back to Ramon.

"Considering the state of my finances? Not really. We will be in New Orleans in a matter of hours, once we begin to move again. I will be able to replenish both wardrobe and purse when we get there."

"I see."

He watched her for a moment, then moved to touch the brass can holding the water. "Come, let's get out of these wet things and make use of this while it's still hot. We can eat later, in bed."

He began to remove his shirt. Lorna made no effort to follow his example. His movements slowed. He stepped in front of her and reached to tilt her chin with one finger. "What is it?"

"I—nothing." Warm color seeped upward into her cheeks. She kept her lashes lowered, refusing to look at him.

"Not an attack of modesty, not after what has been between us."

She jerked her chin away. Turning from him, she said, "Is that so strange? I hardly know you. It's one thing to speak of sharing a stateroom but another to actually be alone here with you."

"You have been alone with me for hours," he pointed out reasonably enough.

"It seems different somehow."

"If you are suggesting that I sleep elsewhere, on deck for instance—" he began in hard tones.

"No!" She turned swiftly, her gray eyes widening as she realized that the last thing she wanted was to be alone. "No, I couldn't ask you to do that."

He stared at her, his dark gaze on the pallor that had crept

under her skin, moving to the pure lines of her mouth with its
tinge of blue, and the damp, raw silk of her hair shimmering
with the quick rise and fall of her breathing. Frowning, he said,
"If that is what it will take to please you—"

"No," she said again, "only, could you turn your back?"

He had offered to do that once before. It seemed this time
that he would refuse, would take some drastic step to force intimacy upon her. Then with an abrupt turn, he moved toward
the door. His hand on the knob, he sent her a long glance. "I
will be back in five minutes. If you are not bathed and in bed
then, I'll put you there myself, modesty or no."

It was more like ten minutes before he returned. Her clothing
lay draped over a chair. The heavy china basin sat upon the
washstand where she had used precisely half the hot water before pouring it away in the slop jar. Her hair, combed out as
best she could with her fingers, was spread over the pillow on
which she lay, while the covers were pulled up to her chin.

He closed the door behind him, his gaze flicking over her,
resting on the bed on which she lay. "Is it comfortable?"

"Yes, but cold."

There was an obvious retort to her words; she realized it as
soon as they were said. He did not make it. Moving to the foot
of the bed, he sat down and took off his boots; then, standing
again, pulled the shirt from his trousers, removed the studs, and
tossed everything onto the washstand. Taking the brass can, he
poured water into the bowl.

Lorna had glanced at him, then looked quickly away as he
began to undress. Now she allowed her gaze to wander back to
the broad expanse of his bare back as he leaned to sluice his face
in the warm water. His torso was burned brown, as though he
was used to going shirtless in the sun. Idly, before she caught
herself up, she wondered if the rest of him was the same. His
muscles stretched, rippling under his skin as he reached for soap
and a cloth. Watching his reflection in the mirror, she noticed a
great bruise at his narrow waist and another higher under his
heart, the second the place where Nate Bacon had hit him. That
this man had held her in the most intimate of embraces, not
once, but twice, was amazing. That she had allowed it, had even
wanted him to do so, was beyond belief. Moreover, if he were
to turn now, if when he got into bed he were to reach for her,
she was not certain she would have the will to deny him.

What power was it he held over her? Was it a mere enslavement of the senses, a need born of desperation? Or was it, could it be, something more?

She glanced at his face, reflected in the gray-spotted mirror, and found him watching her. She removed her gaze in haste to the post at the foot of the bed, staring at it as if it were the most fascinating object she had ever beheld. Nor did she look around when he removed his trousers and came to slide between the sheets beside her.

"Here," he said, "take this."

He had their supper tray in his hands. She struggled upward, clutching at the sheet to cover herself, tucking it under her arms as she held out her hands. He set the tray, instead, on her lap, then took his own pillow, placing it on top of hers so she could lean back. Leaning on one arm, he took away the napkin that covered the food.

There was fried chicken and boiled potatoes, along with a small loaf of bread, a few pickled peaches in a dish, and half a bottle of wine. It was not sumptuous fare, but it was more than adequate and, considering the times, better than Lorna had expected at this hour. Taking up the plate of chicken, she offered it to Ramon.

She had forgotten how hungry he must be. His self-control as he took a piece and bit into it was like a rebuke. She felt the urge to apologize for keeping him waiting the few short minutes longer than necessary. She said nothing, however. Breaking off a chunk of bread, she began to eat, discovering in the process that she was famished herself, hungrier than she had been in weeks.

There was not a morsel left, not even a crumb, when they were through. Ramon tossed aside the remains of a chicken wing and reached for a napkin to wipe his fingers. He surveyed the pile of bones on his plate with a rueful expression before asking, "Did you have enough?"

She nodded, then, lifting the last of her wine to her lips, swallowed it before placing the glass back on the tray. During the meal, he had shifted to sit up in the middle of the bed with his legs under him like a tailor and the sheet making a tent over his knees. Now he uncoiled and, taking the tray in one hand, stepped from the bed to place it on the washstand.

Lorna, watching him, found herself thinking of the depictions of Greek statues she had seen in her uncle's library. His body had the same muscular grace and perfect proportions, although she feared that a fig leaf would be somewhat inadequate for a covering. . . .

She looked quickly away, rushing into speech with the first thing that came to mind. "I . . . I've been thinking about tomorrow."

"Is there somewhere I can take you, someone who will help you?" He stepped to the foot of the bed and reached up to lower the wick on the lamp so that the room was plunged into darkness.

She shook her head, then, realizing that he could not see, said, "No, there is no one."

"Friends? Relatives?"

"No one."

"Not even the uncle who came looking for you that evening?"

"Especially not him." He did not press it and, because he did not, but only waited, standing there in the dark, she told him briefly of her Uncle Sylvester and Aunt Madelyn, and of what must be their reaction to what she had done.

"Then what of tomorrow?" he asked.

"I thought perhaps you would take me to the convent of the Ursuline nuns, that they might take me in."

"You realize you would have to tell them why you are running away?"

"Would I? I had not thought."

"It would be unfair to expect them to extend their protection otherwise. Even so, I doubt they would be able to keep Nate Bacon from you, or any officer of the law he might bring with him if he chose to seek you out."

"He might not think to look for me there."

It was a moment before he answered, but then his tone was quiet, reflective. "I am beginning to see that it might well be the first place he would look."

"But what else is there?" she asked, her tone etched with apprehension. "There is little hope of employment; the dressmakers and milliners of New Orleans are not working, for lack of goods or customers to buy. People have shut up their houses and hired their servants out as maids and cleaning women in the few such positions available. In times like these, no one thinks of drawing or composition lessons for their children—"

"Don't!" he said harshly. "Try not to think of it. It will do no good now."

The bed creaked, tilting in his direction as he got into it. She turned her head toward the sound. "But how can I not?"

"Go to sleep. The problems will still be there in the morning, but you will look at them in a different light."

"I can't!" she said, a trace of despair creeping into her voice. "I keep seeing Franklin, lying there after I hit him. His head—"

There came the rustle of the bedcovering as he turned toward her. "Maybe I can help."

Her muscles stiffened at his touch. "What do you mean?"

"I only want to warm you."

"No, I don't—I'm not cold." The intimacy with this man that had seemed so natural such a short time ago now felt awkward, clandestine.

"Liar," he said with a soft laugh as he slid his hand beneath her, encircling her waist and scooping her across the bed toward him. He turned her with her back to him, fitting her into the curve of his body so that her hips were pressed against his pelvis and the muscular ridges of his legs lay against her thighs. With care, he tucked the sheet and coverlet under her chin, securing it beneath her shoulder that was against the pillow.

She had not realized how cold she was until she felt the contrast of his vital heat. Gooseflesh broke out along the entire length of her body and, as he wrapped an arm around her, closing a hand upon the soft mound of one breast, the nipple contracted beneath his fingers. Her words were strangled as she forced them from her throat. "This . . . isn't necessary."

"It is to me."

She lay still, expecting marauding caresses, a physical invasion. It did not come. Her breathing slowed, her tense muscles relaxed by degrees. She shifted a little, making herself more comfortable, nestling against him. She closed her eyes as the chill seeped from her. Even her feet, resting against his ankles, were losing their iciness. She had never known how soporific human warmth could be. On the edge of sleep, she made a discovery: He had indeed helped to distract her.

She was running. She wore her wedding gown. It was torn and stained with blood. Her veil mingled with her unbound hair, streaming out behind her. She looked over her shoulder, and it was Franklin who pursued her. He was grinning, and in his hand he held a marble bust. Behind him in a carriage came her aunt, hanging out the window, screaming. The coachman on the carriage box was Nate Bacon, and he was naked. Franklin was gaining on her. He reached out and grabbed her veil and the

*ends of her hair, twisting them, pulling her to a halt. She cried
out and swung at him, slapping, clawing to free herself.*

"Lorna, wake up! For the love of God, *chèrie*—"

Ramon held her wrists, shaking her as he bent over her. His
eyes were dark with concern and a frown drew his brows together. There was a vibration running through the bed, and she
could hear the dull and regular thump of the engines; they were
moving. Hard on that discovery, she saw that there was daylight
beyond the one small window the stateroom boasted.

"Are you all right?" There was an urgent note in his voice.

She brought her gaze back to his face, then lowered her lashes.
"Yes, except for . . . for my hair. I think you are on it."

He released her with a quick exclamation, lifting himself up
to take his weight from his elbow that had been resting on the
silken strands. "I am sorry."

"It doesn't matter. I . . . I must have been dreaming. Did I
hit you?"

"You tried," he answered, his expression lightening. He
stretched to retrieve the covers dislodged by her struggle. With
his hands holding the quilt, he stopped. His curses then were
soft, but as lurid and drawn out as those of any stevedore.

It was only then that she realized the bedclothes had slipped
down past her waist. Following Ramon's gaze, she saw what
had disturbed him, something that had not been so apparent in
the dimness and haste of the night before. The fair, pearl-like
texture of her skin was marred by great blue and purple
splotches. The bruises spread across her hips and waist, extending upward to her breasts, livid and angry injuries. She flushed,
reaching for the sheet, tugging at it to cover herself.

He would not release it. His imprecation ground to a halt. He
spoke one other word. "Franklin?"

"Yes," she whispered.

"He must have been more of a mad animal than anyone
guessed. If you had not killed him, I think that I would have
been obliged to do it, seeing this."

"He . . . he thought he had the right, that I had wronged
him."

He allowed her to draw up the covers, though there was a
grim set to his features as he watched. "Then it's my fault."

She shook her head. Lying back on the pillow, she watched
her own fingers carefully smoothing the sheet as she answered.
"No. If it had not been that, it would have been something else,

I think. He enjoyed hurting people—women. It made him feel more a man.''

When he finally spoke, the word was abrupt. "Why?"

"It was an accident, I swear it. I was so afraid!"

"Not that," he said with a sharp gesture of one clenched hand. "Why did you marry him? I thought is was the money, especially when I found out that half the luxury goods I brought through the blockade this last time were consigned to Bacon, including your wedding gown. Even when I saw you on the steamboat going upriver, in the tow of that aunt and uncle of yours, it still seemed likely. You were so aloof, so cool, and your aunt such an obvious snob. I was standing in the doorway of my stateroom one morning after an all-night poker game, and you walked by as if you didn't see me, the future duchess ignoring the common herd, the young woman pointed out by everyone as the future bride of the son of the richest man along the river.''

"I didn't see you. I was too busy searching for some way out of it—the marriage, I mean. There was none. But I thought, at the old house, that you seemed to recognize me. That's why you did it, isn't it? Just like Nate Bacon said. You knew who I was, and you used me to strike at him.''

"I can't deny it.''

She had thought that he would, had wanted him to, and the realization added fuel to the anger flaring inside her as she swung her head to stare at him. "It was a terrible thing to do. What would you have done, how far would you have gone, if I had fought you?''

He stared at her a long moment, his dark gaze unflinching, before he spoke. "To be honest, I don't know. I had some idea of a pleasant dalliance, of laying a siege that might persuade you to cuckold your husband-to-be, or might do no more than make you dissatisfied with your bargain, causing discord in the new marriage. There was no set plan; it was an impulse born the moment I saw you.''

She wrenched over in the bed, pushing to one elbow as she glared at him. "You swine! You reached out, just like that, and destroyed my life.''

"Swine though I may be," he answered, a hard smile curving his mouth, "I have never taken a woman yet who was unwilling. Let us remember that you, Madame Bacon, did not resist. Would you care to explain that oversight?''

She flung away from him back upon her pillow, throwing her forearm across her eyes. "No."

"Shall I say it for you?" he asked quietly, leaning closer. "You regretted your bargain, you had seen something about your bridegroom that you could not like, something that made you afraid of your wedding night." He caught her arm, pulling it away, forcing her to meet his dark gaze. "Compared to that, anything was preferable, isn't that right?"

Tears rose from somewhere deep inside her. Above the gathering tightness in her throat she whispered, "There was no bargain."

"Then why? Tell me why?"

She told him, the words coming in bursts, bringing such relief that it was a measure of the strain she had endured, but could now share. Finally she stumbled into silence. Lifting a hand, she wiped at the moisture seeping from the corners of her eyes.

He made no immediate comment. Sitting up, he reached for the bell rope that hung beside the bed, giving it a hard pull. When a steward tapped on the door a short time later, he ordered coffee and rolls, and handed their clothing out to be cleaned and pressed. His movements were swift and decisive. Magnificent in his nakedness, he seemed no more aware of it than another might have been of a favorite coat. Swinging back toward the bed when the steward had departed once more, he sat down on the edge beside her. For this first time, there was a trace of uncertainty in his manner.

"Would you like a formal apology or would it be an insult? I am sorry for the damage done, the pain you have suffered, but cannot say that I regret the moments we shared."

Nor did she. But that realization did nothing to restore her self-respect. In stifled tones, she said, "You helped me to get away from Beau Repose. That is enough."

"Hardly. If you had let me stay where I was, you might have gone quietly and not been missed until—well, until this morning. Instead, you chose to set me free. Since you had no reason to care what became of me, it doesn't make sense."

She shrugged, lowering her gaze to where she picked at the stitching on the quilt. "Call it a whim, if you like."

"I don't like."

As she remained stubbornly silent, he continued. "I can always suppose it was for the sake of my *beaux yeux*—or something about me that you enjoyed."

She sent him a quick look and caught the gleam of deviltry

in his eyes. "Nothing of the sort!" she said with a gasp. "It was because Franklin told me what they were going to do to you!"

He studied her. "You blush so charmingly at the least mention of anything indelicate. Shall I guess, then, that I would not have enjoyed what my friend Bacon had planned?"

"No, but it doesn't matter; it didn't happen."

Chapter 6

They were interrupted by the arrival of their breakfast order. A civil inquiry from Ramon elicited the information that it was well past midday, however; it was the darkness of the overcast sky that made it seem earlier. The steward, bowing, informed them that the packet had been making good time since just after daylight that morning. He allowed as how it would be no more than two, maybe two and a half, hours before they were steaming into New Orleans. Would M'sieur and Madame care for a bite of the late luncheon being served at that moment in the grand salon?

They declined, and the man departed with another of Ramon's coins as an incentive for speeding the pressing of their clothing, and also for procuring a clean and guaranteed new comb for their use.

When they were alone once more, Lorna asked the question that had been troubling her. "What do you mean to do now?"

He came and flung himself back down on the bed beside her. "Rejoin the *Lorelei*, my ship waiting in New Orleans, and make the run back to Nassau."

"Through the blockade fleet at the mouth of the river."

"It's the only way."

"They say the danger is so great now that almost none get through."

"It's no pleasure outing. I lost a man on the run upriver, a stoker who came up for air just as a Parrott shell took away part of the bulwarks. The delay while the damage was repaired was one of the reasons I came back to Beau Repose. I had the time, and I wanted to look at the old place.''

"It had been some time since you had seen it then?''

"Ten long years. I was at the naval academy when my father died. He never wrote of his difficulties with Bacon; the first I learned of them was when I received papers from my father's lawyer after his death, showing the transfer of the property. I wrote, made inquiries, but everything seemed legal enough.''

"So you stayed on, in the North?''

"I had no family; my mother died when I was young and my father never remarried. Even after I graduated and had leave, there seemed no reason to return.''

She lifted her gray gaze to stare at him. "You are one of the naval officers who resigned to fight for the Confederacy then. I hadn't realized.''

"Not for the Confederacy,'' he corrected.

"Perhaps not in a regular way, but everyone knows the South could not survive without the men who run the blockade, and you risk your life to bring in the arms and ammunition so our armies can fight.''

"For a price.''

She frowned. "But that's—''

"Profiteering? So it is. Also good sense. This is a war we can't win. I've been north of the Mason-Dixon line, and I know. They have the factories, the iron and coal and steel, the raw materials of war, while we have—''

"The best fighting men the world has ever known!''

"Oh, I'll grant you that. They should be, since most of them have spent all their lives out of doors, hunting, riding, working in all weather. But flesh and blood and gut-courage can't stand against ball and steel and exploding shells. The federal army is going to gather itself and roll down upon us like a juggernaut, destroying everything in its path, and it will be the federal navy, like the blockading fleet in the gulf, that will see to it that we have nothing to use as a defense.''

Since the war had begun she had heard little except assurances of victory, and a swift one at that. Even those who did not agree that it must soon be over were certain that the South, with its superior leaders and fighting force, would make the struggle too costly and unpopular for the government in Washington to continue. Was it possible that it could go against them?

She turned her head away. "It will be too terrible to bear thinking of, if we should lose."

"That is why I intend to have a fortune in gold when the conflict is over. Places like Beau Repose will fall like ripe plums into the hands of those who are there to catch them. The home of the Cazenaves will return to the rightful owner. I'll burn that imitation Greek monstrosity to the ground and clear the wasps nests and spiders webs out of the house where I was born. Then maybe my father can rest in peace."

She did not approve of what he was doing; still, she had seen the old house with its wide and shaded galleries in the French manner, could understand his anger at the way it had been used. The edge of bitterness in his tone caught at her attention. "You think there was something wrong about the way Nate Bacon gained possession of the property?"

"I didn't, at first, but since my stay these last few days, I'm convinced of it. You know the tale of how my father lost money to Bacon in a card game?" At her nod, he went on. "That's the explanation generally circulated. What isn't so well known is that he was robbed while on his way to repay the debt, set upon by a gang of men not two miles from the run-down plantation where Bacon was living at the time. Nathaniel Bacon pretended to great understanding, and they entered into an arrangement whereby my father gave him a note of hand against the plantation, pledging himself to pay what was owed plus interest when the cotton crop that had just been planted was harvested."

When he paused, Lorna asked, "What happened then?"

"A crevasse, a break in the river levee that inundated the fields at Beau Repose, burying the new cotton under tons of mud."

A crevasse was a terrible thing, a rushing, thundering flood that could send families in panic-stricken flight or else force them to scramble to the rooftops to escape it. People and animals were drowned, the bloated bodies floating, bringing disease. With the land so flat, there was almost nowhere for the extra water to run off, and so it formed a great lake, allowing the silt borne in the floodwaters to settle out, leaving thick, rich mud when the water was gone. The next year, the soil would be incredibly fertile, but that did not help the man who had lost a year's work and the investment in seed and labor that had gone into it.

"These things happen; they can't be helped."

"Maybe, maybe not. I began to hear stories in the last year or two. Friends from new Orleans that I met from time to time while on duty in the ports of Europe and New England spoke of other men who had been prevented from making good what was owed to Nate Bacon—of foreclosures, of property bought for the taxes that had, unaccountably, gone unpaid. The case of your uncle is an example. It was most unfortunate for everyone that his cotton crop burned in that warehouse—everyone except Bacon, who was having trouble finding a wife for his son in the normal way."

"Yes," she said, frowning, "I had not realized."

"Think about it. It might help you to see that you are the victim, not the criminal."

"And your father?"

"The slaves at Beau Repose say the levee there was in excellent repair that spring, that it was deliberately cut, just as they say that it was Nate Bacon who hired the men who robbed my father."

Lorna made no answer, only staring straight ahead as she sipped at her coffee. For its flavor the brew owed more to an infusion of chicory than to coffee beans, and was sweetened by molasses, but it was strong and hot. By the time she and Ramon had drained the pot and eaten their rolls, the steward had returned with their clothing. It had not been washed but had been brushed and spot-cleaned before pressing, so was at least more presentable than before.

Ramon seemed in no hurry to dress. He lay across the bed, talking, watching the expressions that flitted across her face, teasing her until a smile rose into her gray eyes and color stained her cheeks. It was as if he were attempting to distract them both, to forget that the end of their journey was fast approaching. It was a curiously peaceful time, one in which she learned of the exotic corners of the world he had seen, of the adventures he had enjoyed. She told him something of her childhood and of the more comical things that had happened while living with a house full of girls under her aunt's stern eye. By common consent, they did not speak again of the recent past, nor of the future.

It was a surprise when a tapping came on the door and the

steward put his head into the room. "Shall I pick up your break-fast tray, M'sieur? Captain likes everything tidy when we come into port, and we'll be making New Orleans in half an hour." As they agreed, he came into the room. Tray in hand, he started out again. "Funny thing. There's smoke up ahead from the di-rection of the city. Don't reckon somebody set her afire again, do you?"

"What?" Ramon exclaimed. He jumped to his feet and stepped to the door, moving out onto the deck to lean over the railing, peering at the sky ahead of them.

The steward moved after him. Just as Lorna was beginning to feel somewhat nervous about the door's being open while she was in a state of undress, there came a muffled feminine shriek from somewhere farther along the deck. Ramon, with an im-patient glance at his nude state and heightened color under the bronze of his face, swung back into the room and closed the door behind him.

"You had better put your clothes on," he said, reaching for his trousers. "I'm going to see what's going on."

She flung back the covers. "Do you think the steward was right, or could it be some kind of assault on the city?"

When he did not not answer, she looked up to find him watch-ing her, his gaze resting on the tip-tilted globes of her breasts and the satin smooth flesh of her abdomen. Perhaps it was his own disdain for modesty that had influenced her in so short a time that she felt no desperate urge to cover herself, or it may have been the urgency of the moment. Meeting his dark gaze, she demanded, "Well?"

"He . . . may be," he answered, almost at random. Then, averting his gaze, he fastened his trousers and began to look for his boots.

She was still in camisole and pantaloons when he was ready to leave the stateroom. He dragged the comb for which he had paid so dearly through his brown-black waves, flung it on the washstand, and strode out the door. She followed as quickly as she could, but it took some time to bring order to her wind-tousled hair and twist it into a knot at the nape of her neck. The deck was crowded with people, all craning to see, when she emerged. She made her way toward the prow. Catching sight of Ramon's dark head near the railing, she pushed her way to his side.

She was just in time for the rounding of the wide, crescent-shaped bend that curved in front of the older section of the city known as the French Quarter to the American residents, and the Vieux Carré, or Old Square, to those of French descent. They cleared the wide curve, steaming down the middle of the great, yellow-brown river. Smoke, gray and acrid, blew toward them, lying low on the water. Through it could be seen the sullen orange-red of flames. They seemed concentrated along the levee, in the area of the wharves and warehouses, though they were also dotted here and there over the surface of the river itself. Beyond the town, in the direction of Bayou St. John, where lay a number of great plantations, could be seen spiraling yellow smoke columns, as if from fires just started.

It was raining again, a feathery wetness that blew in upon the crowd hanging over the railing of the steamboat. It was this, on top of the soggy wetness of the past days, that was causing such greasy billows of smoke to lie over the town, rising from the fires.

Around her, Lorna heard the babble of speculation. She glanced at Ramon and saw his face was grim, his attention narrowed on the ships that lay at anchor along the levee. Turning back, she saw activity along the snaking length of the waterfront. Carriages bowled here and there, and knots of men were gathered, brandishing torches in the gloom. More men were rolling huge barrels of sugar and hogsheads of molasses from the buildings. They were breaking these open with axes, letting the richness pour into the streets, while women and children scooped up the spilled goods in buckets and baskets, pots and aprons, ignoring the falling rain as they scavenged. At one point farther along, wounded men with stained bandages were being unloaded from a steamer, carried on stretchers or helped along on crutches, and put into ambulance wagons backed up to the levee.

"What is it? What's happening?" she asked, catching at Ramon's arm.

"At a guess, I would say the federal fleet has fought its way past the forts at the mouth of the river and is on its way upstream. Looks like somebody has given orders to burn the coal and steamboat wood, as well as the cotton and other supplies stockpiled in the warehouses, to keep them from falling into enemy hands."

He was right. The news was flung at them in a dozen clamoring voices as they reached the wooden dock built out from the levee. Anxious friends and relatives, come to meet those disembarking from the river packet, told of how the Yankee fleet, numbering some twenty mortar schooners and gunboats, and seventeen warships for a total of more than 350 guns under the command of Captain Farragut, had attacked Fort Jackson and Fort St. Philip. The garrisons of the forts had not been captured, but the federals had been able to break the chain barrier laid across the river channel and, despite heavy fire, steam past the first and only line of defense for the city of New Orleans. Farragut's fleet had been damaged by Confederate rams during the engagement, but sheer numbers had carried the day, and the federal commander was now steaming slowly toward New Orleans. He would be there in a matter of hours.

It seemed impossible. The ships of the federal fleet had been there, off the coast below the city, for so many months. At first an annoyance, then, as the effectiveness of the blockade grew, a hardship, they had never seemed a real threat.

New Orleans must fall. The people in the crowd, some babbling, others staring at each other in shock, some few women crying into their handkerchiefs, accepted that fact without question. Because of the surrounding flat terrain and the lack of fortifications, the city was indefensible. The best thing that the Confederate forces garrisoned there could do would be to retreat to avoid capture, with the hope of rejoining the Army of the West and reoccupying New Orleans at a later date. When they left, the people of the town would be left defenseless before federal invaders. What they would do, how the townspeople would be treated they did not know. It was possible that the city would be looted, plundered; as for the women, heaven alone knew what they might be called upon to suffer.

Ramon paid no attention to the chaos around him. His gaze was fastened on a ship a few yards farther along the levee. She was a side-wheeler, but there her resemblance to the clumsy riverboats such as the *Rose of Sharon* ceased. Long and narrow, with the pointed bow of an ocean-going vessel, she had truncated masts and a single stack that could be telescoped out of the way when she was under sail. The housings for her side-wheels were enormous, with steps and railings built over them by way of a promenade. Her color was not white but a dirty shade of mist-colored gray. At her stern she flew the Union Jack of Great Britain. She did not flaunt her name with huge lettering and painted designs on her paddle boxes, but marked it instead in scrolling gold letters high on her prow. She was the *Lorelei*.

Ramon was the first man across the gangplank when it was finally let down. Lorna, half-walking, half-trotting at his side, wondered if he even remembered she was there. She was certain she had been forgotten a few minutes later when, nearing the ship, he was spotted by a man patrolling the deck with a shotgun in his arms.

A whoop of joy broke across the levee, followed by a rapped-out order to lower the gangplank. The young man who had spoken was short and slender, his brown hair covered by a uniform cap that came down on his brow to the wire-rimmed spectacles he wore. He swung up to stand on the stacked cotton bales that crowded the ship from stem to stern. "Hey, Captain," he called, "I had a bet with Frazier you'd show up before dark. He's been grumbling like an old grandpa, but we've had steam up for two hours, since we fought off the bunch of riff-raff that tried to set fire to us. We were going to take her out into the river, if they tried it again."

"Good man, Chris," Ramon called. "Is everybody aboard?"

"Every man-jack of us!"

"The repairs?"

"Done, since yesterday! Are we going to run for it?"

"What do you think?" Ramon shouted, his face slashed by a grin of anticipation. His words were echoed by a yell from the gathering crew of the steamer.

In spite of Lorna's misgivings, he had not forgotten her. He turned to her as the gangplank was run out to thud gently onto the top of the levee. "Tell me quickly," he said, "is there anywhere I can escort you? Is there anywhere you think you might find safety."

She glanced at the ship that waited, then back to his face where impatience to be gone was overlaid by his concern for her. She shook her head. "No. You should go, now, with your ship. You don't want to be caught here."

He was gentleman enough not to show his relief, nor to take the easy way out. "We never decided what you would do, where you would go."

"I think . . . it must be the convent. It isn't far from here. You needn't worry."

He sent a hard glance a hundred yards down the levee to where a group of men, shouting drunkenly, were rolling whiskey barrels from a shed, smashing them in the street even as the shed began to burn above their heads. He took her arm. "Come, I will walk with you."

She shook him off, holding out her hand. "No, it isn't necessary. You don't owe me anything. I will say good-bye now."

"Ma chère," he said, slowly taking her cool fingers in his strong, warm grasp, "To say farewell and leave you here, like this, it troubles me."

She forced a smile, looking away from him to where the *Lorelei* rose and fell with the river's current, the rain dappling the surface of the water. Her habit was growing wet again, but she did not notice. Attempting to withdraw her hand, she said, "There is no need."

He did not release her. "I wish . . ." he began, his voice low and tense, "I wish there were something I could do for you. I would take you with me if the risk were not so great, and if I thought you would go."

Her gray gaze met his dark eyes briefly, then flicked away again. "No, I understand."

He swung, calling. "Chris, do you have any specie on you? Whatever you have, bring it here."

"I don't want your money!" she said, anger tightening her voice. "I won't take it!"

"Don't be a little fool!" he said in grating tones as he spun back to her. "It isn't for services rendered, you know. You will need something to live on until you can find a position, or someone to take care of you."

Her chin rose. "I can take care of myself. I don't need your money. I don't need you or anyone else."

The officer he had spoken to came over the gangplank and stopped at Ramon's side, holding out a leather purse. Ramon took it from him and, reaching for Lorna's hand, slapped it into her palm.

"Take it and, for the love of *le bon Dieu*, use it! Let me do this as a salve to my conscience, if nothing else!"

She did not agree, but neither did she refuse the money again. Her fingers curled around the stiff leather, feeling the rough suede with heightened sensitivity. He released her hand; then, almost against his will, he clasped her forearms, drawing her toward him. His kiss was warm and deep, a farewell flavored faintly with chicory and so infinitely tender that she felt the rise of salt tears in the back of her throat. He released her with a ragged sigh and stepped back. His dark eyes held her silvery gaze, and his voice was rough when he spoke.

"Good-bye, Lorna."

She summoned a smile, though a shimmer of tears dimmed her vision. "Good-bye."

He turned sharply and stepped to the gangplank, striding across. The order was given to cast off, and men leaped to obey. Their feet thudded back across the gangplank. Another order was called, and she heard the creak and rattle of chains as the plank was run in. The deep blast of a steam whistle shook the air, sounding once, twice, three times. The paddle wheels began to churn. The ship inched backward. Across the widening gap of water, she sought and found Ramon, standing with his hands braced on the railing. Warm tears spilled from her lashes, and she turned sharply away.

Behind her, she thought she heard his rough oath. The rattle of chains came again. Swinging back, blinking hard, she saw Ramon spring to the moving gangplank jutting out over the water and leap to the levee. He strode toward her, and bent to thrust an arm beneath her knees, lifting her high against his chest. Before she could move, before she could protest, he took a running step toward the moving ship and vaulted the open stretch between the shore and the blockade steamer.

He landed hard on the bolted planking. Eager hands reached out to steady him, to catch and pull him back onto the deck. He glanced around him with a lifted brow, and the men drifted away, suddenly remembering important tasks that needed their attention as the ship headed into the river channel.

He glanced down at Lorna then, and his gaze was unfathomable. The muscles in the arms that held her were like coiled steel. Rain clung to his lashes and beaded his hair so that it curled over his head, falling forward onto his forehead. The rain surrounded them in a curtain of mist, gentle, protective. A slow smile carved deep indentations in the planes of his face and crinkled the corners of his eyes. With great care, he set her on her feet. Looking up, he located the officer who had brought the money, the spectacled youth who was overseeing the coiling of the hawsers some distance away.

"Chris," he called, his voice sure and deep. "Show this lady to my cabin, then let's run for Nassau."

What Ramon had failed to mention, and his men had accepted with such high good-humor, was the fact that, rather than evading the blockade squadron at the mouth of the river, to reach the gulf the *Lorelei* would have to sail past the federal fleet now ascending the river. Slipping by thirty armed ships, any one of which could blow them out of the water, would be no sinecure. The coloring of the ship, designed to make her invisible in fog and sea mist, would be an advantage in the lightly falling rain and the early darkness that was fast approaching, but the risk had increased a hundredfold.

Lorna, left alone in the captain's cabin, faced the danger squarely. It did not dismay her, any more than it did Ramon's crew. Whether from confidence in his ability to surmount a difficult obstacle, from an inability to grasp the possibility of her own mortality, or from sheer refusal to accept the fact of the Yankee victory, she was not afraid. Her only wish was for something to do, some way of passing the hours that lay ahead.

She looked around at Ramon's quarters with a certain curiosity. They appeared to serve all his needs in one compact area. A wide bunk took up one wall, with an oil lamp in gimbals swinging at its head and a large brass-bound trunk at the foot. Another lamp was attached to the wall above a table that sat under a pair of fair-sized portholes. It illuminated the charts spread over that surface, which was also set with a silver and brass condiment holder containing salt, with its own tiny silver serving spoon, a shaker for pepper, and wide-bottomed cruets for oil and vinegar. There were two heavy chairs with turned legs at the table, while on the floor beneath and extending to the four walls of the cabin was a matting of woven straw for coolness in tropical ports.

Minutes after the vessel had cleared the port, leaving the smoking, panic-stricken city behind them, a meeting of the ship's officers was convened in the captain's cabin. Ramon entered first, explaining to her in a few terse sentences what was about to take place. He gave no indication that he wished her to leave; still, she could not be comfortable as the men filed into the small room.

The first to arrive was the executive officer, second in command after Ramon. A tall, rather gangling, sandy-haired man with sky-blue eyes, his name was Earnest Masters, though he answered, also, to Slick. As he was introduced, he spoke to her in a slow and confident drawl that had the sound of the hill country of northern Louisiana. Behind him came Frazier, the supercargo, an older man, short, pot-bellied, with a bald head polished to shining and edged with a fringe of salt and pepper hair that trailed down his jawline forming magnificent mutton-chop whiskers. He was an islander, from the Bahamas, and their pilot in those waters. Finally, the second officer, who also served as navigator, joined them. This was Christopher Sanderly, whom she had seen before. Quiet, almost shy as she returned his bor-rowed purse, he radiated intelligence from the hazel eyes behind his spectacles, an impression confirmed by Ramon's claim that he was a genius with numbers.

There was time for little more than a smile and nod of ac-knowledgment for each man as he entered, before the door swung open again with a bang.

"*Mon Capitaine!* They say you are back, but I must see it with my own eyes, me! Hey, you one welcome man, I tell you. What for you stay away so long?"

The new arrival was a small and lively Frenchman with the rakish look and the scraggly beard of the sailing men of Mar-seilles, allied to the happy disposition of the Acadians of Loui-siana. His name was Cupid, and he had been a seaman for nearly thirty years, most of them before the mast, though an injured shoulder that had caused his arm to wither had turned him into a cook. He preened at having the spotlight as he was made known to Lorna and, by way of approval for her appearance, rolled his eyes expressively at Ramon. His next move was to offer ham sandwiches and hot coffee all around, to fortify them against the night ahead. As Ramon accepted, the Frenchman took himself from the room, but not before he had given a quick wink to Lorna.

She took one of the two chairs the cabin boasted, placing it out of the way in a corner before she sat down. Ramon took the other and, turning the seat toward him, set one booted foot upon it, leaning his wrist across his knee.

There was no need to outline the situation; they knew it well enough. The details Lorna had not known, Ramon had given her before the others had made their way to the cabin. They were cruising at half-speed, with visibility cut to no more than a few yards, and a rain storm on their beam. If that weren't suicidal enough in a river known for shifting its sandbars over-night and carrying enough downed timber any day to build a fair-sized town, they were without a river pilot and heading into the teeth of the best fighting ships the North had to offer. At their present speed, allowing for the effect of the flood current, and if they were lucky, they would make the 150 odd miles to the gulf in approximately fifteen hours, just in time for ships of the rear guard of Farragut's fleet, no doubt patrolling the river's mouth, to use them for target practice at dawn. Before that could happen, they would have to get past Farragut himself.

"The floor is open," Ramon said with an easy smile. "Does anyone have any idea when we may be expected to come upon the main fleet?"

The supercargo, Frazier, cleared his throat. "They were saying on the docks that Farragut started past the forts in the early hours of this morning. If he came straight on after the battle, that would put him just about on New Orleans's doorstep."

"He would have to travel at the speed of the slowest ship in his fleet, say maybe nine of ten knots an hour, moving upstream against the current," the second officer said. "It stands to reason that he would proceed with caution since he wouldn't know the river and couldn't afford to put complete trust in any southern river pilot he might be able to hire. Under those conditions, and given the number of ships he has with him, it would be foolish to risk steaming at night; too much chance of their fouling each other if there were some kind of accident."

"Then there are the batteries at Chalmette. It's likely he will want to pass them near dawn, as he did the forts." That piece of informed deduction came from Slick, the executive officer, who stood with his lanky form braced against the wall.

Ramon gave a short nod, his eyes narrowed in concentration. "We can reasonably expect to run into him two or three hours downstream, then, either making slow headway or tied up for the night. The question is, what do we do about it?"

There was a moment of silence. Christopher Sanderly looked from Ramon to Slick, then back again. He opened his mouth, closed it, then finally spoke. "There are all these ships that have been set on fire floating on the river right now, plus nearly a score of cotton runners like ourselves, and then that many again of river packets, even a Confederate iron-clad. From what we heard, there will be more. I say we rig barrels or something with wet cotton in them to make a smoke screen, make it look like we're just another burning hulk. If we cut the engines and float down on the federals, they'll steer clear of us and let us go right on by."

"Good thinking, Chris," Ramon said. Then, as the second officer began to grin, he continued, "There are only two things wrong with it. The first is the danger of any fires set getting out of control, and the second is that ships like the *Lorelei* have an irresistible appeal to the federal navy. They are still in need of every ship they can lay their hands on, and nothing would make them happier than getting hold of a fast runner to use to chase down others of her kind. So long as there were no actual flames, no sign of structural damage to the ship as it went by, it's all too likely a boarding party would be sent out. The minute the fighting started, we would be exposed and reinforcements would be sent.''

The supercargo shook his head so that the lamplight overhead gleamed on his shiny bald dome. ''That's the truth, sure enough. What I say is, we ought to ease off down this river until we sight the federals; then, saying they're still moving, we slip over to the bank and tie up. What with the rain and the dark, they'd never spot us. Them blue boys would sail right on by, and as soon as the last one got around the bend, we could slip our lines and run for the gulf.''

Ramon looked toward his executive officer. ''Well, Slick?''

The tall man shrugged. ''I'd say there're going to be plenty of lookouts on the decks of the fleet, what with the fired ships coming down on them, and them in enemy waters, not knowing what to expect. What happens if one of those hulks, burning like merry hell and lighting up the night, comes floating past just as a gunship skates by, or if the good Lord sees fit to send a flash of lightning so that some eagle-eyed Yankee catches a glimpse of us and sets off a calcium rocket to take a better look? It would take us a few minutes to get steam up again and move on. In that length of time, we'd be as easy to hit as a tired turkey at a snipe hunt. I think stopping would be a mistake.

''These are deep-draft ocean vessels for the most part,'' Ramon said slowly. ''It's probable they will proceed upstream in single file, keeping to the main river channel, strung out over ten or fifteen miles of river. If we are discovered, if one ship starts to fire, then the others in the line will be alerted. We would have to run the gauntlet with a vengeance.''

''That's true,'' Slick said. ''The Yankee ships down the line would be ready and waiting for us, and there would be no place to run. But if I've got to get mine, I'd just as soon take it running free. The *Lorelei* will do fourteen knots, maybe a bit more at full speed, and this flood current will add another couple. I say we barrel down on them and slide past before they can get their foot back, much less bring their guns to bear.''

Lorna glanced at the others, seeing in their faces silent agreement with the sentiments expressed by the tall executive officer. From the faint smile on Ramon's face, she thought he too was satisfied. He stood up, twisting his chair back around under the table.

''That's the way we'll do it then,'' he said.

Hard on the words, Cupid returned with the coffee and rolls with thick slices of ham pushed into them. The men talked as they ate, completing the details of the plans for the night ahead, while Cupid, tray dangling from his fingers, stood listening, content that he had managed to get in on the end of the meeting. When they were finished, they left as unceremoniously as they had come, Ramon returning to the deck with the others.

The men did not glance at Lorna as they left; indeed, had barely acknowledged her presence during the entire conclave. The business that had brought them was vitally important, of course, and their position much too grim to allow for social formalities. Still, she could not help wondering how much her position as the woman who was to share their captain's cabin had to do with their manner toward her.

She got to her feet, taking a turn about the cabin, stopping to glance at the charts on the table before moving on to stare out the small window, from which she could see the orange flares of burning ships some distance away, moving down the river.

She was being ridiculously sensitive. It was probably so common to see a woman here in this cabin that it had not required comment. Since Ramon was their commanding officer, it would have been impolite, not to say insubordinate, for his officers to accord her too much attention. If she felt like an interloper, it was not to be wondered at; she was. If she was treated as a pariah, it was her own fault for allowing Ramon to see so plainly that she was at a loss, here in New Orleans, as to what to do or where to go.

She should never have let him see that she was disturbed at parting from him. She should have protested at his sudden abduction, refused the place he had assigned her. She had done none of those things and so could not complain.

Why hadn't she? Why had she permitted him to take charge of her? She could plead exhaustion and confusion at the violent upheaval of her hitherto dull life. She could say she had not realized what he meant to do, that it had happened so quickly she had not had time to think. Neither was strictly true, though each had contributed a small part. The fact was that when she had thought of Ramon sailing away free and unencumbered down the river, leaving behind the degrading events of the past days and their frightening consequences, she had wanted to go with him with a longing that was disconcerting in its intensity. To escape, to sail into blue skies and sunshine, away from everything and everyone she had ever known, away from her desolate childhood and the ugly memories that had followed, beyond the reach of the law and Nate Bacon, had been a burning need inside her. She had known Ramon could satisfy that need; that was why she had wanted to go with him. It had nothing to do with him as a man, or of what had passed between them.

Of course it had not! How could there be any attraction between them, other than a brief carnal pleasure, when they had known each other no more than a few short hours, and those under only the most adverse circumstances. He had used her, and now she was using him. It was as simple as that.

Now that she was here on the blockade runner, steaming into danger, was it really what she had wanted? She didn't know. It was so difficult to sort out her feelings. It was not only her life that was changing, disintegrating, but the world as she had known it. She was not unhappy; she was even relieved, if a little fearful of the future, and of the man who had taken her from New Orleans.

In the end, however, it was simple. There was no one else she would rather be with, no place else she would rather be.

Chapter 7

Time dragged past. The steamer seemed to be creeping along. Rain lashed at the decks overhead, and thunder growled. The wooden hull with its thin sheathing of iron creaked as the ship wallowed in the wind-whipped current. The lamps swung, casting swaying shadows on the walls. Lorna could not bring herself to undress and lie down. If the *Lorelei* was hit, she did not want to be caught unclothed, half-asleep. She moved about the cabin, sitting down on the bunk, jumping up again. Catching sight of herself in the mirror of the shaving stand, she grimaced at the unkempt sight she presented. In need of distracting herself, she paused before the trunk at the foot of the bunk, then reached to lift the lid.

Inside, on a tray, lay the jacket of a uniform of dark blue with gray flaps on the pockets, epaulettes sporting gold bullion, and down the front brass buttons embossed with the depiction of a ship under steam and with the word *Lorelei* in scroll underneath. To match the jacket, there were gray trousers with a dark blue stripe down the side of each leg. Under the top tray was more casual clothing, jackets and trousers in somber hues, light-colored waistcoats, silk cravats, and stiffly starched shirts.

She saw these at a glance, but then her gaze was caught by a canvas bag pushed carelessly under the linen. Prodding it gently with one finger, she felt the contents slide, heard the solid, metallic clink of gold. There were more bags deeper down, she thought, though she looked no further. Lying in that trunk, un-locked, in plain view in a cabin that was also unsecured, was a fortune in gold. No wonder Ramon had not minded the few coins he had distributed for service on board the *Rose of Sharon*.

She let the lid of the trunk fall shut and turned sharply away. Blockade running was a lucrative business; she had known that. Seeing the hard gold, always demanded by the runners instead of the Confederate script that had been steadily losing value since its issue, brought home certain realities to her as nothing else could have done. She thought of all the gold pouring from the South into the hands of the blockade runners and their back-ers, and from there into the coffers of the English merchants from whence came the goods that were brought in, and she knew a moment of dismay. The states forming the Confederacy had been rich, incredibly so, before the war began; still, how long could they afford to disburse such a stream of wealth while the cotton and the sugarcane fields that had produced it lay fallow? And when the money was gone, what then? Defeat?

The South had to win, and soon; it had to. The losses, the changes any other outcome must bring, were unthinkable. The *Lorelei* had to get through, then. Regardless of the fortunes they made, men like Ramon were still the South's one hope.

It was impossible to realize, standing there in the warm, dry safety of the cabin, that the ship might be blown into splinters before morning, left to sink to the bottom of the river. The mind, in self-protection, rejected the idea. Yet that same intelligence recognized with dread the fast-approaching moment when the first federal ship must be sighted.

There was a bookcase holding neat rows of volumes above the bunk. Lorna glanced over the titles: Scott's *Ivanhoe*, a thick tome of famous naval battles, collected poems of Edward Young and Alexander Pope, Defoe's *Robinson Crusoe*, Michaud's *History of the Crusades*, Thierry's *History of France*, a treatise by Chateaubriand, and others by Dumas, Flaubert, and a half dozen more. She picked up *The Three Musketeers* and, moving to one of the chairs, sat down, turning the pages.

She read a few lines here, a few there, went back to the first of the book and began again, but the words were without mean-ing. Flinging the book aside, she crossed her arms on the table-top and leaned to rest her forehead upon them. Her eyes were burning and her head ached. As she sat there, the aroma of coffee, as well as the smell of food, reached her from the tray left on the table when the men had gone. She was not hungry, had not taken more than a few sips of coffee earlier, but a weakness in her knees told her it was time she put something in her stomach. Straightening, she reached out for a roll with a thick slice of ham inside and poured herself a cup of lukewarm coffee.

It was as well that she had eaten. A short time later, the French-Acadian cook knocked and stepped inside. He had come, he said, to collect the dishes. It was a rule. The *capitaine* did not want glass flying about if there was shooting.

"Your name is Cupid, I think," she said, her smile wry as she recognized her feeble attempt to hold the ship's cook in conversation.

"*Oui, Mademoiselle.*" He stepped to the table and began to stack the remains of the makeshift meal on the tray he carried. "I apologize, me, for coming so late to remove these things. I thought to prepare enough to eat so that it would be ready in case of battle. There can be no fire then, you comprehend. I almost forget, me, that I left the coffee for you to finish. We are not used to women on this ship, no."

She shook her head with a light laugh. "You don't expect me to believe that."

"But yes." He lifted a brow as he sent her a look of surprise. "It is not allowed. Ramon, he always say that the females only cause trouble. What a man does on shore, that is his affair, but he will not bring his *amours* onto the ship, not in the so beautiful form of a woman, not in the lovesick sighs and moans."

His disdain was amusing, but she did not permit herself to smile again. "He . . . is a hard captain, M'sieur Cazenave?"

"*Non, mais non*, did I say so? He is always fair, always generous, but some things he requires—a clean ship, hot food, a close schedule; some he will not allow, the women, loose plates and cups during action at sea, and . . . talking behind his back."

The rebuke was pointed, even if made with a shrug and a wink. She accepted it, changing the subject. "I don't suppose the federal fleet has been sighted yet?"

"*Non, Mademoiselle.* You would have known by the sound of the engines, by the quiet and the dark. But soon, I think."

When Cupid had gone, Lorna moved to lower the wicks on the lamps so as not to alert the federals by a show of light through the portholes. That done, she resumed her pacing. Perhaps a half hour later the rain ceased. It died away so quietly, it was hard to tell when it had passed. It had become such a constant background sound the last few days that it was some moments before Lorna noticed its absence. That it should desert them when it was so badly needed for cover for the ship seemed a betrayal.

For the dozenth time, she moved to a porthole and stood staring out. There was still nothing to be seen, however, no glimmer of light, no shift of movement. She felt so shut away there in the cabin below decks. Now and then she could hear the others moving about above her, could catch their muffled voices, the passing in subdued tones of an order. It was stuffy in the cabin, heavy with the smell of coal oil and soot from the extinguished lamps. The need for fresh air, the urge to know what was happening, was too strong to be denied longer. Turning abruptly, she crossed to the door and let herself out.

The passageway was cool and dark, without lights. To the left lay the cabins of the other officers and the crew's quarters; to the right, if she remembered correctly, lay the companionway down which she had come when she was led below. Sliding her hand along one wall in the darkness, she made her way forward. She stubbed the toe of her riding boots on the bottom step of the ladder-like stairway. Lifting her skirts, she began to climb.

The thumping of the beams that turned the great paddle wheels was like a giant heartbeat, a thunderous sound echoed by the splash of the water cascading back into the river. It filled the night, deafening in the stillness. Though the rain had ceased, the decks were wet, reflecting the flashes of lightning behind them in the northwest. The shallow-draft blockade runner was hugging the east shore as closely as possible, at the edge of the channel. Lorna could just make out the dense shape of the tree line, hear the sighing of the wind through the branches. That same wind billowed her skirts around her and slapped the collar of her jacket against her cheek. It flung the cool dankness of the river into her face so that she drew in her breath with the fresh shock of it.

She did not want to get in the way; still, she wanted to see. Keeping close to the deck housing, she worked her way toward the prow of the ship. She could hear the low murmur of voices. A few steps farther, and she had left the protection of the housing. The wind struck her like a blow, and she staggered a few steps, coming up against the rail before she regained her balance.

Ahead of her lay the river, like a huge, winding black alley.

The water itself seemed a shade lighter than the banks on either side, gathering and reflecting what little light there was in the cloudy night sky. The flicker of lightning gave an eerie, intermittent light but at the same time seemed to drain the color from the landscape, leaving it gray and black. They appeared to have outdistanced the burning ships, for there was none to be seen around them. The river stretched clear and empty, its surface ruffled into whitecaps in the flashes of light.

Without warning, the rain returned, closing in with the thick darkness of a blanket. In that sudden contrast, she saw it, a pinpoint of light that bobbed and darted, drawing nearer. At the same time, a quiet but carrying cry sounded overhead.

"Ship away! Dead ahead!"

She half expected some violent reaction, a flurry of commands, crewmen running here and there to man stations. Instead, there was only a drop in the speed of the engines, the soft gurgle of steam being blown off underwater, and the decreasing cadence of the paddle wheels. Somewhere nearby a lantern's light was snuffed out with a pierced cover. The only gleam left on the upper deck came from the binnacle, though it was shielded by a solid wood screen.

Thunder rumbled and rain splashed down. The orange light at the masthead of the warship swam closer in the gloom. Lorna stood watching it with her hands clenched upon the railing and rain driving into her face.

A footfall sounded close behind her. She whirled to see the dark form of a crewman standing near her, his body tense, as if he had seen an apparition. He whirled, moving quickly out of sight. A moment later, she heard his voice in low warning. "Cap'n. . . ."

Almost at once, Ramon materialized out of the darkness. His voice was harsh as he demanded, "What are you doing up here?"

"I only wanted a breath of air."

"I must ask you to go below at once. Get in the bunk and cover up, even your head. Don't move until someone comes for you."

She hesitated, then asked the question that had been troubling her. "But what if we are hit, what if the *Lorelei* is sunk?"

He took her meaning at once. "There will be plenty of time to bring you topside before she goes under. The greatest danger by far is from exploding shells, flying glass, and wood splinters.

There is no time for argument or gentle persuasion. Will you go now, or must I carry you?''

''I will go, of course,'' she said, her voice quiet in counterpoint to the sharp impatience of his tone. ''I would not like to be a handicap to you.''

''Since you are still up, I suppose the cabin lamps are still burning?''

She had turned and taken a step back the way she had come. Now she swung around. ''No. Even I can see the need for turning them out.''

As she whirled from him again, he said, ''Wait.''

''What is it now?''

''Would you like to see Farragut's flagship?''

''You mean. . . . '' She faced him there in the darkness, glancing uncertainly toward that shining beacon ahead.

''It's there, the *Hartford*, Farragut's pet ship, the first in line. It looks as if they have tied up for the night.''

She stepped forward, straining her eyes to see, scarcely noticing when Ramon moved to her side with his back to the wind, shielding her from the main force of the rain. The light grew, blossoming, separating into a second lantern in the rigging of the ship, and a third. Their glow outlined the masts and spars, still stripped for action of all except fore, main, and mizzen topsail yards, and with the sails clewed up, dripping in the rain. The vessel that lay at anchor was a screw sloop of twenty-four guns with twin stacks, but it carried the graceful lines of a sailing ship.

''She's a beauty,'' Ramon said, his voice shaded with reverence.

A beautiful thing dedicated to destruction, Lorna thought, though she did not say so. ''You are going to run past her, then?'' she asked as the *Lorelei* continued her slow forward progress.

''Slip past, I hope, and pass, too, whatever else is behind her.''

''Pray God, the rain keeps up.''

''Yes,'' he answered, his voice distracted as he watched Lorna beside him in the wet darkness.

They were nearly upon the ship. Lorna felt that she should move, should offer to go below, but she could not seem to make herself do it. She stood rooted, watching the flagship looming toward them, waiting for the cry that would mean they had been sighted, braced for the roar of guns. It did not happen. The ship lay quiet, swinging on her cables, enduring the pounding rain in sullen stillness. The men on her would be exhausted from the battle they had fought that day and the work of repairing the damage in the aftermath; they would be lying as the dead in the forecastle. There would be the injured to see to, the dead to be prepared for burial either in the river or when they reached New Orleans. No one would be expecting a cotton runner to be insane enough to try to race by them in the storm-swept danger of the night.

The Creole blockade runner beside her remained still, lending his presence, his protection, without fanfare, embodying the courage of every man on the ship. Lorna grew aware of a sense of camaraderie, of shared danger that seemed to bring them close, closer than she had ever been to any human being. It was a disquieting feeling, one she could not welcome, for it seemed that when it was withdrawn she would be more alone than before.

They were past and leaving the *Hartford* behind. Ahead could be seen another signal lantern on the prow of another ship. "I had better go below," Lorna said in low tones, "but I am grateful to you for letting me stay this long."

His voice was abrupt, almost as if he regretted the impulse, as he answered, "My pleasure."

If the minutes and hours had been slow in passing earlier, they scarcely seemed to move at all now. In the cabin, Lorna stood at one of the portholes for a time, but could see nothing since it was on the port side of the ship and the federal fleet lay at anchor to starboard. No sound could be heard on the steamer except the slow hammer strokes of the boom, mingling with the thunder and the rain-like splash of the water from the wheel. She found after a time that her muscles were tensed, as if waiting for a blow. Unable to see or hear, consigned to idle waiting, it seemed the best thing she could do was to follow Ramon's suggestion. She moved to the bunk and lay down, staring into the darkness, her hands clenched into fists held stiffly beside her.

There formed in her mind a mental picture of the steamer ghosting past an endless line of ships, black hulks heaving on the breast of the river, lashed by rain, marked only be their wavering lights. She thought after a time that she could tell when they passed one; there was a change in the sounds of the night, a compressed quality with the hollow ring of an echo. As it came again, and yet again, with no challenge to the *Lorelei*, she began to relax. The gentle rise and fall of the vessel in the water was soothing. As her tension eased, it was replaced by a vast tiredness. Her legs and arms felt heavy, weighted to the bunk. Her eyes burned, and she lowered her lashes for an instant.

The night exploded with a bursting report that reverberated from one tree-lined shore to the other. Hard upon it came a crash overhead and the tinkle of breaking glass. The ship rocked from the blow so that she was thrown against the wall. The starboard paddle wheel, lifted from the water, beat a wild measure as it spun, then the vessel settled again with a rumbling crash. As Lorna clung to the sides of the bunk, she heard the shrill whistle as air was blown through the tubes connecting with the engine room. Immediately, the beat of the paddle wheels accelerated.

Again came the shattering boom of big guns, the sound rolling across the water. The shells made great splashes nearby, as if they had fallen short. In the interval that followed, it seemed to Lorna that she could hear the shout of distant orders on board the federal ship away to their right; then came the third crash of gunfire.

It sang as it approached, a high-pitched and deadly whine that passed harmlessly overhead. She did not move, though it was the hardest thing she had ever done. The need to leap up, to do something, anything, was a rage inside her. She felt so useless lying there, a burdensome responsibility, of neither benefit nor aid to the men of the ship, or to herself.

Was it all to end here on this wet April night? It was possible that she deserved no more. The wheels of the gods might not always grind slowly. With wide eyes, she breathed a silent prayer and waited for the next shot. It did not come. With paddle wheels thrashing, the *Lorelei* plunged into the rain-drenched night, intent on her heedless, yet calculated, run to the sea.

It might have been the sun that woke Lorna; it might have been the sound of footfalls in the corridor outside. She lay dazed but with her eyes open as Ramon stepped into the cabin. He met her gray gaze as he swung the door to behind him. Releasing the knob, he moved to pull out a chair from the table and dropped into it with the heaviness of exhaustion. He sat for a moment, before beginning slowly to remove his boots.

"We are safe, then?" she said, her voice husky.

"As safe as we can expect to be, with the federal navy on the prowl."

"Are we in the gulf?"

"Just leaving the Mississippi Sound, heading out into dark blue water, but past the danger point." He dropped one boot to the floor with a thud and began to tug at the other.

He seemed hardly conscious of what he was saying. It was not surprising. Other than the few snatched hours aboard the river packet, he must have had little rest in nearly three days. Her next question came without thinking, born, she told herself, of no more than natural concern for a fellow human being. "Have you eaten?"

"With the men, yes." He set the other boot aside and got to his feet, dragging his shirt from his trousers.

She lowered her lashes. "I thought, from the sound of it, that we were hit last night."

"We were."

"Was anyone hurt?"

"Only a few scratches. A shell ventilated the wheelhouse, nothing major."

"We were lucky then." From the corner of her eye, she saw his shirt as he flung it across the chair in which he had been sitting.

"It was one of the last gunboats that fired on us," he said. "There were two others, river steamers converted into gunboats, but they couldn't get our range, or else they never really got a good look at us."

There came the rustle of his twill trousers as he stepped from them, throwing them to join his shirt. The bunk jarred slightly as he sat down on the edge. Lorna shifted with a quick, scooting motion, making room, and he slid beneath the sheet. His broad form took up nearly three-quarters of the available space. The calf of his leg touched hers, and she drew away, huddling on her side against the bulkhead, facing him as though on the defensive.

He smelled of fresh salt air with an undertone of warm maleness. His eyes were bloodshot, and the stubble of his beard made a dark shadow beneath the bronze of his skin. As she watched, he let his eyelids fall shut, and so tightly did they seal that his lashes, black and curling, tangled together. She could feel the warmth emanating from his body. It made her uncomfortably aware of the habit she still wore, with the long skirt twisting around her knees and thighs. She had not been able to bring herself to remove it, not even when it had seemed they might be safe. Now that the rain had been left behind and the sun was out, the air in the cabin was close, freighted with warmth.

"Could we let in a little air?" she asked.

His answer was an indistinct sound, but she took it for an affirmative. Clambering over him, she struggled upright, shaking out her skirt. She crossed to the porthole and turned the heavy bolt that held the frame closed, swinging the sash with its thick glass wide on its hinges.

The gulf breeze swirled into the small cabin, filling it with the tang of the sea and the somnolent heat of the bright day. It caressed her face with a gentle touch, lifting soft tendrils of hair, fluttering them about her cheeks. She reached up and released the soft knot of her hair, spreading the silk roll of it with her fingers so that it hung wild down her back in a shining curtain. Working at a tangle, she stared out the opening where she could see the water, dancing in sun-struck waves, stretching to the far horizon. It was as deep and impenetrably blue as Spanish ink, or as the painted eyes of a china doll she had had as a child. There was no land in sight, nothing except endless reaches of water. Louisiana, the occupied city of New Orleans, and Nate Bacon all lay far astern.

At the thought, she felt a lightening of her spirits, the relaxing of close-held fear. She flung back her hair in a sudden gesture of freedom, shaking it so that the soft wind fluttered the ends. Abruptly, a yawn caught her and she stretched, bending an arm to massage the stiff muscles of her neck even as she filled her lungs with clean, warm air.

How lovely it would be to feel the breeze upon her skin. She turned to fling a quick glance at Ramon, but he lay unmoving, his eyes closed. With nimble fingers, she unbuttoned the bodice of her jacket, shrugging from it. She tossed the jacket to lie with Ramon's clothing on the chair, and began to unfasten her skirt.

Standing in camisole and pantaloons, she stretched again, wishing she dared to throw herself down naked to sleep, like Ramon. She might have, if she had been alone, but the fact remained that she was not, and the habits of a lifetime were difficult to break. Eying the space on the other side of him, loath to wake him or, in truth, to share his bunk, she wondered if there was some other place where she might sleep.

"Will you stop dithering and get in the bunk?"

She was so startled by his sudden request that her answer was sharper than she intended. "I'm not sure I want to."

"That makes no difference. It's the safest place for you just now."

"Safe? What danger could there be?"

"There are twenty-six men on this ship, twenty-six good men. I'm not saying you would be assaulted if you stepped beyond the door alone, but you would be a definite enticement. I don't intend for the ability of my men to work as a unit to be jeopardized simply because you aren't sleepy anymore."

She drew in her breath with an angry gasp. "If you think that I am in the habit of dispensing my . . . favors . . . to all and sundry, then I take leave to inform you that you are wrong!"

"No." His eyes flew open and he heaved himself over, bracing on one elbow. "I never said such a thing nor hinted at it. My concern is that, in trying to attract your attention, my crew will forget their duties. If the notice of the man on lookout strays, or the man at the wheel, or a stoker who should be in the hold watching the boilers, it could mean disaster. I can't help it if you are sensitive on the subject of your favors, but I did not raise it."

She could feel a tide of color as it swept to her hairline. He was correct, she was sensitive to the charge she had thought he was making so obliquely. That was something she had no intention of acknowledging, however. "Anyway," she said through set teeth, "I don't see how you could think I meant to go outside dressed like this!"

A smile tugged at the corner of his mouth. In dulcet tones, he said, "It should have occurred to me, but since a good three-quarters of the men on this ship are wearing less this morning, it escaped my notice."

"Did it indeed?" She narrowed her eyes, trying to decide if he were deliberately teasing her. It was a novel idea. Such a thing, along with horseplay and practical jokes, had been discouraged in her aunt's household.

"Perhaps I should have said I was in no condition to allow myself to notice," he amended, a smile creeping into his eyes. "Are you, in truth, weary of sleeping already?"

She shook her head. "Not really."

"Then come."

He moved closer to the edge, making more room for her

between himself and the bulkhead before lying back on the pillow and clasping his hands behind his head. She approached the bunk, keeping a wary eye upon his long form. He was watching her closely, his gaze resting on her chest. Glancing down, she saw that the tucked and lace-inset lawn of the camisole was not as concealing as she had imagined. Plainly through the soft and much laundered material could be seen the rose-pink shadows of her nipples.

She turned her head with a quick movement, and her hair cascaded forward over her shoulder, falling down her breasts in a silken, concealing curtain. She put one knee on the edge of the bunk and leaned across him. Placing her hands on the resilience of the soft cotton mattress, she rested her weight upon them. As she lifted up her other knee, drawing it across his body, the inner surface of her thigh brushed across his pelvis. She was aware, suddenly, of the open crotch of her pantaloons, those garments always constructed with a split seam for ease in attending to the functions of nature while clad in the voluminous fashions women wore. She refused to look at him to see if he had seen. Instead, she dived across him, at the same time lifting the sheet and slipping beneath it.

She half-expected some comment about her ungainly haste. It did not come. For long moments he lay still, staring at the close-matched boards of the ceiling. He threw a glance at her lying so stiff beside him, and an expression crossed his face that seemed composed of equal parts of amusement, concern, and irritation. He lowered his arms and reached across to close his hand on the smooth roundness of her shoulder, drawing her nearer to him. As he pillowed her head on his shoulder, his voice was deep and rough against her hair.

"It's all right. Before God, I promise it. Go to sleep."

She was hot. She felt as if her skin were melting. The air she breathed had a cook-stove heat. It stirred around her, but so warm was it that it had no power to cool. She was swathed in covering, wrapped to the point that she could hardly move. There was a pounding inside her head, allied to a rocking motion that seemed unceasing. It was funny; she didn't feel ill.

She moved her head, lifting her arm from the coils of hair that bound her in its damp skeins, and she woke at once. She opened her eyes, and the cabin steadied around her, swaying only with the movement of the ship, while the steady beat of the paddle wheels took on an ordinary, muted cadence. She turned

her head on the pillow, and perspiration trickled along her hairline. She lay alone in the bunk, though the moisture along her
side was enough to tell her that it had not been long since Ramon
had left her.

A tinkling sound drew her attention to the foot of the bunk.
The lid of the trunk that sat there was raised. Above it, she could
just see the top of Ramon's head as he knelt in front of it. From
the sounds, she thought he was searching for something. It
seemed obvious that he was looking for fresh clothing, until he
slammed the trunk lid down and got to his feet. In his hand, he
held not a clean shirt or pair of trousers, but a roll of bandaging.
His movements were stiff, and he held one arm clamped across
his chest.

"What is it?" she asked, flinging back the sheet, pulling her
hair from beneath her with an impatient gesture as she raised up
in the bunk.

"My rib," he said shortly. "I was thrown against the wheel
last night when we were shelled. Must have struck the same
place your fine father-in-law hit me."

"Is there anything I can do?"

"Now that you ask, *ma belle*, there is. The thing needs strap-
ping down."

He came to sit on the edge of the bunk, one brow lifted in
silent challenge as he proffered the roll of cotton stripping. She
took it gingerly. "I would be glad to help, but I'm not sure I
know how."

"There's nothing to it. You just wrap that around me nice
and snug and tie it tight." He watched her as he spoke, and the
bright look in his eyes was a reminder of her disheveled state,
of the dew of perspiration across her upper lip, and the way in
which her damp camisole clung to her upper body.

She sat up, drawing her legs under her, sitting on her heels.
She flung her hair back over one shoulder and, keeping her
attention on what she was doing, began to unroll the bandaging.
He turned toward her, obligingly raising his arms. Reaching
around him at the level of his heart, she caught the end of the
strip of cloth and began to carefully unwind the roll, smoothing
it with her fingers against the sculpted planes of his chest. There
was a livid bruise to guide her as to where to place the greatest
thickness. She covered the center of it, continuing to his back
where, leaning close so that the top of her head brushed his
chin, she secured the end and began the next round.

His chest rose and fell with his steady breathing. His skin seemed to tingle under her fingertips, as though he were more alive than most men. She found herself lingering, gliding her palms over the muscular sheathing of his back, while a peculiar disturbance grew inside her, and her blood sang in her veins. She sent him a quick glance from under her lashes. He was watching her with narrowed attention.

She swallowed hard. "Does it hurt?"

"Only when I breathe."

The words were without inflection, a simple statement of truth. "Am I getting this too tight?"

He shook his head. "Feels better already."

She suspected a hidden meaning to his words but did not care to press it for fear she was right. "It didn't seem to bother you last night, or rather, I should say, this morning."

"I suppose there was too much going on to worry about it."

Considering the rigors of the night, this did not seem unreasonable. After a moment, driven by the need to find distraction and keep some semblance of ease between them, she said, "I didn't hear the *Lorelei* return the fire of the gunboats last night."

"She didn't."

Lorna sent him a quick, frowning glance. "Why not?"

"The ship is unarmed."

"What?"

"No blockade runner is armed."

"But—I don't understand. Isn't that dangerous?"

"Not as dangerous as being caught with guns abroad. When a blockade is in force, any ship entering or leaving a closed port is considered a hostile belligerent and is liable to be treated as such by being fired upon with, in the event of capture, imprisonment for the crew. That is the rule of maritime warfare, and has been for centuries. If a ship is armed, however, and fires in her own defense, her crew becomes pirates and can be hanged out of hand."

"They can slaughter every man on board and sink your ship, but you can't fire a shot in return? That must be maddening!"

"It can be, yes, but our goal is to get merchandise into port, not fight federal cruisers. If we wanted to engage the enemy, we could have ourselves commissioned as a ship of the Confederate navy, a commerce raider, and go out and sink northern shipping, both commercial and naval."

"That would not be profitable," she commented with a shade of derision.

"No."

"But don't you ever feel like hitting back? Don't you long to sink the ships that are trying to sink you?"

It was a moment before he answered; then he gave a grim laugh. "Sometimes I would like nothing better."

It was odd, how pleased she was with the sentiment. She was quiet while she considered it. She finished a second, lower row of bandaging and began a third, neatly overlapping the other two, before she spoke again. "How long before we reach Nassau?"

"Six days, more or less, if we don't run into trouble."

"Trouble?" She flicked him with a frowning glance as she began to double the rows for added holding strength.

"A storm. Or a federal cruiser that we have to veer off course to evade."

"What . . . what will you do when you get there?"

If he was impatient with her questions, no trace of it showed in his voice. "The same thing I've been doing for the past six months: arrange for a new cargo and, probably, sit out the time until the dark of the moon while the wheelhouse is being rebuilt."

"Until the what?" On the lower strip of bandaging, she had to bend down in order to pass the roll behind him. Each time she did, the warm fullness of her breast brushed his side, with only the thin lawn of her camisole preventing contact with his bare skin. She tried to avoid that touch by extending her arms, but he only leaned closer, as if he thought she might be having difficulty reaching around him. His deep voice rumbled near her ear as he spoke.

"Ships are much too easily seen when there's moonlight on the water. During the early days of the blockade, the steamers ran into the ports without worrying about it, but since the cordon of federal ships has tightened around Charleston and Wilmington, Savannah and Mobile, most only go out during the dark phase of the moon."

"Most?"

"There are a few who still make moonlight runs."

"You among them," she said, her conviction strengthened by something in the timbre of his voice.

"When the money is right. There's not a great deal of difference, except the timing has to be better. You run into a coastal inlet between dusk and moonrise to avoid the federal line, then head for port in the few hours between the time the moon sets and daylight comes.''

''And if you can't find a convenient inlet?''

''You do, if you have a good pilot.'' He lifted his shoulders in a shrug. ''If not, it's like being caught naked, whether under the moon or in the dawn. You pray you can reach cover before anybody sights you.''

A facetious question concerning his experience with that state crossed her mind, but she dismissed it. ''A cautious captain doesn't make that many trips in any given month, then.''

''True, but the danger is greater, and therefore the cost is higher—''

''—So the money remains the same,'' she ended for him.

''Very good,'' he said, his tone honeyed as he ignored her sarcasm. ''Maybe Lansing and Company can find you a job in their accounting office, since you have such a flair for business.''

''Women are not given positions on accounting stools,'' she informed him through tight lips.

''You would be surprised at what's going on in Nassau these days. There's a black female stevedore on the docks who can match any man loading, bale for bale and barrel for barrel. There's a woman who raises and sells fresh butter and eggs and fruit and vegetables for the steamer crews, and she is making more money than many a blockade captain. I swear I saw her take a gold eagle for a sack of oranges the last time I was in port. She may be getting twenty dollars apiece for them now.''

There was skepticism in Lorna's gray eyes as she met his solemn brown gaze. Her voice was flat as she said, ''Really.''

''Really. I could speak to John Lansing about a position, if you like. He would consider it, as a favor.''

''That would get me out of your hair very nicely, wouldn't it?'' She tugged on the bandaging, pulling it snug.

''Ouch,'' he said, wincing.

''Sorry.'' She could sense him staring down at her, but refused to look up.

''You needn't be in a fret about Nassau. It's a beautiful place, and one of the most exciting in the world just now. The town is booming, the streets crawling with speculators and commission agents from half the countries of Europe. Confederate officers and federal diplomats, courtiers and statesmen rub shoulders in the rooming houses and hotels. There are seamen of every nationality you can name on the streets, and women the same. Fortunes are being made and spent every day. New houses, grand mansions, are going up on every corner. There's a constant round of entertainments, of cotillions, dinners, sailing parties, balls, and picnic excursions.''

''I fail to see how any of that concerns me, since it hardly sounds like a place where it would be safe for a woman to go out on the streets, and I will not be going into society.''

''The only way you can fail to enjoy it is if you are so stubborn that you refuse to have a good time. I was joking about the position, but Edward Lansing is a friend and business associate of mine. He's one of the best-known men in the islands, a Londoner who came out a few months ago and has since built a home above the harbor. His two daughters are the belles of Nassau, and I'm sure that Charlotte and Elizabeth will take you in hand and see to it that you find a place.''

''They will, naturally, be happy to sponsor a woman who murdered her husband.''

''That's in the past,'' he said, his voice hardening, ''and should be forgotten. I see no need to mention what was no more than an unpleasant episode. You are young and beautiful. In Nassau, there are so many men and so few women that the men stand ten deep around every girl even slightly presentable. Before the month is out, you should have so many proposals that you will be hard put to decide among them.''

''That will be wonderful, for you, since you will be relieved of any responsibility for me.''

She was near the end of the roll. By main strength, she tore the last few inches in two, tied them upon themselves, then wrapped one end back in the opposite direction before forming a flat knot just under his breast bone. He waited until she was finished before he spoke.

''Is that what is bothering you, the fact that I have no plans to keep you with me?''

She swung from him, settling back on the bunk. ''Of course not! Why should I want to stay with a mercenary blockade runner whose only interest in me is as someone to use to avenge himself upon an enemy, particularly when you will probably be blasted out of the water by the next Yankee frigate that sails over the horizon?''

"Put that way," he said gravely, "it certainly makes no sense at all."

"Still, you might have given me the pleasure of refusing your suit," she said in goaded tones, sending him a scathing glance before looking away again. "Under the circumstances, it would have been the honorable thing to do!"

It was a moment before he answered; then there was a grating tone in his voice. "Oh, by all means, let us be honorable."

She felt the bunk move, heard the creak of the supporting ropes, then he was on one knee before her, picking up her hand. He carried it to his lips, and she felt their warm brush on the sensitive tips of her fingers before he turned her palm upward and placed a kiss in its hollow. A tremor ran up her arm, and she controlled it with an effort. "Ramon—"

Disregarding her breathless appeal, he said, "Would you give me the great pleasure of becoming my affianced wife?"

Chapter 8

Sitting on the low bunk, her head was very nearly on a level with his own. She stared into his eyes, seeing in their dark brown depths a glimpse of self-derision, and of undoubted pain. An instant later, they were devoid of emotion as he knelt there, swaying in perfect balance with the rise and fall of the ship. She could hear the splash and rush of water against the bulkhead behind her, and it seemed that in its gurgling there was the sound of laughter.

"It would serve you right if I accepted, but of course I refuse." She had meant the words to carry a sting. Instead, they had a shaky, uncertain sound.

"Of course." He took a deep breath and let it out slowly, then, in a smooth reflex of well-conditioned muscles, came to his feet.

"What I don't understand," she said slowly, almost to herself, "is why you came back for me, why you are taking me with you."

Several seconds elapsed before he spoke. "After what you had done for me, how could I leave you behind?"

"Easily," she jibed. "But what does it matter if I am set down in New Orleans or Nassau? I have no one in either place."

"You see no difference between a conquered city and one in the midst of plenty? Anyway, as I told you, I have friends who will look after you. I can't do that myself, I have a job to do, a commitment to regain Beau Repose, men who depend on me, such as Edward Lansing and my crew. There has never been a place in my life for a woman beyond an affair of a day or a night, and now, while the North and South are tearing at each other's throats, is an unlikely time to make one. That doesn't mean I won't be keeping an eye on you, seeing that you are all right. I owe you a debt, more than that, I have done you much more harm than I dreamed, or intended, that afternoon. I would not insult you with more apologies, but I will give you my most solemn oath that reparation will be made. I will make it.''

Duty. That was what it came to in the end. He had taken her aboard his ship not because he wanted her with him but out of a sense of guilt and the need to appease it, out of duty.

What else had she expected? She could not have said, and yet the idea filled her with dismay. Her voice quiet, she said, ''I see.''

''Your needs will be provided for, a place to stay, new gowns, bonnets, slippers; whatever it takes to rig you out *à la mode*. I will attend your bills until. . . .'' He paused, then shrugged and went on, ''Until some other man relieves me of the expense. I don't expect that to be long.''

''You have it all planned, it seems.''

''I have tried to think ahead,'' he agreed.

''No doubt the idea came to you in all its detail just before you jumped off the *Lorelei*.''

He came erect, frowning. ''Are you suggesting that there is another reason I went back for you?''

Emboldened by the compressed timbre of his voice, she glanced up at him. ''Isn't there?''

There was a flash of sudden gold deep in his brown eyes, and a tight smile curved his mouth. ''If you mean that I wanted you,'' he said, the words spaced with deliberation, ''then you are correct. There should be no surprise in that. As you well know, I have wanted you from the minute I first saw you, and have scarcely had you out of my mind since.''

That was not what she had meant—or was it? In the confusion of her thoughts, it was impossible to be certain. She only knew that she was mortified by his intention of seeing her established in another man's keeping.

''That doesn't matter,'' she said, her gray eyes as dark as a storm from the northwest. ''I need nothing from you. I want nothing. There is no need for reparation, I assure you. I'm not sorry to have had my marriage ended, regardless of the causes that brought it about, though I deeply regret Franklin's death. If you are in my debt, then I am also in yours for helping me escape from Beau Repose. But now, I would as soon forget the whole thing. When we reach Nassau, you may go your way and I will go mine.''

He reached for her arm, hauling her upright so that she stumbled from the bunk, falling against him. Before she could regain her balance, he pulled her closer, molding the slender curves of her body through camisole and pantaloons to the muscular hardness of his frame.

"Even if I could agree to such a proposition," he said, his voice deep, "which I can't, and won't, there would still be the matter of the days between here and the islands.''

He ran his fingers in her hair, clenching them on its satin softness, tilting her head back. His firm mouth descended to shape the smooth contours of her lips to his hard demand. His hands upon her, gliding, exploring, were like spark to tinder. She felt the beginning flame, knew her own yearning toward its consuming heat.

She wrenched away with desperate effort, dragging her mouth free, bracing her hands on his chest. The knowledge of how close she had come to yielding brought fiery color to her face. "No," she exclaimed, despising the tremor that shook the word. "You can't mean to . . . to act as if nothing we have said makes any difference.''

"It doesn't," he murmured, drawing her closer, bending to nuzzle the tender nape of her neck as she turned her head away from him.

Could he be right? Involuntarily, she remembered the moment on deck when they had braved the might of the federal fleet anchored so near, their hours in the storm-buffeted skiff and the perilous race against the dogs and mounted men at Beau Repose. Shared danger was a powerful bond, and a violent spur to desire.

"You can't," she cried on the edge of coherence. "I can't—"

His lips burned a path along her neck to her shoulder, where he slid aside the narrow sleeve of her camisole, letting it fall down her arm. "Consider it," he suggested as he peeled the fine material lower, exposing a rose-tipped breast to his attention, "as the price of passage.''

It was an excuse, she recognized that in the remote recesses of her mind. Still, it was one that held a peculiar validity. She had no other coin in which to pay, no right to ask for or expect costless favors from this man. Nor did she want to be beholden to him.

He sensed the moment when resistance left her. He lifted her against him, standing for a moment so that she was rocked in his arms by the ship's movements.

"Your rib," she whispered, placing her hand on his chest, feeling beneath her fingers the cloth binding and, under it, the strong thudding of his heart.

"Damn my rib."

He put his knee on the bunk, then leaned to place her on the mattress before easing down beside her. He picked up a curling strand of her hair, like raw silk, and carried it to his lips. His eyes were watchful, almost black as they rested on her face. Placing the lock out of the way across his shoulder, where it linked them together like an ecru satin tether, he gathered her close and buried his face in the silken waves that lay on the pillow around her. Blindly, he searched for her lips, found them, and the sound that vibrated in his throat might have been a murmur of either triumph or despair.

Nassau was the favorite base of the blockade runners, primarily because it was the closest neutral port to Wilmington, North Carolina, which was, in turn, the nearest harbor, with the best rail access, to the Confederate capital at Richmond. The distance to Wilmington was 640 miles, the distance to Charleston only 560, with the current of the Gulf Stream an added boost on the heavily laden outward journey. In addition, the chain of islands belonging to the Bahamas extended more than a hundred miles in the direction of the southern ports, lending the protection of its neutral waters for that distance.

Bermuda was another base much used, but it was farther from the important Atlantic ports of the South, with less direct communication with England. Another drawback was the strong winds often encountered near that lattitude as the ships headed northward. Being so heavily loaded with war materials and, especially, the tremendous amounts of coal needed to make the round trip, these gales were more to be feared than the sighting of a federal frigate.

Havana was used by many runners who traded with the gulf

ports of Mobile, New Orleans, and Galveston, but the distance
to the area where the main battles were being fought at this time
being so great, the traffic was mainly in civilian goods. The
Spanish government was cooperative, though venal; still, the
merchant firms lacked the dispatch and drive of the English and
Bahamian companies at Nassau on New Providence Island.

The result of such natural and commercial advantages was a
harbor so crowded that it looked impossible to get another ship
into it with a wedge and maul. There were frigates and barques
and brigantines; yachts and yawls, schooners and sloops; and,
darting here and there, a few skiffs with sails colored orange
and blue and green. The tall masts made a wild cross-hatching
against the intense blue of the sky, and among them loomed the
smokestacks of the steamers, the lead-colored ships like so many
gray ghosts among the brighter craft: So closely were they all
anchored, indeed, that it looked as if it might be feasible to walk
across the harbor by moving from deck to deck.

Lorna stood in the prow of the *Lorelei*, holding to the rail,
her eyes narrowed against the wind that flapped her skirts and
thrummed in the rigging above and behind her. She had watched
as the Bahama Islands had risen slowly out of the sea, low-lying
mounds gray-blue with distance, turning slowly to a vibrant jade
green edged with the white of their beaches. She had seen the
dark, purple-blue of the deep water turn to magenta and turquoise as they neared land, changing to aquamarine and pale
celadon green along the creamy shoreline as they steamed past.
They had kept to the channel, easing past countless small islands—mere dots in the vastness of the ocean, with palm trees
waving above their arid sands—and larger masses of land with
scant habitation. Finally, they had steamed between the shores
of low-lying Hog Island on the left and the larger hillock of New
Providence on the right.

Now the port of Nassau itself lay before her, a long, semicir-
cular bay with warehouses of weathered limestone or rough,
new-sawn planking crowding the water's edge, and houses with
wide verandas climbing the low hill behind them. Church towers
stood out, shining in the sun, and the graceful crowns of royal
palms, silk cotton trees, sea grapes, and deep green sea pines
waved over cool, secluded gardens enclosed by limestone walls.
Against the white stone and green vegetation could be seen bright
splashes of lavender and orange, crimson and yellow and pale
blue, where tropical flowers bloomed.

Small in the distance, carriages and people moved to and fro on the street that bordered the waterfront. The closer the ship drew in, the more frantic seemed the activity. There were stevedores, their black torsos glistening in the tropical sun above knee-length breeches, loading and unloading the vessels drawn up to the docks. Men in frock coats and stovepipe hats strode from one stuccoed building to another, talking, gesticulating with the canes they carried as they walked, while between them darted clerks with bills of lading fluttering in their hands.

A squad of men in the red of British uniforms, shouldering bayoneted rifles, marched along. A maid in white apron and boldly printed kerchief, carrying a napkin-covered silver coffee pot in her hands, crossed hurriedly in front of them. Women bearing woven trays of fruit and vegetables swayed with languid purpose from quay to quay. On a boat just in, Bahamian fishermen cleaned fish and twisted conch from their brown and pink shells, throwing the refuse into the water. Ladies in foaming crinolines, holding delicate satin-and-lace parasols tilted to protect them from the strong rays of the morning sun, were being driven here and there in open landaus. Dogs swarmed, while rooting pigs kept a wary eye upon them. Gulls circled the harbor, screaming as they fought over garbage in the water, and above them floated the angular black shapes of frigate birds.

Across the bay could be heard, too, the chanting of work songs sung by the gangs of stevedores, the barking of dogs and squealing of pigs as they were chased, the rasping of saws and pounding of hammers as new buildings were thrown up, the shuffle of feet and rattle of carriages. The smell of new lumber, sharp and resinous, drifted seaward along with the rich and ripe aroma of flowers and decaying fruit, of fish and verdant growth and open sewage.

The *Lorelei* was hailed by ship after ship as she made her way toward her anchorage. Other vessels farther along ran up greetings with signal flags. The ship's crew, bringing her in with practiced ease, shouted and yelled, their spirits boisterous, as if it was only now that they felt safe at last. The whistle down the tube communicating between the wheelhouse and the engine room shrilled. The ship lost headway. Her engines shuddered to a stop with a burst of steam as pressure was released from the boilers. The paddle wheels stopped turning with a last cascade of water. Chains rattled, running free, and the ship swung to her anchor. They had arrived.

There was an endless delay while port officials came on board. Later, Ramon swung down into a boat and was rowed to shore, where he was to negotiate for the disposition of the cargo of cotton the ship had brought in and its eventual unloading. It was well after the noon hour when he returned.

Lorna watched from the deck as he was rowed back out to the ship. He sat at ease with the inshore breeze ruffling his dark hair, and his features relaxed as he exchanged quick banter with the men who manned the oars. It was a change.

During the last few days of the voyage, he had grown tense, with lines of strain about his eyes, and they threaded through seas that were known to be patrolled regularly by federal warships. Twice they had sighted sails and had turned their stern to them, piling on the smokeless anthracite coal and dropping them well below the horizon before they continued on their way again. The passage among the islands of the Bahama chain had not been much better, for it was lined with sharp and deadly formations of ancient coral reefs that could rip the bottom from even an iron-clad steamer like so much gold foil from a bon-bon.

It had not been particularly comfortable being around him during that time. His temper had become uncertain, his manner brusque to the point of rudeness. All he required of her, it had seemed at times, was the mind-dulling solace of her body, snatched moments of surcease from the demands of duty. Once he had gone to sleep with his head pillowed on her breasts and his hands tangled in her hair. Another time, she had awakened in the dawn hours to find him dressed to go back on deck, kneeling beside the bunk watching her, only watching her, in the pale gray light. He had come to her less often after that, and when he had taken her in his arms it was as if he was driven by a compulsive need and the anger of self-contempt.

What would he be like, now that they had reached their destination? She searched his face for an answer as he climbed the rope ladder let down over the side. He gave her a brief smile before swinging inward, onto the deck. His manner was preoccupied; still, he stopped beside her.

"I suppose you are anxious to go ashore?" he asked.

"I guess so."

"It won't be long now. I would like to see you settled at the hotel before dark; that will be the Royal Victoria, the newest on the island. I met Edward Lansing while I was ashore. We are invited to dinner this evening, and to the musicale to follow.''

She sent him an incredulous glance. ''Any rooming house will do for me, but you must make my excuses for tonight. You must know I have only what I stand here in to wear. It would not have been suitable in the best of times, but now is quite impossible.''

She had long ago discarded her habit jacket of heavy poplin for one of Ramon's shirts, which was much more comfortable in the warm weather. With its collar left open, falling to a depth on her smaller frame that plumbed the hollow between the creamy curves of her breasts, and with its sleeves rolled to the elbows, the shirt would hardly have done for an evening function, even if her trailing habit skirt had not been irreparably stained by river mud and sea water.

''I had not forgotten,'' he said with a brief smile. ''There should be time to visit one of Nassau's best dressmakers on the way to the hotel. I'm sure something can be arranged.''

The chances did not seem good to Lorna, considering the unimpressive size of the capital of the Bahamas; still, when the time came to leave the ship, she walked beside Ramon, picking her way along the streets. On a quiet thoroughfare away from the waterfront, they stopped before a small West Indies-style house of pink-painted plaster over limestone blocks. The girl who answered the door had threaded needles thrust into the bib of her apron and a pin cushion strapped to her wrist. Bobbing a curtsy, she invited them in a broad cockney accept to step inside and poured out cups of tea for them to drink while they waited for the owner of the shop to join them.

The mistress of the establishment was an overblown woman with shining black hair, a quick laugh, and shrewd eyes. Informed of their need for an evening costume, she clasped her hands before her, pursed her lips, and began to demure. It was impossible on such short notice; human hands could not accomplish the sewing of a gown in less than three days' time. Men were such volatile creatures, so demanding, but Captain Cazenave must understand—

Ramon took a purse heavy with the weight of gold eagles from his jacket and quietly placed it on the table beside his chair. ''This lady,'' he said, ''has no time to waste, nor do I.''

''I see.'' The woman, who had introduced herself as Mrs. Carstairs despite the lack of a ring on her finger, looked from the gold to Lorna. "I see," she repeated, her mouth curving into a wide smile. "I suppose something might be done. I have one or two gowns stitched, awaiting only the final fitting. If the young lady will come this way?"

She moved to the doorway through which she had entered and, holding aside the portieres of pale yellow silk that draped the opening, waited for Lorna to precede her.

"Is it possible you have something in black?" Lorna said quietly.

"Black?" The woman's tone held disbelief.

"Not black," Ramon said at the same time.

Lorna swung on him. "But surely . . ." she began.

"No. There is nothing that compels it, and everything to advise against it. Those dressed in mourning must be ready to explain the cause."

Her gray gaze caught and held his opaque, black stare. She was aware of the dressmaker's watching them in frank curiosity, aware too of the undercurrent of meaning in Ramon's words. Choosing her reply with care, she said, "You think, too, that it would be a mockery?"

"I think it would be a sacrilege. Mourning is worn only for those who matter. If you don't regret the death, then don't drape yourself in black."

It occurred to her that, if he was to be rid of her, she must be attractive to other men. People could hardly be expected to take notice of a female in mourning, one who might well turn lachrymose at the least provocation. She inclined her head in a cool nod of acceptance and, turning, allowed herself to be shown into the fitting room.

So disturbing were her thoughts that she paid little attention to the gowns brought out from a back room, beyond noting that they were all of the latest fashion, one not yet seen in Louisiana. When the woman held one up, she merely nodded, then stood staring over the heads of the dressmaker and her assistant as they bustled around her, helping her from her clothing, pulling off her riding boots and substituting a pair of white kid slippers in order to better judge the length of the gown. She was aware of the women's sidelong glances at the bruises that still lingered in yellow and green profusion on her arms and her back above her camisole, but Mrs. Carstairs, turning away with tight lips, asked no question, and Lorna volunteered no answers.

When she was in her underclothing, a new Victoria corset

with a steel bust and front hooks for easier fastening and removal was brought out and fitted snugly about her waist. Next, a Douglas and Sherwood cage crinoline of spring steel clad in graduated rows of cloth tubing was lifted over her head, followed by three petticoats of lawn and one of taffeta, each of them edged with lace and bound at the hems with ribbon. The dressmaker then carefully placed a gown over Lorna's head, drawing it down into place. Standing back, she issued instructions while her assistant pinned the excess material in place upon Lorna. When they were done, the older woman turned Lorna slowly around so she could see herself in the great cheval mirror of mahogany and ormolu that stood in one corner.

The gown was of plum silk with short sleeves hidden under epaulettes of ribbon rosettes, and with a pointed bodice above a full skirt set with more rosettes of ribbon about the hem. The color was over-bright and the rosettes large for Lorna's taste, but it was the décolletage the was the real trouble. Set off the shoulders, it dipped low and wide across the breasts, leaving the blue-veined globes exposed to the very edge of their rose-pink aureoles.

"I don't think . . ." she began.

"Perhaps the gentleman should judge?" Mrs. Carstairs suggested, her head tilted to one side and a roguish smile on her generous mouth.

The implication was that, since Ramon was paying, he should have the final say in how he meant her to look. It was an unpalatable idea, but there was a certain cynical wisdom in it.

"Very well," she said.

The young assistant held back the portieres that had been dropped into place as a curtain over the doorway during the fitting. With her head high and her face a trifle pale, Lorna swept through the opening, compressing her crinoline, then allowing it to billow around her as she turned with slow majesty before Ramon. Facing him, she lifted her chin as for a blow, awaiting his verdict. Mrs. Carstairs stood to one side with her hands clasped in front of her and a benign smile of anticipation on her face, while her assistant hovered beside her.

Ramon frowned, surveying Lorna with slow care from head to hem. His dark gaze rested on the smooth curves of her shoulders. The lines about his eyes tightened.

"No."

Lorna released the breath she had been holding. He flung her a quick glance, and she looked away, unwilling to permit him to see her gratitude. She had been afraid he meant to parade her as a woman of less than pristine virtue, to make a spectacle of their intimacy as a means of attracting another man to—as he so inelegantly put it—pay her expenses.

"Certainly not, sir, if you don't wish it," Mrs. Carstairs said, a shade of anxiety in her voice as her gaze flicked to the purse of gold eagles. "It doesn't truly suit the young lady. I have another that will, I'm sure, be much more appropriate."

In the fitting room once more, Mrs. Carstairs joined the assistant in snatching out the pins. She scolded the young girl for her clumsiness and went down on her knees to let out the hem once more, then heaved herself upright again.

"I apologize, my dear," she said to Lorna as she lifted the gown off over her head. "I quite misunderstood. It isn't often I make such a mistake, but these are trying times, and everything is turned topsy-turvy. A body never knows which side is up, so to speak, with sleepy old Nassau being overrun with reckless, lawless folk who flock where there's gold to be had. But there, I'll say too much, if I don't take care. Let me settle this one on you. I think you'll find it more what the gentleman had in mind."

It was certainly more what Lorna had expected. A true dinner gown, rather than partaking of the nature of a ball gown, it was of a peculiar shade of silk that the dressmaker chose to call pearl-colored. It was nearer to being gray, however, a pale and silvery shade with a shimmering hint of pink in the folds as it floated over the hoops of Lorna's crinoline. That touch of color was repeated across her cheekbones as she stared at herself in the cheval mirror.

Never had she worn a gown of such richness, of such elegance. It had a double skirt, the lower one comprised of two deep flounces and finished with a *plissé*, or ruching, of pearl satin ribbon. The bodice was plain, with revers at the throat *à gilet*, or waistcoat fashion, edged with ruching and showing a frill of lace at the neckline. The sleeves were full and long, with ruched demi-revers at the elbow. which allowed the under-sleeves of fine lace to be seen.

"It's perfect," she said, her voice low.

"So it should be," the woman said with a wink in the mirror. "It was made to resemble one worn by a fashion doll brought just last week from France, one designed by Worth himself, couturier to Empress Eugénie."

"You mean you copied it? How talented of you."

"One does what one must to make a living." The other woman lifted a well-padded shoulder before turning to a nearby table heaped with silk flowers and lengths of ribbon, with fans and lace caps and tiny parasols. She extracted from the pile a small posey of pink silk rosebuds set with leaves of moss green velvet and nestled in a circlet of fine, handmade lace. This she held to one side of Lorna's head, then muttering beneath her breath, reached to take up a length of pearl ribbon to form a small, many-looped bow about the roses. She tucked the flowers deftly into the soft knot of hair at the nape of Lorna's neck. Standing back, she surveyed her handiwork with satisfaction.

"You are pleased?"

"Oh, yes!"

"Will you show the gentleman, then?"

Lorna's smile faded. After a moment she answered, "It might be as well."

The woman gave her a guarded glance. "He seems a generous man. I have here a walking dress of *tan d'or* in plain silk, just a shade darker than your hair, my dear, and piped in gray at the cuffs, the jockey, and waistband. There is, too, a cream poplin with a most *soignée* pardessus cloak of lightweight black silk lined in cream satin and braided with the same material. If you were to smile and be prettily grateful for the gown you are wearing, perhaps—"

"I couldn't," she answered flatly.

"She wouldn't," came the echo in deep-pitched tones from the doorway. Ramon dropped the portiere he had drawn aside and strolled forward. "She wouldn't," he repeated, "but we will take them anyway, provided you can deliver them to the Royal Victoria in two days' time."

"Two days! Impossible!"

"Indeed? Perhaps another dressmaker might find it within her power."

"It would mean sitting up all night . . ." the woman began, her resolution, wilting under his imperturbable and wholly charming smile.

"A drudgery for which you will, of course, be well paid."

Mrs. Carstairs closed her mouth with an audible sound. "Yes, sir. Certainly, sir."

"You may add whatever you think necessary in the way of undergarments and, ah, feminine accoutrements."

"Bonnets, sir? There is a friend of mine who has a lovely way with such scraps of straw and lace and ribbon."

"Bonnets will be necessary, I don't doubt," he agreed with the lift of a shoulder.

"And kid slippers, perhaps handkerchiefs, silk stockings by the dozen pair, veiling against the tropical sun, a parasol for outdoor excursions, hair ornaments; then there are nightgowns and caps, an assortment of undersleeves to protect the gowns from the ill effects of the wearer becoming over-warm—"

"As you say," Ramon agreed, exasperation making his tone short. "I will be waiting outside. Remember, if you please, that while we are prepared to wait two days for the remainder of the wardrobe, the gown she is wearing must be ready within the hour."

"The hour!" Mrs. Carstairs interrupted her blissful flow of accessories to scream the words.

"Within the hour," he said firmly and, turning, left the fitting room.

Somehow, it was done. The silk gown was delivered, along with three sets of camisoles and pantaloons of the finest lawn trimmed with Alençon lace and pale blue ribbon, and the new corset and hooped crinoline. There was also a wrapper made with the fullness of Watteau pleats in white batiste trimmed in blonde, and a matching nightgown that made Lorna think of her Aunt Madelyn's contention that attractive nightwear was a sign of depravity. Tucked into the wrapper's folds was a silk shawl, a drawstring purse of black silk net, a fan of ivory and lace, and a tiny vial of perfume that, when opened, spread the fragrance of madonna lilies on the air. Finally, there was a box of rice powder for the face and a milk-glass pot of French carnelian rouge. As she drew the things one by one from the small straw trunk, hand-woven on the island, that the dressmaker's assistant had delivered, Lorna thought Mrs. Carstairs was trying Ramon's words with a vengeance.

He was not there to object. After seeing her ensconced in the hotel room, he had gone back to his ship. He would change into his evening wear on board and return for her in a carriage. They would then proceed to the Lansing mansion.

It should have been a relief to be alone, and it *was* a real pleasure to have space to move around in and privacy again. She could not, however, escape a sense of having been deserted. Why, she could not have said; she was nothing more to Ramon

Cazenave than an encumbrance, a source of nagging guilt, and certainly he was nothing more to her than the man who held the distinction of being the recipient of her virginity.

It was ridiculous to think that they should be together, especially after his rejection of even the most remote possibility. She had no wish to hold him, none at all. And yet, he was the only person—other than the officers and crew of the *Lorelei*, men to whom she had barely spoken while on board—whom she knew in Nassau, the only connection with all she had ever known. It was that, of course, which left her feeling so bereft.

For the convenience of its guests, the Royal Victoria boasted large, fresh-water bathrooms. Leaving her room, Lorna went in search of them with her wrapper over her arm and a bar of castile soap in her hand. They were located on the south side of the building, at the end of a long walk along the railed verandas and over a long bridge to an adjoining building. Fitted with zinc tubs encased in mahogany, they were most luxurious when finally reached. An attendant filled the tub with heated water and laid out towels before drawing a curtain around the bathing alcove and leaving Lorna in privacy.

She soaked for long moments, letting the warmth of the water seep into her muscles, draining away tension and sundry small aches, floating away the invisible encrustation on her skin left from saltwater bathing while aboard the ship. Sitting up at last, she soaped herself with the fresh-scented soap, rubbing the lather into her skin, reveling in the cleanliness. Last of all, she wet her hair and worked a rich lather through the tresses dulled by fatigue and salt-laden mists. She had several hours yet before she must be ready, and she did not intend to hurry.

It might have been better if she had. When Ramon returned to the hotel some time later, she was still struggling with the myriad small hooks that closed the back of the pearl silk gown. She opened the door to him with one hand twisted behind her to hold back from gaping wide, keeping the décolletage from falling open. There was temper in her gray eyes and a flush on her cheeks from her efforts.

"Ready?" he inquired, his gaze resting on her face, his tone light.

"Do I look it?" The words were indignant, and she swung to give him a glimpse of her problem before turning back again. "I was going to ring for the maid."

"Perhaps I can be of service." Stepping into the room, he

closed the door behind him. He placed his high-crowned hat, cane, and gloves to one side, then put his hands on her shoulders and wheeled her gently around in her wide skirts, so that her back was to him.

It wasn't fair, the wave of weakness that moved over her at his touch. His fingers were warm against her skin, his movements quick and accomplished. As an antidote to the sensations that gripped her, she said, "You are very good at this, you must have had practice."

He stopped, his knuckles resting against her back just above her camisole. "A bit."

"More than a bit, I would say." She felt as if she were drowning in the spicy aroma of the bay rum he had used to counter the burn of his straight-edged razor.

There was lazy amusement in his voice as he answered, and his fingers began to move again, though with a slower, more lingering touch. "Feeling waspish, are you? You needn't fret; the Lansings will welcome you, just as they have hundreds of others in the past few months."

"Especially the Lansing sisters?"

"Charlotte and Elizabeth are charming young ladies. I think you will like them, and I see no reason why they shouldn't be good friends to you."

"No doubt, since you ask it!" She seemed driven to jibe at him, irritated as much as affected by his warm breath brushing across her shoulders.

He fastened the last hook, then catching her forearm, swung her to face him. "What is the matter with you? So what if you are invited tonight for my sake? You need these people to help you make a fresh start here, the right kind of beginning that will lead to a respectable alliance."

"Respectable? Are you sure? Mrs. Carstairs, this afternoon, wasn't so certain I was respectable, simply because I was with you! What do you intend to tell the Lansings to account for the fact that you are paying my bills? That I'm your sister, or maybe your cousin? And do you actually think they will believe you?" She had not been aware of the doubts festering inside of her until they came spilling out under the pressure of anger.

He scowled. "I will say that you are the niece of an old friend, an orphan, single, of course, who was entrusted to my care in order to get you out of New Orleans before it fell to the Yankees. I can't think why the question of your expenses should arise, but if it does we can always say that I am handling your funds for you. Whether they believe it or not doesn't matter, so long as no one challenges the story."

"That's all well enough," she said with a scathing glance, "but why didn't my so convenient uncle make his escape with me?"

"He stayed behind to look after his holdings, naturally. Your aunt could not bear to leave him. Their own children are married, no longer at home. They were concerned for your safety whether you stayed or went, but with your beauty, your fervent belief in the cause, and your somewhat fiery nature, they feared you must draw the attention of the northern soldiers."

The irony in his last words was not lost on Lorna. "I was the most even-tempered of females—until I had the misfortune to meet you!"

For a fleeting instant there was an expression in his eyes as if she had struck him. His voice was hard as he said, "With me out of your way soon, perhaps you will be again."

It seemed better to ignore that brief exchange. She whirled from him, searching for something to say and marveling, at the same time, at the thought he had given to the story they must tell. Moving to the washstand, she checked her appearance in the mirror, noting without surprise her flushed countenance and the darkness of her eyes. She tucked a tendril that had become dislodged back into place in her low chignon before she spoke again.

"Doesn't it bother you, foisting a murderess upon your friends?"

"For the last time, you are no murderess," he answered with aggravation, taking a swift step toward her, grasping her arm to swing her around to face him. "It was an accident and you are not to blame. Let it go. Forget it."

"I . . . I can't," she said, her voice low. "It's always there at the back of my mind, in my dreams."

"You can, and you will, if I have anything to do with it." He gave her a small shake, his grip tightening, his thumbs smoothing over the silk-clad roundness of her arms.

She lifted her lashes and, placing her hands against his chest, stepped back, straining to break his hold. Her voice low, she said, "But it isn't your affair, is it?"

He retained his grasp, his gaze resting on the tender curves of her mouth for the space of a long-drawn breath. Abruptly, he released her. "No, it isn't."

What had she expected? More to the point, what had she wanted? She pushed the knowledge from her, removing herself from proximity to him with a fierce twist. Gliding with self-conscious grace to the washstand, she picked up her fan and the drawstring purse that lay ready, containing her room key and a handkerchief. Lifting her head, she said, "I am ready."

Chapter 9

As promised, Ramon had hired a carriage to transport them to the Lansing home. Of the type known as a victoria, its hood had been let down so that they rode in the open, enjoying the mild night air. The man on the box set the vehicle along at a sedate pace. Their progress took them in an easterly direction along quiet, shady streets above the harbor, beyond the reach of the few gas streetlamps newly installed near the town square. On the right, rising high due to the upward slope, were large houses with lamplight gleaming through the jalousies that covered the windows beneath the wide verandas, while on the left snaked a high limestone wall that concealed the rear gardens of the house along the lower side of the street. Soft voices called in the night, music played, and the heady smell of citrus trees in bloom mingled with the scent of dust.

Lorna cast a glance at the man beside her. In the light of the carriage lamps he appeared virile and darkly attractive. For the first time she had leisure to note his well-cut evening clothes of black broadcloth and waistcoat of cream-colored satin and a gray cravat gleaming against the pristine white of his shirt. Aloof, preoccupied, he gazed out into the night.

She looked away again, her attention caught by the clatter of a carriage coming toward them. As it drew even, she stiffened, staring straight ahead; then, as it moved past, she turned in her seat to stare after it. Swinging back to Ramon, she exclaimed, "That was a naval officer, a federal naval officer!"

"So it was."

"I know this island is under British control, and therefore neutral, but it seems so odd to see one going peacefully about his business, when others like him were trying to kill us only a few days ago."

"It's odder than you think. I expect the man is on official business with the governor this evening. Ordinarily, the United States Navy isn't too popular with either the officials or the citizens of the Bahamas."

"It isn't? Why is that?" It was a relief to hear the even tone of his voice, which seemed to indicate his willingness to forget their quarrel earlier.

"Several reasons, first among them being that Nassau harbor itself is very nearly in a state of blockade, with the federal ships attempting to stop vessels of foreign registry coming in from Europe, as well as those going out toward the southern ports— anything they can catch beyond neutral waters. For another, there is the *Trent* affair. A Federal naval capitan by the name of Wilkes boarded the British mail steamer the *Trent* on the high seas and took into custody two Confederate diplomats who had been sailing out of Havana to their posts, one in France, the other in Britain. England came close to recognizing the Confederacy out of outrage over federal tampering with Her Majesty's vessel. The last reason is simply that without the South, and the blockade runners that supply its armies and its people, Nassau would be little more than a sleepy town on a sand spit in the middle of the ocean, where the descendants of pirates, wreckers, and American loyalists try to eke out a living."

"So you aren't forced to associated with Federals every day?"

"You think that would trouble me?" he asked, turning his head so that his dark gaze caught and held hers. "Why should it? I've known some of them since my academy days, and met others during my years in the Mediterranean. They are men, no more, no less. I've talked to one or two who said that, if they weren't assigned under orders to the blockading fleet, they would like to be commanding a cotton runner themselves,"

She turned her gaze forward, staring at the back of the driver. "You make it sound so reasonable—so civilized. How does it come about that men like you, and those back there, are killing each other?"

"An idea, nothing more or less. That's the usual basis for war."

"It's a stupid reason!" she cried.

"So it is, but ideas are what make the difference between existing and living; why should men not die for them?"

"Some do," she said before she could stop herself. "and then some live and die for gain."

She thought he would argue with her, would remind her of the use he would make of the money he acquired. Instead, he pressed his lips together in a firm line, turning away.

They did not speak again until the carriage had pulled up before a terraced Palladian mansion. Newly built, the home of Edward Lansing and his family was set in the midst of tropical vegetation that had not yet been tamed into the English idea of a garden, despite evidence of efforts in that direction. A groom in tailcoat and white gloves waited to hand them down, then passed them into the keeping of the dignified footman who stood on the landing before the house.

Edward Lansing was one of any number of Englishmen who had seen the opportunity inherent in the conflict in the United States and had moved to take advantage of it. Many of the investors had formed into companies and sent out representatives to look after their interests. Lansing had decided to oversee his particular venture himself; once his fortune was made, he could always return to London, taking up the place among the gentry to which his birth entitled him, though in considerably improved circumstances. In the meantime, he and his family were not adverse to being the leading social arbiters of life in the fast-growing tropical port; they were considered second only to the governor and his lady. Mrs. Lansing enjoyed her role as a hostess whose cards of invitation were much sought after, and the daughters of the house were, quite naturally, in demand.

This much Ramon had made plain during the voyage out from New Orleans, but he had not prepared her for the Lansing scale of hospitality. The butler, correctly stiff, with collar and cravat starched and white enough to do credit to a lord, bowed and welcomed Ramon with dignified familiarity before escorting them to the massive front door where he gave them into the hands of the butlers who waited in the front hall. That worthy, in the evening wear of an old-fashioned gentleman, took their names and ushered them toward the reception room.

The floors of the entrance hall were of polished marble checkered black and white; the walls were plastered and frescoed with scenes of palm trees, blue seas, and old Spanish galleons. A winding, unsupported staircase curved upward into the private reaches of the house. To the right was a library, plunged in gloom, while to the left was the brightly lighted room, hung with yellow silk and with floors of polished parquet studded with flowered Brussels carpets, where the dinner guests were gathering.

As they paused in the doorway, their names were shouted to all and sundry. There formality ended, for hard on the call came a girlish squeal, and a young woman, whirling in her enormously wide skirts of pale green muslin, turned and bore down upon Ramon.

She was a minx; that could be seen with half an eye. Her hair, of an unremitting shade of red, was drawn back in a style that was much too sophisticated for her age and piquant features. Her eyes of sherry-brown were tilted in her face, and her smile was saucy, displaying no hint of uncertainty over the sincerity of her welcome.

"Ramon," she cried, "I could not believe it when Papa said you were to come tonight! You have been away so long I was afraid you were feeding the fishes on the ocean bottom."

"What a revolting idea," he chided her, though there was affection in his eyes as he reached out to take her hands. Lorna, watching, thought his gesture was as much to keep the girl from flinging herself into his arms as part of the undoubted warmth of his greeting.

"So Elizabeth tells me," the girl admitted. "She says I am without sensibility, but I think it better to laugh at such things, for the more one dreads the worst, the more likely it is to happen! Don't you find it so?"

"Always," he agreed lightly, then turned to Lorna, performing the necessary introductions. When the acknowledgements had been made, gracefully on Lorna's part but with mere politeness on that of Charlotte Lansing, Ramon asked, "And where is your father, and your sister?"

"Oh, Papa is strolling on the terrace, talking business with the charming Mr. Lafitt from Trenholm and Fraser and Company. I am pledged to go and break it up at any moment, since word has come from the kitchens that dinner will be done to perfection in five minutes. And here is Elizabeth."

Trenholm and Fraser, the name was familiar. Searching her

mind, Lorna thought she recalled a southern import-export company by that name. Though based on the Atlantic seaboard, it was such a large operation that its stencil markings were often seen on boxes and barrels on the New Orleans wharfs. It made sense that the firm would be actively involved in the running of goods through the blockade.

"How delightful to have you back among us, Ramon," the second Lansing sister said as she approached. Her voice was smooth, bell-like in its tone, a perfect complement to her impeccable appearance. A dark beauty, she was consciously elegant, her manner cool. Her hair was waved back from a center parting and drawn up into a Psyche knot. The gown she wore was of blue silk, with a wide band of tartan plaid in green, blue, and black caught over one shoulder, held by a brooch at the waist, then falling over the flaring skirts in a style made popular by Queen Victoria's enchantment with Balmoral.

Her words were echoed by a tall, blonde Englishman who sauntered up to them in Elizabeth's wake. "By all that's holy, it's grand to see you again. We heard of the fall of New Orleans and suspected you would be embroiled in that fiasco, one way or another."

"You heard?" Lorna exclaimed. "But how?"

The dark blue gaze of the blonde-haired man rested upon her with interest. "By wire to Washington, then by ship and signal through the blockading fleet, which couldn't wait until we had heard of it here. Ramon, old man, aren't you going to make me known to this charming creature?"

"I wouldn't if I could avoid it," Ramon said with a grim amusement, "but since that's impossible—Lorna, may I present, first of all, Elizabeth Lansing, and also Peter Hamilton-Lyles, otherwise known as Captain Harris."

Lorna greeted the couple, then glancing from one man to the other, queried, "Otherwise?"

"My *nom de guerre*," the Englishman said, inclining his head, "though a worse-kept secret would be hard to imagine."

"I'm not sure I understand."

It was Ramon who enlightened her. "Peter is on furlough from the Royal Navy. Since England is officially neutral, his capture as a blockade runner would be an embarrassment to Her Majesty's government. That being so, he sails under an assumed name, with the agreement that he will expect no aid if he runs into trouble."

"Don't look so concerned," Peter said quickly. "Neither I nor any of the other chaps like me intends to be caught in a Yankee trap."

Charlotte, her voice subdued, said, "I'm sure none of the men who have gone aground, been captured or sunk, intended it to end that way either."

"I think it is time you fetched Papa," her elder sister said, a slight frown marring her features. The younger girl's face flushed scarlet in embarrassment for the gaffe she had made in speaking seriously of death in front of men who faced it each time they went to sea; still, she was not ready to leave them. As she opened her lips to protest, however, Elizabeth lifted a brow, and Charlotte flounced away to do her bidding.

"Could we talk of something more cheerful?" Peter said, his tone plaintive, though ready amusement lurked in the depths of his eyes. "For instance, Elizabeth, who is it you have to entertain us tonight?"

"I trust he will not disappoint; I considered that our guests might be weary of the usual tenors and string quartets," she answered, going on to tell them of a man from one of London's most famous music halls, one noted for his wit as well as his singing voice. In honor of the southern cause, he would be giving them a medley of ballads by Stephen Foster. They spoke of minstrel shows and favorite tunes, of showboats on the Mississippi River and the French opera house in New Orleans, of London's Covent Garden and the Victoria Theater. The conversation was interesting, but so disparaging was the young Englishwoman's smile at the mention of American entertainment, so animated her attitude when speaking of that of her own country, that Lorna was relieved when dinner was announced.

Peter chatted easily as he led Lorna into the dining room, moving after Ramon and Elizabeth in an arrangement the older Lansing sister had made with smiling deftness. He wanted to know how she came to be in Nassau, and listened with flattering interest to the agreed-upon tale as they took their places. That he was to be on her right hand at the table was a pleasant discovery, since Ramon was some distance away, near the head of the table, with Elizabeth on one side and Charlotte, her good-humor restored, on the other. It was diverting to watch the sisters vie for the dark and handsome Creole's attention, interrupting each other and sending daggered looks across him in a manner that was, Lorna thought, painfully obvious.

"Poor Ramon," Peter said, leaning close. "He walks a fine line. Which one of the sisters, do you suppose, would wield the sword if a Solomon decreed he should be divided between them?"

A smile came and went at the corners of her mouth before she answered. "Surely they wouldn't go so far?"

"Nothing more likely! Just wait until it comes time to choose seats for the musicale. I strongly suspect you will find Ramon searching for your skirts to hide behind. He will be out of luck there, I hope, for I intend to monopolize you for the rest of the evening."

The words were so lightly said that it was impossible to take umbrage. Still, she made an attempt to put him in his place. "With or without my permission?"

"Oh, with, by all means, if you will grant it. If not, I will trail along behind you like a faithful spaniel, all sad eyes and drooping tail, until you take pity on me."

She laughed, and was surprised by the soft sound she made, so long had it been since she had felt so light of spirit. Her reprimand was equally light. "Don't be ridiculous!"

"Why not, if it makes you smile at me? Perhaps I misunderstood, and your smiles are reserved for Ramon?"

"Not at all," she replied, though she could not prevent a covert glance at the other man down the table.

"Good," Peter took her up at once. "I'm glad we settled that. Now we can concentrate on how I am to entertain you while you are in Nassau. What say you to a meal al fresco in some deserted cove, or a moonlight sail?"

The expression in his sea-blue eyes was warm and shamelessly blandishing as he gazed down at her. It was a moment before she realized that his shoulder was pressing hers. She moved away. "You must be mad. I hardly know you."

"That can be remedied, given time."

"I'm not sure I want it to be!"

A look of infinite sadness closed over his face. He sighed dramatically. "I am cut to the quick."

"Of course you are!" she rallied him, "and bleeding inside, too, I don't doubt. I'm sure that except for the small matter of a hardy appetite you would go into a decline."

"Cruel, cruel," he mourned. "Why is it that the most beautiful women take such pleasure in inflicting wounds upon the egos of us poor defenseless males?"

She opened her eyes wide. "Because you ask for it, and there is no other way to be rid of you."

"If my suit is distasteful to you . . ." he said, drawing himself up in injured dignity.

"Your suit?" she queried softly.

"All right, all right, my attentions," he amended, abandoning hauteur for an aggrieved sigh.

A laugh broke from her, a free and delectable trill. Hearing it, Ramon swung his head in her direction, dividing a quick glance between the delight in her face and the man at her side. A frown gathered between his brows and, though Charlotte spoke to him, and he answered, he did not turn his gaze away.

Whether to avoid pursuit, as Peter had suggested, or from a sense of duty, Ramon did indeed seek her out when they left the dining room. He was on her right, with Peter on her left, as they re-entered the reception room that had been transformed during the meal into a music room with a Pleyel piano at one end and rows of small gilt chairs set before it.

Additional guests, who had not been lucky enough to be asked to dine, had gathered, sitting in groups here and there. There were a number of empty chairs located near the end of a middle row nearest the door, and Ramon led her toward them. Peter, true to his word made in jest, sauntered along beside them. When Ramon had shown her to a seat, taking the end chair beside her, the Englishman rounded the row and took the place on her other side. The look he sent the other man was bland. Ramon returned it with a hard stare, but within moments the three of them had fallen into spirited conversation while they waited for the room to fill. They talked of cargoes and of exorbitant freight rates and of the items in shortest supply, those most direly missed by the ladies of Lorna's acquaintance. They spoke of Lafitt of Trenholm and Fraser and of his need for experienced captains to see the arms and ammunition ordered through the firm by the Confederate government into Wilmington harbor. They discussed, too, the fortune made by one shrewd commander on a single run, carrying his own private cargo of toothbrushes, calomel pills, and corsets.

They were interrupted by Edward Lansing, who appeared beside them, asking to be introduced to Lorna and making his apologies for not being on hand when she had arrived. A slight man, his evening clothes were supremely well-tailored, and there was about him an air of the aristocrat. He presented his wife, as that lady, rather embonpoint, a bit vague, and vastly good-natured, paused beside him. She spoke and smiled, but it was plain her mind was on her role as a hostess, and she soon fluttered away in a drift of caramel-colored skirts. Their host did not ask about the voyage just completed by the *Lorelei*. He did invite Ramon for a drink the following afternoon, with some indication that business would be discussed, but it seemed more in the nature of a courtesy than because of any real interest in the degree of profit that might have been made by the ship in which he was an investor.

"You are lucky to be associated with Lansing instead of my firm," Peter said, a shading of envy in his voice. "You can do much as you please instead of having to answer to a board that pinches pennies as if they were ladies bot—ah, your pardon, Miss Forrester—as if their lives depended upon it. Would you believe they have been complaining about the price of anthracite? They sent out a lovely little memorandum suggesting that we use more bituminous, just as if burning the stuff outside Bahamian waters wouldn't be the same as sending up smoke signals the way your American savages do, telling the Yankee cruisers to come and get us."

They were joined at that moment by Charlotte, laughing and vivacious, who took the chair in front of Ramon and turned to brace her arms on the back. The girl chatted gaily, moving from one subject to another. Her mother had invited several chance-met acquaintances without informing either Elizabeth or the staff, and so they were short of chairs. Her sister, it seemed, would be playing the piano for the evening, a signal honor, since she would be accompanying a professional singer and joining musicians brought out at great expense from London. She had been practicing for days, until the household was sick to death of the pieces about to be presented, but her sister was not nervous. Elizabeth was never nervous.

Shortly after the last information had been imparted, the dark-haired Lansing sister entered the room and seated herself at the piano. The other musicians made their entrance, carrying their instruments, two violins and a French horn. The entertainment began.

Two hours later, it was over. On the return journey to the hotel, Ramon was silent. Lorna sent him an oblique look once or twice. He sat with his arm resting on the door of the open carriage, staring out into the night. In the dim light, it was impossible to tell whether it was weariness or preoccupation that held him silent.

"You didn't have to see me back to the hotel."

"Yes, I know," he said, his voice tinged with irony as he flung her a quick glance. "Peter would have been happy to do it for me."

"Isn't that what you wanted, to have some other man take on the responsibility for me?"

"With Peter, I expect it would be a temporary thing."

"Do you indeed?" she exclaimed. "That isn't very complimentary!"

"It wasn't meant to be. Peter enjoys women, women in their variety, and, though you were the most stunning woman there tonight and he may have half a mind to fall in love with you, he won't forget that he is the second son of a peer of the realm and expected to marry someone of his own class."

"He . . . he never mentioned such a thing to me."

"He would hardly be likely to boast of his bloodlines."

"Or to consider them over-much, I would think," she said heatedly, "if he loved a woman."

It was a moment before Ramon replied, and when he did his tone was stiff. "That may be so, but the possibility is so remote that I would advise you to tread lightly with him."

"Very well. You will, I hope, inform me when I am introduced to someone you think suitable!"

He turned in the seat to face her. "There's no reason to get on your high horse just because I tried to advise you."

"Advise? It sounds as if you mean to choose for me," she snapped, sending him an incensed look. "I have had some experience of other people's choices, thank you! And this time I prefer to make my own."

He watched her a long moment without speaking, then wrenched his gaze away at last. The accent was strong in his voice as he said, "As you please."

The Royal Victoria Hotel was an imposing building in the prevailing neo-classical style built of warm, cream-colored plaster over limestone blocks. It was four stories high, the bottom three of which were surrounded by verandas, the same airy porches that were known as galleries in Louisiana. On the eastern exposure, they wrapped around the end of the hotel, which was curved like the bow of a steamboat, and continued along the rear of the building. It was one of the highly advertised attractions of the resort that there were more than a thousand feet of promenades to be enjoyed. On the west end, at the third-floor level, the main building was connected by a covered walkway to an older structure where the baths were located. In the same section, at the second-floor level, was a wide staircase leading down to the gardens that fronted the edifice. The front entrance was graced by a pedimented porte-cochere that featured an arched Romanesque arcade around its four sides, with a gentlemen's parlor built out over it, and an open piazza topping that on the third floor. Gracing the roof of the long building was an octagon-shaped belvedere designed to give a commanding view of the sea and the ships beating into the harbor.

The carriage stopped outside the arcade. Ramon alighted and helped Lorna down, then, bidding the driver wait, turned with her into the hotel. They crossed the brick-floored arcade, passed through the entrance doors open to the sea breezes, and entered the lobby with its large Turkish carpet, sputtering gaslights under crystal globes, potted palms and cast-iron planters, cushioned wicker chairs, and plush ottomans encircling the support columns. The lobby was virtually deserted at this hour. A few men sat playing dominoes in one corner, while the desk clerk looked over their shoulders. That was all.

At the foot of the stairs leading upward to the guest rooms, Lorna reached to catch one of the higher steel hoops of her crinoline, lifting it and the skirts over it as she placed her foot on the first step. Ramon reached out to cup her elbow in his strong hand. The contact, even through the silk of her sleeve, was vibrant, unsettling. She resisted the impulse to jerk away. Assuming a distant air as a cover for the sudden increase in her heartbeat, she mounted the stairs beside him.

Never had a staircase seemed so complicated by turnings and landings, or a corridor filled with such echoing emptiness. The moment when they arrived at her door on the third floor had the feel of deliverance. She drew away from him on the pretense of searching for her key in her drawstring purse.

"Allow me," he said, his voice deep and low.

Taking the purse, he extracted the key. He inserted it in the lock, twisted the knob, and pushed the door open. He did not stand aside for her to precede him as she had expected, but instead stepped into the room. Moving to the brass gaslight near the marble-topped washstand, he lighted it and adjusted the flame before sending a searching look around the room. He went then to the French doors that opened onto the veranda. Finding them locked, he twisted the mechanism and set them wide, fastening the glass-paned panels back against the inside wall and drawing the jalousies shut over the opening, latching them.

Without turning, he said, "Does it trouble you, being alone here?"

"No, I don't think so," she replied.

"I don't like these doors. Any man with a room on this floor could force the jalousies and enter at will."

"I . . . I had not considered it."

"In ordinary times, there would be little to worry about, but there are some unsavory characters in Nassau just now, scavengers coming in to pick up what they can where money is being thrown around."

She moved to a rosewood table against the wall, which was covered by a piece of friezework. She put down her purse and fan, and began to unbutton her gloves. Over her shoulder, she said, "If you are trying to terrify me, you are succeeding."

"It would be better if you did not have to sleep with these doors open."

"It can't be helped," she answered, sending him a frowning glance from under her lashes. "I would stifle otherwise."

"True." A grim smile moved across his face as he turned and moved toward her. "Of course, someone to guard you would be equally effective."

She paused in the act of stripping off a glove, her gray gaze searching his face. Choosing her words carefully, she said, "I doubt the people who run this hotel would understand the need."

"Must they be consulted?"

The warmth of desire was in his eyes, but the smile that curved his mouth seemed to hold self-derision. There could be no mistaking his meaning. She swung from his path with such abruptness that her hoop jerked around her and her skirts sailed in a wide circle. A few steps away, she came to a halt, facing him in the center of the floor. Her breasts rose and fell with an anger that was allied to a peculiar chagrin. With great effort, she kept her tones even as she spoke. "The risk is too great. I thought it important there be no sign of intimacy between us. More than that, I seem to remember that you have no use for anything other than a brief affair, one lasting no more than a day or a night."

"I may have been wrong."

The timbre of his voice was raw, though his strained smile was beguiling, appealing. Lorna resisted it.

"I think not. I mean nothing to you, nor . . . nor you to me. We turned to each other because of a situation that no longer exists. I am grateful to you—"

"It's not your gratitude I want."

"It's all I have to give you! As you pointed out—"

"Will you stop throwing my words in my face? I know what I said, but I am willing—"

"I am not! You made it plain that once we reached here there would be no place for me with you. Very well. Now we are here. You have made it possible for me to start over, and that is what I intend to do." She paused a moment, her hands clenched on the glove she had removed, her voice trembling. "I would rather not have accepted anything of value from you, but, as you so rightly pointed out, it was necessary. Regardless, I would not have you think that because if it, I owe you—"

"Stop!" His features were harsh as he rapped out the command. "You owe me nothing, nor do I want anything from you that is not freely given."

"No?" she shot back at him, her gaze unflinching. "I seem to remember a charge for passage."

He took a step toward her, then halted as she retreated in haste. With spread legs, he said, "It was a gesture, a way to allow you to accept your own needs without lowering your pride. I thought you understood. Before God, woman! The debt I owe you far outweighs anything I may have done in return, while as for the damage—"

"I don't count it so!" she cried, raising her right hand, which still in its pale gray glove, was clenched in a fist. When he made no reply, she let her gaze move over his shoulder, feeling the rage draining from her. As she spoke again after a moment, her voice was without heat. "It would be best, I think, if we forget everything that has occurred between us, except the money you have spent on my clothing. That I will repay as soon as I—as soon as possible."

"The money is less than nothing. Try repaying it, and I will throw it into the sea."

"It is yours. When the time comes, you must do as you will."

He was so near that she could feel the radiating strength of his personality, a force that seemed to draw her toward him. She wanted to succumb, to walk into his arms and remain there, but that was an impulse he must not guess. It may have been the effort of refraining, or the bitterness of it, that left her so spent. She took a sustaining breath, forcing herself to wheel slowly toward the open French doors.

"I must ask you to leave now," she said.

"What makes you think that I will agree?"

Her mouth curved in a weary smile that he could not see. "You are a blockade runner and an opportunist, also something of an adventurer with a quixotic twist; but, most of all, you are a gentleman."

He stood unmoving for long, tense moments. Abruptly he gave a short laugh, and the sound of his footsteps moved away in the direction of the door. As he pulled it open she heard his answer.

"To my sorrow," he said.

The door closed behind him. She allowed her shoulders to sag. Moving to the opening of one set of French doors, she leaned her head against the frame of the doorway. She had done the right thing, of that much she was certain. There could only be pain and regret in surrendering yet again to Ramon Cazenave. This attraction for him would pass. In a few days, or weeks, she would forget what it had felt like to be held in his arms, to become a part of him, and he of her. She must.

She straightened, turning back into the room. She would not think of it. She would not think of him. She would not think.

It was a fine resolve, but one that proved impossible to keep in the hours that followed. The remainder of the night was a long section of dark time in which she tossed on the sheets, a prey to stealing images of foresworn pleasure. The responses of her body that Ramon nurtured were deeply engrained. She longed for his touch that would bring them rising, burgeoning inside her, and woke time and again from dreams, not nightmares of terror but dark seances of desire that left her devastated when she found herself alone. It was the tradewinds of dawn, sweeping into the room, that lulled her to sleep.

She slept well into the day. Rousing, finally, she rang for a meal that might serve as both breakfast and lunch. She did not dress at all, but spent the time in her wrapper, lying on the bed and staring at the tent of mosquito netting around her, trying to think what she must do, or else standing at the French doors. From that vantage point, she watched the ever-changing face of the ocean and the gulls that wheeled, the sun on their wings, over the waves. The seabirds followed the ships that came and went; cargo vessels under clouds of sails from England, the smaller crafts that made their way between the islands, and fishing boats manned by sun-bronzed natives.

The second night was no better than the first. She was awakened at mid-morning by the cries of street vendors hawking bananas and oranges and pineapples. Those fruits were a part of her breakfast and she enjoyed them immensely, eating once more in her room. Afterward, she dressed in her habit and Ramon's shirt, but did not go out. Instead, she read the *Bahamian Guardian* and the *Illustrated London News*, which had been delivered with her morning repast. Later, she sat watching the people that came and went before the hotel; the maid, in kerchief and apron over a gown of calico held out by makeshift rattan hoops, who strode regally past with her head crowned by a basket of laundry; the vendors of straw, women practicing the craft of weaving that had been learned by their mothers and grandmothers years before, who set out their wares daily in the hotel's arcade; the invalids in opulent wheeled chairs who were pushed here and there, using the hotel for its original purpose as housing in a salubrious climate away from the damp and cold of more northern climes. From her room she also enjoyed a view of the garden, and of the gardener who raked the paths, removed spent blooms, and trimmed the shrubbery. One of his most constant tasks, it seemed, was the whitewashing of the tree-house-like balcony that was built in the largest of the giant silk cotton trees in the garden. Though she saw him applying the lime wash with slow, careful strokes a number of times, he never seemed to complete the job.

As the day advanced, men appeared of erect bearing with sun-burned faces, eyes narrowed as if from gazing out over great distances against the sun, men who might have been taken for the captains of the blockade runners in the bay. Once she saw Peter Hamilton-Lyles approaching the hotel. Fearing that he meant to call, she had hurried to the mirror over the dressing table, tucking up the loose ends of her hair, twisting at her habit skirt, brushing ineffectually at the spots that stained it.

Her preparations had been for nothing. There had been no summons to the lobby and, after a time, she had seen the Englishman leave in the company of two other men. She was relieved, yet, at the same time, disappointed. She did not want to see anyone in her present state, did not feel like making aimless conversation. Still, the incident was enough to show her that she was not satisfied with her self-imposed solitude. She had been too much alone of late, too much at the mercy of her own thoughts and memories. The sea beckoned, and she felt a great need to stroll along its verge, to touch it, to taste it, and even, perhaps, to walk into it. She wanted to explore the island, to see what was beyond the town, on the other side of the hill, or even what waited on the low island that guarded the harbor. She was tired of being the prisoner of her own morbid fears, tired, too, of her high-ceilinged room with its rosewood furniture and Haughwouts china fixtures. Tomorrow she would sally forth, with or without the benefit of the proper clothing, with or without Ramon's blessing.

It was fortunate that Mrs. Carstair's assistant arrived on the morning of the third day with her arms piled high with dressmaker's boxes. After she had hung the gowns away, the young girl offered to stay and help Lorna dress. There were three muslin gowns her mistress had tucked into the boxes just in case Lorna might need them. Her aid was accepted, and Lorna donned the walking costume of *tan d'or*, after being assured it was the very thing that the fashionable ladies of Nassau wore while visiting in the morning.

When the girl had gone, Lorna brushed her hair back in waves from a center parting and caught it in a brown chenille snood. Satisfied that she appeared neat and modish; she picked up her drawstring bag, dropped her key into it, and swept from the room.

She heard the gathering before she came upon it. Even as she left her room, moving toward the stairs, the babble of cheerful voices, the clink of coins, and an undertone of rollicking melody could be heard. It was coming from the piazza on the same floor that jutted out over the porte cochere. Gathered there was perhaps a score of men seated in rattan chairs, each with a brass cuspidor beside it. A few wore uniforms, but most, in deference to the warmth of the day, wore open-necked shirts tucked into their trousers and sandals of woven straw upon their feet. Here and there a man plied a fan of plaited palm leaves, but the most common item used to stir the air was a straw hat with a vivid cloth band. The clanking of coins she had heard signified a table of poker set up on the veranda, near another where men played at dominoes. At the other end, a fast-paced game of pitch-penny was in progress.

The music was being supplied by a trio of Bahamians who squatted on the steps with wide grins lighting their brown faces. One of them strummed an ancient, box-like guitar; one slapped a small hide-covered drum; and the last shook a pair of gourd rattles in one hand and a tray filled with coins in the other while he sang. Their music had such an infectious rhythm that Lorna could not prevent a slight movement to it that made her skirts swing. As she hovered in the doorway, the man with the gourds caught sight of her. His eyes brightened, and he gave a quick nod. Without losing the beat or the melody of his song, he improvised an introduction for her:

> Lady with hair like the sun on the sand,
> Rain-colored eyes shine like promise land;
> Dress like the angel, and 'pon her hand,
> Ain't no sign of a wedding band!

A laugh bubbled up inside her, though faint color appeared across her cheekbones at the blatant flattery and the swiveling heads of the men lounging in rattan chairs behind the veranda railing. Three jumped up to beg her to join them, offering their seats; among them was Frazier, the islander who was also super-cargo of the *Lorelei*, with his salt-and-pepper side-whiskers. His smile was warm, if a shade familiar. It crossed her mind to wonder, as she acknowledged the men Frazier took it upon himself to introduce her, what he thought of her brief sojourn with his captain, and what, if anything, he would say about it here on the island.

She was seated next to the supercargo in a cushioned lounge chair of wicker, and a glass of lemonade was pressed upon her from a tray that stood to one side. The men, though with many covert glances, returned to the pastimes she had interrupted. It was only then that she noticed that the coins the men near the end railing were flipping in the air and passing so blithely back and forth were gold eagles worth ten dollars each, and that the stack of coins in the center of the poker table nearby were double eagles. With the dropping value of Confederate script, it was as though they were wagering with fifty and one-hundred-dollar bills merely to while away the hours.

Her expression must have mirrored her astonishment, for the supercargo, sitting forward in his chair with his wrist braced on his knees, followed her gaze. "It's an amazing sight, isn't it? But don't worry, you'll get used to it."

"I couldn't. When I think the things that the money lying out in plain sight here would buy in the South. I feel a little . . . ill."

His face earnest, Frazier said, "I'll grant you it seems like a lot, but they earned it, you know."

"I know that the job they—you all—are doing is a dangerous one, but surely it can't pay so much."

"You would be surprised. A good captain these days earns better than three thousand a trip, and it goes up every month. Some say it will be five thousand in another year, if the war lasts that long, and that's not counting what a man can make if he owns his own ship, or what he can turn shipping cargo in his cabin."

"Captains like Ramon?" she inquired.

He agreed with a smile and a shrug before he went on. "A pilot, now, about the most important man on the ship after the captain, takes maybe three-quarters as much, and so on down the line to the crew. A good ship will make two trips a month, sometimes three. When you consider that few ship's officers in peacetime ever see as much in five years as they make here in a month, you can understand why they are just a bit free with it."

"That doesn't sound as if it leaves much for the men who invest in the cargo," she commented.

"They make plenty, believe me. It's not unusual for the profits from a single run to top seven hundred percent. There are men who are making fortunes, literally fortunes, every time a ship makes it through the blockade, and the only thing they have at risk is their money."

Her voice low, she asked, "Is the danger truly so great?"

"As the money gets better, the danger gets worse. The big, heavy-moving sailing vessels, the made-over tugboats and square-built river steamers are being weeded out. Ships like the *Lorelei* have the best record, though even she will be obsolete before too long. I hear they are building a ship now on the Clyde with a screw propeller and a steel-plated hull. That's what we'll be running next."

Lorna sipped at her lemonade, staring at the pulp floating in the tart liquid. She glanced at the musicians, who were singing a slow and hauntingly beautiful song about the sea and the sun.

"What is it they are playing? It's a type of music I have never heard before."

"It's island music, some of it goombay, some calypso, made mostly by the descendants of the slaves brought from Africa. Kind of grows on you, doesn't it? That was a nice verse the singer there made for you. I've been listening to them all my life, and it's uncanny how they can describe a person or a thing in a few rhyming words, as if they snatched them out of the air. They seem to see things other people miss. I don't know, maybe it's because they look closer."

"I appreciate the compliment, but I can't accept it."

"I didn't mean it that way," he answered, his gaze troubled.

"Oh, my mistake, then." Her tone was light.

A dull brick color crept under his skin, even to his bald dome. "Not that I don't think you're everything the song said, it's just that—"

"Never mind, I shouldn't tease you, but it's such a glorious day. Are you from this island then? I hadn't realized there were so many different ones until we reached them."

"Oh, no. I'm from Eleuthera, and so am a real conch, as we who were born in the islands are called," he answered, and Lorna was forced to hear in detail about that miniature paradise in the Bahama chain.

After a time, he trailed off into silence. Lorna drank the last of her lemonade, looking away, her gaze drawn by the dry scrapings of the palm trees that grew at the corner of the hotel, their deep-cut fronds waving in the tradewind blowing into the piazza.

"I . . . I suppose it seems strange to you and the other men on the ship, Ramon's decision to bring me to Nassau?"

"Not particularly. Anyone with half an eye could see that it would be dangerous to leave you where you were."

She made a slight movement with her shoulders. "It wasn't as if New Orleans were going to be sacked and pillaged, as in some barbaric conflict in the Middle Ages."

"But your safety couldn't be assured, and your uncle wanted you carried to a quiet place for the time being. It seems natural enough."

It was the story they had agreed upon, she and Ramon. "I see," she said slowly, "that you are in Ramon's confidence."

"You might say so. He explained it to all of us, the officers and men of the *Lorelei*, along with a warning that any man caught speculating about the affairs of the passengers, or of the captain, would be dismissed. That's a powerful incentive for leaving the subject alone, I can tell you. Nobody wants to lose a good berth.''

She had not realized her apprehension was quite so evident. Nonetheless, she was gratified by his oblique reassurance, and by Ramon's thoughtfulness in seeing to it that there was no damage done to her reputation by his crew. She had opened her mouth to thank Frazier, when behind them came an accented drawl armored with a hint of steel.

''Exchanging secrets?''

Chapter 10

It was Ramon, with Peter, the so-called captain Harris, at his side, who had stepped out onto the veranda from the doorway behind them.

"No, sir. Good heavens, no!" Frazier said, starting up from his seat and turning to face the two men.

"No need to be defensive. You wouldn't be the first man to say too much to an attractive woman who knows how to listen."

"It was nothing like that."

Peter entered the conversation then, his puzzled gaze resting on Ramon's set face before he turned to rally the supercargo. "Then you must have been bending poor Miss Forrester's ea' about your dashing family." He winked at Lorna. "I don't know why it is, but he seems to think having a pirate or two swinging from the limbs of the family tree makes him irresistible."

Frazier shuffled his feet, his bald head turning pink once more. "Wreckers and sponge fishermen is more like it, though there was a great-great-grandmother who claimed to have known Teach, old Blackbeard himself, a little better tnan she should."

"How interesting," Lorna said, trying to do her part to relieve the tension Ramon had brought with him, to put their impromptu gathering on the friendly footing it should have had.

"New Providence was the home base for most of the pirates in the Caribbean during the late seventeenth century and early eighteenth. They were finally cleaned out about, oh, a hundred

159

and forty years ago, more or less. Since that time, we have managed one way or another to make a living here in the islands.''

"One way or another,'' Peter said in mock confidence and sotto-voce to Lorna, ''meaning luring unsuspecting ships onto the coral reefs by lanterns tied around the necks of wandering goats.''

"Well,'' Frazier said with an unrepentant grin, ''I admitted they were wreckers, didn't I? I have to say in their defense that the men who watch for wrecks save many a life.''

"Men who watch?'' Lorna asked. "You mean there are still wreckers?''

"There are still shipwrecks, aren't there?'' Frazier answered with great reasonableness.

"A pilot like you, old man, is what's needed,'' Peter said. "An islander who knows the cays and the North West Channel as well as he knows Bay Street. I don't suppose you'd like to ship with me the next time out—at a higher wage, of course?''

"Talk about piracy!'' Ramon complained with an irascible glance to his friend. "Did your ancestors sail with Drake by any chance?''

As Peter merely grinned, Frazier said, "I reckon I'll stay with the *Lorelei*, sir. She's been a fine ship. But it's times like these that I know this war between North and South is the best chance we've had here in ages to see the color of gold.''

"And others are taking advantage of it,'' Peter declared. "Why just yesterday, in my innocence, I gave a laundress a dozen shirts to launder. And how many did she bring back? Eight! She swore I miscounted, but more than likely she made a tidy sum on them on the black market. There are entirely too many men in Nassau, and not enough tailors to go around.''

While Peter talked, Ramon had pulled up chairs for his friend and himself and signaled a waiter to bring drinks. He waved Frazier back into his chair and, as he took his seat, said to Peter, "You may be right about the tailors at any rate. Didn't I see your coat circulating again last night at the government house reception?

"You did indeed,'' the Englishman said bitterly, "on three separate backs, along with the choice rosebud, one of the few on the island, that I had plucked from a garden wall for my buttonhole.'' In an aside to Lorna, he explained, "My frock coat is one of the few of its kind in the islands and enjoys great popularity for formal occasions. I doubt I've spent more than ten minutes at one of the governor's receptions since I've been here; somebody is always snatching me out of a window and stripping my coat from me so they can pay their respects. My shirts are constantly being borrowed, too, as well as purloined. I dare say that by the time I get back to my lodgings I won't have one to wear this evening, either!''

Ramon shook his head as he paid for the drinks he had ordered, then leaned back at ease in his chair. ''You are too good-natured by half. Why do you lend them out?''

''It isn't I!'' Peter protested. ''It's my man. He will believe any story a British naval officer tells him, and my friends on leave here are some of the most outrageous liars the service has ever known! If this keeps up, my laundry bill will be astronomical, or else I, begging your pardon, Miss Forrester, will be walking around in the suit I was born in.''

''That should enliven Bay Street of an evening,'' Ramon observed.

''Hah! You think they would notice on the waterfront among the dens, dives, and bordellos? I wouldn't care to place my yellow boys on the chance!''

''You could always try your luck on East Hill Street.''

''The draperies and lace curtains would twitch like mad, but I doubt there would be any, uh, signals raised.''

Their banter continued in the same vein. Lorna was glad of it, for it gave her time to recover from the stiff embarrassment she felt in Ramon's presence. She was aware of his dark gaze resting upon her, even as he exchanged quips with the other men, of his weighing her words as she was drawn into the exchange of easygoing insults. She wished that she could think of something light and amusing to say to him to banish the stiffness between them, but her mind was blank.

She turned her attention instead to Peter. She liked the Englishman more every time they met. His humor and self-deprecation were most attractive features. He was, in addition, a handsome man, in a smooth, refined fashion. His features were somewhat angular but well-defined, with a strong nose and wide mouth. Despite the general preference, all too evident in the men that lined the veranda, for facial hair, he was, like Ramon, clean-shaven.

Lorna came in for her share of the teasing. Frazier told the others of the goombay singer's descriptive verse, and the musicians had to be called closer and asked to repeat it. The lyrics were considerably embellished under the influence of a coin or two and a round of drinks. The Bahamians were beginning on a fifth, even more vivid, rendition against her laughing protest, when a gay hail floated up to the veranda from the drive below.

It was the Lansing sisters, sitting in an open carriage with a driver on the box. Charlotte was waving and calling, while Elizabeth tried in vain to restrain her. At the younger sister's imperious order, the vehicle drew to a halt before the hotel. Without waiting for assistance, Charlotte jumped down and entered the hotel. Elizabeth followed with greater dignity.

"So here's where you have been hiding, Ramon!" Charlotte greeted him as she emerged from the stairs and tripped out onto the piazza. "We were worried when you did not come for dinner last night."

"Charlotte, if you please," Elizabeth said, joining them, "one does not take an invited guest to task for not putting in an appearance." With meticulous grace, she spoke a cool greeting to the others, giving her gloved hand to Lorna and also to the men who had risen at the approach of her sister and herself. She turned last to Ramon. "Charlotte is correct, however; we were concerned. There is so much illness in town these days, with so many ships coming from foreign ports."

It was almost certainly true. "Yellow Jack," the dread yellow fever, and also Asiatic cholera, typhoid, and a half dozen other less virulent diseases were always a danger in a tropical port, especially among people who were not acclimated. Since they had arrived, there had been signs of the burning sulphur in the holds of the vessels, one of the means used to prevent the spread of contamination.

"How pleasant it is here," Charlotte said artlessly. "One can see everything that is happening, all the ships and the people coming and going, and, of course, everyone knows all the captains congregate here when they finally summon the strength to leave their beds of a morning."

"Charlotte," Elizabeth began.

"Won't you take my chair?" Frazier invited, his gaze admiring as he eyed the younger girl's flaming curls, which could be seen under the brim of her bonnet. "I was about to leave, have to get back to the ship to see to materials for the carpenters working on her."

"Perhaps you ladies will join us?" Lorna invited at the same time.

It was Elizabeth who, abandoning yet another admonition, answered before Charlotte could sit down. "I think not. We were just on our way to visit the shops."

Charlotte gave Frazier a pretty, apologetic smile, then, as he left them, swung back with animation to the others. "The most marvelous thing! You will never guess. We are to have a cotillion in two weeks' time. I will tell you the theme, though you are all to promise you will not breathe a single word. It is to be a dark-of-the-moon ball and will be held on the night the moon changes its phase. Isn't that a wonderful idea? It was my very own!"

"With so little time, we have many errands to run," Elizabeth said.

"And we must order our gowns," Charlotte, irrepressible, added. "Something mysterious to suit the occasion, we thought. We would value your opinion, Ramon, if you would care to give us your escort?"

With a quelling glance, her elder sister said, "And you also, Peter, and Miss Forrester. We will expect to see all of you at the ball."

Peter lifted his hands in a fighter's gesture of fending off a hit. "No shopping for me, though I will venture the dance. The last time I advised a female on what she should or should not wear, I was struck over the head with a parasol."

"You must have been more maladroit than usual," Lorna murmured.

"The soul of tact, I assure you. I merely said I had never seen a sorrel mare yet that looked good in a magenta blanket!"

Ramon, ignoring them, turned to pick up his glass, lifting it in a small salute as he answered. "You will accept my excuses too, I hope; I'm much too comfortable here to stir, but perhaps Lorna would find a round of the shops entertaining?"

"Oh, but Ramon," Charlotte cried before she could answer, "if you do not come, we will have to keep the carriage, for Papa will not allow us to walk unescorted through the streets."

"Very wise of him, though any man stupid enough to attack three such Amazons as you will be would have to be desperate indeed."

"Ramon," Charlotte pouted.

"Ramon!" Elizabeth remonstrated.

"Besides," he said ruthlessly, "you will need the carriage to carry the packages."

Lorna sent him a speculative look that he returned with a bland smile. Swinging to Elizabeth, she said, "Though it sounds delightful, you must excuse me from both cotillion and shopping excursion. I did not come prepared for such merriment, and I fear I must practice economy as well."

"Gone through your allowance again?" Ramon queried, then went on without giving her a chance to answer. "Never mind. For a special occasion such as this, I don't think your uncle would mind if I advanced you enough to cover whatever you may choose."

She turned her head to stare at him, a frown between her winged brows. "You are too generous. I couldn't possibly accept."

"I insist."

"No, really, it isn't necessary."

"Permit me to know what is necessary and what is not. This affair has all the earmarks of entertainment of the season. You would not want to miss it." He put his hand in his pocket and pulled out a fistful of gold eagles. Reaching for her hand, he placed them into it.

She tried to withdraw from his grasp but could not without an undignified struggle that must make them both conspicuous without guarantee of gaining her release. A quiver ran along her nerves, and she was still. She stared at him with resentment in the depth of her gray eyes, wondering why he was doing this, longing to ask what he thought he was buying. In his dark gaze she saw his determination to prevail allied to amusement for her plight, and something more that made her catch her breath.

"Goodness, Ramon," Charlotte exclaimed brightly, "would you like to be my guardian?"

Elizabeth's lips tightened, through her narrowed eyes were upon Lorna. "Since it appears you are coming, would you care to bring your parasol? The sun is bright indeed today, and Charlotte and I never go out without ours."

"Yes, you will need a parasol," Ramon said, "and a purse." Having had the last word, he reached to take the guitar from the goombay player and, cradling it in his arms, began to pick out a soft and sensuous tune.

The Lansing sisters may have been forced to include her in

their shopping expedition, still, once they were in the carriage, they made good use of that circumstance.

"What an exciting voyage you must have had with Ramon from New Orleans," Charlotte said, her eyes wide. "Do tell us about it."

"There isn't a great deal to tell," Lorna began with caution, briefly sketching in the events.

"How I would have loved to have spent so much time with him upon the seas. So romantic, being all alone on the ocean."

"We were not alone. There were the other officers and the crew."

"But there must have been time that you could spend together? He is so charmingly foreign, by far the most interesting man in Nassau. Don't frown at me so, Elizabeth. You know you find him so yourself! Don't *you*, Miss Forrester, or may I call you Lorna?"

Agreeing readily to the use of her name in exchange for freedom with theirs, she replied, "Ramon is certainly attractive, though not particularly foreign to me. It's Peter I find rather different."

"Peter?" Charlotte crowed. "Oh, no!"

Elizabeth smiled, suggesting, "Perhaps Ramon does not seem strange to Lorna because she has known him for some time?"

The probing, direct from one sister, more delicate from the other, went on, interrupted only briefly while they stopped at a millinery shop, a perfumer, and a warehouse specializing in feminine falderals. At the last, they inspected scarves and fans, delicate little aprons of silk and lace, glove tops to decorate the obligatory kid gloves, fichus to fill in the necklines of gowns, and miles and miles of ribbon to set off an ensemble. Lorna could not resist a pair of undersleeves and a collar of neutral colored Brussels net trimmed with a double fall of point Duchesse, the set to be used to change the appearance of the gown she was wearing. But she could not be persuaded to buy the necktie of cherry-colored silk embroidered with gold braid and spotted with gold beads and bugles that Charlotte pressed upon her, nor would she look at muslin nightcaps, evening coronets with stars and feathers on buckram, a Zouave jacket and Garibaldi shirt, a short nightgown, coming merely to the knees, or an embroidered pen-wiper. Charlotte herself made no attempt to resist, nor did Elizabeth. It was almost better to endure more questions than to watch the thoughtless extravagance of the Lansing sisters.

As they were returning to the carriage, Charlotte suddenly caught Lorna's arm, dragging her to a halt. "Look, there!"

Lorna turned in the direction indicated and saw a small, dainty woman dressed in black, wearing a black bonnet hung with veiling on her chestnut hair. She was just going into an apothecary shop.

"Yes?"

"That is Sara Morgan, or so she calls herself. They say she was a courier for Mrs. Greenhow and rode with messages between Washington and General Beauregard before the Battle of Bull Run."

Rose Greenhow was a heroine revered throughout the South, a woman now imprisoned in Washington as a dangerous spy because of her activities.

"Miss Morgan doesn't look well," Lorna said.

"Perhaps it was the crossing. She has only just arrived from England, and they say she is looking for passage on a fast runner going to Wilmington. Can you imagine riding by yourself through enemy territory in the middle of the night? I think it's the bravest thing I've ever heard! How I would adore to do the same, carrying messages rolled up in my hair."

"I don't suppose there was much danger," Elizabeth said. "It's doubtful in the extreme that a young and attractive lady would have been stopped, much less searched."

"That doesn't matter, though I can't think it is entirely true," Charlotte protested. "Only look at Mrs. Greenhow. And if there were no danger, it would not be half so romantic."

"Get into the carriage," Elizabeth said, her voice astringent, "and do not be ridiculous."

Their petty quarreling and quibbling did not cease until they drew up before the dressmaker's. As the carriage came to a halt, Lorna knew a moment of trepidation; it was the shop of Mrs. Carstairs, the same she had visited with Ramon. She need not have worried, however. The woman greeted her as a valued customer on a footing equal to that of the Lansing sisters and without reference to the circumstances of her last visit to the shop.

Bolts of material were brought out, as were back issues of *Godey's Ladies Book* and the Parisian journal *La Mode Illustrée*.

Much time was consumed in choosing fabrics, styles, and colors, but finally it was done.

Charlotte was leafing through one of the fashion magazines as Mrs. Carstairs made careful note of their choices. The young girl gave a small leap in her seat, crying, "Elizabeth, Lorna, pray look. I must have it!"

The gown was of Swiss muslin strewn with dots made of copper thread. The style was simple, with a square neckline filled in with plain, gathered muslin, a buttoned bodice, ruffled sleeves to the elbow, and a gored skirt. Neckline, sleeves, skirt, and a matching shawl were banded with copper ribbon, and a copper satin sash finished the waist.

"Very nice," Elizabeth conceded.

"It's perfect!" Charlotte enthused. "So cool, so light, and marvelous for my coloring. Only think how divine it would be for a picnic."

"If you are suggesting—" her sister began.

"Think what fun it would be! It's been an age since we had one."

"But so close to the ball, remember! Mama will never agree."

"It need not be elaborate, only four or five couples. We could ride out to the caves. It will be so pleasant this time of year, and later may be too hot. Say you will help me persuade her, Elizabeth. Say you will!"

"Well, perhaps," Elizabeth conceded, a speculative gleam in her eyes. "A picnic would be amusing; the gentlemen prefer the informality. And, as you say, we need not go to a deal of trouble."

The parade of carriages left for the caves five days later. They were preceded by three wagons carrying provisions for the meal; the china, crystal, and silver utensils; the linen, tables, and baskets of food and wine; also canvas chairs for lounging, large sun umbrellas, and the equipment for lawn croquet-and-roque and for badminton. There were also three footmen and a maid for serving and clearing away, and the Royal Victoria's goombay musicians for entertainment. Behind the wagons, traveling a safe distance back to avoid the dust, came the carriages. Seven in number, each bore at least two ladies, sometimes three, with here and there a gentleman to keep them company. The other men of the party had elected to ride. A few kept pace with the carriages, exchanging comments and raillery with the occupants, while others raced from one end to the other of the slow-moving cortege.

Lorna rode with Charlotte and Elizabeth in the forward seat of the landau. What had at first seemed a trial, since she had to ride with her back to the horses, had turned into an advantage; she could face Ramon and Peter as they rode on either side, speaking to them without having to crane her neck to see them around the wide brim of her leghorn hat. Charlotte had not foreseen the difficulty when she had chosen her own bonnet of white chip straw with an extra wide poke. Elizabeth was in a better position since, depending on her parasol for protection from the sun's rays, she wore only a Stuart cap of lace that came to a point on her forehead, falling in a graceful, lightweight cape over her shoulders.

It was a bright day, one of a seemingly endless series on the island. Lorna was glad of her hat, which shaded her eyes from the sun's glare. She had bought it from one of the island women who displayed their wares in the arcade. Lightweight but strong, with a muslin band and ties, it had cost a fraction of what she would have had to spend at a milliner's. Though it was not fashionable, it was immensely practical, since it allowed the circulation of air through its loosely woven crown, and was not unbecoming with her simple muslin gown. Ramon and Peter wore similar headgear in the planter's style, from the same source.

Those two were occupied in conversation with the Lansing sisters, Ramon's features relaxed in something approaching a grin as he listened to Charlotte's chatter, and Elizabeth softening under the influence of Peter's banter. Lorna looked around her. She had not been out in this direction before, west of the town. She stared with interest at the bulk of old Fort Charlotte, built in the latter part of the previous century to protect Nassau from the Spanish. Beyond it was a number of homes perched on the ridge that ran down the center of the island. Over their limestone walls could be seen the papery purple of bougainvillea, the waving green of palms, the wind-fretted leaves of banana trees, and, here and there, the brilliant orange of poinciana trees just coming into bloom.

The sun poured down, bright and unrelenting. The blinding white road wound away behind them as they moved in and out of patches of shade, and dust rose to powder their faces and clothing. Lorna scarcely noticed. Turning from the landward side, she gazed to her left where now and then between the thick growth of sea grape trees and casuarinas that closed off the sea breeze could be seen the turquoise and emerald of the ocean, and the flat blue line of the horizon.

It was a scene that never wearied, never bored her. Contemplating it gave her a feeling of serenity, a sense of boundless space and limitless time. She must have seen the sea as a child, on the trip from Georgia to New Orleans, but she had no vivid recollection of it, certainly not of such marvelous shifting shades of blue and green. To think that she might have spent her life without gazing upon this sight was sobering. It was not that she was happy to be gone from Louisiana, but that she was becoming more resigned with each passing day to making a life for herself far from its green and fertile shores.

"Lorna? Lorna do stop daydreaming!"

She turned with a start toward Charlotte, smiling a little. "Sorry."

'I wanted to ask you if you will change places with me. I am getting a wry neck from trying to see Ramon when I talk to him.''

Before she could answer, Ramon broke in, saying with mock severity, "Unconscionable brat, why should Lorna be the one to suffer, just to please you?''

"But she isn't talking," Charlotte pointed out, not at all displeased by the familiar term of address.

"She might, if you gave her a chance.''

"She never has much to say.''

"Oh, I don't know," Ramon answered, his gaze resting upon Lorna. "She has a way of making her wishes and opinions known.''

"And when she opens her mouth, a man can be certain he is going to hear something sensible," Peter added, breaking off what he was saying to Elizabeth to enter the conversation.

"Well! If I am not to be appreciated, I will remain silent!" Charlotte, in high dudgeon, sat back on the carriage seat with her arms folded, facing straight ahead. An instant later, she caught sight of an iguana lizard beside the road, exclaiming at its size and urging Ramon to catch it as a pet for the gardener's son. When the two men burst out laughing, she flushed, but had the grace to join in the laughter at her expense.

The caves were limestone formations hollowed out by the action of the sea in some ancient time when the island was nearly covered with water. It was said that the early Indian inhabitants,

the Lucayans, had used them for shelter during the great hurri-
caines, and later, when the Spaniards had come to enslave them.
It was certain that someone had done so at some time not too
distant, for the ceilings of the stone hollows were black with
smoke, and there was a litter of coals and bones, sea shells and
broken bottles on the floor. It was cool and dry inside, despite
the holes in the top that allowed light to enter from above. Some
moisture lingered there during the rainy season, however, for
the roots of trees and shrubs growing over the caves pushed
down through the openings as thick and sinuous as snakes, and
small ferns grew around the outside entrances.

The caves were near the end of the island's central ridge, with
a rocky headland some twenty-five or thirty feet high jutting out
into the ocean before them, and with the beach, carved into
small coves, below. The knoll that crowned the top was covered
with thick, tough grass and a scattering of sea grape trees, wind-
blown into stunted, twisted shapes. Between the drop-off and
the caves was an open area, bounded by the sandy roadway, that
was shaded by tall trees. Here, games could be played, the
al fresco meal could be laid out, and the lounge chairs set up to
take advantage of the breeze at these heights.

Mrs. Lansing, and another obliging matron who had joined
the party as chaperone, commandeered the lounge chairs and
took out their needlework, settling in for a long gossip. The
goombay musicians found a comfortable outcropping of limestone on which to sit while they played. A fire was built on which
to heat the water for tea and coffee. Croquet mallets, balls, and
wickets were unloaded and set out, ready for play. A net was
erected for badminton, though it was judged too windy for the
moment to make a game practical. To refresh the picnickers
from their arduous journey out from town, lemonade, tea, and
coffee were served, along with a selection of cakes; then the
servants got down to the serious business of setting out the repast.

The solid whack of mallets striking wooden balls carried on
the salt-laden air. The cries of young men and women in frustration, triumph, and defeat mingled with the distant murmur of
the surf and the calls of the gulls that skimmed now and then
along the coastline. The odd rhythms of the goombay band lent
lightness and gaiety to the day. Challenges were made and accepted, wagers won and lost, forfeits demanded and paid, though
the last most circumspectly under Mrs. Lansing's indulgent eyes.

One or two couples wandered away, climbing up through the trees above the caves, or meandering down the road toward a path that lead to the beach. After a time, other couples were sent after them to bring them back.

By the time the picnic was laid out, appetites were sharp once more. The heaped platters of cold meats and fried chicken; the dishes of seafood, including a salad of conch, boiled egg, and palm hearts; the crusty loaves of bread; the pickles and relishes; the great iced cakes and trays of tarts did not last long. The wine, kept on ice, was delicious, but had a slightly soporific effect upon susceptible individuals. A few sought the shade and, adjusting veils, hats, and handkerchiefs over their faces, succumbed to the urge to nap. Others gathered around Ramon, who had picked up the guitar of one of the musicians and began to strum it quietly.

"Would you care to stroll a bit?"

It was Peter who asked, standing above Lorna where she sat a small distance apart. He held out his hand to assist her to rise. She smiled, placing her fingers in his. "Perhaps I had better before I fall asleep."

She stumbled a little as she gained her feet, and he steadied her, his fingers lingering on her arm and a crooked smile on his wide mouth. "You may nod off at any time, with my compliments. I won't mind."

"I hope I won't insult you so."

"On the contrary, I would consider it the highest flattery, since it would mean I had your trust."

She gave a light laugh. "Dear Peter, you always know just what to say to make a woman feel good."

"I said it because I mean it."

She glanced up at him and saw an unusual gravity in his dark blue eyes. "I know," she said, "that's what makes you so nice."

"Nice! Nice, I ask you!" His mood instantly turned whimsical again as he clutched his fist to his breast in a dramatic gesture. "You might have said suave, or gallant, or polished—anything but nice!"

"Forgive me?" she murmured, her gaze soulfully entreating.

"Anything, anything, if only you will look at me that way again! Theft, piracy, murder, anything—Lorna, what have I said?"

She recovered with an effort, banishing the stricken expression she had been unable to prevent, searching for something with which to allay his concern. "Nothing, really, I . . . I must have stepped on a sand burr with the side of my slipper."

He went down at once on one knee beside her. "Place your foot here, on my knee. Let me see."

Lorna sent a quick glance at the others behind them, still in full view. "Don't be silly. I'm sure it . . . it didn't stick. Get up, please!"

"And lose my chance to fondle your ankle? You must be daft. Let me see."

"You're the daft one," she said crossly, and lifting her skirts a few inches, did as he asked.

"No," he said mournfully sliding his fingers over the leather of her slipper. "It didn't stick. No opportunity to render service to the divine one by enduring pain for her sake, no reward."

On impulse, she kissed the tip of one finger and touched it to the end of his nose. "There, consider yourself rewarded."

Catching her finger before she could draw it back, he brought it down to his mouth. Pressing the moist place her lips had touched to his own, he said, "Now I can die happy."

"Now you can get up," she snapped in mock annoyance, snatching her hand away.

He laughed, springing to his feet, and they moved on, but behind her Lorna was aware of the primitive and passionate chords of Spanish flamenco reverberating from the strings of a guitar.

The path along the northern slope of the headland led to the cove but also wandered parallel to the water below, descending in a series of terraces to the beach farther along the coast. They took the less strenuous trail, coming out on a narrow promontory of limestone that supported a lone sea grape with a stretch of grass beneath it. As they paused, Lorna leaned against the tree, gazing out over the sea spread beneath their feet.

"Just think," she said after a moment, "that a pirate may have stood here a hundred and fifty years ago watching for Spanish galleons laden with plundered gold from Mexico."

"I hope he had as lovely a companion as I have."

She sent him an exasperated glance. "I'm speaking of history, of someone who lived and died before we were born."

"I'm not."

"You're hopeless!"

"Not quite, though there is something about you sometimes, such as that moment back there, that makes me despair."

She gave an uneasy laugh, not quite looking at him. "You mistake my meaning."

"No mistake," he said deliberately.

She turned then to look at him as he stood so tall and so very English at her side. The sea breeze ruffled his fine blonde hair and molded his shirt to his frame. His blue gaze was direct, without humor.

"I don't think I understand."

"Don't you? You are a woman in a thousand, beautiful and intelligent, made for loving. But there are secrets behind your eyes, and barriers. I would like to draw out the secrets and break down the barriers, but they can't be touched. Not yet. If the day comes that you would like to be rid of them, I want you to know I will be there."

"Peter," she began against the slow pressure forming in her throat. She had seen much of him in the last few days. He had appeared nearly every morning on the veranda of the Royal Victoria and usually wound up escorting her for a walk or a shopping expedition along the more respectable end of Bay Street, or strolling with her through the gardens of the hotel. Still, his declaration took her by surprise.

"I don't need or expect an answer." He smiled with a wry twist to his mouth. "As a matter of fact, an answer might spoil everything."

"It . . . it's a good thing," she said, her mouth curving with a hint of a tremor, "since I don't know what to say. It's all nonsense, you know." If the time should come when she was ready to think of another man, then she would have to explain her past; to do otherwise would not be just. For now, she could not bring herself to think of it.

"Is it? Then there's no harm done, is there?"

She shook her head. His features grave, he took her hand and raised it to his lips, brushing them across her knuckles. As he released her, he smiled a little, then turned to face the sea. He placed his arm across her shoulders in a light embrace as he moved to stand beside her, and so casual was it, so without threat, that she did not protest.

"Oh, there, a ship," she said after a moment, as her gaze settled on the only feature on the blue rim of the horizon.

"A frigate. Federal."

"It's so far away, how can you tell?"

"By the shape of her, and the set of her canvas, her sails."

The topic was a safe one; Lorna relaxed imperceptibly. "I suppose it is waiting for the dark of the moon, too."

" 'Like patience on a monument,' as the bard said."

Like patience on a monument, smiling at grief. She controlled a shiver as she recalled the quotation. "Does it bother you, knowing they are out there, waiting for you?"

"Gives me the most juvenile desire to thumb my nose at them."

He suited action to his words, and they laughed together in the comic release of tension. They could hear the surge and wash of the waves against the foot of the limestone rock below. The ocean breeze caressed them, lifting Lorna's light muslin skirts, billowing them about her, rattling with a dry sound in the round, tough leaves of the sea grape that tossed over their heads. To the right, the coast line sent a curving arm out into the sea, while to the left beneath them was a small cove lined with sharp coral rock where limpets clung, and edged with cream-pink sand. The salt tang of the sea joined with the sun-warmed scent of the grass they had crushed as they walked, the faint, acrid taint of wet limestone, and the delicate fragrance of madonna lilies that came from Lorna's skin.

Peter inhaled deeply, a small smile playing about his mouth, before glancing down at her. "Shall we sit down for a few minutes?"

She nodded, and he took out a large handkerchief, spreading it on the grass conveniently near the trunk of the sea grape, which would serve as a back support. When she was seated, he sank down beside her. Breaking off a blade of grass, he sat nibbling at it as they talked of first one thing then another, using it to gesture as he made a point, tickling the backs of her knuckles as her hand lay on her full skirts to prevent the breeze from getting under them. After a time, he stretched out full-length, placing his head on the hem of her gown in a pretense of helplessness. When she turned to speak to him a few minutes later, she saw that his eyes were closed, the spiked gold of his lashes resting on his cheeks. He was asleep.

How long she sat there watching the shifting, changing face of the sea, while the son of an English peer slept at her feet, she did not know. Her thoughts drifted, turning, coming to no conclusion. She took off her hat, there in the shade, tossing it to one side as she leaned her head against the rough tree trunk behind her. She may have dozed lightly, lulled to somnolence by the ceaseless sigh of the waves and the warmth of the afternoon.

She was roused by the sound of a voice, feminine and rather breathless. "How impetuous you are, Ramon! Such hurry is unseemly and quite unnecessary. We are far enough from the others, in any event. Why go farther?"

Lorna turned her head. Ramon, with Elizabeth clinging to his arm, was advancing toward her. His face was set, and the pace at which he was moving forced the woman at his side to some exertion to keep up with him. Ignoring the comments of the elder Lansing sister, he stopped a few feet in front of Lorna. He looked down at Peter, his eyes were dark and his voice hard as he spoke.

"Your *cavalier servant* seems to have had a strenuous . . . walk."

The innuendo could not be mistaken. Her voice cold, Lorna answered, "It would appear to have been rather boring, if anything."

Roused by their voices, Peter opened one eye, surveying Ramon. "Oh, it's you."

Ramon shifted his point of attack. "Who did you expect? Mrs. Lansing? You do realize that you have come near to compromising Lorna?"

Peter opened both eyes, then, as if suddenly aware of where he was, sat up hurriedly. "No!"

"I assure you it's the truth."

The Englishman shook his head, less in negation than in an effort to clear it of sleep. He looked up at Ramon standing over him and glanced from him to Elizabeth, who stood looking on with an expression composed both of chagrin that Ramon had obviously not brought her walking for the purpose she supposed, but as a blind, and of avid pleasure at the prospect of trouble between the Louisianian and his protégée.

"What do you want, old man, an apology? Or are you waiting for an offer in form? I have trouble picturing you as the outraged guardian, but if I thought Lorna would accept—"

"That won't be necessary," Ramon broke in, his accents incisive, cutting across Peter's words. "If you can find the energy to help Lorna to her feet, we will return to the others. They are ready to go back to town."

The drive to Nassau was accomplished in silence for the most part, as with most return journeys when the enjoyment is past and tired people look forward to the quiet and comfort of their own surroundings. Charlotte was sulky, stifling yawn after yawn in her corner of the carriage. Elizabeth spent the time between worry over the redness across her cheeks and nose, gained while playing croquet, and snapping at Peter for his tactless suggestions for remedying what she considered to be the disfigurement. Ramon rode in silence, a crease between his eyes. Lorna glanced at him from time to time, thinking of the way he had behaved earlier.

He took his responsibility for her seriously. But if he was determined to see her in a ''respectable alliance,'' as he chose to call it, why had he not allowed Peter to complete the offer of marriage he had been about to make? For all the expectations of his noble family, she thought that, once the Englishman had made public his intentions, he would not have denied them or sought to avoid the consequences. Surely Ramon had realized that also?

It had almost appeared, in that moment on the headland, that he was jealous. Could it be? It hardly seemed likely, in view of the blithe way in which he had parted from her. If so, however, it was most perverse of him. What right had he to discard her at will, yet prevent Peter from claiming her hand? She was of a mind to encourage the Englishman for all she was worth, just to spite Ramon. Peter was too nice to be used in that manner, of course, but it would give her great pleasure to see Ramon's face as he was informed of their plans to wed.

She turned to glance at Peter, who was unconscious of the smile of wicked anticipation that lighted her gray eyes. He grinned back, enjoying the benefits of it even if he did not understand it. Ramon, intercepting the exchange, scowled.

In her room at the hotel, Lorna ate a light dinner and prepared for bed. She lay reading for a time, a novel she had picked up in a stall of used books outside a shop. It held her attention only to a degree, for the heroine was insipid, the hero overbearing, and the story filled with unlikely events and coincidences. Still, it was better than the irritating company of her own thoughts. The night stillness drew in. A cluster of moths flew in the open doors from the veranda. They fluttered about the gaslight, courting death and each other in a graceful aerial ballet. Delicate, fearless creatures, they lived for so short a time and were so easily damaged.

Sighing, she set her book aside and got up to turn off the gas at the fixture, plunging the room in darkness. The moon was waning; in a few more days, little more than a week, it would be gone. Its gleam was pale far out on the heaving surface of the sea. She paused for a moment in the doorway with the night wind gently shifting the folds of her gown and the ends of her hair around her, before closing the jalousies and moving back to her bed.

It was then she heard it, the soft music of a guitar in an old Andalusian love song. Coming, she thought, from the hotel gardens, it was a melancholy yet stirring refrain in a minor key. It spoke of love and desire, of duty and of parting, an endless lament that throbbed in the darkness, tearing gently at the heart.

She tried to shut it from her mind, as she lay in bed staring through the gauze of her mosquito netting at the bars of moonlight created by the doorway, but it crept insidiously inside. She thought of Ramon, playing a guitar on the afternoon they had met. Had it been the same song? She could not remember. Twisting in the bed, she allowed the images, the feel and taste and smell, the pounding crescendo of the lovemaking she had shared with him to invade her thoughts. She ached with unfulfilled need and loss, with suppressed anger and a pervasive fear of the future. Tears crept from under her eyelids, dampening the pillow and her hair, and she slept finally with the haunting notes of the guitar still in her ears.

She was late the next morning in making her way to the piazza. Through the doorway, she saw Peter, and also Slick and Chris, the officers from the *Lorelei*, as well as Frazier. Summoning a smile, she moved toward them, and the chair beside Peter that was held ready for her. She was halfway across the open piazza when a man spoke, the voice drawling, freighted with heavy irony.

"My dear Lorna, aren't you going to wish me a good morning?"

She knew before she turned. She knew, and the knowledge made her stiff and unnatural, made her skin prickle with dread. She knew, but there was nothing to do except answer.

"Good morning, Mr. Bacon."

His loose mouth curved in a smile that was not reflected in his pale eyes as he leaned back expansively in his rattan chair, sipping his mint julep before he replied. "There's no need for such formality, now is there, my dear? You may call me Nate."

Chapter 11

The dance cards for the Lansing cotillion were in the shape of full moons, with spaces for the names of the men who would request the listed dances on the lines of the rays around them. Yards of navy blue netting sewn with silver spangles had been gathered and tented under the ceiling to form a canopy of stars. At the end of the ballroom, above the long table holding the punch bowl, was a huge full moon of isinglass lighted from behind by a trio of lanterns and suspended in swaths of clouds formed of gray cotton wool. Other than these arrangements, the long reception room used for the ball was much the same, with its long line of glowing chandeliers, banks of greenery, and massed bouquets set on tables between the rows of gilt chairs that lined the walls.

Charlotte, glowing with excitement and the satisfaction of seeing the theme of the ball she had suggested much admired, told a chosen few, Ramon and Lorna among them, that they must watch the moon. As the evening progressed, it would gradually darken until, at the chosen hour, it would be eclipsed. There would then be a surprise dance, after which the ball would be over.

The young girl scintillated in white silk scattered with diamanté. Her elder sister was in royal-blue silk, only a shade lighter than the ceiling canopy and with a similar scattering of the tiny cut-glass stones known as diamanté. Lorna had declined the glitter on her own costume, choosing instead a gown of soft lavender-blue tulle, the color of a distant shore as seen from the sea at dawn, though, in keeping with the theme, she wore a headdress of lavender satin in the shape of a coronet that was centered with a small gold moon, the radiating beams of which were formed of long, thin beads.

As the long room filled, the atmosphere was one of suppressed anticipation and excitement. It was not the prospect of the ball's finale, however brilliant it might be, that charged the air, but the knowledge of the danger the men in the room would be facing when it was over. Charlotte, flitting up to Lorna where she stood alone for a moment, expressed it best.

"The men look different tonight, don't you think? You see it even in those who are not in uniform, though they are not so dashing. I suppose it is knowing they may not return, and that they count the game worth the risk."

"Yes, I suppose so," Lorna answered.

"I admire that in a man," the girl went on, her eyes alight with discovery, "but I suppose most women do. We are really elemental creatures, aren't we? It is important that the man who may claim us be not only able, but willing, to protect us."

"It doesn't always follow that a man who will risk his life for gain, or even for a cause, will do the same for a woman," Lorna pointed out.

Charlotte opened her eyes wide. "But of course he would! A gentleman always protects a lady, only some more . . . more handily than others."

"If that is so, then who is it we must be protected from?"

"From men who are not gentlemen!" With a gay laugh and a flounce of her skirts, the younger girl whirled away.

It was a simple philosophy, one that Lorna had been raised with, though she had reason now to doubt its validity; one that she had used as a weapon against Ramon that night nearly two weeks ago. Unconsciously, she sought his tall form and dark head in the growing crowd. She caught sight of him with Edward Lansing; they had come early, that he might discuss a few final points about the forthcoming run with the man who was his partner. Ramon was one of those in uniform, like those he had designed himself for the officers of the *Lorelei* in order to make them easier to pick out from the crew in time of need. The blue coat stretched across his broad shoulders, while the blue stripe down the dark gray leg of his trousers made him seem taller and more erect. The severe cut of the dark color gave him a lean grace that was heightened by the gold bullion on his shoulders and gold-fringed sash holding a dress sword at his waist. It was fairly obvious whom Charlotte had been thinking of when she had spoken of men made dashing by such attire.

Lorna took a deep breath against the tightness gathering in her chest. It was ridiculous to allow herself to be affected by what was not more than a costume, one that had no connection with country or cause. As for the danger Ramon faced, his was no greater than that which threatened any of the many men in the room who would be putting to sea at midnight.

The musicians, behind a screen of palms and ferns, had tuned up and now began a spritely Chopin piece to welcome the arriving guests. Lorna glanced at her program, but it only showed her what she had suspected, the first dance would be a waltz, following by a polonaise and a polka, and then another waltz to finish the first set. Ramon had put down his name for the second waltz; on the day of the picnic, he had been placed in a position where he could not escape asking Elizabeth for the first, and Charlotte for the polonaise.

"Permit me, if you will?"

She stiffened, her grasp tightening instinctively on her program, but Nate Bacon wrenched it from her fingers. Taking the small, attached pencil in his grasp, he scrawled his name beside the polka.

"There," he said, handing the moon-shaped card back. "I don't think you will be able to avoid me while you are in my arms on the dance floor. There are a few things that need discussion between the two of us."

"I hardly think a gathering of this sort is the time or place," she said, retaining the cool indifference of her voice with an effort.

"Oh, I will admit it isn't what I would have chosen, but you have not answered my notes requesting a more private interview, and you are always surrounded by admirers."

"In any case," she went on as if he had not spoken, "I have nothing to say to you."

"No? Well, I have quite a bit to say to you, and to ask, about the death of my son."

Lorna sent a quick glance around her, aware, even as she did so, that the thickset man beside her had spoken in overly loud tones in order to make her nervous. "You knew Franklin, knew what he was like. Can you not guess what happened?"

"Guessing isn't knowing."

She sent him a harassed glance tinged with pain. "He became violent. We fought. It was an accident that he was killed. What more do you want to know?"

"Several things," he said, his voice taking on a hoarse note, "like whether the marriage was consummated, and if you are now carrying his child?"

"No!" she said with a disgust that she did not trouble to hide.

His face took on a reddish-purple hue, and his chest seemed to swell. "That's both bad news and good. I wanted a child, but if there is not to be one, then there is no need for care in my dealings with you."

"Dealings? As far as I am concerned, there will be none."

"Oh, but there will. You are wanted for murder; I myself swore out the warrant. What do you think fine people like the Lansings will say when they hear of it, as they will if you don't cooperate? No, I think we will deal together, and I expect the association to be most pleasant." The look he gave her, his hot gaze moving over the soft curves of her shoulders, was the exact opposite.

"That . . . that's blackmail!"

"You know, I believe you are right, but then I see no reason to be too nice in my methods. You certainly served me a dirty trick, using Cazenave to get away from me."

"It wasn't you I was running from."

"Wasn't it?" he asked, and smiled his loose-lipped smile.

Abruptly she knew he was right. Franklin, and Nate's hopes for an heir through his son, had been a buffer between her and her lascivious father-in-law. With him dead, there had been nothing. There was nothing now.

The answer must have been reflected in her eyes, for he went on, "You know better, don't you. I meant to have you from the moment I saw you sitting at your uncle's table beside your meek cousins. I might have married you, if it weren't for my invalid wife, and gotten my heir directly while enjoying you yourself. That wasn't possible, so I arranged to marry you to Franklin and prepared myself to wait a respectable time before approaching you. You ruined my plans, destroyed my son, but it doesn't matter. I'll have you yet. Nothing will stop me, nothing. Do you understand?"

It occurred to Lorna, as she listened to his low-voiced threats, that the instability of Franklin's mind might not all have stemmed from his childhood accident; a portion might have been inherited. "You must be mad if you think you can do with me as you please. Ramon will not permit you to carry out such threats."

"You are not as close to him now as you once were, I hear. I will admit I don't understand why, but it works to my advantage. Since he seems to have lost interest in you, he may not be so quick to come to your aid. Regardless, he will be leaving Nassau in a few hours and won't be returning for more than a week. By then, it will be too late."

Before she could form a reply, he bowed abruptly and strode away. He must have seen Peter approaching, coming to claim her for the waltz just beginning; for, a few seconds later, the Englishman came to a halt in front of her.

"I don't like that fellow," he said, staring after Nate.

"Nor do I," Lorna answered fervently, then, as he turned to stare at her, forced a smile and lowered her lashes, shielding her distress from his too clear gaze as she pretended to study her program. "Why, I believe this is your dance, sir!"

"So it is!" he agreed in theatrical surprise, leading her onto the floor, though his expression was watchful as he took her in his arms.

He had reason to be suspicious, Lorna told herself with a suppressed sigh as they whirled to the strains of Strauss's "Roses of the South." Instead of the evenhanded way in which she had treated him earlier, spacing her time in his company with time spent also with Frazier, Slick, Chris, and also, on occasion, Ramon, she had sought him out for protection from Nate's attempts to speak to her alone. It was not entirely by choice; the *Lorelei*'s offficers, including Ramon, of course, had been embroiled in the last-minute details of seeing that the ship would be in working order after her repairs, and ready to sail.

Still, it wasn't fair to Peter to use him; never mind that he made it so very difficult not to. He was always there, or so it seemed, and such easy company that it would have required a tremendous effort to avoid taking advantage of him. For the moment, with Ramon occupied elsewhere, her need was too great to permit such altruism.

So distant had Ramon become of late, in fact, that mentioning him to Nate as her possible champion had been merest bravado. Whether from annoyance at her refusal of his advances or from irritation at her conduct on the picnic, he had kept his distance for the last few days. It was only the ship and the forthcoming run to Wilmington, she had tried to tell herself. Naturally, he was concerned with these things, since the lives of his men and himself, plus his plans for the future, depended on his efforts and vigilance now.

Often at night, however, she still heard the guitarist in the garden, softly playing his tender songs of love and lament. She was not certain whether it was only because she knew Ramon played the instrument or also because of the promptings of vanity, but she sometimes pretended the guitarist was Ramon, serenading her as she drifted off to sleep. She had never tried to discover if she was right. It was not possible to see into the darkness of the garden from the veranda outside her room, and the guitarist was heard only after she had retired for the night. She could have waited, could have crept downstairs to see. But on consideration, she had decided each time that she would as soon not know, in case the man was a stranger, or the music not meant for her at all.

"Will you miss me while I'm gone?"

She brought her attention back to Peter with an effort. "Certainly I will. It will be so dull here without our court jester!"

"Ah," he intoned mournfully, "first the kiss, then the slap."

"I didn't kiss you," she said, drawing back in mock hauteur.

"No. Would you? That is, would you permit me to kiss you?"

His clowning cloaked the seriousness of the question, but it lay there, in the blue depths of his eyes. For the flick of an instant, she remembered Ramon that day at the old house: He had neither asked for permission nor required it. In an effort to keep the conversation on a light level, she inquired demurely, "Good-bye?"

"Or hello, or whatever you please. A proper kiss, mind, none of your pecks on the cheek or, heaven forbid, the nose."

"I . . . will have to think about it."

He pounced on the hesitation. "For how long?"

"I'm not sure. Tell me again, now, when does your ship leave?"

"Heartless, heartless woman, you know very well the *Bonny Girl* will leave with the others!"

"Indeed I do, and it was cruel of me to tease you. Of course you may kiss me, dear Peter!"

Staring down at her, his expression gloomy, he said, "Why

do I have the feeling that I am going to be fobbed off with a brotherly smack again? I am nobody's brother, except for a great lout who will be the eighth earl, and a covey of brats younger than I am.''

Over his shoulder, Lorna saw Ramon, sedately turning with the eldest Lansing sister. At the same time, he was watching her, a scowl between his eyes. Had he overheard her laughing permission? She could not tell, but the empty feeling in the region of her breastbone told her it was possible, if not probable. She could not worry about it now, however. Besides, what business was it of his?

"Peter," she began, the amusement leaving her as concern took its place.

"Never mind," he said hastily. "I didn't mean to bring clouds to those gray eyes of yours. You may kiss me any way you like; isn't that magnanimous of me? Also, any time you like, and as often as you like. I am nothing if not thorough. It's one of my chief, and many, charms; one I trust you will grow to appreciate. Ah! Don't look now, but we are being honored with the presence of the heroine of Bull Run.''

"Not Sara Morgan?''

"None other. I wonder how it was managed; she hasn't been out much while she has been here. A bit under the weather, I hear.''

It had been managed with careful calculation, Lorna knew, since she had been present while the campaign was mapped out on her first shopping expedition with the Lansing sisters. First had been sent a note of welcome, accompanied by a basket of fruit and cakes, and a large bouquet of flowers. After a few days, a call had been paid. Finding the lady unwell, as the servants' grapevine had foretold, the sisters had left flowers, expressions of admiration and condolence, plus the offer of a carriage to use while taking the air of an evening. Later, the physician who treated Mrs. Lansing on occasion had been sent to call. He had prescribed a tonic for the southern lady's indisposition, which appeared to be consumption, recommending also that being among people would be beneficial to her rather melancholy turn of mind. The Lansing sisters had then called again, with the invitation to the ball grasped firmly in their hands. The poor woman, weighted down with authoritative advice and obligation for favors received, could hardly have refused to lend her presence to their soirée.

"She doesn't look very happy," Lorna said.

"A handsome woman, nonetheless."

"And I thought you preferred fair women," Lorna said with an air of injury, and could not quell the laugh that rose in her at his hasty reassurances. She was still smiling, inquiring about his famous, much worn and society-prone coat, when the music ended.

The polonaise belonged to Ramon's executive officer. Slick's performance on the floor was polished, in contrast to what might have been expected given his long-limbed frame, rather sloping walk, and faint air of the backwoods. He had five sisters who all loved to dance, he said, and a bevy of cousins who played with ease any musical instrument they picked up or sat down at. Dancing was a regular Saturday night occurrence in the hills of north Louisiana, portions of them at any rate—the Baptists around the towns frowned on people kicking up their heels, drinking hard liquor, or having fun in general. Said it all led to sin, while, truth to tell, it kept 'em from it—as well as out of the bushes and the swamp bottoms, and places like that. Most of the dancing was done in squares, but the other, slower dances served to let the girls catch their breath in between.

Regardless, when the polonaise, a Polish dance in triple time, was done, Lorna was somewhat breathless and glad for the offer of a glass of punch. While Slick moved away through the crowd to get it for her, she found a place to stand near the wall. Spreading the fan that hung from one wrist, she began to ply it. She had made no more than a half dozen strokes when she heard her name called and, looking around, saw Charlotte bearing down on her.

"Come with me quickly," the young girl said, catching her arm, "before the polka begins. Mrs. Morgan wishes to meet you!"

A moment later, Lorna's hand was being taken in the frail ones of the heroine of the evening. Her gaze rested upon the pale and thin face of Sara Morgan, made even more striking by the contrast with her widow's weeds, while the woman's shrewd, measuring glance ran over Lorna in turn.

They exchanged the conventional greetings. Then Sara Morgan said, "Indeed yes, I can believe you ran the fire of the federal ships at New Orleans; you have that steadfast look. I heard something of it from the Misses Lansings, of course," she paused to smile at Charlotte hovering beside them, intently listening for once, "but I would enjoy hearing more details some time."

"I did nothing except cower in my cabin, in all truth," Lorna said with a wry smile. "It doesn't begin to compare with your adventures, I'm afraid."

"I was never under fire, nor likely to be, and there were others who also carried messages in those days and hours before Bull Run."

"You must have run the blockade, too, on your outward journey to England?" Lorna suggested.

"Yes, but that was some months ago, before the strangling cordon of ships began to tighten. There were several women, and even children, on board as passengers then, so little was the danger considered. I understand it is quite different now."

"Apparently so."

There was no opportunity to say more, for Nate Bacon approached and, moving deliberately to Lorna's side, nodded to Sara Morgan and Charlotte before turning to her. "I believe the next dance is mine."

"Yes, certainly," Lorna agreed in pleasant tones, "but perhaps you will excuse me, since I have just met this lady and there is much for us to talk about."

The smile Nate turned upon Sara Morgan was smooth, urbane, but, though his words were tinged with self-deprecation, there was iron beneath them. "I'm sure the lady will understand my reluctance to release so beautiful a partner? I am not a patient man, and I have waited no short time for this moment."

"Of course," the woman in black agreed, rather at a loss as she glanced from Lorna to the man beside her. "There will always be another time to chat."

It was then that Slick reached her side, carefully maneuvering the two cups of punch he carried. Behind him there was a stir as the dancers took their places for the polka and the first notes of the music began. Nate swung toward Lorna in triumph and haste. His elbow struck a cup, and punch cascaded in a pale yellow stream down the side of his trousers to the shining toes of his boots.

Slick did a marvelous balancing act to save the other cup. Charlotte gave a small scream, dancing out of the way with her skirts pressed down in front. Lorna, stepping back instinctively, received no more than a few drops on the hem of her gown. Nate cursed, then turned to glare at the executive officer as if he suspected Slick had done it on purpose. Glancing at the look of exaggerated concern on the north Louisianian's face, Lorna was not certain he was wrong.

Ramon's timing, then, was perfect as he joined them. "Charlotte," he said, a trace of mockery in his tones, "if you are done with checking for spots, you might signal for a servant to attend to the mess and detail someone to sponge down your father's guest. The punch you still hold, Slick, shall be your reward. Mrs. Morgan, Lorna, may I escort you both to a less sticky neighborhood?"

"Hold on a minute, Cazenave," Nate grated. "This polka is mine."

"Now don't tell me you expect a woman to permit herself to be clasped to your damp apparel?" Ramon surveyed Nate with a lifted brow that was an insult in itself.

"We can sit it out. I have a thing or two to say to my . . . to Miss, uh, Forrester."

"Later," Ramon answered, giving his hand to the woman in black as he helped her to rise and step over the sticky puddle on the floor, "when you are in better condition for the debate."

Offering his other arm to Lorna, he swept them away. They skirted the dancers, moving toward the long windows at the front of the house that opened onto the terrace. Mrs. Morgan, after a brief glance at Lorna, broke the silence. "It was good of you to come to our rescue, Captain Cazenave."

"My pleasure," he answered, dividing a smile between them, "and my gain. I saw your trunks brought on board this afternoon. I assume you are ready to sail?"

"As ready as I'm likely to be," the woman answered. "It's not a voyage I look forward to."

"That would be too much to ask, but I hope it will prove uneventful, for your sake."

Lorna had not realized that Mrs. Morgan would be leaving tonight, though she should have expected it. On that first day that they had seen her, Charlotte had mentioned she was looking for a runner willing to take a passenger.

"For all our sakes," the woman said, her voice low. "I trust I will not be a hindrance to you."

"It seems unlikely," Ramon answered, the smile that carved indentations in the bronzed planes of his face warmly encouraging.

Envy, dark and blighting, caught at Lorna. She wished with

a fervor that was astonishing that she was going to be sailing with the *Lorelei*, that she could be a part of the adventure of the run. It was going to be so hard to watch the ships steaming out of the harbor and into the night, one by one, gray ghosts that might, or might not, return. Then would come the waiting, the watching. That had always been the woman's part in times of war, but now it seemed beyond bearing. Sara Morgan would not have that idle endurance forced upon her, not she.

A turn in the night air was suggested and accepted. They strolled up and down the terrace, inhaling the scent of flowers from the gardens and of freshly scythed grass, mixed with the omnipresent salt sea tang and the smell of cigar smoke from where two men had retreated to smoke near one wall. While the gay strains of the polka issued from the room behind them, they talked of this and that. Lorna, oddly disinclined toward the exchange of social commonplaces, allowed the widow and Ramon to carry the conversation. Her attention was snared at last, however.

"I understand," Mrs. Morgan said, "that there will be two ships carrying gunpowder on this run. Will your vessel be one of them, Captain Cazenave?"

Lorna stifled a gasp, swinging to stare at him. There was no more dangerous cargo. If the ship were struck in the wrong place, if a spark from a detonating shell reached the hold, the vessel would explode into a hundred pieces, leaving little more than debris floating on the water.

He flung Lorna a quick glance before he turned back to answer the widow. "Your information is correct as far as it goes. Surely you know the answer to your question also?"

"Then it will be," the woman returned with composure. "I had hoped my informant was right, but one cannot take these things for granted. President Davis and his generals will be pleased. A modern army can fight without many things, but gunpowder isn't one of them."

"As a passenger, the knowledge doesn't disturb you?"

She smiled. "You have the reputation of running a lucky ship, Captain; I can think of now other I would rather trust myself to. And if I should cavil at taking passage along with so valuable a contribution to the cause, I would not count myself much of a rebel."

The polka jolted to a stop inside the ballroom. Pleading fatigue, Mrs. Morgan turned back into the house. As she was seated in a chair near the windows, she turned to Lorna. "Perhaps we may talk about New Orleans a bit later, Miss Forrester. For now, I'm sure there is an anxious man somewhere searching for his partner."

"The man is here, Ma'am," Ramon said with a small bow.

The widow laughed. "Then do not let me keep either of you."

It was indeed Ramon's waltz. He led her out onto the floor, drawing her into his arms as the opening measures of a Strauss melody began. They circled in silence for a moment. She looked up at him finally to find him watching her, his dark eyes black with intensity as his gaze rested on the gentle curves of her mouth. Did he realize, she wondered, quite how overpowering was the aura of his masculinity, the sense of strength and purpose that he exuded? Did he have any idea of how easy it would be for him to reach out and take her, if he wanted her, easily overcoming her halfhearted resistance? He must, for he had done just that once. A tremor ran over her.

To banish the tenor of her thoughts, she said in silken tones designed to bait, "How very gratifying it must be, to be sure, to find yourself carrying such a *valuable* cargo tonight."

"Someone has to ship it."

"Doubtless it will pay well, being so dangerous?"

"The regular rate plus a large premium."

"A few runs like that, and you could turn the *Lorelei* into a fishing boat, or wind up at the bottom of the ocean. Too bad I didn't accept your proposal; I might have been a rich widow in no time!"

"Tell me," he said, his accent growing more marked, "Have you read this lecture to Peter?"

"Peter? You mean he—"

"His *Bonny Girl* is the other ship with a consignment of arms and ammunition for Messieurs Trenholm and Fraser, representing the Confederate government."

"Oh."

"What is the matter? Did you think our English friend was in this for the glory only, with no concern for so mundane a thing as the money?"

Stung by the lash of his sarcasm, she flung up her head. "At least he is not a southerner, draining the wealth of his own country!"

"I provide a service badly needed, for which I am paid. What is wrong with that?"

"There are thousands of men in the South who are doing the same in less comfortable circumstances and without hope or expectation of gain."

"They are fools; courageous, I will grant, and generous with their substance and lives, but fools nonetheless."

"Would you have them accept the dictates of the North, or allow a foreign army to remain on Confederate soil in defiance of repeated requests to leave it?"

"Do you think that is the cause of this war? It isn't. The cause is money. The North, fearful, and rightly so, of the wealth and aristocratic position gained by the South using the slave system, seeks to dismantle or at least curb it. The men of the South, especially those small farmers just starting out, coming from Europe where advancement is impossible, are determined to protect a system that offers them the chance to use their own endeavors to move up in the world, to build something of substance in a generation. The rest is patriotic and moralistic nonsense."

"What of states' rights?"

"The constitutional amendment setting forth the right of seccession is simple enough for a child to understand. Anyone denying it is spitting in the face of the men who drafted it. Doubtless Lincoln is correct in expecting chaos to follow on the division of the union, but, if he manages to preserve that union, it will be an the expense of true freedom."

"The slavery question?"

"Any southerner knows, if he will admit it, that the institution is morally wrong, but the precedent for it goes back as far as recorded history, and so enjoys quasi-respectability. The climate in the lower states makes it a necessity, if the fields are to be made to yield, while the investment in it is too great to be liquidated easily, too large for fair recompense from the United States Treasury. It will be abandoned naturally when the time comes and some other form of labor, such as the immigrants in the northern states, becomes cheaper than buying and keeping slaves. More, the practice is still legal in several northern states, including the District of Columbia itself—which seems a little like a man sneering at his neighbor's dirty linen while his own filthy nightshirt hangs out the back of his trousers. Raising slavery as an issue for this war is mere hypocritical drum beating."

"According to you, then, we are right, but they must win."

"That is my assessment."

It was one far different from those she had heard in the last year while men pounded tables and struck heroic poses. Irrefutable in its simplicity, it was also far more depressing.

"You are something of a cynic," she said slowly, "but have you no feeling for the place where you were born, no impulse to fight to keep it untouched?"

It was the custom, in waltzing to the Strauss tune the musicians were now playing, for the dancers to whirl clockwise to the first half, then, when the repeat came, for the room to "turn," or for those on the floor to stop and begin spinning counter-clockwise. Ramon waited until the turn was completed before he answered.

"I feel it sometimes, yes," he admitted, a distant expression in his dark eyes as he gazed over the top of her head, "but if I ignore it, it goes away."

What could she say in answer to such callousness? She made no reply. Perhaps it was as he intended, for he glanced down at her, changing the subject.

"Has your father-in-law been a trial? Slick, and Peter also, report that he has not forced himself upon you at the hotel during the day."

"They have been very good at keeping him at bay, Peter especially. He was a bit unpleasant earlier this evening, however. I confess, I was surprised to see him here."

"He came with one of the cotton factors, who sent a note to Edward without giving the name."

"I see." His words seemed to indicate that he had warned the Lansings against Nate. It was good to know that he had gone to the trouble.

"There have been no other problems, at night for instance?"

"None, which has been an unexpected blessing." The look of satisfaction that flitted over his face, then was gone, alerted her. "You wouldn't know anything about that, I suppose?" When he did not answer, she said, "Ramon?"

"It . . . was only a precaution; I didn't want to alarm you."

"What was? Since I know that much, you may as well tell me the rest."

His lips tightened, then he said, "A healthy bribe to the desk clerks, both of them, not to give out your room number, and an effort to have whoever escorts you to your room be certain you are not followed.''

''And?'' she persisted, as he paused.

''A guard in the corridor at night, and another on the veranda.''

A sudden certainty gripped her. Before she could stop herself, she said, ''And one with a guitar in the garden?''

The darkness of his eyes was opaque and his frown faintly puzzled as he stared down at her. ''A guitar?''

''Do you deny it was you?''

What reason could he have for doing so, if he had been doing no more than protecting her? True, she had first heard the serenade on the night before Nate Bacon had arrived. Possibly, then, his presence could be taken as an admission of interest in her. But Ramon had made it plain enough that he desired her on the evening she had sent him from her room. Why should this be any different?

''Don't tell me you have a lovesick fool who sits serenading you beneath your window every night, and you haven't even been curious enough to find out who he is?'' The light in his face was mocking, daring her to accuse him.

''I wouldn't want to frighten him away,'' she said with a coolness she did not feel. ''I have enjoyed his playing too much for that.''

''If you had invited him in, you might have enjoyed his company more.''

She looked away over his shoulder. ''So I might, but men seem to tire easily of what is easily attained.''

His grip tightened and she heard his swift-drawn breath, but, before he could answer, the waltz came to its abrupt, swinging close. Around them, couples began applauding with gloved hands, laughing, chatting, moving from the floor. As she drew away from Ramon, Lorna turned to see Elizabeth in her dark gown making her way toward them through the crowd of dancers.

''Lorna, could you come with me? It's Mrs. Morgan. She has been taken ill, and she wishes to speak to you.''

''To me?''

''She was most insistent that you should come to her as quickly as possible.'' That the request was a mystery, and something of an annoyance to the elder Lansing sister, was obvious from the stiffness of her manner.

Lorna glanced at Ramon. His face was impassive, but the slight narrowing of his eyes indicated cogent thought. In answer to her glance of mute inquiry, he merely shrugged.

Though the woman was virtually a stranger, it was impossible to refuse her appeal. With a brief gesture of assent, she followed Elizabeth across the floor and out of the room. They made their way along a long hallway toward the back of the house. At a door near the far end, the other girl paused, knocked softly, then ushered Lorna into a small sitting room.

Sara Morgan lay on a fainting couch of rosewood covered in mint green brocatelle, her head resting on a bolster of the same material. Her eyes were closed and her face drained of color, almost gray. In one hand she clutched a small, silver-capped bottle of smelling salts; in the other, a stained handkerchief. A maid crouched at her side, holding a basin in which swirled the pale red of blood mixed with water.

"Mrs. Morgan?" Elizabeth said, moving forward to hover over the couch. "Miss Forrester is here."

The woman opened her eyes. Her colorless lips curved in a smile as she found Lorna. "So good of you to—come," she whispered. "I must talk to you—if we could be left in private."

"Oh, really, are you certain you are well enough?" Elizabeth asked.

"I . . . must be. If you please?"

"Well, of course, if that is the way you want it. Come, Clara!" Elizabeth waited for the maid to open the door for her, then swept with her from the room. But not before she had sent Lorna a look of supercilious outrage.

"Come closer, here beside me."

Lorna moved at once to kneel in a billow of lavender blue skirts beside the fainting couch. "Tell me what I can do for you," she said quietly.

Mrs. Morgan reached out to take her hand. Her hazel eyes searched Lorna's face with minute care, probing, meeting her gray gaze and holding it as if she would look into her mind. At last she said, "I must have someone I can trust. Can I trust you?"

"I don't know, but I would hope so."

A fleeting smile crossed the woman's pale face. "An honest answer, much better than instant reassurance, since you have no idea what I would ask of you. I—one moment."

As Mrs. Morgan fumbled with the cap of her smelling salts, Lorna took them from her, opened them, and placed them in her hand once more. The woman took a deep breath with them under her nose, choked a little, then pushed herself up higher on the couch. She lay still, inhaling and exhaling slowly, evenly, then looked at Lorna once more.

"I thought I was strong enough for this undertaking, but I was wrong. If only this attack could have held off a few more days—but perhaps it is better this way. I might have been taken ill on the ship, and that would have been most uncomfortable for everyone. I could not ask men intent on saving our very lives to play nursemaid to an invalid, and without that my mission might not be completed. It is vitally important that I succeed, you see."

The woman waited, as if expecting some comment while she caught her breath. After a moment, Lorna said, "Am I to understand that you are . . . that you have a message to deliver, as you did with Mrs. Greenhow in Washington?"

"You are quick; that is good." The woman closed her eyes for a moment, smiling faintly, then went on. "But what I carry are dispatches from the confederate envoys in Britain to President Davis concerning the negotiations for British recognition. You see how important it is that they be delivered?"

The recognition of the Confederacy by Great Britain could mean international legitimacy and, perhaps, military aid, in much the same way that France had sent aid to the struggling United States during the Revolutionary War. The assistance of the British fleet would neutralize the blockade, even destroy it. That, plus adequate supplies of the materials of war, would mean almost certain victory.

"Yes, I do see," Lorna answered slowly. "but why me? Why could you not entrust them to, say, Captain Cazenave?"

"He is a man and, in the event of the capture of his ship, would certainly be searched, then sent to some northern prison. You are a woman, and a most attractive one, if I may say so. You would not be molested and in all probability, if you asked it as a favor from gentlemen to a lady, would be put ashore, if not in the Carolinas, at least in the nearest northern port. From there, you would be able to make the contact that would see the dispatches into the right hands."

There was a long silence. The woman waited, her eyes on Lorna's face while she struggled with the problem. In the quiet,

Lorna thought she heard a rustling sound, as of someone breathing. She stared for a moment at the other woman, then pushed to her feet, moving quickly to the door. She hesitated, feeling slightly foolish, before putting her hand on the knob and jerking the panel wide.

There was nothing, no one there. Behind her, Mrs. Morgan said, "It is best, always, to be sure."

"Yes," Lorna said, frowning, still listening, wondering if she had imagined that soft sound, like a door being eased to, somewhere along the hall. Nerves, she told herself, brought forth because the need for secrecy was so apparent. Turning, she said, "If I take your place, I will have to leave tonight, within the next hour."

"A servant can be sent to pack a trunk for you and deliver it to Captain Cazenave's ship, taking mine off at the same time. I'm sure our host, or rather his daughter, would not mind giving the order."

"I have no idea what to do when I reach port, who I must turn the dispatches over to, or where, or when."

"I will tell you that. It is not at all difficult."

"Someone must inform Captain Cazenave of the change of plans and passengers."

"You seem to be on terms of some friendliness with the gentleman; so it should be easily arranged. One woman, or another, it can make no difference to him."

"I suppose not," Lorna said slowly, "so long as he realizes the importance of the dispatches' getting through."

"No! On no account must he be told of the dispatches. Captain Cazenave may know of my past activities; in truth, the story seems widespread enough, but, as far as he is aware, I am only a woman anxious to return to her family after a visit to Europe to consult physicians there."

"Oh, but surely it would be more convenient, and just, for him to be told?"

"By no means! Should his ship be taken by a federal cruiser, your safety, and his own, may depend on his being able to answer with natural and honest indignation to any charge of aiding a Confederate courier. It is not beyond reason that he might be tried as an accomplice should it be proven that he was in your confidence, with the penalty for that crime carried out at sea. This is wartime, and such a hanging would scarcely cause a ripple in official federal circles, given the cause."

"Hanging!"

"For a man, it is not unthinkable. For you, the penalty would be imprisonment, as was the case for Rose Greenhow, who is still being held in Washington. If I have frightened you, I am sorry, but I cannot stress the danger strongly enough. It is much better for you to depend only on yourself, and on your frailty as a member of the weaker sex. I believe, if Captain Cazenave ever discovers the subterfuge, he will thank you for it."

Lorna was by no means certain of this last claim, but it was a problem that would have to be faced when the time came, if it came. She smiled, then, with the determination and excitement burgeoning inside her turning her gray eyes to silver. "I can think of no other objection, so I suppose I must go."

"Good." Mrs. Morgan lay back, closing her eyes in weariness, then opening them again. She lifted her skirts, drawing them up until her black petticoats were exposed. Taking a packet wrapped in oilskin from a pocket concealed in the ruffling, she placed it in Lorna's hands. She drew deeply on her smelling salts again, then said, "Listen to me, now. Listen carefully."

Chapter 12

There was an expectant hush in the ballroom when Lorna made her way toward it again. As she stepped inside, she saw men and women with champagne glasses in their hands, all turned facing the end of the room. The isinglass moon had gone dark, the hour for leaving was at hand. Before the moon, however, stood Edward Lansing, drawn up with a glass of champagne held high. His voice rang out clear as he began what was, apparently, a well-known toast.

"Here's to the Confederates who produce the cotton," he proclaimed.

"Here, here!" came the reply from the crowd, in deep masculine voices.

"To the Yankees that maintain the blockade and keep up the price of the cotton," he went on.

"Here, here!"

"And to the British who pay the high prices to buy the cotton!"

"Here, here!"

"So three cheers for all three—and a long continuance to the war and success to the blockade runners!"

In the shouts of hurrah that followed, the soprano voices of the women rose higher, surpassing those of the men as they gave vent to their admiration and apprehension for the men who would soon be leaving. It was some time before the babble of voices died away, leaving quiet enough for their host to make himself heard once more.

"I would like to ask the ladies to line the walls, one beside the other, while the gentlemen remain in the center of the floor. This last dance of the evening will be a choice dance, not included on the program. At the signal, the gentlemen will attempt to reach the ladies of their choice before some other scoundrel gets there first. And remember, if you will, that the idea for this was not mine, so I am not to blame for any disappointments! For the sake of the ladies, I will explain that the signal will be the complete lowering of the lights. Is everyone ready? Now!"

This was, without doubt, Charlotte's surprise, Lorna thought as the lights died slowly while servants with candle snuffers on long wands moved down the room, extinguishing the flickering lights. As the last candle was snuffed out, there was a rush of booted feet, a nervous laugh, an assortment of gasps and cries. Then, abruptly, Lorna was caught in a firm clasp and whirled out of reach of other, grasping hands. Her flying skirts brushed the legs of yet another man, and above her head she heard a low chuckle.

"Peter," she said as best she could with his arm constricting her waist.

"A near miss," he said, his lips near her ear.

"Who—"

"Bacon, I think, I saw him looking in your direction. As for the other, I'm not sure, but I can guess."

Had it been Ramon? There had been nothing to tell her, one way or the other, It might just as well have been Slick or any one of a dozen of the blockade runners she had met in Nassau during the last weeks. Before she could demand an answer, the glow of candles grew in the end of the room where the musicians were seated, and they struck up the "Hesitation Waltz."

They danced in silence then, slowly revolving, pausing, revolving. The few dim candle flames shone in the crystal lustres of the chandeliers, gleamed on the silk of the women's gowns, and were reflected in the glass of the French doors that stood ajar down the room. It barely illuminated the faces, absorbed and solemn, of the men and women taking part in that peculiar ritual. It might have been supposed to be exciting, faintly titillating, that dance in near darkness; instead, it only underscored the melancholy of the partings to come.

The man who held her was deferential, his touch gentle as he guided her. He watched her, his emotions naked on his face. Lorna met his dark blue gaze for long moments but could not sustain it. Looking away, she saw Ramon, leaning with his shoulders against the wall near the doorway. As their glances clashed, he pushed away and, swinging, left the room.

The music died away and, with it, the candlelight. In the darkness, Peter's hold tightened. He tilted her chin, and his mouth descended, resting warm against her lips, parting to deepen the kiss, seeking her response. With her lashes still upon her cheeks, Lorna gave it, longing to feel some trace of desire, some inclination toward love. There was, instead, only sweetness and the gentle stirring of affection.

The blockade runners, captains and officers, left in a mass, their booted feet thudding across the terrace and down to their waiting horses and carriages. With them, too, went those men who had no plans to go to sea that night, partially because of the laughing threats made against them should they stay, and partially out of full knowledge that their lingering would be an anticlimax for all involved. There were cries of good-bye, exuberant shouts and calls, the waving of handkerchiefs. The dust rose in choking clouds on the drive as the mounts and vehicles departed. The pounding and rattling died away again, and all was quiet.

With drooping shoulders and eyes dim with tears, the women turned back into the house. They sat about finding wraps and evening purses, straggling here and there, slowly brightening as they talked of the evening. By twos and threes, they climbed into the carriages arranged for them by Edward Lansing and, still congratulating the Lansing sisters on the brilliance of the evening, trundled away into the night.

Lorna was among the last to leave. She had returned to be with Sara Morgan for a little longer, trying to be certain of what she must do. The widow had been prevailed upon to spend the night at the Lansing home to save her strength, and Lorna sat beside the bed where she had been installed, talking quietly, reassuring the woman that all would be well, until, finally, the invalid slept.

In the carriage, Lorna wrapped her pardessus cloak of black silk closer around her, feeling chilled now that the moment was upon her. For the dozenth time, she reached to touch the slim, oilskin-wrapped package tucked into her cloak pocket to be certain it was safe. She tried to think what she would do when she reached the ship, how she would persuade Ramon to allow her to come aboard without telling him the reason for it. Her mind would provide few arguments, none convincing. She would have to wait upon the moment, and hope that inspiration would come when she was face to face with him.

The *Lorelei* lay at the dock, where she had finished loading late that afternoon when the last touches to her repairs had been done. Around her, there was a bustle of activity as men shouted and cursed, wheeling barrels and bolts and bales here and there on barrows, trying to get cargoes on one or two other ships. In the harbor beyond, the gray steamers sat on their bright reflections in the water, they were lit from stem to stern as final preparations were made, smoke rising from their stacks. Even as Lorna's carriage pulled up opposite Ramon's ship, she saw one weigh anchor and move slowly out toward the channel, extinguishing its lights as it went. Watching it for a moment, she wondered if it was bound for Charleston or Wilmington, and, if the latter, whether it and the *Lorelei* might find themselves in company when the moment came to make the dash through the line of the federal blockade toward that port.

There was a lantern with a smoked globe hanging on a stanchion beside the gangplank. As Lorna passed beside it, stepping across the wooden apron, one of the ship's officers standing toward the prow turned to look her way; Chris, she thought, from his size and build. He was expecting a woman passenger, however, one in widow's black, so did no more than touch the brim of his cap in a salute and point out the companionway leading below, directing her to her cabin.

Lorna inclined her head, indicating her thanks, since she did not trust her voice to give her away. She was swinging from him, when Ramon appeared, stepping from the wheelhouse. She stiffened, instinctively drawing the hood of the cloak closer around her face, covering her hair. He acknowledged her presence with a nod, then turned to his officer, dismissing her as he issued rapid-fire instructions. A few minutes later, Lorna was safe in her cabin.

There was not a great deal of room allotted to passengers aboard the blockade runner, the cargo being by far the most important commodity transported on a run. There was a common cabin for men forward, and one for women aft, with the officers' quarters in between. Lorna, being the only woman on this trip, had the women's cabin with its stacked bunks, small washstand, and slipper chair to herself.

She lit the lamp in its gimbals over the washstand, took off her cloak and hung it on a hook on one wall, then looked around for her straw trunk, the same one her new gowns had been delivered in. With nothing else to attend to, she sat down.

Fatigue washed over her, as if it had been waiting for this moment when she could go no farther by herself, when the exhilaration of the evening had drained away and it was too late to go back on her agreement. What had she gotten herself into by taking this mission?

Prison. Hanging. The words Sara Morgan had used rang like warning bells in her mind. And yet, she could not have refused; it would have been impossible, even if she had wished it.

She did not think she was particularly brave. What, then, had made her accept? A love for the region where she was born? The need to do something to further the southern cause? Pride that would not allow her to appear a coward? A simple need to get out of her hotel room, to be doing something useful? Any of those things, perhaps all of them. Was this, just possibly, the way men felt who had marched away to war, full of doubts and fears and dogged determination?

If Ramon knew, he would say it was because she was a fool. He did not know, must not know. What was she going to say to him, then, to explain her presence? What?

She rose to her feet, pacing to the end of the cabin, swinging around so that her skirts belled around her, then pacing back again. The problem was not what she was going to say but what he was going to think unless she came up with a reasonable explanation. It would appear that she wanted to resume their relationship on his terms, that she would take any risk to be with him. So long as she could not tell him the truth, he would be perfectly entitled to think just that.

Sara Morgan could not have foreseen that difficulty, of course. Lorna had recognized it, but it had not, at the time, seemed insurmountable. Now, there was nothing she could think of to account for her being on the ship that did not sound weak and contrived, a mere excuse.

She could not say she meant to settle in North Carolina, for it was patently untrue; she had no friends, no place to stay, and would be forced to make the return voyage. A message to relatives of Mrs. Morgan concerning that lady's illness, and the delay because of it, could much more easily have been written and given to Ramon himself to be put in the mail rider's pouch; there would have been no need to employ her to carry it. Her fears over the threat posed by Nate Bacon, he had already put to rest. What did that leave? A desire to see Wilmington? One did not travel for pleasure in wartime. Boredom with Nassau? Far too silly, since she had barely arrived.

The thud of the beam and slow beat of the paddle wheel impinged upon her furious concentration. The ship was moving. At least if her being on board did not suit Ramon, it would now be troublesome for him to put her off. After a time, an hour or two, it would be better for him to allow her to remain than lose the time in putting back. The three-day run had to be carefully calculated so that the federal fleet could be penetrated at night, and the mouth of the Cape Fear River, below Wilmington, reached before the light of dawn exposed them as a sitting target.

Moving to the small cabin porthole, she watched as the lights of Nassau drew away, gradually growing dimmer, winking out one by one. The dark coastline stretched, marked by the line of the surf that was a gray streak in the starlight. When even that sight faded into the night, she began to relax, to think that she might be undisturbed until morning, to consider undressing and getting into bed.

A knock came on the door. She whirled, then lifting her chin, moved to open the panel. It was Cupid who stood outside. He stared at her, his mouth open in surprise, before, blinking, he closed it.

"Yes?"

"Mam'zelle Lorna! I came, me, to ask if the lady needs anything, as the *capitaine* says. I did not know the lady was you."

She summoned a smile. "No, it was a . . . sudden change of plans. But I need nothing, thank you."

"You are sure? The *capitaine*, he said the lady in the cabin has been sick, very sick, and I must take special care. You do not look sick to me, but it would give me much pleasure to serve you."

"It's very kind of you, and Ra—Captain Cazenave, to be concerned, but I am fine."

"I think it, me, and I will tell him so. He will be most relieved."

"No—that is, you need not trouble him. I'm sure he has no interest in my health, one way or another."

"You do not know, Mam'zelle; everything is of interest to him, every small thing. But I am happy, very happy, to have you with us. He will be better now, I think."

"Better?" she inquired before she could prevent the curious question.

"Of sweeter temper. He has been like the raccoon with a sore paw since you left us. Perhaps you will sweeten him again, *bien*?"

With a wink and a nod, he left her. She stood irresolute in the middle of the floor, conscious of a feeling of impending crisis. If there had been a place to go, she might have run, but there was not. Her mind was blank, her knees stiff. She clasped her hands in front of her, the fingers entwined so tightly that her knuckles were white. She stared straight in front of her but failed to see the small picture of a child and a dog that hung on the wall, swinging steadily with the movement of the vessel.

When a knock fell on the door again, she started, then moved slowly to answer it. It was Cupid once more. His smile was gone, and his dark eyes were shrewd, watchful, as he spoke.

"The *capitaine* would like to see you in his cabin."

The Acadian cook led her along to the door of Ramon's cabin, tapped on it, then retreated. Lorna took a deep breath, then turned the handle and stepped into the room. It was the same, except for the guitar that lay on top of the trunk, replacing the one he had lost at Beau Repose; everything was neat, severe, and achingly familiar. Surveying it gave her something to do in those first unnerving seconds, but at last she was forced to turn and face Ramon.

He got to his feet, pushing back his chair from where he had been seated at the table with a chart spread in the pool of pale gold light cast by the lamp in its gimbals. He sent her a hard glance, then threw down his pen. Indicating the chair across from him, he said, "Sit down."

If she did not, he would be forced to remain standing, and she preferred not to have him towering over her. Summoning a cool smile, she moved to the chair and, adjusting her crinoline, sank onto it. Moistening her lips, she said, "You did not expect to see me again so soon, I think."

"No, it was the last thing I expected." His tone was dry,

noncommittal, of no help to her at all as a gauge of his reaction. He returned to his seat.

"I . . . trust you do not mind?"

"That depends."

"Oh?" She tilted her head inquiringly. "On what?"

His answer was soft, threaded with steel and inevitability. "Your reasons for being here."

"Mrs. Morgan was taken ill, and so could not come," she said, lowering her lashes, taking up the pen he had discarded and turning it in her fingers. "I knew her place would be vacant, so—I decided to take it."

"Just like that."

She nodded, swallowing hard. "More or less."

"Charming," he drawled, "but it isn't a reason."

She glanced up to find him staring at her, his dark gaze resting on the soft curves of her breasts most tantalizingly revealed by the draping of the tulle at the neckline of her gown. She felt a slow heat move along her veins. She threw down the pen. With a catch in her voice she asked, "Must there be one?"

He came to his feet so quickly that his chair skidded backward. "Don't play me for a fool, Lorna. Two weeks ago you turned me out of your room. Since then, you have been keeping Peter on a string. Not two hours ago, I left you in his arms in the dark. What happened? Did you mistake the *Lorelei* for the *Bonny Girl*?"

"Of course not!" she cried, springing up with color flooding into her face. "How can you suggest such a thing?"

"Easily! It springs to mind full-blown, with visions I would as soon not describe, when I think of the two of you together."

"It was nothing like that. I . . . I'm not sure why I came. It was an impulse, that's all! I sailed with you once; why not again?"

"If you don't know the answer to that one . . ." he began, then stopped. He took a step toward her, skirting the table. "But maybe you do? Maybe that is, in fact, what you came for?"

He reached out to close his fingers around her forearm, drawing her to him. She wanted to protest but could not find the words, could gather no strength with which to resist him. With parted lips and wide eyes, she watched as he lowered his head, blotting out the light.

His mouth touched hers, teasing the sensitive contours. She felt the warm flick of his tongue along the moist inner surfaces before he pulled her closer, increasing the pressure, probing deeper. Languor welled within her, and she closed her hands on the material of his uniform jacket, feeling its roughness beneath her palms. Her lips softened, burning, and she tasted the honeyed warmth of his desire. Swaying, she clung to him, intoxicated with the promise of surcease long denied, knowing that she was lost, unable to care.

A sigh shuddered through him, and he lifted his head, pressing a kiss between her brows, brushing her eyelids. He lifted his hand to cup her cheek, smoothing the tender shape of her mouth with his thumb, easing her lips apart and swooping to try that vulnerable sweetness.

His hand strayed to her hair, where he pushed his fingers into the massed curls, searching for and finding the pins that held the coronet with its tiny golden moon, discarding it as he sought those that also supported the weight of her hair. He scattered them so that they fell to the floor with small, musical sounds, and her hair slipped, cascading over his hand and arm, falling down her back in a pale gold shimmer. He brushed his hand down the silken length, closing his fingers in it, wrapping it around his fist, before he released it, letting it tumble to her waist once more.

Drawing her with him, he returned to the chair on which he had been sitting, guiding her onto his lap. With a delicate touch, he ran his fingers over her shoulders and along the exposed curves of her breasts. He traced their contours through the tulle of her gown, finding the top edge of her corset that pressed them upward, gently cupping them, flicking the sensitive nipples with intimate, knowing care. Moving to the valley between them, he slipped his fingers inside her décolletage, stroking, fondling.

His mouth seared a trail along the plane of her cheek and down the delicate angle of her jaw. He pressed his face into the curve of her neck, breathing deep of the lily fragrance concentrated there, rising from her hair. He shifted his free hand to her waist, and let his lips slide with warm kisses to the enticing hollow he had quitted. Behind her back, under the fall of her hair, he began to loosen, one by one, the hooks that held her gown. With the easing of the strain across her chest, the bodice slipped lower. He took full advantage of that relaxation, drawing aside the narrow sleeve of her camisole to bare the thrust of a breast, teasing the peak to tautness with the moist surface of his tongue.

So exquisite were the sensations he aroused in her, so compelling was his spell, that Lorna hardly knew when he released the last hook, when he slipped free the bow that held the tapes of her crinoline and petticoats. She only became aware as he drew the sleeves of her gown down her arms and pushed her heavy skirts over her hips, lifting her from them as he stripped them down and kicked them away. For the first time, too, she felt the brass buttons of his uniform digging into her. She shifted, and with lowered lashes, reached to undo the first of them. With only the fine linen of her pantaloons cushioning her body from his, she was forced to recognize for the first time, too, the vibrant rigidity of his manhood beneath her.

He paid no attention to what she was doing, still less to the urgency of his need. Like a man entranced, he explored, through the thin linen, the warm curves and hollows he had unsheathed, closing his hand on the roundness of her hip, stretching the fingers of one hand to span more than half of the narrow turn of her waist in its confining corset. The sleeves of her camisole trailed down her arms, and he peeled the fine cloth from the swelling thrusts of her breasts, baring them in the lamplight. They gleamed with the soft luster of fine satin, the veins a fine tracery of blue under the skin, the rose-pink of the aureoles and raspberry contractions of the nipples an enticement he made no effort to resist.

Her hands trembled slightly as she pushed them inside his jacket, removing the utilitarian buttons of his uniform shirt from their holes with more haste than care. She spread the edges of the open front wide, pressing her palms to his chest. The roughness of the curling hair that grew there tickled between her fingers, and a smile, tentative with dreams, curved her mouth. She brushed his paps with the pad of her thumbs, and felt the tensing of the hard muscles of his thighs under her. Felt also the slide of his hand between her legs, and the insinuating twist of his fingers as he found the open crotch of her pantaloons.

The flat expanse of her abdomen rippled at his first caress, then tightened to board hardness. She caught her breath as her senses expanded. Her heartbeat increased, and heat suffused her. With spread finger she held to him, her grip slowly compressing. Her loins ached with fullness, yet deep inside she was empty, so very empty.

A fantasy in shadow images crossed her mind of the guitarist from the garden, wearing Ramon's face, climbing up to the ve-

randa outside her bedroom as she slept, entering, coming to her
as she lay unprotected. It was brief, that drift into unreality, yet
the surge of wantonness was so great that she made a soft sound
in the back of her throat, turning her face into the strong curve
of his neck.

He reached to unbuckle his belt, releasing the buttons of his
trousers. He stripped them down, prizing off his boots, pushing
both trousers and boots from him. At the same time, he put his
thumb under the garter that held her rolled silk stockings, loos-
ening them at the knee one at a time, removing them as he swept
her slippers from her feet. She smoothed his jacket and shirt
from the broad expanse of his shoulders, freeing his arms as he
straightened. Blindly, she drew him to her, pressing her bare
breasts against him so that they were flattened upon the unyielding hardness of his chest. As he leaned forward to wrap his arms
about her, she eased the jacket and shirt from behind him and
dropped them to the floor.

"Lorna, *ma chère*," he whispered. "*Mon Dieu*, how I have
missed you."

"And I you, oh, and I you."

The need she felt to have him inside of her, a part of her
being, grew. She pushed her fingers through the soft, curling
hair that grew low on the nape of his neck, clenching her hand
upon it. Parting her lips, she brushed them over the lobe of his
ear, touching it with the tip of her tongue and breathing with
quick pants as he slid his hand once more inside the slit opening
of her pantaloons. Her heart thudded against her ribs. She could
hear the singing race of her blood in her head, feel its pulsing
where his fingers touched with warm and relentless persistence.
Her skin glowed with moist heat. The depth of her longing was
amazing; she had not known herself to be so sensual a creature.
So alive was she that her every nerve ending felt exquisitely
sensitive. At the same time, she was aware of being boundlessly
vulnerable, as if she had abandoned her defenses and would be
unable to regain them.

She trailed her fingers down his chest to the flat tautness of
his belly with its narrow line of dark hair, following it to where
it widened to a triangular mat. His body, with its hard planes
and resilient, jutting firmness satisfied some deep, questing expectation. His chest swelled at her touch, and he turned his
head, finding her lips, his mouth hard with the force of his ardor.

He slid his hand under her thigh, drawing her higher, spreading her legs so that she straddled him. Gently he parted her heated flesh and, positioning himself, eased into her. He brought her closer with both hands on her hips, pushing deeper. She caught his shoulders, and with a twist of her body, took him farther inside, bearing down upon him.

He held her then, smoothing the tumbling waves of her hair down her back, whispering her name against her lips as the movement of the ship, rising and falling, pressing and receding, brought them slowly to feverish arousal. Their mouths clung, devouring, bruising. The pressure of his arms tightened until she could hardly breathe. She raked his shoulders with her nails, lightly scraping with the tips only, so that he shuddered in the grip of desire held tenuously at bay. The movement set up a vibration deep inside her, and she felt the hot concentration of her very being, the dark, engulfing moment of pleasure bordering on pain, the jolting contractions of release.

She moaned, pressing herself to him, entwining her tongue with his. He held her in that moment of paralyzed need, then gathering his feet under him, he surged upward. Stepping to the bunk, he put a knee on the sheeted surface, sinking to one elbow with controlled strength, carrying her with him without withdrawal. He turned with her, raising himself above her, plunging into her warm moistness with hard, powerful strokes.

She felt the leaping return of desire, more vivid, more overwhelming than before. She raised herself against him, swept by dark frenzy. Her hands clutched at his arms, feeling their trembling as he sought to stretch the boundaries of their passion, sliding on the dew of perspiration that enveloped them both. She spread her fingers wide, running the sensitive palms over the corded muscles and sinews of his forearms. She was soaring, sinking, flying, falling, towering, tumbling, rising, dropping. She was drowning in ecstasy beyond bearing, but neither could she bear for it to end.

It exploded with piercing, heart-stopping grandeur, a violent crescendo that burst upon them, spreading outward in waves of molten joy. Pure, magnificently carnal, it was an ancient upheaval, wondrous. It ended their striving, stilling movement at the last, deep thrust. They reveled in its magic power, bewitched, voluptuous, clinging, their chests heaving with effort: their eyes, black and gray, locked, glances mingling, close; as near to the touching of souls as they were allowed to be.

She was in love with Ramon. She had known it for some time

but would not allow herself to accept it. It could be denied no longer. Not that it was a piece of knowledge she intended to share. Ramon's attraction toward her, while undeniable, was physical. He had no use for a more vital emotion. He would see it as an attempt to fetter him, and pride would not allow her to give even the appearance of such a tactic.

"What is it? What's wrong?" he asked, watching the play of expressions across her face.

"Nothing," she said at once, but he was already tugging at the wild silk strands of her hair that were caught under them both, easing the tension on her scalp that she had scarcely noticed. His searching hands brushed the corset constricting her waist, and he cursed softly.

"I should have known better," he said with remorse. Heaving himself up, he began to unfasten the steel hooks that held the front of the undergarment, the backs of his fingers brushing the curves of her breasts. "I can't begin to see how you breathe in this thing in formal times, much less—"

"It's all right," she protested, but he paid no attention.

"Why do women wear gear like this? It distorts your natural shape, cuts off your air, and compresses your organs, as any doctor will tell you, besides being damnably inconvenient."

"I can see your concern is entirely for my health." She sent him a glance from under lowered lashes, doing her best to prevent him from seeing the relief it was to be released from that whalebone prison.

"Entirely," he said, whipping off her corset and flinging it to one side, then in the same movement, dragging her camisole off over her head. Gently, he began to massage the long red marks where her stays had compressed the skin.

His touch was soothing, and she did not think she had reason to be wary of his motives, not so soon. Despite the length of time it had been since she had lain nude before him, she had no consciousness of it at that moment. She relaxed, inhaling deeply as she had needed to do for some time. He snorted in what might have been sardonic amusement for her pretenses, or satisfaction that she had abandoned them.

A languid feeling crept over her. She watched him through narrowed eyes, her gaze following the movements of his smooth gliding muscles as his hands swept along her sides. Her attention drifted to the flat sheathing of brown skin over his abdomen, the sculpting of the muscles there, and the sharp line of demarcation where the bronze of his upper body met the ivory paleness of the lower. And yet, his skin tones were not so white as her own, due to the olive skin of his Creole ancestors. The faint mantling of perspiration from his exertions and the tropical night gave a gilded sheen to his body in the lamplight. Almost unconsciously, she reached out to touch him, then followed the musculature of his belly upward to the planes of his chest, stopping with her fingertips just over his heart. Its beat was strong and steady, pulsing under her hand, throbbing through her nerves until it combined with the race of her own blood.

She allowed her touch to drift a fraction lower. Swallowing with difficulty, she said, "It healed all right, your rib?"

"Fine."

"I'm glad."

"Your concern, of course, being solely for my health?"

"Solely," she answered, but could not prevent the smile that flickered like silver lightning across the gray of her eyes.

"I was afraid of that." He had found the tapes that held her pantaloons and slipped the bowknot. His fingers smoothing the red line left around her waist, he brushed the fine linen lower, and lower still. When it bunched under her, he shook his head in mock annoyance, and slowly drew the material down over her hips, his gaze dropping to the taut surface of her belly as the wheat-straw gold triangle at the apex of her legs appeared.

Under his warm appraisal, she felt naked indeed now. "I— my nightgown. It's in the other cabin with the rest of my clothes."

He came to his feet, and, swinging in rampant, aroused maleness, moved to extinguish the lamp. There was a hint of laughter in his voice as he came toward her in the darkness. "Don't worry," he said, "you won't need it—or them."

Chapter 13

Ramon was right. She did not need either nightgown or clothing until far into the next morning, well after they had left the protection of the channel between the islands and moved into the open sea. It was then that a federal cruiser was sighted. Ramon threw on his clothes and went above, grudgingly giving the order for Cupid to transfer her trunk from the ladies' cabin to his own. By the time she had dressed, put up her hair in a coil on top of her head against the force of the wind, and followed him topside, they had run into a squall. Taking advantage of the rain and low-lying cloud bank, they had changed course, leaving the cruiser behind.

It was a rough trip. The *Lorelei*'s engine labored as she rolled in the waves. The decks stayed wet and slippery, and lines were left up both topside and along the corridors for handholds. It was the safest kind of weather, according to the men. Poor visibility for the federal frigates on the lookout for runners, and therefore good for making time, since they did not have to be constantly turning tail and running from the Yankees. It was not the best for comfort, however. Lorna did not feel truly seasick from the pitching, but neither did she feel at her best. She spent much of the time in the bunk, reading by the fitful light of the swinging lamps during the gray days when a light could be shone; staring at the ceiling, thinking, after dark.

She had for company in the cabin stacks of bonnet boxes. She had not paid them much attention that first night, but as the ship pitched, the lightweight boxes, made of thin wood covered with paper painted in floral scenes, had a tendency to slide back and forth across the floor, tumbling from their stacks, rolling about the cabin. The tissue-wrapped bonnets spilled out, shining in their rich satin and taffeta and lace, with trims of feathers and gilt cord and silk flowers. Lorna had picked them up, holding them in her hands for a moment before thrusting them carelessly back into their boxes. The more she saw of them, the more her anger with Ramon grew. What use were bonnets for fighting the Yankees or feeding hungry people? The extra space in the cabin could have been much better utilized for transporting cloth for uniforms and good leather boots, or cotton cards to remove the seeds from the cotton so it could be turned into thread on the spinning wheels being brought from the attics all over the South—anything except bonnets to please the vanity of the few women who could still afford such luxury.

It was true that he was performing a great service by shipping the gunpowder so badly needed by Confederate forces, but his reason was purely monetary. What could be admirable about endangering his life, and that of his men, for gain? That flaw in his character troubled Lorna as she lay alone in the bunk, but when he stepped into the cabin, on those few occasions when he could leave his duties, and came toward her with his dark eyes alight with desire, she put aside her misgivings.

Toward the evening of the third day, the sky cleared. The rose-pink light of sunset lay across the water, turning it to an opalescent purple on the horizon and giving a rose tinge to the ship's gray paint. It outlined a ship, small due to distance making headway on their right.

Lorna, moving to stand beside the executive officer at the railing, waited until Slick had lowered his glasses before asking, "What is it?"

"Another blockade runner, Ma'am," the north Louisianian drawled, sending her a quick glance. "I'd say, from the look of her, the *Bonny Girl*."

Peter's ship. Slick might be curious as to her reaction, knowing she had received attention from the Englishman, but she did not intend to give anything away if she could help it. In truth, she felt a bit strange, a little anxious for Peter. For the *Lorelei* and herself, she felt no such trepidation. Her trust in Ramon's skill and judgment was complete, regardless of her dislike of his principles.

To direct the conversation into other channels, she asked, "How far are we off the Carolinas?"

"No more than an hour or so. We are at half-speed now, if you will listen to the engines, idling along so we don't come up on the federal fleet before good dark. Actually, we've passed the mouth of the Cape Fear."

The Cape Fear River, rather like the Mississippi River below New Orleans, was the entranceway to Wilmington, though the city was only sixteen miles upstream instead of the one hundred fifty that separated New Orleans from the gulf. "Passed it?"

The officer turned, smiling a little, ready to show his knowledge. "The river is named for the point of land, or cape, that juts out just here on the coast. At some time or other, it made itself two different outlets to the sea. There's an island, Smith Island, as if the tip of the cape had broken off and floated out a piece. One river channel goes to the south of it, and the other to the north. There are two fortifications, Fort Caswell to the south, and Fort Fisher to the north, protecting the channels. The blockade fleet is strung out across both entrances, stationed at close intervals, if you can picture that."

"Yes, I think so," Lorna said, frowning in concentration.

"All right. During the day, the federals lie at anchor, but at night they patrol, keeping in touch with the flagship, which stays put. The batteries at the north fort, Fort Fisher, are so strong they can pick off the Yankee ships like sitting ducks if they aren't careful; so, up there, the gunboats have a tendency to stay farther out from shore. The idea, for runners like us, is to steam north of the entrances, run around the end of the fleet, and come down the coast inside the line of vessels. Being more shallow-drafted, we can steam closer in. When we get near the river's mouth, where the Yankee ships are the thickest, we run under the guns of the fort and are home free."

"You make it sound so easy."

He shook his head. "It is, and it isn't. You have to have a navigator who can find the mouth of a river only a half-mile wide in the dark, a pilot who can sound the bottom and tell you by the color of the sand whether you are too far north, or not far enough. You need a captain with the nerve to decide if navigator and pilot are right, and a ship with a good, steady engine that won't quit on you or blow off steam at the wrong moment.

Most of all, you have to have luck. Any ship without it is going to wind up forty fathoms under or beached on the sand with sea gulls roosting in its ribs.''

Night came on with incredible swiftness, or perhaps it only seemed so because of the apprehension the executive officer's words had stirred inside her. The lights on the ship, ordinarily doused at dusk, were double-checked. Tarpaulins were used to cover the hatches of the engine room, in spite of the hellish heat and lack of air below. The binnacle was closed off with only a funnel-shaped aperture left through which the man at the wheel could see the compass. Warnings against even the smoking of a cigar were issued to the few male passengers who gathered on the deck. The cook's fire had long since been allowed to go out, and Cupid passed around cold meat and bread, and wine to wash it down with, just before they stopped to cast a lead, taking a sounding of the bottom, then proceeding faster.

The night was fairly clear, but a mist lay on the sea. A vagrant night wind, neither cold nor yet warm, drifted over the decks. Lorna stood with her black cloak wrapped around her and her back to the wheelhouse, in the shadow of the smoke-stack. Nearby, a pair of the men passengers crouched behind the bulwarks at the prow so that their silhouettes could not be seen against the gray of the ship. The smell of the coal smoke wafted warm on the air, but, though she craned her neck to watch, no spark flew past overhead from the anthracite being used in the boiler room.

She should be below, as she well knew. The silent darkness was claustrophobic, however, especially when she knew that every man on the ship was on the main deck, save those laboring to keep the engines running. She would take her chances in the open, no matter what Ramon said. She did not want to be a hindrance, but he had no right to command her, particularly if he did not ask the other passengers to abide by the same rules.

There was a rustle of sound near her; then a voice hissed in her ear. ''Black snake!''

She spun around in a sweep of skirts, at the same time recognizing Ramon's voice. Still her tone was sharp as she asked, ''What?''

''Black snake,'' he repeated, laughter threading his low voice. ''It's what the federal naval sentries on board the cruisers call when they see a blockade runner, instead of 'Sail ho!' It implies the sighting of something sneaky, also fast and elusive.''

"And what, may I ask, has that to do with me?"

"You know well enough."

"You mean because I am here, instead of in that dark, stifling cabin."

"Correct."

"I won't go," she said after a moment, her voice quiet, "and, if you were truly concerned for me, you wouldn't ask it."

"I've told you before, it's the flying glass, the splinters, the fragments of shell that are the greatest danger."

"I know, but you risk it and so do the others."

"I'm not a woman, nor are they."

"What has that to do with anything?"

"The consequences—maiming, death—are not as important."

"Why? We are all human beings."

"I don't have time to argue philosophy with you. It's a fact, something every man recognizes and most women are happy to acknowledge."

She ignored his comment for lack of an answer. "I won't get in the way, I promise. Nor will I scream or faint or cause any more trouble than the other passengers should we be fired upon."

"Lorna—"

"Please?"

He did not answer at once but weighed her request. She sensed a certain tension about him that was caused, she thought, partially by the weight of responsibility upon him at this juncture, partially from concern for her safety, and to no small extent from irritation that she was causing difficulties. She shifted slightly, half-turning toward the companionway to go below, when he reached out and caught her hand.

"This way," he said, "to the wheelhouse. At least you will be beside me."

The pilot was already there beside the helmsman, staring into the darkness, a North Carolinian who had taken Frazier's place on this leg of the run. He turned to glance briefly at Ramon and Lorna, then swung back to strain his eyes into the blackness ahead of them. There was nothing to be seen except the faint shifting of the water and the pale drift, like a soft silk scarf, of the mist around them. They pressed on, with the beat of the paddle wheels and wash of the water cascading from them sounding increasingly louder. Long minutes passed. Perhaps an hour later, the pilot shifted uneasily.

"Better cast the lead again, Captain."

The order was given to stop. The engines ceased. Silence closed in as they waited with held breaths for the hiss of steam blowing off, a sound that would carry for miles. It did not come. The shadow figure of a man slipped forward into the forechains. The report came back in a minute or two. They were free of the speckled-mud bottom, the indication they had been waiting for that meant they were far enough to the north.

"Starboard," Ramon ordered, "and go ahead easy."

They turned in a long gentle sweep, moving in toward shore, and began to creep down the coast. There was not a sound now except the regular beat of the floats on the paddles, dangerously echoing on the water though blending somewhat with the rush of the surf as they proceeded at the pace of a snail. On the right lay a line of sand dunes, pale and ghostly pyramids in the night. The shortened masts of the ship, denuded now of sails since they were moving away from the open sea, were no taller than their sandy peaks.

The minutes passed. A quarter hour, then a half. The night was fleeting, and Lorna wondered if they would have time to reach Wilmington before dawn at the plodding rate they were traveling. If they were caught in this trap between the shore and the blockade fleet when dawn came, they would be as helpless as a target barge towed behind a slow frigate.

"There! On the port bow."

Before the pilot's voice had died away, Ramon's quiet order came. "Starboard a point. Steady."

It was only then that Lorna saw the long, black shape in the water, lying absolutely still. It carried no lights, nothing to alert the runners to the presence of a federal ship. A sloop, it rose and fell with the swell, not a hundred yards away, its masts and spars waving as if trying to help keep balance.

They slid past in dead quiet. Not a man seemed to breathe. Lorna stood still, as though her immobility was a protection. Her hands were clenched, the nails cutting into her palms. Ramon was a dark statue beside her. The pilot's head turned slowly as he kept his eyes on the blockader. Somewhere a man, possibly one of the passengers, stifled a cough.

The *Lorelei* drew ahead half her length, her whole length, double that. They steamed on four hundred yards, eight hundred. The sloop was swallowed up in darkness and mist, dropping away behind them. They were safely beyond her, and had not been seen. No man spoke or offered congratulations. Certainly none cheered. They were only beginning to run the blockade.

Where was Peter's ship? They had not seen the *Bonny Girl* for some time, not since just before sunset. Was he ahead of them or behind them? Was he even taking the same course? There were other passages into Wilmington, Lorna knew, for she had heard the men speak of them these last weeks. This was the safest, the preferred course, but was perhaps more closely watched because of it.

Her eyes were burning from trying to penetrate the encroaching gloom. She closed them tightly, then opened them again. A stir of movement in the mist caught her attention, resolving into the vague outline of a ship steaming slowly across their bow. She reached out to clutch Ramon's arm. At the same time, he said quietly, "Stop her."

The engines stopped, and there came the quiet bubbling sound of steam blowing off under water. The paddle wheels ceased. The ship glided a short distance under her headway, then sat on the water, wallowing in the swell. Ahead of them, the Federal ship materialized out of the murkiness of the night, moving at an angle from the featureless shoreline to seaward. She showed up, a black mass, the smoke from her stacks a dark veil above her shot with tiny red sparks, proving beyond all doubt the wisdom of the blockade runners in painting their ships the soft gray of ghosts, and the value of good Welsh coal.

The noise of the Yankee vessel's paddles was muffled but carrying. They sat listening to it long after she had moved on, disappearing into the darkness. It was only after Ramon gave the quiet order to re-start the engines that Lorna began to breathe normally and realized that her heart was pounding, beating with deafening strokes that sounded in her ears with the same feathery thudding of enemy paddle floats.

They altered course to steam as close to shore and the dim line of the surf as they dared, as far from the line of federal fleet as possible. It was some time later that the pilot grunted, pointing out a mound of earth about the size of a tall tree, and perhaps as big around. Called Big Hill or, sometimes, the Mound, it was a landmark used to tell how far they were from Fort Fisher. It would not be long now before they could expect the aid of the batteries against the ships drawn up near the mouth of the river. They were always thicker and more heavily armed in this area.

Minutes passed, and they saw nothing. The night was hushed, though the faint sighing of the surf could be heard away to starboard. The darkness was oppressive, a weight that they had been fighting for hours, or so it seemed. The tension was a palpable thing. Despite the coolness of the night, Lorna felt a beading of perspiration on her upper lip. She was not certain if she was glad or sorry she had stayed on deck. It might almost have been better not to have known what was taking place, to have remained ignorant of the close brush of danger. But no, the wild play of imagination would have been worse by far, that and the feeling of being shut away, denied a part in the events of the night.

Somewhere ahead of them there came a distant shout, no more than a human sound without words at that far remove. It was followed by a hoarse, whistling sound. Light flared, a great yellow bloom that soared upward to explode in a red glare, reflecting from the deep mist with an orange sheen. It hung in the sky, fading only slowly, a calcium rocket illuminating the scene below.

It showed the embankments of Fort Fisher, sullen earthworks above the river, facing out to sea. Surrounding it at a healthy distance were six or seven gunboats. In the stretch of water in between was a ship just getting up full steam after her slow approach, her paddles beginning to churn and sparks flying as fresh coal was thrown into her furnaces. A thudding boom sounded, and there was a flash of light from the gunboats. In its last gleams could be seen the geyser of water that spewed up on the beam of the ship running toward the fort, the blockade runner *Bonny Girl*.

"It's Peter," Lorna whispered.

"Full speed ahead!" Ramon called, no longer bothering to lower his voice. To her, he said, "So it is Peter, but you had better be worrying about yourself. Get down!"

Hard on his words came a growling explosion, followed by a high-pitched whine. The shell fell in front of them, spouting water upward so that it fell on the deck. The calcium rocket had lit the area, catching them as well as Peter in its glare.

Lorna had not needed Ramon's hard hand on her shoulder to bring her to her knees. She remembered too well the whistle and scream of musket balls around them on the night they had left Beau Repose. Now, crouching, she flattened her skirts around her. The pilot dropped down beside her, hunkering with one hand on the deck as another shot burst overhead and bits of hot metal rained, rattling, down onto the steamer. The concussion of the explosion was hot, numbing. Lorna saw Ramon grab for a brass bar to haul himself erect. Hard on that blast, mingling with it, was another. Wood screamed as the shell tore into the deck. Splinters flew, pinging on the hatches, clattering. Lorna felt a tug at the folds of her cloak but did not bother to look. Foremost in her mind as she knelt with the deck vibrating beneath her hands was the thought of the dynamite stored in the hold beneath them, waiting for an errant spark.

The vessel was picking up speed, her wheels beating the water to a froth, the thud of the beam increasing in tempo. They were racing toward the fort, sprinting, straining with every ounce of power and particle of pride in the ship. It was almost as if the *Lorelei* were alive, could sense the desperate need to reach safety; that she reacted to the orders of the man who guided her by voice alone, without need of mechanical guidance. Behind them, a shot fell short. A broadside, deafening in its staggered booming, scattered around them so that they ran through a rain of water spouts, but were unhurt.

A rocket flared, soaring into the heavens. Lorna could not resist the need to see its progress, to judge the distance they must go. She pushed herself upward, balancing on the plunging deck. At that same moment, a salvo roared from the fort ahead, whirring past them. The *Bonny Girl* was beneath that beneficent shower of shot, dashing homeward.

Not so, the *Lorelei*. Ahead of them was the white water of a shoal, and, though Lorna had not heard the order given above the shelling, they were moving out from shore in the direction of the gunboats.

"Port, hard, for the love of God!"

She saw then what Ramon had seen. It was the hulk of a blockade runner, half-sunk earlier in the night perhaps, lying waterlogged in the mist. Near impossible to see until the rocket had lighted the sky, it lay across their way. There was no time to stop, and none to pass behind it; they would plow into it, risking tearing the bottom of the ship out on the jagged stern. There was just room, if they were lucky, to slip by between the sunken bow and the shoals to starboard. Ramon had given the only possible order, and he stood now, the planes of his face set and hard in the yellow-red light.

She thought they were going to make it, skimming past with inches to spare on one side and white water foaming around the paddle wheel on the other. The gunboats thought so, also, for they sent out a double broadside that whistled and screamed around them, toppling the aft mast so that it crashed to the deck and a man yelled in pain. Then there came a whispering, scraping noise, a ringing of the ironclad hull like the thumping of a tin kettle. The *Lorelei* shuddered. They struck.

Lorna hurtled forward, coming up hard against a warm chest. Strong arms closed around her as they sprawled, rolling, slamming into the windowed side of the enclosure. Ramon grunted; then, as a shell exploded above them with the shattering tinkle of broken glass, he pinned her beneath him, covering her with his body.

The firing stopped. Ramon rolled from her, springing to his feet. He issued terse orders to settle the crew and get the grounded ship moving. The pilot and helmsman regained their feet, the last daubing at his bleeding neck as he caught the spinning wheel. Lorna pulled herself up, backing out of the way. Around her in the dimness was torn decking and splintered railing. The stern of the boat had a crippled look with the downed mast lying at a grotesque angle over the side. Somewhere a man moaned, and she left the protection of the wheelhouse, moving toward the sound. She found him, one of the passengers, a Scotsman from Edinburgh. His right arm was broken and he had a gash in his head. She knelt beside him for a moment, wiping ineffectually with her handkerchief at the blood running across his face. Rising, she looked around for one of the officers, anyone who might tell her where medical supplies could be found. The ship, in common with most runners, carried no surgeon.

It was then she saw it, a long boat in the water with a lantern amidship. It carried a complement of blue-clad soldiers, their muskets at the ready and an officer of rank glittering with braid at the prow. She was standing, staring at it still, when Ramon appeared at her side.

"We are about to be boarded," he said, his voice abrupt. "You had better go below."

She indicated the passenger moaning at her feet. "But this man is hurt. Someone needs to see to him."

"He'll be taken care of."

"I—when they come aboard, you don't intend to resist?" It would be suicide as they sat there under enemy guns, besides branding them as pirates rather than merchants.

"No," he said, the single word etched with the acid of bitterness, "but you can never tell what might happen."

He took her arm then, forestalling further questions or argument. At the door of the companionway, he left her, striding aft to deal with his crew and the situation that awaited him.

Lorna hesitated, holding to the door frame, staring back toward the injured man. She heard then the thump of the grappling hooks as a rope ladder was secured to the side. A moment later, there came the sound of rough, self-important voices.

She did not care to witness Ramon's humiliation at having his ship seized, at his being taken prisoner. In the hectic pace of events, it was only beginning to come to her what this grounding of the ship meant. They were caught. The *Lorelei* would never run the blockade again. They would be taken aboard one of the federal ships, and Ramon's gallant vessel confiscated. A numbness gripped her, but of the kind that gave warning of pain when it wore away. She turned, thinking distractedly of the things she would have to do to make ready to be taken off the ship. Behind her, the arrogant voice of a federal officer rang out.

"I understand you have on board a female passenger, one Miss Lorna Forrester, a known Confederate courier. I have orders of search and seizure for this woman, and demand that she be turned over to me on the instant."

Lorna heard Ramon's hard denial, his questions, but she did not wait for the result. She plunged down the companionway and along the corridor to the cabin. Search and seizure. The implications of the term were plain; the meaning of it in connection with her name, and on the lips of the federal officer, would have to wait. Inside, she swung her gaze around the small space. She dragged the oilskin packet of dispatches from her cloak pocket, weighing it in her hand as she sought a hiding place. Her trunk was the first place they would look, and doubtless Ramon's the second. Under the mattress was too obvious; likewise under the straw matting on the floor. To put it among Ramon's papers would be to implicate him, the last thing she wanted to do.

Outside she heard the clatter of booted feet on the companionway. There was no time to be clever. She took a step forward,

and her slippered foot kicked against a hatbox, one of several
scattered over the floor by the force of the grounding. She had
become so used to them, she had scarcely noticed them in the
dark. Now she swooped to pick up a bonnet that had spilled
from its nest of tissue paper. A confection of black lace with
long veiling, it was peculiarly appropriate for wartime, a mourning bonnet. She thrust the oilskin packet into the crown, wadded
the tissue paper around it, and crammed it back into the box.
She was just putting the lid back on when the door crashed open
behind her.

She swung around, fixing a startled look on her face as she
confronted the officer at the head of the detail of men in blue,
one of whom carried a lantern. Pitching her voice higher than
was normal for her, she said, "Oh, you gave me a fright."

"Miss Lorna Forrester?" The officer was tall and clean-cut,
nice-looking in a wholesome way, with brown hair tinged with
mahogany and hazel eyes. He was not, she thought, more than
twenty-six or twenty-seven.

"Why, yes."

"I must ask you to come with me, Ma'am."

After the first brief glance tinged with admiration, the officer
had stared somewhere just over her head. With a small, helpless
gesture, she inquired, "Whatever for?"

"Order of the commander of the fleet, Captain Winslow,
Ma'am."

"The fleet commander? I am honored," she said, touching
her hair, smoothing loose strands, "but I'm so untidy, and this
cabin is such a mess—"

"This way, if you please, Ma'am."

She gave a small shrug and set the hatbox aside. Still fussing
with her appearance, brushing off her cloak and patting her hair,
she swept from the cabin ahead of him.

Cupid stood in the passageway outside. He bobbed his head
at the federals, stepping out of the way. As Lorna met his black
gaze, he gave her a sly wink that seemed to carry a message.
She smiled, grateful for the encouragement, before turning toward the companionway.

Lanterns had been lighted and set about on the deck. Soldiers
with muskets were ranged along the railing behind the federal
commander, while Ramon stood facing him. The ship's officers
were ranged behind Ramon, with the crew gathered beyond
them in the prow. Cupid, who had undoubtedly been ordered to

point the way to the cabin where Lorna was, now followed her topside and joined the others. Lorna moved to stand at Ramon's side, facing the fleet commander. The naval lieutenant stopped a pace behind her, while his detail ranged themselves on one side.

Captain Winslow was a man of medium height with a craggy face half-concealed behind a brown beard that jutted out at an arrogant angle from his chin. Barrel-chested, he held himself erect with his hands clasped behind his back. As he looked Lorna over, his eyes burned with zeal, and there was in his expression something of the implacability of the Puritan faced with a suspected witch.

"Miss Forrester, sir," the officer who had served as her escort said.

"Humph." The commander cleared his throat before beginning. "According to my information, Miss Forrester, you are a known courier of the insurrectionist Confederate government, carrying dispatches destined for Davis. I demand that you give those documents into my possession."

"I would be happy to comply, sir, if I had such things, but I'm afraid I haven't the least idea in the world what you are speaking of. May I ask who may have given you such vicious and erroneous information?"

"You may not. And I warn you not to play games with me, Miss! I will not be taken in by an air of innocence or coquetry, however prettily done. You will turn over the papers you carry willingly, or I will have you searched for them. Is that understood?"

Ramon took a step forward. "You are exceeding your authority. This is highly irregular. When did the United States government begin harassing ladies as a pastime?"

"This is no pastime, I assure you. The ladies of the South would be quite safe from harassment if they would stick to their embroidery and refrain from involving themselves in the conduct of this war. As to my authority, I assure you it is valid, though I see no reason to bandy words with an ex-officer of the United States Navy turned traitor!"

"What happens, sir, if you are wrong?" Lorna asked, summoning an injured frown. "Who will restore my self-respect after being submitted to such an ordeal?"

"You will have the apologies of the United States Navy, Miss Forrester," the commander said with heavy irony, "but I foresee no need for them. For the last time, will you volunteer the dispatches you are carrying or must we search for them?''

''I have told you, I am not what you think. You have been misinformed. If I cannot convince you, then I am afraid you must do as you think best.''

Even as she made the small, poignant gesture of defenselessness that accompanied her consciously brave words, she was aware of Ramon's sharp glance in her direction. He knew that angry defiance was more in character for her than this fragile acceptance. What he did not realize was how important it was for their search to be cursory, if undertaken at all.

''You leave me no choice,'' the commander said, his features hard. He nodded to the officer behind her. ''Lieutenant Donavan, see to it.''

''No,'' Ramon stepped forward, putting his hand on Lorna's arm. ''Couldn't this wait until you are ashore, where a woman could be brought in?''

''And give Miss Forrester time to dispose of the dispatches? No. Lieutenant?''

The lieutenant took a step toward her, then stopped, eying in something akin to dismay the bulky garments Lorna wore.

''She will have to disrobe,'' the commander said with impatience. ''Take her below.''

''I will go with her,'' Ramon said.

The commander's frown hardened and he lifted a brow. ''I fail to see how the presence of another man will be of use to Miss Forrester. No. I require that you remain here. There are matters to be discussed concerning the cargo you carry, and then I am of a mind to go over this ship with the view of making her my flag vessel. That's if her speed and seaworthiness prove satisfactory, which I have no doubt they will. If everything is in order, you will be needed to see her free of the shoals.''

Ramon paid no attention, moving to Lorna's side as she turned toward the companionway. At a snapped order, the soldiers at the rail brought their weapons to the ready, pointed in his direction.

''Need I remind you, Captain Cazenave, that you are my prisoner?''

It was Lorna who came to an abrupt halt. ''I think you had better do as he says,'' she said quietly. ''I will be all right.''

''*Chérie*—''

She made a quick, silencing movement. The visions that

haunted him she could only guess at, but they could not be helped in any case. If the papers were not found, all would be well, but if they were it would be best if he were not present. She remembered too well, now, Sara Morgan's warnings. She would be sent to prison for a time, months or years, if she were discovered. For Ramon, however, the penalty would be death. Sara Morgan had also said she would be immune from search as a woman, and she had been wrong. What else she might be wrong about, Lorna did her best not to think.

In the cabin once more, the officer held the door for her to enter. "This is new to me, Ma'am," he said, his hazel eyes troubled, "but I think it would be best if you were to take off your things and hand them out to me. If you will light a lamp and pass it out first, I'll be able to make my search out here."

"Yes, I'll do that, Lieutenant Donavan," she said, real gratitude in her low tones. There were men to whom a woman, once she trespassed beyond the bounds normally reserved for her sex, was fair game. The ordeal before her might have been made much more unpleasant had the man been so inclined. It crossed her mind that his chivalry left much room for deceit, if such a thing had been necessary, but she pushed the realization from her. Removing her cloak, she put it in the lieutenant's hands, then stepped into the cabin.

As she undid the buttons of her gown, Lorna heard thumping, thudding sounds vibrating through the ship. The soldiers were in the hold, examining the cargo, she thought. The Union armies would doubtless be able to make good use of the gunpowder and other arms and ammunition. It was to be hoped they had no use for bonnets. She thought of seizing the packet from its hiding place and pushing it out the porthole. If they could not find evidence of her guilt, they would be forced to release her, wouldn't they?

Whether it was because of a reluctance to give up her mission for lost or of a simple need to deal fairly with the officer who had treated her with such courtesy, she did not make the attempt. Rather, she skimmed from her clothing with quick movements, passing it piece by piece out the door until she stood in her camisole and pantaloons. As she hesitated over handing them out, she heard a murmur of voices. After a few moments, a knock fell on the door.

"Ma'am?"

"Yes, Lieutenant?"

"Beg your pardon, but the commander has sent orders that I am to do a body search."

"A what!"

"I'll be as quick as possible."

He did not wait for a reply but turned the handle of the door and stepped into the room. She backed away from him with her arms crossed over her breasts covered only by thin linen. There was a grim line to his mouth, and his face was beet-colored. His gaze was steady, determined, though focused on a point just above her head.

"I'm sorry, Ma'am, but orders are orders. If you'll hold out your arms, like this," he said, demonstrating.

The officer's embarrassment in some way mitigated her own. Lorna forced herself to comply. Her color was high, but her gray eyes steady as she watched his advance. A faint sheen of perspiration appeared on his face, and he swallowed so that his Adam's apple bobbed. Still, he stepped closer, hands extended. As he touched her sides, he closed his eyes. With a quick, patting motion, he felt up under her arms, pausing the merest fraction of a second at the soft roundness of her breasts, then moved quickly back down along her waist and over the curves of her hips. He knelt, sliding his hands along first one leg, then the other, then came erect, stepping back as if from a hot stove.

"I must ask you now to take down your hair," he said.

She might have expected it, remembering Charlotte's comment about carrying messages in the coils of her tresses. Apparently it had been a favorite method of Sara Morgan. Lifting her arms, she removed the pins and let the shining, wild silk length slip, unfurling, down across her shoulders.

"Is that satisfactory?" she asked, her voice tight.

"Beautiful—I mean, that's all right, then. I . . . if you will tell me that . . . that an internal search is unnecessary, I'll swear it was done."

If it was possible for the heated flush that spread over every inch of her body to become darker, it did. The only compensation was that his did the same. "I can assure you it isn't necessary."

He nodded and, swinging around, dived from the room. Outside the door, he scooped up her clothing in his arms and thrust it toward her. "I'll leave you to dress while I report to the commander. And again, Miss Forrester, Ma'am, my most abject apologies."

He left her as if it were he who had been released from sur-
veillance instead of she. That there was no guard, and that he
had not seen fit to post one, could have been taken as an indication either of her presumed frailty as a woman, or of his belief
in her innocence. Lorna frowned over the omission as she righted
her gown and petticoats, her hoop and corset, and got back into
them. Now was the time to be rid of the packet, to throw hatbox
and all out the porthole, she tried to tell herself, but could not
bring herself to act. Instead, she put up her hair once more and
slipped her cloak back on, preparing to mount to the deck.

At a tap on the door, she glanced up sharply, then moved to
open the panel. Lieutenant Donavan stood outside. He gave her
a quick look, as if to be certain she was dressed once more,
then directed his gaze over the top of her head again.

"I have been detailed to guard you, Miss Forrester, and to
institute a thorough search of your quarters."

She should have known the Yankee commander would not be
so lenient. She thought with irony of her earlier idea that her
treatment left room for deception. There was nothing she could
do now, however, except step back, allowing him to enter. She
left the door swinging open and moved to take one of the chairs
at the table, spreading her skirts around her. The officer stood
irresolute, then stepped to Ramon's trunk and lifted the lid.

There was a great noise of tramping feet and heavy thudding
overhead. After a few minutes of watching the officer in blue
lifting out Ramon's clothing, carefully going through it item by
item, she spoke.

"Is it permitted to ask what is happening?"

"They are shifting the cargo aft, lightening the stern, hoping
the ship can be backed off without having to jettison too much."

"She wasn't damaged when she struck?"

"An opened seam or two, nothing major. She'll float all right,
if she can be freed, though we may have to wait until high tide."

"Your commander has decided to use her as his flagship
then?"

"Yes, Ma'am. He's been waiting for a ship like her, something fast and sleek, like a race horse, that can chase down other
runners. He's gone now to arrange for the transfer from his
present ship to this one."

"In the middle of the night?"

"That's when we do most things these days, during the dark

of the moon, at least. Besides, there may be another runner or two before dawn to chase and board. Good God, what's this?''

He had found the gold. ''The captain's . . . uh, ill-gotten gains, I suppose you would call it.''

Whistling, he hefted a sack of the heavy, clinking coins. ''I knew running the blockade was a money-making venture, but this sure brings home just how much of one.''

To be sitting there talking easily to a man who was the enemy, a Yankee, one moreover who had inflicted the humiliation of searching her was beyond belief. Strange things happened in time of war, strange affinities, strange sympathies. She did not have time to think about it, however. ''I've heard it said that quite a few federal officers would like the chance to run the blockade if things were different. Does the idea appeal to you?''

A boyish grin lit his features as he half-turned to face her. ''They say it's like nothing else, more exciting and a better test of nerve than hunting, pig-sticking, steeplechasing, or big-game shooting. If I had a ship of my own, one like this one, I wouldn't mind trying it.''

The engines of the *Lorelei* began to strain in reverse. The paddle wheels thrashed. The ship shuddered through every bulkhead, and Lorna caught hold of the anchored table as the deck shifted, canting at an angle. The lid of the trunk fell, and the lieutenant only just got his arm out in time. He squatted, holding to the end of the bunk. Slowly, grindingly, the ship began to move.

''She's going to make it,'' Lorna said in amazement.

''She's made it,'' he answered, and it was true. The hard contact with earth was gone, and they were righting, floating free.

It made no real difference. The moment of brief exultation over, her captor continued his search, moving to her own small trunk, which he examined minutely, kicking aside hatboxes as he stripped the bunk and meticulously made it back up again, shifted through the charts and papers kept in a small chest under the table, rifled through the books on the bookshelves. Lorna, watching him with a growing sense of strain, managed to continue to talk, but each time he set a hatbox out of his way, she could feel the tension inside her tighten, squeezing at her stomach until she felt ill.

Turning from the bookcase, the lieutenant stared around him. His frowning attention lighted on the hatboxes at his feet. He picked one up, lifting the lid, peering inside. Clapping the lid under one arm, he began to pull at the tissue paper, letting it drift to the floor. He looked up as the door swung open, banging against the wall. Lorna swung, alarm coursing along her tense nerves.

Ramon stood in the doorway. In his hand was a navy colt revolver. He did not point it at the federal officer, but the threat was there. His eyes were black as obsidian as his glance swept the cabin, resting for an instant on Lorna's pale face, noting the neat bunk, coming to rest on the man who stood before him.

"You have a choice," he said, his voice soft, "you can surrender or you can play the hero. Under the circumstances, my friend, need I say which I would prefer?"

The lieutenant set the hatbox aside, straightening to his full height. His voice colorless, he said, "I take it there has been a change in the status of the ship."

"Most assuredly."

"The men?"

"There are a few broken heads among them, but they will hardly notice the pain, considering the way they have been downing the liquor stores carelessly left out where they could get to them."

"You realize that you will be hunted down as a pirate after this?"

Ramon shrugged. "What odds? As long as I'm being shelled there might as well be a good reason. But enough. Will you travel to Wilmington with us or will you end it here?"

The words they threw at each other could mean only one thing. Ramon and his crew had retaken the *Lorelei*. Lorna rose to her feet, moving to his side. She reached to place her hand on his arm before turning toward the man in the center of the room.

"Lieutenant, can you swim?"

"Passably," he answered, his voice stiff but a sudden stillness on his features.

She looked back to Ramon. "Let him go."

"What?" He scowled down at her.

"I am asking you to let this man go. He . . . he could have made these past hours terrible to endure, but he did not. I feel I owe him this much."

He stared at her, weighing the request, giving it full attention even in the midst of the crisis he held so tenuously under control.

She thought she saw an easing of the leashed rage that gripped him as his gaze moved over the white oval of her face. Abruptly he nodded.

They mounted to the deck. The ship was moving, idling along, circling the length of the gutted ship that had caused her to ground, seeking open water. Out on the sea could be seen the long boat with the shape of the fleet commander standing in the prow, returning to the ship he thought was going to carry his flag. Behind them, in the wheelhouse, Slick was at the helm with only the pilot beside him. There was no one else in sight. They moved farther aft, away from the slowly turning paddle wheel. The lieutenant pulled off his boots and uniform jacket, and stripped out of his shirt. Ignoring Ramon, he turned then to Lorna.

He took her hand. "My most fervent thanks," he said, "and again, my apologies."

"Accepted, for the second; for the first, there is no need."

"There is, you know, and I won't forget it."

His hazel eyes steady, he held her gaze, then raised her hand to his lips. Releasing it, he stepped back.

"Take care," she said.

He nodded, turned, and vaulted to the railing. He stood poised for an instant, then dived, hitting the water with a clean splash. In a few seconds, they saw him in the waves, his arms pulling strongly, heading toward the long boat.

"Satisfied?" Ramon asked, his voice hard.

"Yes, thank you."

"Save your thanks; it was no gift."

"I don't understand."

"It requires payment. I will include it in the price of passage."

There was in his dark eyes the promise of a reckoning and something more, a doubt so foreign to him that it cast a dark shadow over his bronze features. Now was not the time to explore it, however.

Turning from her, he strode toward the wheelhouse. In a moment his voice rang out in an order that was passed down the speaking tube to the engine room. The paddle wheels began to slap the water with their swift beat, kicking up foam and spume. For an endless stretch of time, the federals seemed not to notice; then came the whine of a shell. It fell short, sending up a geyser where they had been seconds before. It exploded as it hit the water, and the concussion made the ship buck as if it had been kicked in the backside. Lorna went to her knees, clinging to the railing, but not before she had seen the long boat bearing Captain Winslow dancing on the thrown up waves, nearly turning end on end. The fleet commander was gesticulating, berating a very wet lieutenant on the seat beside him, oblivious of the danger. Another gun roared, and the shell passed overhead; then there were no more.

The federal gunboats had ceased firing for fear of endangering the life of their commanding officer. As the reason for their forbearance reached Lorna, she got to her feet once more, moving forward toward the prow of the ship. Holding to the rail, she turned her back on the Union fleet. Narrowing her eyes against the wind, she swung to look toward Wilmington.

Chapter 14

Half-hidden behind the tender green of the foliage of oaks and maples and an occasional jack pine, the port town of Wilmington climbed the hill above the waterfront. A roof here, a wall there, could be glimpsed through the thick mantle, along with the Gothic spires of churches and the square shapes of chimneys. High on the rise could be seen a classic facade of Corinthian columns that was pointed out to Lorna as the town hall. Near the waterfront was the squat and dingy building of the customhouse, while beyond it loomed the tower set with columns that marked the town marketplace which was said to house a full-scale theater. Compared to Nassau, it seemed a peaceful and quiet place, far removed from war. Still, there was a certain amount of bustle around the dock area where the blockade runners were being unloaded and their cargoes shuffled into warehouses.

The *Lorelei* had landed at Fort Fisher. There they found the *Bonny Girl* waiting. As Ramon and Lorna stepped into the sand, Peter had been there to embrace them both. In his shock at finding Lorna had been on the ship, his guilt at being the cause of their discovery by the blockaders, and his relief at their escape, he was almost incoherent. The story was soon told, however, Ramon brushing past the reason for Lorna's presence. Regardless, Peter had not missed his possessive arm about her, or the challenge in his friend's eye. He had glanced once at Lorna, then looked away, his face pale.

In company with the fort commandant, Colonel Lamb, they had broken out champagne to celebrate. All officers and crews were included in the toasting, especially Cupid, who, on Ramon's orders, had seen to it that the liquor stores were conveniently open to tempt the federal boarding party of marines, even including a keg of rum sitting unattended in the galley. Excluded were the marines themselves, who were marched from the hold and given into the custody of Colonel Lamb.

Afterward, Peter had gone on, while Ramon, with Slick and Chris, inspected the ship for damage, making those repairs necessary, leaving the rest until they had better access to materials in port. By mid-morning, they had passed the inspection against quarantine for yellow fever and other tropical diseases and been given their pratique, taken on a local pilot to guide them through the unbouyed channel of the Cape Fear, and were steaming for Wilmington. Two miles below the town, they had reached the Dram Tree, an ancient cypress hung with moss standing in the river. As they passed, they had not drunk a salute in recognition of a safe voyage, a tradition not to be flouted.

There were four blockade runners in already, too many to be unloaded at the limited docking area. The *Lorelei* dropped anchor and sat waiting her turn. Lorna stood on deck, watching the activity on the waterfront, the plying back and forth of the Market Street ferry, a flatboat operated by sweeps; the activity around a shipbuilding yard some distance away; the graceful passage now and then of a sloop belonging to one of the many plantation houses they had passed on their journey upriver. She lifted her face to the mild river breeze and warm noonday sun, listening to the calls of the birds in the trees that masked the town, aware of an intense joy in being alive after the dangers of the night.

After a time, she was joined by the other passengers. They carried on a desultory conversation as the gentlemen tried to decide if they should ask to be taken ashore or wait until the ship could run in and lower her gangplank. Among them was the Scotsman who, though he wore a bandage wrapped around his head and carried his arm in a sling of black silk, was as anxious as any to get into town to transact his business.

Also lying at anchor was the *Bonny Girl*. Lorna waved to Peter once as, like Ramon, he attended to the details of the making ready to go ashore. He had lifted a hand in return, then swung away in a sudden show of efficiency.

The men were not the only ones with matters to attend to in town. The thought of the duty she had accepted rested heavily on Lorna. The sooner she had discharged it, the easier she would feel. It would be as well if she were ready to find the place and the person to whom she must pass on the dispatches as soon as they were free to go ashore. At the thought, she straightened from the rail. Murmuring her excuses, holding her shawl close around her in the breeze, she went below.

She closed the cabin door carefully behind her, then looked around her. Cupid had been in to set the place to rights, it appeared. The chairs were in their places by the table; the lamps had been taken from their gimbals, polished, and refilled, the remains of the combination breakfast and luncheon she had eaten alone while Ramon remained on deck had been removed. The hatboxes had also been collected and stacked against the wall, out of the way. She moved toward them, frowning as she tried to decide which one held the black bonnet in which she had hidden the dispatches.

The oilskin-wrapped packet was in the seventh box she picked up. The contents of the other six were strewn on the floor around her, the bonnets lying in drifts of tissue paper, by the time she found it. With the packet in one hand, she stuffed the black bonnet in which she had hidden it back into its box, and began to push paper around it when the door swung open. She made a convulsive movement, as if she would thrust the packet out of sight, then was still as she realized it was too late.

Ramon did not speak, but closed the door behind him and came toward her. His face was bleak, as he took the packet from her hand, untied the oilskin, and unfolded the papers it contained. His perusal was swift, cursory. When he spoke, the words were like a lash.

"What in God's holy name do you mean by this piece of folly?"

She drew herself up, lifting her chin. "I meant to aid my country. What else?"

"Do you realize how close you came to paying the full price for it?"

"I should, I think, since I was the one who was subjected to search in this very cabin!"

"A trial that could have been avoided if you had had the sense to decline acting like a heroine in a melodrama."

The sarcasm in his voice was a severe test of her temper; still, she clung to it. "I could not refuse to complete Sara Morgan's mission for her. It is important, vitally important, that these dispatches reach President Davis."

"Someone, anyone, else could have taken them. There was no need for you to run the risk."

"There was every need! And why should I not? As a woman, I should have been immune from search, and would have been if there had not been some advance warning of my coming. How it became known, I can't imagine, but—"

"The wallpaper sprouts ears in places like Nassau, and signals are easily flashed to the frigates patrolling the coast. A federal ship setting a course dead on Wilmington, without having to worry about being chased and shelled, could reach the blockade fleet at the mouth of the river ahead of us. No, the how is plain enough; it's the why that sticks in my gullet. You thought it would be a lark, didn't you? You thought it would be so easy to dupe me into taking you with me. And it was, wasn't it? *Mon Dieu,* how easy I made it for you!"

"No, it . . . it wasn't like that."

He paid no attention to her words or the plea in her wide gray eyes. "What I don't understand is why it was necessary for you to let me believe you came for my sake. You could have told me the truth and saved yourself a great deal of trouble. You might even have been able to sleep alone, instead of trading your favors like a whore for my goodwill."

"I was told that, if you knew, it would mean your hanging if the dispatches were discovered," she said, her voice hard, her gaze on his face, which was dark with rage and passion.

"How laudable, so unselfish," he jeered. "Do you think they would have believed for a single instant that I did not know the woman who shared my cabin was a courier?"

"It's true, I tell you. As for the sharing of your cabin, I didn't think how it would look. I never meant to—"

"Now we come to the truth, do we? You never intended to come to me. You thought you could sneak on board and stay hidden all the way here, I suppose?"

"I didn't think at all! There was no time!" she said, her voice rising.

He threw the packet onto the bunk and caught her arms, dragging her against him. "I thought you came because you felt the same pull of obsession for me I feel when I look at you, because you couldn't stay away, any more than I can stay away from you. That makes me a fine fool, doesn't it?"

"No, Ramon, listen to me—"

"Well, as long as you're laughing, add this to it," he grated, his eyes dark with derision. "Even knowing what you have done, the one thing I feel like doing at this moment is to take you to bed and make love to you until you beg me to stop."

"Love?" She infused scorn into her voice despite the trembling that ran through her. "You only want to punish me."

"You think so? Either way, I want to feel you naked and writhing under me, to watch your face while I am inside you, to see you lose control."

She stared at him, trying to ignore the tide of color that rose to her hairline. "What would that solve?"

"Nothing. Isn't it a good thing that there is nothing to be solved, that you have brought your dispatches through and we are safe in Wilmington, that it doesn't matter any more what I think or feel, only what I want?"

She watched as if mesmerized as, with his black eyes burning into hers, he lowered his head to take her lips. At the last moment, she turned her head. His mouth seared her cheek, moving to the curve of her neck. "You . . . you are angry with me," she said with a catch in her voice, "and I don't blame you, but you can't do this."

"Who will stop me?"

"I . . . I'll fight you."

His voice soft, his breath warm just beneath her ear, he said, "Is that what you did while you were down here with the naval lieutenant?"

She jerked away so violently that she broke his grasp, but he was upon her in an instant, catching her shoulders. She brought her hands up to throw off his grasp, but he swung her around, sending hatboxes flying as he thrust her against the wall and pinned her there with his body. She suppressed a cry.

"I have never felt such cold fear in my life as when he was sent below with you with the order he was given. He had carte blanche to treat you as he saw fit, even encouragement to do it. I wasn't close enough to overhear what passed between him and his commanding officer when he returned the first time, but I made a point of being there for the second. *"Nothing discovered in the body search or internal examination, sir,"* was his report, and he nearly died for those words. He would have, if Slick and Chris and Frazier had not been close enough to keep me from going for his throat."

The images his words evoked filled her with distress, but she would not let him see. "How can you blame me?"

"Oh, I didn't, not until I came down here and found the two of you chatting and smiling, as cozy as two old maids at a tea party."

There were shafts of gold in the depths of his eyes, and his lashes were tangled from the wind. The lines radiating toward his temples were tight with strain. In sudden discovery, she said, "You were jealous."

"Why not? I'm not in the habit of sharing my women."

The arrogance of his tone, the neat way he had sidestepped her accusation, sent anger flaring through her. "I'm not one of your women!"

"You are for now, and until we get back to Nassau if you expect to make the return in the *Lorelei*. But you haven't answered my question: What happened between you and the lieutenant?"

"Nothing," she snapped. "Less than has happened between us since you came barging in here."

"Tell me about it." The command was harsh, permitting no denial.

She obeyed, stressing the sensitivity of the federal officer, his concern for her modesty, and his honorable conduct. Some of the tension left him, but even through her full skirts she could sense the heat of his need, sense the violence that drove him.

"You are sure? You would not change the facts out of embarrassment—or fear?"

"I would not! Why should I be afraid of you or care what you think?"

A grim smile crossed his face at her defiance. "It would be as well if you could bring yourself to both."

She did not dignify that comment with an answer. Staring him straight in the eyes, she asked, "If you were so certain that he had mistreated me, why did you let him go?"

"You asked it so prettily, and it was a means of being rid of him—there always being the chance that you enjoyed his . . . treatment. Then there was the strong possibility that he would drown."

She drew a swift breath, her gray eyes silvery with rage. "Just because I once let you make love to me without screaming or falling away in a dead faint doesn't mean I accept the same from any man!"

"No? Why should I consider myself special?"

"You know why. You know—" She couldn't speak past the sudden hurtful tightness in her throat, the burgeoning of pain that he could doubt her, that it was necessary to defend herself to him.

His gaze dropped to her lips, moist and parted, tremulous at the corners. "Yes," he said, his voice deep, threaded with weariness, "I know."

He lowered his head, taking her mouth, molding it to the hard contours of his own, thrusting past her defenses to a deep and complete possession. His hand moved downward to brush the firm roundness of her breast beneath the muslin of her bodice, outlining it, testing its soft resilience before closing his hand upon it. The pressure of his kiss lessened. His mouth moved upon hers, questing, urging a response. By degrees, as if compelled, she gave it. She spread her hands upon the rough cloth of his uniform jacket, sliding them upward, touching the strong column of his neck with her fingertips as she pressed herself against him.

A knock sounded on the door. Hard on it came Chris's voice. "Orders to dock, Captain!"

Ramon's imprecation was soft but vivid before he released her, stepping back. He moved to the door. With his hand on the handle, he turned. In his dark eyes was a smouldering promise. "We will finish this later. Remember it."

How could she forget it? The thought of it remained with her as she dressed in her walking costume of *tan d'or*, put the oilskin packet into her purse, and went back up on deck. It lingered in the back of her mind as she waited for her chance to leave the ship, and also as she took it. It hampered her concentration as she made her way to Governor Dudley's mansion. For the few minutes necessary for her to relinquish the precious packet into safe hands, she was free of it, but it returned to haunt her once she was back on the streets again. So persistent was it, she was quite unable to feel the relief she had expected at being done with the task appointed her.

She did not want to go back to the ship. She wandered about the streets as the afternoon waned, watching the once familiar activities: a maid sweeping off the front steps with deliberate strokes, a gardener pulling weeds from a border; a pair of boys in short breeches, rolling a carriage wheel down the street and chased by a trio of dogs of no discernible breed. Through a doorway, thrown open to the air, she saw a group of women busily at work, obviously a sewing circle, though the material that lay across their laps was the gray of Confederate uniforms. Away from the residential area, nearing the waterfront once more, she paused before the window of a bakery displaying breakfast rolls, arrowroot crackers, and pilot bread; of a druggist advertising dye stuffs, perfumery, and soaps, as well as the filling of prescriptions from medical men. She glanced, too, at the display window of a "Photographic Room" where could be had photographic portraiture of every known style, beautifully colored in oil, pastel, watercolor, or India ink. Farther along, her attention was caught by the shop of M.N. Katz, who offered staple and fancy dry goods, including silks, merinos, alpacas, and French millinery, also Balmoral and hoop skirts, double elliptical skirts, and mourning and fancy veils, with prices quoted in gold and Confederate scrip. His stock did not seem much less complete than was average before the war had begun. It appeared that the blockade had not made that great an impression here as yet, or else M. Katz was a preferred client of the blockade runners.

"What do you fancy? A length of silk? A clutch of feathers for a bonnet? Or how about the seed pearl collar to hide a scraggly neck. Oh, I do beg your pardon, Madame. The last would be most inappropriate!"

"Peter, you idiot," she said, a smile rising to her eyes and sounding in her voice even as she turned. It died away as she faced the Englishman—and Ramon, who stood at his side.

"True, I must accept the title," Peter replied somberly though with a gleam in his eye, "but even the best of us have these failings. Forgetfulness seems to be yours. I do wish you had told my friend here where you were off to; he's made a damned nuisance out of himself beating my quarters and looking in my pockets for you."

She sent a quick glance at Ramon's stiff features. "Yes, I suppose I should have."

"Definitely you should have. On the other hand, if he means to keep you, he should either use a longer rein or else refrain from frightening you into flight.'' The concern and the query were there, couched in his easy banter.

"It wasn't like that. I . . . I had a message to deliver."

"Oh, I see. If I had known you had business in Wilmington, I would have been happy to have you travel on the *Bonny Girl.* She's a fine lass, my ship, but you would have been an ornament to her.'' He paused only a fraction of a moment for an answer and, when it did not come, went on without missing a beat.

"But that's neither here nor there. I find my fellow countrymen have rented a house to use during their time in Wilmington, a place where they plan to hold revel this evening, following the performance of the Thalian Association at the market house. I am told the quality of the play-acting will be near professional, so high, in fact, that the officers from the federal fleet have been threatening to sneak into town to see the show. The bill features the bard's *Taming of the Shrew.* I don't expect a great deal of Katharina with a languid southern drawl; still, it should be entertaining. Will you do us the honor of joining us, both of you?''

"I don't know," Lorna began, glancing at Ramon.

His dark gaze raked her face before he turned to fling a look at his friend. "We will be delighted.''

"Good," Peter said, flashing a smile. "We will have supper after the play, so you need not worry about that. You can walk tø the market house, and to our little pied-à-terre afterward, or a carriage can be arranged. There is still an amazing number of equipages around with fine horseflesh not yet commandeered by the army.''

"We will walk—that is, if this house you mad Englishmen have rented isn't too far from the theater?'' Ramon said, his tone casual.

"No more than a step or two, just far enough to stretch your legs after sitting.''

He nodded and stepped to offer his arm to Lorna, who took it automatically. "We will see you there, then.''

"Yes, see you there," Peter repeated, but his voice had a deflated sound as he watched Ramon turn with Lorna back toward the ship. He stood, still looking after them, until the downward slope of the street hid them from sight.

Lorna felt a tightening in the pit of her stomach as they neared the *Lorelei.* She glanced up at the man strolling beside her, aware of the corded muscle of his arm beneath her fingers and the controlled strength of his movements. She could not help wondering if now was the time when they would finish what they had begun, while they were supposed to be dressing for the evening before them. Did she want it, or did she not? She could not decide, but neither could she deny the sense of perilous anticipation that rushed through her veins.

At the gangplank, he faced her. "This is one more thing that will have to be accounted for, soon."

She saw little use in pretending to understand. "I had something of importance to attend to, as you well know. There was no point, and considerable danger, in dragging anyone else into it."

"You might have mentioned it."

"You might have guessed," she countered. "It was a responsibility, one I had to meet myself. In any case, would you have let me go alone?"

He reached to take her hand, smoothing his thumb over the backs of her fingers. His voice was quiet as he spoke. "So independent. What will you do when you discover that in this world you need a man?"

"The same as other women, I expect." She had already made that discovery, but she did not intend that he should know it.

"You aren't like other women."

"Of course I am," she said tartly.

"No." He dropped her hand and stepped back. "I still have a few things to attend to before the evening. I will join you in a little while for the walk to the theater. Wait for me."

He gave her no chance to answer, but swung and strode away. So abrupt was his manner, and so disturbing, that Lorna did not watch him. Snatching up her skirts, she boarded the ship and swept below to the cabin.

Her mind seethed with the things she should have said, with angry accusations and bitter reminders. At the same time, she found herself standing suspended, the compliment he had paid her running through her mind. He was an infuriating man, blowing hot and cold. What did he want of her? He had given no indication that he had changed his mind concerning a permanent relationship, therefore he must want her as his mistress. He felt something for her, thought it might be no more than a case of snatching at the morsel the other dogs were fighting over.

What a revolting comparison. She shook her head and went to fling herself down on the bunk, staring wide-eyed at the ceiling. Was a man necessary to her? Could she, perhaps, learn to be as independent as he had called her? There must be something she could do to earn her way, provide a roof over her head and food to eat without having to depend on Ramon's bounty or the favor of any other man. She was a fair seamstress; Aunt Madelyn had seen to that by requiring that she help with the mending and occupy any leisure time that might have been spent in idleness on fine embroidery. She spoke fair French but, due to her aunt's indifference to learning for females after the age of twelve, had not the grounding in other subjects that might be expected of a governess. She was strong and had no objection to work. She could scrub, take in laundry, anything.

The light inside the cabin grew dim with the approach of dusk. Noting it, finally, Lorna sprang up and moved to the door, calling for Cupid to arrange for a bath. Still, even when it had arrived and she had settled into the copper hip bath filled with fresh, not salt, water, the nagging question would not go away. What did Ramon expect of her now? That she would occupy his bed, forfeiting all claim to respectability, holding herself at his beck and call? Did he expect her to be satisfied with the gratification of her desires, enthralled by his masterly sway over them?

And if she could abandon self-respect and be what he expected, what then? Obsessed, he had called himself. Was it so, or was it merely that his possession of her had been complicated from the beginning, that she had spurned him, then used him as no other woman had dared do? How long would his need for her last? What would become of her when it faded?

In the strict social sphere in which she had moved all her life, there was no place for a woman who had been kept by a man without the sanction of marriage. She would be forced to take a lower position, to go on catering to the desires of men, to become a woman of the shadows. To think that Ramon would casually demand that sacrifice of her brought rage rising to her brain; more than that, it brought anguish.

She was still crouched in the short tub with its sloping back and brass handles, when he returned. He stopped just inside the door as he saw her, then came into the cabin more slowly, closing the panel behind him. He lifted a brow, a faint smile at one corner of his mouth as he crossed to the bunk and sat down.

"Are you about finished?" he inquired, his voice mild. "I could use a quick rinse myself."

"Yes, you can have it, though you had better ring for more water."

"I'll use yours."

It was amazing, the sense of intimacy his words suggested. From beneath lowered lashes, she watched as he pulled off his boots and began to undo the buttons of his jacket. There had been little chance for moments such as this in the time since they had left Nassau. After that first night, Ramon had been constantly on duty, snatching only interrupted moments of sleep. It had not been a great deal different on the run from New Orleans; always there had been the need for vigilance. What would it be like, she wondered, to see him completely relaxed and at ease? What would it be like to see love on his face instead of the dark desire for revenge or the brooding need of possessive jealousy?

Her thoughts were so disturbing that she surged to her feet, reaching for her towel. It was snatched from under her fingers. Ramon, wearing only his trousers, stood holding the width of Turkish toweling, ready to wrap her in its folds. As long as she stood up to her knees in water in the bath, he was enjoying watching her, his black gaze moving over the wet curves of her body, resting on the froth of bubbles that glided slowly, with the rivulets of water pouring down her, along the shapely turn of the inside of her thigh.

"Give it to me, please?" she managed to ask.

"Come and get it."

She mistrusted his smile. "Really, we don't have much time."

"We don't do we?" he agreed pleasantly. "But then, I don't think this will be wasted." His gaze flicked to her face, then traveled deliberately lower, as if assessing her points one by one.

Irritated beyond bearing by his manner, she shot her hand out to grab the towel. He caught her wrist and hauled her from the tub so that she stumbled, falling against him. He accepted her full weight, cradling her, wrapping the towel around her. She pushed away, coming erect, but could not evade his grasp. With soothing gentleness, he began to dry her back. He swept his hands up and down along her spine, dropping lower with each stroke. As he reached her hips, lingering on their curves, she squirmed, protesting in his grasp. He allowed her to turn, and, as she did so, proceeded to dry her side, sliding his hand beneath her arm and up to her collarbone, drawing it caressingly down over her breasts. She tried to turn back, but he would not let her. His hand dropped to her waist, massaging, skimming over the flat surface of her abdomen, pressing the small, triangular mat of fine gold to dry it, and sliding quickly between her thighs.

She stiffened, lifting her lashes to glare at him. He smiled, his movements slowing, becoming exquisitely gentle. Any sudden attempt to free herself could be painful. She was still, her muscles slowly losing their tension, her breasts rising and falling with the increasing depth of her breathing, their nipples hardening as they pressed into his bare chest.

Abruptly he released her, bending to swirl the towel around first one leg, then the other. Lorna swayed, placing a hand on his shoulder to steady herself, incensed with herself for that spreading weakness. He raised up, flinging the big damp square over his shoulder. With a tight grin, he said, "We should hurry. We don't want the others having to wait on us."

She turned from him tight-lipped, though she felt more than a little dazed as she went about her dressing. From her trunk, she brought out a fresh camisole and slipped into it, then took the time to dab on a little perfume before turning back to look for her pantaloons. Though she turned the contents of the trunk upside down, she could find none. Turning away, resigned to wearing the ones she had pulled off, she found Ramon already out of the tub, standing on the other side as he briskly dried himself. As she moved toward her discarded undergarments, he picked up the pantaloons, holding them wadded in his hand.

"Is this what you need?"

For an answer, she stepped toward him, hand outstretched. Just as the pantaloons were within her grasp, he let them go. She made a grab for them, but so did he, knocking her hand aside. The leg casings of white linen fell into the copper tub and sank beneath the soap-scummed gray water.

Lorna watched them for a moment, then slowly lifted her gray gaze to his face. "You did that on purpose!"

"How can you say so? It was an accident."

"Where are my others?"

"I haven't the least idea. Maybe Cupid decided to wash for you too, while we are in port; he came this afternoon for my shirts. Anyway, what does it matter? You don't need such things. Go without them."

"It . . . it wouldn't be decent."

"It would be cooler."

That much was true. "I couldn't."

"No one will know—except me."

"And me!"

"You wouldn't want to miss the play, not for such a reason." His tone was persuasive, only faintly shaded with amusement, and something more that she couldn't identify.

"N-No."

"It won't matter, believe me. Who could possibly find out under those haystack mounds of skirts you women wear."

That much was true. By degrees, Lorna allowed herself to be persuaded; still, it felt peculiar, unbelievably lascivious, to put on her corset and petticoats while she was bare below the waist, to walk in the dome of her crinoline with nothing between the nakedness of her legs as she moved. Even fully dressed in her gown of soft lavender blue tulle, with her purse and fan in her hand and her cloak over her arm, she was aware of her nakedness underneath, so much so that she felt the heat of a flush rise to her cheekbones as she met Ramon's quizzical gaze just before they left the cabin.

Was it imagination, or was he affected as much as, if not more than, she by the state of her lower body? The question hovered about her for the rest of the evening. It seemed that he missed no opportunity to touch her, to brush the swell of her breasts with his sleeve or even a fingertip, on the pretense of banishing a mosquito; to spread his hand at the small of her back and lower, where the edge of her corset met bare flesh; to make double-edged remarks about the dress of the actors on stage, which included doublets and skintight hose. She could not concentrate on the play for the sensations that gripped her, for the feel of a draft beneath her skirts, the sensuous slide of the material around her, the warmth of Ramon's breath against her ear as he turned to speak to her.

When she could focus her attention on the stage, it was no better. Every word that Petruchio spoke was freighted with carnal meaning, if not downright lewd. His part was played with swagger and boastfulness and sensual dominance, a violent wooing that carried a hint of tender understanding. Katherina's graceful capitulation in the end was expected, but still disturbing. In order to throw off its spell and forget her own state as they walked along the street afterward, Lorna instigated a running argument with Peter, Ramon, and the others. She laughed to scorn their idea that Kate had really been tamed. She had merely shifted tactics to suit the strength of her opponent, Lorna claimed, like any woman of intelligence. When they protested at the idea, she swore in laughing certainty that the erstwhile shrew had winked at the audience during her last tender speech of submission, indicating that her meekness was but a gentle way of ruling.

Peter's friends and compatriots, a boisterous crowd dressed in every kind of costume imaginable, from correct frock coats to velvet smoking jackets and uniform coats from the Crimean campaign, greeted the suggestion with hooting disbelief. Simply because that was the way southern gentlewomen marshalled those around them did not mean an Englishman would be taken in by it. Kate had gotten no more than she deserved, what any man worth his salt would have given her.

"Is that so?" Lorna inquired, half-serious, half-laughing. "I see nothing particularly worthy about starving a woman into submission."

"He was only attempting to bring her to recognize that she was fed by his efforts," Peter remonstrated.

"And at his discretion! In return for which she must tend his kitchen, see to his comfort, mend his clothes, and bear his children. It seems to me it would have been better if she had foregone marriage and bent her efforts toward feeding herself."

Peter shook his head. "Unlike Kate, my dear Lorna, your lances are made of steel instead of straw; but, regardless, you could never be a shrew."

"How little you know her," Ramon said, his tone dry as he strolled at her side. Peter, sending him a sidelong glance, did not answer.

Was she a shrew, impossible to please, wanting only her own way? The thought was disturbing, but she had no time to pursue it. The English officers, on half-pay, come to the islands and the war-torn states of North and South to gain the experience only conflict can bring, were in too high spirits to allow anyone time for introspection. They flung quips and insults at each other, using an assortment of nicknames, few flattering, that had nothing to do with either their real names or those they had chosen to sail under. Their manner toward Lorna was teasing, though deferential in respect for Ramon's close guard and Peter's hovering concern. Toward the two or three other women who clung to their party, they were less formal, treating them with amused, if rather lustful, contempt. they had reason, Lorna thought. The women were something less than ladies and had a distressing tendency to giggle and turn the conversation toward bonnets and silk dresses they would like to have, and the cakes and wine they looked forward to eating.

They were not disappointed. The fare served up at the house rented by the Englishmen was sumptuous. There was seafood chowder, leg of lamb, roast beef, and fried chicken; vegetables swimming in cream sauces; cakes and custard made with plenty of butter, eggs, and milk. To wash it down were champagne and ale; and, for those not yet interested in alcoholic beverages, ginger beer and soda water. The cook, renown for the lightness of her biscuits, was a freedwoman who had been lured away from a plantation family and sent to one of the best eating places in Charleston for training. As they sat around the board, eating and drinking with a will, all considered she had been worth the expenditure.

Such bounty was not unusual, it was claimed, at least not in the coastal towns. In those centers, people with money still were able to command the luxuries of life. Farther inland, it was different. No one was starving, but imported goods were snapped up before they reached the interior. In many places, women were making do with cakes made of bolted cornmeal; experimenting with roasted corn, rye, and dried okra seeds for coffee; using dried blackberry and raspberry leaves for tea; boiling anything sweet to make sugar syrup; picking out the seams of old gowns to be made over; and making leather out of mule and hog hides tanned and dyed with red oak bark. Medicine was in short supply, and anyone with knowledge of herbal remedies suddenly became popular.

Listening to the recital of such hardships, involved in the flashing repartee that flashed back and forth across the table, Lorna had very nearly forgotten her undressed state under the bell of her skirts. She was reminded as the dancing began, when Ramon took her in his arms. His eyes, as they circled the floor, held a wicked glint. She could not have felt more voluptuous, more piercingly aware of herself as a woman, if she had been completely naked. Her fingers trembled in his hold, and she was aware of heat circulating through her veins. Her gray eyes were dark as she sustained the smiling intensity of his gaze while they whirled to the music.

It was of both relief and annoyance that she was torn from him by the corps of Englishmen, passed in a twirling of skirts from one to the other until she was breathless. Peter rescued her finally, signaling for a slow gavotte and leading her through it. His blonde hair gleamed in the light of the candles that burned in the chandeliers overhead, his smile was easy, the look in his eyes warmly admiring. She asked him about the cargo he would be loading to return to Nassau, and he told her of the cotton, tobacco, and naval stores of resin and turpentine, tar and pitch that he and Ramon were vying for at the moment.

"You could always split it between you," she suggested.

"What would be the fun in that?"

"This is war; must it be fun?"

He shrugged, his smile wry. "Why not? Not everybody wants to have a staring contest with danger. I had as soon be looking the other way in some tomfoolery. Chances are, it will pass me by without a second glance."

He had used the word danger, but he meant death. She managed a light laugh. "It's as good a philosophy as any, I suppose."

The music died away. He turned with her from the floor. "You are enchanting, do you know that? One of the most natural and unaffected women I've ever had the good fortune to meet. Have I told you that—?"

"Has she told you that, for all her enchanting ways, she has been the death of a man?"

Peter looked at Ramon, frowning, as the Creole moved to join them with his smile affable in spite of his cutting words. "I don't believe it."

"I assure you it's true. Isn't it, Lorna?"

The blood had drained from her face as she realized what he had said. Her gray eyes were dazed as she stared at the bronze mask of his face. She thought she had put that terrible night at Beau Repose behind her, but now it rose up before her, and once more Franklin lay dead at her hand, sprawled on the floral carpet. Finally she spoke. "Yes, it's true."

"Fascinating," Peter drawled, his dark blue gaze mirroring concern as he watched her. "I have always had a weakness for adventuresses."

"Oh, the man deserved killing, twice over, but it was a convenient way to be rid of a husband."

Peter stiffened, his eyes narrowing as he looked to Ramon. "Husband? That must have caused . . . repercussions."

"Unfortunately, and they have followed her to Nassau in the person of Nathaniel Bacon, whom you may have met."

"I would like to hear the full story, I think."

"Lorna will tell you, I'm sure, if you are really interested. But not now." He took her hand, tucking it under his arm, covering her cold fingers where they lay on his sleeve. "I think, *chérie*, it is time we returned to the ship."

She allowed him to guide her from the room, to wrap her cloak around her and escort her from the house. She walked beside him without speaking until they had reached the *Lorelei* and were safe inside the cabin. She pulled away from him then, standing in the middle of the floor, clasping her hands in front of her.

"Why?" she whispered, then said louder, "Why?"

"It seemed something it would be best if he knew."

"As a warning? Before he became too involved with a murderess?" She was becoming distraught, but she could not help it.

"As a precaution. You apparently had said nothing." He began to remove his jacket, having difficulty with the top button.

"It isn't something I use to enliven idle conversation!"

"But it is something a man overly interested in you should know." He stripped off the jacket, kicked off his boots, and began to remove his shirt.

"You have no right to interfere." She followed his movements without taking them in, so acute was her distress.

"If he cares for you, it won't matter, and it seemed that he might be able to help."

"Help? Help what, convict me of Franklin's murder by my own admission?"

"To prevent you from being harassed by Bacon when I am not, cannot, be there."

She swung from him the, clasping her arms around her body, moving to stand before the porthole that was open to the river breeze. She breathed deep, feeling as if she had been running, chased by a devil, and found it was only a figment of some vanished nightmare. Vaguely, as if from a great distance, she heard the rustle of Ramon's trousers as he stepped from them, the pad of his bare feet as he moved in behind her. He took the cloak from her shoulders, throwing it to one side, then closed his arms around her, cupping her breasts.

"Berate me in the morning," he said, the timbre of his voice husky, the warmth of his breath against the tender curve of her neck. "Claw my eyes out in the morning. But for right now,

come to bed. I have watched you tonight, thinking of you without your pantaloons until I am half-crazed with wanting you.
The look and feel and scent of you is in my blood like wine.
The more you throw up obstacles before me, the more mad-
dened I become. Come love, and let me love you, or I will take
you on the floor with your skirts about your waist, and never
regret it.''

She swung in his arm, staring at him with the vestiges of pain
and anger clouding her mind. Then she flung herself at him,
twining her arms about his neck, meeting his mouth with feroc-
ity, driven by the passion that leaped inside her as she ground
her lips to his. He caught her to him in a crushing embrace, his
breath stopped in his chest. Slanting, bruising, probing, his triumphant kiss fed her desire. His hands roved over her, tearing
at the hooks of her gown, jerking them free so that it fell open
down her back. He slipped the knots in the tapes of corset and
petticoats, breaking those that resisted as he strove to release
her from the cocoon of the clothing that held her bound. She
aided him, writing, swaying, stepping from the billowing
mound, pressing herself against him from breast to ankle.

The hardness of his body was a sensuous delight, the strength
of his arms a refuge. She was aflame inside, trembling with the
force of a raging fire. She clenched her fingers on the hair growing low on his neck, kneading his shoulders, and closed her eyes
in dizziness as he swung her from her feet and placed her on the
low bunk.

He knelt beside it, bending over her, his hands marauding.
She arched her back, turning toward him, offering her breasts
to the warmth of his mouth. He took one, worrying the nipple
with his teeth, flicking it with his tongue, closing his lips upon
it. The muscles of her stomach quivered, tightening convulsively as his hand smoothed downward. Her breathing grew
ragged, and she made a soft, imploring sound as his mouth
followed, pausing at her navel and the gentle mound below it,
seeking to find that most sensitive, most sensual part of her
body.

Her muscles tensed. Reality receded and she drifted into sharp
ecstacy. Across her mind flitted the image, soft and shimmering,
of Ramon coming to her once more through the French doors
of her hotel in Nassau, silent, god-like, bringer of joy. She cried
out in wanton release, twisting, drawing him up beside her on
the bunk, hovering over him, her loosened hair trailing over his

chest. In her fervent gratitude and the tide race of pleasure in her veins, she tried with lips and hands to incite him to that same fury of desire. He accepted it, with his hands locked in the silk of her hair, testing the limits of control until he could bear it no more.

"God, *mon coeur*," he whispered hoarsely, "let me—"

Drawing her down beside him, he pressed into her, plunging deep as he drew her against him with his fingers digging into her hips. Unsatisfied by the depth of penetration, he heaved aside, pulling her beneath him. She clung to him, drawing him deeper and deeper, her breath gathering in her throat. He lay for a moment, resting his weight on his elbows, finding her mouth, drinking in its sweetness. Then he began to move, fitting her to his rhythm with tender insistence. She rose against him, eyes tightly closed, hands spread wide and flat on the bunk. She soared, weightless, unbound, transfigured. She had no identity and needed none. He was a part of her, and she of him, linked, inseparable.

It burst upon her with the hot moistness of her own release, mingling with his. It was dark mystery, ancient and consuming, a thing to create life or destroy it, to bring surfeit or gnawing hunger, evil or joy. It beat in her blood and vibrated through her body, a violent repletion that left exhaustion in its wake. She burrowed her face into the hollow of Ramon's throat, kissing the firm, salt-tasting skin, murmuring wordlessly in the excess of love she felt at that moment. His arms tightened and his mouth brushed her forehead. He held her, staring into the night. Before her heartbeat had slowed, she slept.

Chapter 15

"I think," he said, his voice warm and lazily content, "that I will throw away all your pantaloons. Maybe your corset. And hoops, yes, definitely your hoops."

They were lying in the bunk with the pure, golden light of morning steaming through the portholes, falling onto the gently moving floor of the cabin. Their bodies were nestled together under the covering of a sheet and light blanket, though Ramon was propped on his elbow, brushing his lips over the sweet curve of her shoulder while, with his free hand, he smoothed up and down the molding of her arm. Lorna had been pretending to drowsiness, in spite of the growing heat of him against her naked back and his gentle caresses. She opened her eyes, stiffening.

"You did do it. I knew you did!"

"Do what?" he asked, his voice silky with innocence.

"Get rid of my pantaloons so I had nothing to wear."

"You were quire adequately clothed, more than adequately."

She twisted from his grasp, pushing herself up in the bunk.

"Of all the lowdown, underhanded tricks, that's the worse I've ever come across!"

"I didn't say I did it," he protested, turning his attention to her shapely and slender knee, which she had drawn up within his range. He draped his arm over her leg and began to trace the crown of her kneecap with the tip of his tongue.

"You don't have to, it's written all over your smug—stop that, it tickles!''

He ignored her squirming efforts to avoid his tongue. "What if I did? Admit it, you enjoyed your . . . unencumbered evening—and everything that followed."

"Oh! she cried and, driven mad by his tickling and his superior attitude, wrenched the pillow from under them and swung it at his head. He dodged, grabbing for it, and they tussled. She leaned over him, and as she found she could not wrest it from him, tried instead to press it down on his face. He surged up, taking the pillow with him. She would not turn loose. He jerked it, leaning, and a moment later she lay facedown across his lap. He released the pillow. She felt, rather than saw, him lift his hand above the vulnerable white skin of her buttocks. Like an eel, she twisted faceup and lay panting, glaring at him.

He grinned, the untrammeled pleasure of their play lighting the darkness of his eyes. The white gleam of his teeth shone against the bronze of his skin. He shook his head. "Don't you know, *ma chère*, that I wouldn't redden even an inch of your beautiful skin?''

"Why should I know any such thing?" The words were sharp if rather breathless.

"I want only to please you."

He placed his hand upon her waist, closing his grip upon it. "To drive me mad, you mean!" she snapped.

"In some ways, possibly," he acceded, pursing his lips as he slid his hand upward to cup her breast. "It seems only fair, since you have not helped my sanity in these last weeks."

"You know—" she began, but he cut her short.

"Yes. Shall we let it go, thinking only of now? I require at this moment simply to know what is your pleasure? If you are dissatisfied, you must tell me what I can do to make you happy."

"I—nothing." She lowered her lashes, feeling the warmth of a flush on her cheeks.

"Nothing? Isn't there anything I have done that you would like again?''

"I . . . I'm not dissatisfied."

"Nor am I," he said, sliding his fingers into the valley between her breasts, letting them come to rest on the swell above her left side where her heartbeat made the soft white mound tremble. "Nor am I, but you have so thoroughly, if sometimes unwillingly, gratified my most fervent desire, that I would do the same for you. Only tell me what it is.''

His voice was low, hypnotically persuasive, oddly musical. The vision she had had of him, coming to her through her open French doors after his serenade, flashed through her mind. She hesitated, then shook her head.

"There is something," he said, his hold tightening, his tone commanding as he said again, "Tell me."

"It . . . it's silly, and nothing you can help now, even if it wasn't too dangerous. It was . . . just an idea, a sort of day-dream.''

"But one that excites you," he said, beginning to smile once more as he stretched out beside her, drawing her into his arms. "Now I have to know. You can't keep it from me; I won't let you.''

When she told him, he didn't laugh, as she suspected he might, nor did he mind that her thoughts had gone tumbling into fantasy while she was in his arms. The sound he made deep in his throat might have been of amazement of exultation. A moment later, he was whispering against her ear, "Wait, just wait.''

Was it the lasciviousness of their thoughts, or the speaking of them aloud that brought them together then with such hunger? The reason did not matter, only the actuality, the strength and fury of the possession, the physical need that was appeased, the human warmth that was exchanged with clinging mouths and enclosing arms. There was another element. It was as if, above the merging of their bodies, there was the forging of a link between their minds; a link that was tentative, fragile, one that might endure or just as easily be broken in an instant.

It was with reluctance that they dressed, finally, and made ready to go into town. Ramon had business to attend to concerning the cargo they would be loading in the afternoon and, in addition, there was to be the auction of the goods brought in by the different blockade runners. He seemed no more ready to leave Lorna on board alone than she was anxious to stay. Wearing her muslin gown, with a shawl over her arms against the spring coolness at this latitude and a parasol to protect her from the bright sun, she left the gangplank of the ship on his arm.

The business was contracted without incident, Lorna being regaled with tea and cakes by a junior accountant while Ramon drove his bargain in the factor's office. As they were leaving, they met Peter and his English friends once more. She knew a moment of dismay as they crowded around, noisy and exuberant, only slightly more sober than they had been the night before. She cast a quick glance at Ramon, but he was smiling, joking with Peter about the cargo he had stolen from under his nose, ready to be entertained. He did not seem to mind the gallantries paid to Lorna this morning, nor the intrusion upon them. If anything, he appeared to welcome the distraction, readily agreeing to wait for Peter and the others as they arranged their business so that they could all go somewhere for a noon meal.

Even after they left the red-brick factor's building near the waterfront, it was still some time before they ate. Their wandering search of a suitable place took them past the photographer's shop. There was a great cry, suddenly, to have their likenesses made, and they descended en masse on the hapless practitioner of the art. A short, slim man with thinning hair that left a lifeless brown peak on his high, shining forehead, he was so flustered by such an influx of business so near to the noon hour that he made a muddle of names and amounts of payment. He posed Lorna, as the only lady present, first. Fussing with the backdrop of dark green drapery, arranging her gown in careful folds, placing her hands just so and tilting her head at a precise angle, he kept ducking back under the black cloth that covered his camera on its wooden leg supports. The color of her gown did not suit him, being much too light, as was her hair in his opinion. Her gray eyes would be a problem too; brown eyes showed up best in photographs, and dark blue eyes did tolerably well, but light blue and gray seemed to disappear. It would be much more satisfactory if they were to have the likeness tinted. There was a woman he could recommend who did an excellent job for a very reasonable fee.

One likeness was not enough. Ramon insisted on having one made for her as well as for himself; and Peter, with a sidelong glance at his friend, requested one too. Not to be outdone, or else as a means of taking a sly dig at Ramon and Peter at the same time, a number of the other Englishmen demanded the same. Lorna sat stiffly smiling, trying not to laugh from the ridiculous advice being thrown at her from all sides as the others watched from behind the photographic artist. As frame after frame was pushed into the wooden box of the camera and pulled out again, as the powder that gave light for each exposure went off again and again, filling the air with acrid smoke that made her eyes water, she began to wonder when it would end.

Ramon, when it came his turn, engaged the harassed photographer in a conversation about the difficulties of taking photographs in the field and of the value of such records on the battlefields of the current conflict. It was a subject the man seemed to feel strongly about, and he settled down to his business, taking with unruffled calm the clowning of Peter and the others as they struck Napoleonic and Admiral Nelson poses for posterity. Nevertheless, it was the contention of the young Englishmen, propounded almost before the door of the photographer's shop had closed behind them, that Lorna had been the cause of the man's initial lack of composure. Her fatal beauty had completely upset his equilibrium, they declared, and they would not be convinced otherwise, no matter how she protested.

Luncheon, served in a brick-floored court in the shade of a fresh venerable oak, consisted of turtle soup, rare roast beef, fresh-baked bread, new potatoes in a cream sauce with scallions, and trifle. It was a hilarious affair, with the quips and the wine flowing in equal proportions. Lorna, her sides aching from laughing, watched them as they lounged along the table there in the court, their faces dappled by the sunlight falling through the leaves of the trees, limning the unconscious daring and quick intelligence found in each one. They were never still, never silent, a tightly knit group bound by the camaraderie of kinsmen in a strange country, engaged in a dangerous calling. She found herself thinking, as she let her gaze move from one to the other, of the trip they must all make back down the Cape Fear River and out past the guns of the blockade squadron on the run back to Nassau. How many of them would make it? A year from now, as the blockade tightened and the danger increased by slow degrees, how many would still be alive? How many would remain in memory only as the fading images on pieces of photographic cardboard?

A species of superstitious horror gripped her for an instant, and she shivered, reaching for her wineglass. It was a relief when Peter glanced at his pocket watch, announcing it was time they made their way toward the auction house if they intended to watch the proceedings.

Lorna had never been to an auction. She was intrigued by the marvelous variety of merchandise standing in bundles, boxes, and barrels from spirits to soft diaper linen for infants, each tagged with their lot numbers and arranged along the sides of the great open room. She looked with interest at the podium and lines of stiff, uncomfortable chairs, and at the men and women who promenaded slowly around the room, pausing now and then to finger a piece of cloth or sniff at a sample of an open vial of perfume or a box of spice. It was difficult, given the amplitude of the goods and the prosperous look of the people, to remember that there was a war on and a blockade in force. That was, until the bidding started.

The auctioneer was hefty and balding; the men aiding him to spot and keep tracks of bids in the audience, eagle-eyed and brisk bordering on rudeness. The selling process began in an orderly enough fashion, with an item, such as a bolt of cloth, being held up while the pitch was made in the fast-running, smooth-tongued request for bids. Then, as again and again the bid was pushed up higher than bidders could pay or the crowd thought reasonable, men began to mutter and women to cry. A rough-clad farmer shouted his contempt; a woman fainted. Two gentlemen, both claiming the high bid, went at each other with their canes, while their wives screamed and hid their faces in their hands. A pair of women who could not be classed as ladies both tried to take possession of a length of tulle edged with silver lamé ribbon. Before they could be separated, they had torn each other's bonnets off and stamped them on the floor, ripping flounces from bodices, dragged hair improvers from curls, and were clawing at each other's faces. The auctioneer pounded his table for order, his helpers shouted, and men with muskets in their hands poured in a back door to stand before the bales of tea, sacks of coffee, and other foodstuffs as the crowd surged in that direction.

Order was finally restored, but those moments of turmoil had been enough to show the fear that lurked behind the pretense of normality, the desperate need to hoard against an uncertain future, the grasping after the things that represented accustomed luxury in the pretense that it was not, could not, be threatened.

Lorna had seen all she cared to see but did not like to suggest leaving since Ramon would feel obligated to escort her. Her head began to ache with the constant chant of the auctioneer, the shouts of the men helping him, and the closeness of the packed room. A few seats down from where they sat, a back-country farmer with a plug of tobacco in his jaw chewed rhythmically, squirting the juice between his teeth into a cuspidor he held between his feet. The odor of the brass container, the monotonous regularity of his bending to spit, the sound of it striking into the nearly full cuspidor, affected her with aversion.

Then came the turn at the auction table for the bonnets Ramon had stacked in the cabin of the *Lorelei*.

They were not to be sold singly but as a whole lot. With the announcement, pandemonium broke out. Women wept and pleaded, their cries rising piteously as several of the Parisian confections were unpacked. There was one of pink straw lined with gathered rose satin and tulle and with a spray of silk roses under the brim. Another was cunningly made of moss green velvet over a wire frame with an open back to expose a woman's coiffure, and with a fluttering, dipping garnishment of peacock and marabou feathers. The third and most fascinating was of black satin swathed in veiling and featuring a spray of jet flowers that lay along the crown and extended on fine wires so that they would lie in the center of the wearer's forehead.

The bidding started high and went higher. There were six or seven merchants competing in the beginning; they were gradually weaned out to three, then only two. The sobs and sighs died away as the price rose to astronomical heights. Woman sat frozen, while their men looked at each other in grim disbelief. Nothing bidded on so far had brought such sums, not tea or chocolate, not bread flour, not material for summer clothing, not tanned leather for shoes. That so much of the resources of a strangling economy should be squandered on something so frivolous, so unnecessary, was appalling, even treasonous, and yet there was not a woman in the room who would not have bartered her soul for one of the bonnets, and not a man who would not have spent his last penny to get it for her.

The hammer fell. The bonnets were sold to a self-satisfied merchant who was immediately besieged by women demanding to know when they would be put up for sale. In the confusion, Lorna stood and, stepping over Peter's feet before he could move, made her way toward the door. Ramon caught up with her, catching her arm in a strong grasp, hauling her to a halt while he pushed open the door for her. When they were outside on the sidewalk, he swung her to face him.

"What is it? Are you ill?"

Tight-lipped, stony eyed, she stared at him. "No."

His dark gaze raked her face, as if searching for signs of the illness he feared. He lifted a thick brow, his features hardening. "It was the bonnets, then."

"Yes, the bonnets! Why did you bring them? Why did you have to make such useless things a part of your cargo?"

"Because, as you saw, it's what women want."

"But they don't need them! They will spend money that could be used so much better for food and clothing, or to supply our soldiers."

"I don't force them to buy them," he answered, his voice threaded with temper held firmly in check.

"Maybe not, but the choice was yours, to bring them or to leave them for something more valuable!"

He studied her, a grim light in his eyes. "It isn't really the bonnets, is it? It's the money."

"Why shouldn't it be?" she demanded. "You have enriched yourself by preying on the weakness of women for pretty things in an ugly time. It's not fair; in fact, it's cruel."

"Why? If the women can afford it, and it helps them to make the best of the stupid quarrels of men? They can cheer just as loudly with a new bonnet on as they could deprived of such things."

"You don't understand," she said, her gray gaze direct, "or is it that you just don't want to?"

Stepping around him, she drew her skirts aside from contact with his boots and swung down the sidewalk. He plunged after her, catching her in a few quick strides, blocking her path.

"I have never pretended to be a glory boy, ready to wave the flag and lead a suicide charge. You knew that before you came on this run. If you didn't expect to see evidence of my mercenary habits, then you should have stayed in Nassau."

She gave him a cold stare, moving around him once more. "I suppose I should."

"And worn that riding habit of yours while you earned your living," he called after, his tone grating.

She stopped for a stunned instant as she realized that he meant to remind her he was supporting her, and on money earned running the blockade. She whirled to face him, her eyes dark with fury and shame. "That can be done too."

"Lorna—" he began, reaching out, the rage leaving his face, to be replaced by wary regret. But she did not listen. Swinging around again so fast that the hoops of her crinoline dipped and swayed, she left him there in front of the auction barn.

The run back to Nassau was hardly a rest cure for the nerves but was without major incident. One of the greatest requirements for a successful runner of the blockade was impudence, the quality of intelligent daring. Ramon had that in full measure.

To break through the line of federal ships that guarded the entrance to Cape Fear on their way out, the scheme hit upon by him and his officers was simple, but sublime. The federal flagship remained in place during the night, while the remainder of the fleet cruised up and down the coast. Because of this, there was a small area around the flagship that was left unguarded. The *Lorelei* moved down the river in the afternoon of their third day in port, creeping up until she could lie hidden behind Fort Fisher. A boat was sent ashore to discover the latest news of the positions of the ships. Then, with the fall of good darkness, they slipped from concealment and steamed for the federals.

They passed the flagship in deepest silence, close enough to hear the sound of a harmonica coming from her decks, but put her behind them without incident. A short time later, they saw a frigate toiling past in belligerent majesty some two hundred yards away. They stopped dead still to allow her to pass, then threshed onward without further incident. Toward daylight, they saw bales of Sea Island cotton floating in the water, where some unfortunate comrade of the sea had been forced to jettison at least his deck cargo. Some suggestion was made of picking up the bales, valued at several hundred dollars each, but it was concluded that there was no place on the ship to store them. So overloaded were they already that from a distance they must appear square and brown with baled cotton, and there was a standing order out to pray for fair weather into Nassau.

It had been Lorna's intention to remove herself from Ramon's cabin. That course proved unnecessary. He did not descend to it once during the three days of the voyage. Constant vigilance was the watchword, as they scanned the seas for sail or smoke, turning away from it until it was below the horizon each time it was sighted. Ramon stayed at his post, sleeping only in snatches, and then flinging himself down on the bales of cotton on the decks.

Lorna came upon him as she took the air on their final day at sea, after they had reached the relative safety of Bahamian waters. He lay sprawled on his stomach, exhausted, his face turned to one side. His features were marked with the strain of the last days, yet they were relaxed, almost boy-like in sleep. The wind rippled the linen of his shirt that was stretched over the rigid muscles of his back. It ruffled his dark hair and stirred the crisp curl that lay on his forehead. A peculiar tenderness rose unbidden inside her. She stretched out her hand with the impulse to brush back the curl as she had seen him do a thousand times.

Her fingers were within inches of him before she snatched them away. She was becoming maudlin. That would not do. Such a weakness was of no use to her, and might well be dangerous. A few feet away, her footsteps faltered and she looked back. The sight of his body sprawled over the bale awakened furtive memories of a rain-soaked afternoon, a flickering fire, a damp, deserted house. Heat flowed in her bloodstream, tingling along her nerves. With her face flaming and her eyes bleak, she turned and, deliberately conquering the need to run, moved away.

By the time they landed in Nassau, Lorna's trunk was packed and she was ready to go ashore. She did not intend to make a clandestine departure; still, it could not be denied that she was glad to see only Cupid in evidence when she emerged on the deck. Explaining that she would send for her things, she left the ship, picked her way across the wharf, and emerged on Bay Street.

Before her lay Parliament Square with its government buildings washed a delicate shade of salmon pink. If she crossed the street and walked straight uphill, past the massive buildings with their porticos and columns, which reminded her of Beau Repose, she would come to the Royal Victoria. Instead, she stood looking around her. It was mid-afternoon, and the wheeled traffic was thick on this main thoroughfare in spite of the rubble that lay here and there where new curbstones were being laid and more gas streetlamps erected. A dog, yelping, fled before a freight dray piled high with crates. A young native boy, a fruit peddler with a cherubic brown face and a sack of mangoes over his back, dodged in front of the fast-moving wagon, hooting at the driver. Two British sailors hanging from a buggy waved and called to her. Strolling toward her came a policeman in his white uniform. He noted her hesitation there on the street corner, glanced at the style of her gown, then stepped out into the street, holding up a gloved hand.

Traffic came to a halt with the rattle of traces and squeal of handbrakes. Horses neighed and drivers cursed. It would have been impossible, after that official courtesy, to refuse to cross, no matter what she meant to do afterward. Summoning a smile and a nod of appreciation for the policeman, she stepped into the white dust of the road and moved to the other side.

Somewhere nearby, perhaps three or four blocks beyond the hotel, in the vicinity of Government House, she thought there were lodgings. She was almost sure she had heard a man one day on the piazza mention them as being more reasonable in price than the hotel. If she could remove to something similar, then she could begin to look for work with which to keep herself. It was galling that she had not done so already in the weeks she had been in Nassau, that she had left herself open to the charge Ramon had leveled in his anger. She had no excuse, no one to blame except herself. It was difficult to see, now, why she had not made the effort. Surely she could not have wanted to be dependent on Ramon Cazenave?

The idea was ridiculous. She had been upset by everything that had happened, unable to think straight, that was all. Well, not anymore. Raising the parasol she carried, lifting the front of her skirts, she set out with a militant step to search for a room.

She did not find one. The tide of Confederate military and naval officers, diplomats, newspaper correspondents, advertisers of various goods and munitions, captains of the British navy, British civilians serving the blockade runners, speculators, gamblers, and ne'er-do-wells seeking an easy living where money was plentiful had filled every nook and cranny in the city. The only thing available was a single bed in a room smelling strongly of rats and with roaches crawling on the walls. Since the other four beds, empty at that hour, were to be occupied by four men, it was clearly unsuitable.

It was getting late. There was nothing to be done except return to the hotel for the night and try again in the morning.

By the time she had reached the hotel, the swift tropical night had fallen. The glow of lamplight shone like beacons from the French doors of the graceful building. The doors of the dining room stood open to the evening air, revealing the diners at their tables beneath the sparkling chandeliers, while the terrace outside was dim and cool, lit by lanterns in the palm trees. A soft, piercingly sweet sound of violins reached Lorna. Suddenly, she was aware of a deep weariness and an inexplicable welling up of tears.

She trod the path that led through the new garden toward the great silk cotton tree with its balcony. Mingling with the smell of damp earth where the gardener had been at work and the scent of growing things, she caught the odor of a cigar. It came from the balcony in the lower branches, she thought, for there was a red glow at that point. As she came even with it, she looked up. The last light in the sky fell on her upturned face.

An oath, harsh, little more than an unbelieving grunt, came from among the limbs of the tree. A man stood there, though he was no more than a solid shadow in the dimness. Lorna, startled herself, spoke a musical good evening. The man did not answer but stood staring after as she walked on toward the entrance of the hotel. She was in her room, preparing to ring for supper, when finally she placed the voice. The man who had been so surprised, so shocked to see her, was Nate Bacon.

She got an early start the next day. She called first on Sara Morgan to report the success of her mission, and found that lady feeling well enough to be thinking of returning to England as soon as she had hired a nurse to care for her on the journey. The task of aiding the Confederacy, she said, could not be carried out in Nassau. Lorna was almost of the opinion that her own task of finding a room was also impossible in Nassau.

Her efforts took her along Bay Street a number of times. She was there to see the *Bonny Girl* arrive and to hear from a stevedore the story of how she had been chased ninety miles off course by a federal cruiser before she could haul for home. From a distance, she saw Ramon. It appeared that he was making the *Lorelei* ready to run again, despite the fact that the moon had changed. Three days to unload and take on another cargo was considered dispatch, she knew, which meant that he would probably be taking the ship out again in two days' time. That information was the sole result of her day.

She saw Peter the following afternoon. His ship had sustained a hit near the waterline that had caused problems with the engine. With the delay for repairs, he would not be going out again. She did not mention her quest. He might have been able to help, but he still believed, or pretended to, in the polite fiction of her uncle who paid her expenses. Since she was not prepared to confide in him, she could see no point in raising questions to which she could tender no truthful answers.

She was having breakfast on the morning of the third day, sitting alone at a table on the terrace, when she saw Nate Bacon again. He noticed her at the same time and changed his course, coming to stand with one hand resting on the stiffly starched white linen of her table, the other holding his high-crowned hat, and his back to the sun.

"You are looking well, Lorna," he said, his voice grave. "You are rested from your trip to Wilmington?"

She ignored his pleasantry, reaching for the knife to butter her roll. "How did you know I had gone?"

"There must be few in Nassau who don't know. Cazenave is

the hero of the hour in Nassau, one of the dashing blockade runner captains who can do no wrong, and this is a small place, a provincial backwater. You were seen boarding his ship, and seen returning. The only question is whether you went for love or for money.''

"I beg you pardon!"

"Forgive me, I put that badly," he said, his voice bland, though the look in his pale blue eyes was not. "I meant to say there was some idea that you may have had an investment in the run, since you are known to be living here on the bounty of a wealthy uncle."

He meant her to know he was aware of the lies that secured her place in Nassau society. But could it be that his snide remarks also indicated his ignorance of her real purpose in traveling on Ramon's ship? Whatever the reason for them, she had no intention of being drawn out. His reaction to her return had caused a virulent suspicion that he might have some knowledge of how the federals had come to learn of her trip as a courier. She could think of no way to prove or persuade him to admit it, however. She turned her attention to his question.

"Let us say," she said, a smile curving her mouth with a hint of fond remembrance, "that I went along for the pleasure."

His face darkened, but the waiter, a long apron tied about his waist and covering his dark trousers, approached to refill her coffee cup, and Nate could not speak for long moments. When the man had gone, Nate put his hand on the back of the chair across from her, saying abruptly, "May I join you?"

She looked at the chair, then raised a limpid gaze to his face. "I think not."

"You little bitch," he said softly.

It was odd that his virulence left her unmoved. Not so long ago, she would have been upset, thrown into dismay. Now she calmly picked up her coffee cup. "If that is the way you feel, I'm surprised that you care to speak to me."

"I would like to do more than that to you."

"That would be difficult here in public. I suggest you go, before I call the waiter and tell him you are annoying me."

He stood staring down at her. There was a quality of menace in his silence that affected her much more than his threats. She wished she could see his expression, but the glare of the sun behind him made his features dim. She set down her cup and it rattled in the saucer. Turning her head, she looked about her for the waiter.

"All right, I'm going," Franklin's father said, "but this isn't the end of it. I thought I could ignore you, since you were so well guarded; that I could get on with transferring my holdings into gold and strike out for Yankee country. There were things more important than a beautiful blonde bitch, even if she did kill my son. I thought I could see to it you paid the price, and that would satisfy me. I was wrong. There's something unfinished between us, and I mean to finish it.

She gave an unsteady laugh. "Fine words. The people of Nassau have little use for people who trade with the Yankees. The government here, to say nothing of the men in gray I've seen, might be interested in knowing your plans. I would be careful if I were you."

"Are you threatening me, Lorna? I hope not. It would be most unwise, considering your own past."

She traced the rim of her coffee cup with a finger. "I wonder who they would be most interested in, a murderess or a traitor?"

"I somehow doubt," he said, a savage undertone to his humor, "that we will find out. On the other hand, you can be sure that I will get my hands on you, alone, someday. Soon."

He left her, striding from the terrace back into the dining room. After a time, Lorna picked up her fork, pushing at the piece of pineapple left on her plate. She bit into her roll, but it was dry, nearly choking her. Lifting her coffee cup, she sipped at the liquid, It was cold and bitter.

Lorna's encounter with Nate left her disturbed, chilled in spirit. She could not seem to bring herself to consider what she must do. She kept to her room, tending to her scanty wardrobe, rinsing out a few things, sending others to be laundered. She stared out the French doors, watching the harbor; looked over the books she had brought from Ramon's shelf in the cabin, and paced, stopping now and then—too often for her peace of mind— to stare at the portraits of Peter and Ramon and herself that had been made that day in Wilmington.

It was a comfort to have the guards in the hall at the end of the veranda, all within call. She had been inclined to resent their presence when they had reappeared on her return, had been tempted to send them away with a sharp message for Ramon. No longer.

If she were able to find another place, would her guards follow her? Would Nathaniel Bacon? Or would she be safer, more anonymous, away from the hotel? She could not decide, and so abandoned the idea of looking further that day. Instead, she concentrated on the prospect of employment. An idea formed slowly in the back of her mind, one connected with Peter's frequent lament concerning his ever declining supply of shirts. She would have to present it to Mrs. Carstairs to see what she thought.

It was peculiar that she had not heard from the Lansings since her return. Or perhaps it was not. She had suspected it was Ramon who had insisted on her name being added to their guest list. If he no longer pressed it, then Charlotte and Elizabeth would doubtless be glad to overlook her. That she should feel hurt by the omission was silly. She was nothing to the Lansings, nor they to her. Instead of letting herself be seduced by such petty concerns, she had best be trying to remedy her situation, even if it had grown late in the day.

Mrs. Carstairs was not in. The door of her shop was wreathed in black crepe, and the maid who answered said that she had been called away to one of the out islands, to Abaco, she thought, for the funeral of a relative. As she was turning away, a carriage pulled up.

It was Peter who jumped down and strode toward her. "There you are! They said at the hotel that you had gone out, and I've been looking for you everywhere. Come on, we haven't a moment to waste."

"What is it?" she asked, as he took her arm and hustled her toward the carriage.

"There's an opera troupe in town on their way to Boston. They will stage one performance of Verdi's *La Traviata*, and one only. We don't want to miss it!"

They didn't, though Lorna flung herself into her gown with only the most sketchy rinse of her face, and they snatched a dinner of fried grouper and chips at a stand near the docks, eating them with their fingers while the carriage rolled away. The music was marvelous, the soprano who sang the difficult role of Violetta, the tragic Lady of the Camellias, superb. The ending brought tears to Lorna's eyes, even as she took pleasure in the evening's escape from her own problems. Peter took out his handkerchief and, complaining in mock exasperation, dried her tears with gentle care.

It was while they were moving slowly toward the exit doors, caught in the crush of people made more difficult by the enormous circumference of the ladies' skirts, that Lorna saw Ramon. He was escorting Charlotte, with Elizabeth moving ahead of them on the arm of a man in the extremely correct evening attire of a diplomat. Edward Lansing and his wife followed. Ramon was staring at Lorna with clenched jaws. As he met her gaze, he looked away to Peter, and the expression that smouldered for a moment in his eyes was murderous.

Charlotte, chatting away, noticed suddenly that his attention had wandered. She followed his gaze, and a haughty mein descended upon her. She looked through Lorna as if she were not there, then tapped Ramon's arm with her fan in an imperious gesture so at odds with her usual vivacity that it made her seem extremely young. He turned back at her summons, bending his dark head as he listened to her.

Lorna felt herself go hot, then cold. Charlotte had cut her as if she had been a social pariah. Such a thing had never happened to her. She could not believe it. Was it possible she had been mistaken? Could it be that the younger Lansing sister had been moved by spite because she knew Lorna had gone with Ramon to Wilmington? That must be it.

It might be cowardly, but she would as soon not give Elizabeth and her mother the opportunity to treat her in the same manner. She wondered if Peter had seen. She sent him a glance from under her lashes as they reached the door, and saw that his long, narrow face was set in lines of unguarded anger. With his usual quickness, he caught her oblique regard. Forcing a smile, he began to complain in put-upon tones of people who could not bear to miss any entertainment offered, who were inconsiderate enough to fill up the aisles of theaters and music halls, and snarl traffic with all their carriages when he wanted to get to his.

He fell silent when they reached the hotel. With his hand under her elbow, he moved with her across the lobby and up one side of the double staircase. Lorna, trailing her fingers along one side of the mahogany railing, was aware of his preoccupation as they reached the first landing and rounded the upper newel to mount the second flight of stairs. By the time they had mounted to the third floor, the feeling had become oppressive. She nodded to the uniformed Negro guard who stopped in the hall halfway between the door of her room and the arched entrance to the piazza, murmuring a quiet good night. Tall and slender, but wiry, he answered respectfully. His gaze remained on the man at her side, however, a fact of which Peter, from his glance of irritation, was well aware. At her door, he took her key and inserted it into the lock, turning it. With his hand on the knob, preventing her entering, he said, "Lorna, I must talk to you."

"All right," she answered.

"Seriously, my love."

Something portentous in his manner warned her this would indeed be no light discussion, even as she heard the lilt of humor in his endearment. "Oh."

He sighed. "Your joy and anticipation unmans me, but I will persevere. Will you have dinner with me tomorrow night, here, in the hotel dining room?"

She stared up at him, meeting his dark blue gaze with an uncomfortable feeling of guilt. "You have been good to me, Peter, and I like you, but I hope I've given you no reason to think—"

He shook his head. "Very little. But I would as soon not discuss it here with your watchdog looking over my shoulder. Dinner?"

"Yes, I suppose so." How could she refuse so reasonable a request? She had the feeling that she should have done so, but it was too late now.

He pushed open her door, then took her hands, pressing his lips to first one, then the other with an endearing lack of self-consciousness, for an Englishman. Releasing her, he stepped back. His voice low, he said, "Until then."

"Yes. Good night, Peter."

He did not reply, but stood watching her as she closed the door. It was a moment before she heard his footsteps receding, fading down the hall.

It was a warm night, giving a hint of the summer to come. Lorna wandered to the washstand and put down her purse, then began removing her gloves. Throwing them down, she moved to the French doors and set them wide to the night air, leaving the jalousies open since there was so little wind stirring. She stood for a moment, staring out at the scattered lights of the city, watching the riding lights on a ship at anchor in the harbor, a coal barque from Newcastle she thought, ready to restock the bunkers of the ships in the harbor. Some of the runners would be leaving tonight, perhaps even the *Lorelei*.

She swung from the French doors. She felt unsettled, on edge. She didn't want to think of Ramon and his ship, or of Peter, of what had occurred this evening, or the untenable position in which she found herself. She wished with sudden fierceness for oblivion. The thought of laudanum drops, such as her aunt had sometimes given her daughters for headaches, toothaches, and their monthly cramping, registered briefly. She had none, however, and no way of getting any at this time of night. Perhaps a bath would soothe her disturbed senses and provide a degree of composure. It must at least help her to feel fresher.

The only trouble was that after the long trek to the bathroom and her submersion in the tepid water, all that was available at that time of night, she was even wider awake than before. Wearing her nightgown of handkerchief lawn with small cap sleeves, and a low-cut, tucked bodice fastened with tiny pearl buttons, she settled down beneath the mosquito netting to try to read.

It was difficult at first, but slowly she became absorbed. Time crept past. At last her eyes began to burn. Putting the book aside, she blew out the lamp, adjusting the sheet over the lower half of her body, and closed her eyes.

As if at a signal, it began, the haunting melody of a guitar coming through the open doorway. Lorna sat up to listen. She had not heard it since her return from the run. She had missed it at first, that midnight serenade, then had thought no more of it. Now the leashed passion of it seemed to strike inside her, tearing at her emotions. It soared in fervent rapture, then sank to throbbing anguish; it commanded and enticed, grated in vital dominance and shredded her heart with such piercing sweetness that she felt the rise of tears—and something more, the flaming touch of desire.

Flinging herself back down on the bed, she caught her pillow and turned onto her stomach with it held over her head to blot out the sound. Still she heard it, almost as if the sound could penetrate the sensitive surface of her skin, vibrating inside her mind, seeping into the marrow of her bones. She cringed inside, torn with a longing that she could not deny, with the need of one man. How could she feel so about him when she could not respect him. when she despised his grasping and cynical nature? It was degrading that she could not control her mental and physical responses. Memories stalked her of Ramon's arms about her, his mouth upon hers, his hands . . . With a stifled moan, she drew up her knees, curling into a ball, her raised arms pressing the pillow to her ears.

She was not sure when the music stopped. Had it died away

gradually or ended with an abrupt flurry of chords? The echoes of it seemed to resound in her ears still, though she knew it for nothing more than an errant fancy. Slowly, she rolled to her back. She released the pressure on the pillow, staring wide-eyed into the dark, listening. No, the serenade was over; she could sleep, Sighing, she relaxed and let her eyelids fall shut.

The noise came a few minutes later. Like the rattle of metal against wood, it had a familiar sound. It seemed to come from outside, at some distance down the veranda, perhaps even on the piazza. Her brows drew together in a puzzled frown. She had heard something similar not too long before. It was not a common noise, not something you heard every day. Where had she heard it? When? She could not recall. How maddening, when it was such a simple thing. Lately she had been here at the hotel, and aboard the *Lorelei*, of course. The squeaks and moans and rattles of a ship were a bit unusual but fairly constant things. The whinning and explosions of shelling had been new, startling, quite unlike anything. . . .

It couldn't be. It couldn't. Her mind was playing tricks. And yet, she would swear that that rattle of metal on wood, suddenly cut off, was exactly like the sound made by the grappling hooks the federals had thrown to secure their small crafts against the side of the *Lorelei* before boarding. Sharp-pronged, the grapnels had bitten into the wood of the deck railing before being pulled taught by their attached ropes.

Her breath caught in her throat. She sat up, swinging her legs from the bed, starting toward the French doors. At that moment, a shadow moved in the opening, detaching from the darkness of the night, etched against the gray velvet of the sky. It was the height, the shape, of a man.

She drew breath to scream. At that first soft sound, he swung toward her, launching himself at her white shape in the dimness. A hard arm snaked around her waist, bruising her ribs as he snatched her off her feet, dragging her backward against him. His hands clamped over her mouth, smothering her cry. She writhed in his arms, painfully aware of how powerless she was against his superior strength. Ignoring her struggles, he held her. She felt his chest shudder in what might have been a laugh of satisfaction. He leaned to whisper against her ear.

"Is this any way to greet a dream lover?"

Chapter 16

She went still. Ramon. Relief swept her, and with it the shock of outrage. Hard on their heels came the realization of what he had said. That foolish fantasy. Why in the name of heaven had she ever confided it to him? Why? It had become, in his skilled and callous hands, a weapon.

"That's better," he murmured, and slowly decreased the pressure on her mouth, lifting his hand away.

"What are you doing here?" she demanded.

"I came at the request of a lady."

His breath was warm against her cheek, his voice husky. He lowered his hand until it came to rest on the curve of her breast above the clasp of his forearm. Through the thin material of her nightgown, she could feel the hard pressure of the muscles of his legs against the backs of her thighs. The clean male smell of him was in her nostrils, along with the salt tang of the sea and the fresh scent of the night. Weakness crept along her limbs, an insidious thing, as if desire were a form of poison. Trying to banish its debilitating effects, she shook her head so that her unbound hair dipped and swayed like a curtain of soft spun silk around her. "No."

"Oh, but yes."

"You are mistaken."

"No. Such a thing, I could not forget. And if you say that

you have, *chérie*, remember that I can feel your heartbeat, and if you lie I will know it.''

Routed from her position before she had even taken it, she was forced to other defenses. Her voice cold, she said, ''Let me go.''

''So you can scorn me and flay me with words. Never.'' He rubbed his cheek against her hair, moving the fine strands aside to nuzzle her ear.

''You . . . you think that this is all you have to do, to touch me, and my resolve will melt so you can do as you will.''

''It isn't your resolve,'' he said, his low voice etched with certainty, ''that interests me.''

Her body was on fire, and it was a desperate effort not to press herself against him in surrender. From the depths of her self-disgust she cried, ''But I despise you!''

''Don't you think I know that?'' The words were rasping as his hold tightened. ''It doesn't matter. I have no resolve, and little pride of the kind that would keep me from you. I am a man bewitched. The need of you is a torment beyond bearing. To stay away is more than I can do, though I tried.''

''Oh, yes, you wanted to see me so badly that you could barely force yourself to go to the opera tonight with Charlotte Lansing instead!'' Any weapon would do as a means of protection.

''Were you jealous?''

''I? Don't be ridiculous!''

''Why else should you mind?''

His thumb was brushing the peak of her breast. She shivered. A ragged sound in her voice, she said, ''I didn't mind! I . . . I only meant to say that I don't believe you have been pining for me.''

''I was jealous,'' he admitted, his voice pensive. ''I could have seen Peter drawn and quartered with pleasure, have hanged him myself from the yardarm, or ordered him keel-hauled.''

''Am I supposed to care? I want nothing to do with you. Nothing.''

''Is that why your heart is fluttering like a wild thing under my hand?''

''Get out,'' she cried. ''Get out and leave me alone!''

''After going to such effort to come to you? How can you suggest it?''

He shifted his grasp and she felt herself lifted with his arms beneath her knees. He turned toward the white bulk of the bed and strode to duck beneath the looped mosquito netting, placing her on the yielding surface of the mattress. The moment she felt its softness, she threw herself from him, sliding, reaching for the other side. He lunged after her, pinning her to the bed with his weight. With the fury of a cornered wildcat, she struck for his face. He turned his head so that her fingers sank into his thick hair. She closed her hand, only to have him catch her wrist, snatching her grasp free. He had her other arm beneath him. Shifting to put his knee across her flailing legs, he lowered his head then, seeking her mouth.

His victory had been so easy. Panting with exertion, trembling with rage and something more that she refused to name, she waited until his lips touched hers, then she sank her teeth into the lower one.

He jerked back, his elbow sliding on the satin length of her hair that was spread around them. He shifted, and his shoulder with his weight behind it pressed into her breast. She gave a soft moan of pain.

Instantly, he pushed from her, swearing under his breath. He released her and wrenched himself to a sitting position on the side of the bed. A moment later, he came erect and moved to the French doors, where he stood in the opening with one hand braced on the frame and his head down, his breathing harsh.

Over his shoulder, he said, "I'm sorry. I never meant to hurt you."

With his retreat, his sudden freeing of her, she felt peculiar, almost as if she had been deserted. She drew her knee up and turned to her side to stare at his tall figure silhouetted against the sky in the window frame, at his square shoulders and bent head. As if the words were forced from her, she said, "I know."

"I didn't mean it now, nor that afternoon at Beau Repose, and especially not when I brought you to Nassau. It was just . . . something it seemed I had to do. You have every right to blame me, even to hate me."

With the threat of physical coercion removed, she could think rationally once more. She ran her tongue over her lips, sending him another swift glance. "I don't—hate you, that is."

He turned slowly, his movements concentrated, as if he were weighing the sound of her words. "But you blame me."

"Not entirely." Honesty compelled the answer. If she had not gone riding that earlier afternoon, if she had turned and left the deserted house the instant she had heard the sound of his guitar, if she had stated plainly that she would not permit intimacies, then her position might now be different. It might, in fact, be worse.

"I want you," he said, the words strained. "The need of you is like a fever in my blood. I could force you to respond to me, or take my pleasure without it, but that isn't what I want."

She could deny nothing he had said. Wasn't the turmoil fading from her veins proof that he had only to touch her to bring forth a response, regardless of the strength of her will? And she could not claim that it was the frustration of being denied the pleasures of the body that drove her. Peter's touch had left her unmoved beyond the warmth of compassion and friendship. Still, she said nothing; there were times when it was best not to press honesty too hard.

His clothing rustled as he moved toward her. The foot of the bed sagged, the bed ropes complaining, as he put one knee upon it. "I would ask you to forget what has been between us. Pretend, if you will, that this is no more than a dream. Make me a part of it, *chérie*. Permit me to share your dream with you; only that, nothing more."

No doubt he meant what he said, for the moment. The trouble was that the moment would pass, and then what? His plea, passionate though it might be, had contained no hint of permanence; if anything, quite the opposite. And yet, the night was dark and soft, and the need to become lost in it strong. Given the flaws in his character and her reaction to them, was she certain she wanted to be with him always? If not, how could she fault him for not offering something she did not want?

Even as she considered, he closed his warm hand upon her ankle. He sat down on the bed and leaned to rest his weight on his elbow, his thumb moving in slow circles upon the sensitive instep of her foot. It was an oddly soothing motion, certainly not as if he were touching her more intimately. She lay still, hearing the strength and timbre of his plea echoing in her mind. She did not want to deny it, but how could she agree? Whether from an urge to distract him, or herself, she finally spoke.

"They say you will be making another run."

"Yes."

"When?"

"Tonight."

"So soon?"

"It has to be soon or not at all." His voice was steady. His fingers inched higher, stroking her ankle, circling it, his grip so sure that she felt it would be difficult to break. He bent his head and pressed his lips to the delicate arch of her instep. She felt the moist flick of his tongue.

She controlled a shiver. "You . . . you will be going to Wilmington again?"

"Uhmm."

His breath, ticklish and warm, touched her ankle. His tongue flicked the hollow just below it. So novel was the sensation that it was a moment before she realized his hand had crept higher, pushing aside the hem of her nightgown, massaging her calf and the turn underneath her knee.

"Your cargo," she said, grasping at a subject, "is it a dangerous one?"

"Hardware."

It sounded innocuous enough, but she knew that was the term used on the manifests of the runners to indicate arms and munitions consigned to the Confederate government. Her voice almost a whisper, she said, "Gunpowder?"

"Not this time. And no bonnets."

The last barely penetrated the lassitude that had crept over her. "Are you certain it's safe enough? The moon is nearly at the quarter already."

"Why? Are you worried that I might have to stay in Wilmington until the next dark moon?" His hands were upon her thighs, the heated wetness of his mouth at the bend of her knee.

"It could happen," she said, the words little more than a whisper, "if the reloading is slow."

"It won't be, I'll have to sail under a half moon, but will gain and leave port before moonrise."

"But the risk!"

"They won't be expecting us. We'll catch them napping."

"Ramon, no, I—" She scarcely knew to what she meant to object, his going, his calculations of the moon phases, or the insistent, invasive play of his hand.

"Yes, *chérie?*" he mocked her gently, a husky note in his voice.

The hem of her nightgown was at her waist, his touch, feather-light, ceaselessly caressing, was on her hips, while he gently nipped the tender skin of her inner thigh with his teeth. She moaned, a low sound instantly stifled. She put her hand on his shoulder, trying to halt his upward progress. He paid no heed, and after a moment her fingers spread, closing on the knotted muscles she found there.

His hold tightened, drawing her toward him, and he pressed his face to her, seeking and finding the warm, honeyed entrance to the depths of her body. He slid his hands to the slender indentation of her waist, spanning it, kneading, hovering over the fluttering muscles of her abdomen. Gently marauding, inescapable, they moved to the mounds of her breasts that shuddered with the pounding of her heart, fastening upon them, teasing the nipples until she was caught in a triangle of fire, her pulse leaping with molten desire.

She wanted him; she could not help herself. She arched toward him, her leg muscles stiff and her breath sobbing in her throat. She plucked at his shirt, and with slow reluctance he released her, shifting to draw her nightgown off over her head. She helped him then to divest himself of his own clothing, pausing as she explored in sensual wonder the ready maleness of his body. Then he caught her to him, molding her to his hard length.

She took his face between her hands, setting her mouth to his in hunger, boldly probing its firm contours with the tip of her tongue, thrusting inside. His grasp tightened, and he rolled with her, bringing her on top of him. He ran his hand down the tapering slimness of her back to her hips, and, twining her legs with his own spread them wide as he pressed into her.

The scented cloak of her hair fell forward around them. Of her own accord, she moved upon him, wanting, needing that sweet and fervid friction. Pleasure mounted to her brain, intoxicating, overriding thought. He aided her, his hands encouraging, inflaming, taking the strain of her weight from her. She was soaring in an ageless rhythm, transfigured with the delight that sang in her veins. Only her own frailty, her inability to sustain the pace, held her earthbound.

He shifted, turning with her so they lay on their sides, gently but surely taking from her the responsibility for her pleasure, and his own. He stepped up the pace, making it faster, more vital, so that she clung to him, motionless, suspended in splendor, feeling the dissolving of her being. Love was an ache, a joy, inside her and she buried her face in his neck, whispering his name, parting her lips to taste the salt of his skin.

With a hoarse sound in his throat, he heaved himself up and over, turning her to her back. His penetration was deep and violent. The shock of his thrusts rippled over her in waves of pleasure. Her eyes flew open and she caught his arms, feeling their trembling as she rose to meet him. Together they strove with fevered effort and hoarse, ragged gasps for air. The surface of their skin burned and perspiration made their bodies slippery to the touch.

It burst upon her abruptly, a wondrous thing, a tumult of the senses that defied petty reason, a voluptuous reveling in bodily gratification, bliss so intense it affected the nerves, being perilously near pain; joy that verged on despair.

With a strangled cry, Lorna went still, her fingers frozen on Ramon's arms. He gathered himself and plunged deep, pressing her down, holding her as the dark explosion gripped them.

Long moments later, he eased from her and rolled to his side. He drew her against him, freeing the ends of her hair, smoothing back the tangled tresses from her face as her head lay pillowed on his shoulder. His chest rose and fell in a sigh of deep contentment. He was still. Lorna's hand clenched his side, then relaxed. Like one near unconsciousness, she slept.

It might have been a quarter of an hour or an hour later when she awoke. Ramon lay tense, listening, beside her. After a moment, she heard what had alerted him. It was the scrape of footsteps. They came from the veranda beyond the open French doors, though farther along, back toward the piazza from her room. There was about them a deliberate sound, as if someone was moving slowly, trying not to awaken the people sleeping. With each alternate step, there was the creak of strained shoe leather.

Ramon brushed a hand over her shoulder in reassurance, then with swift grace rolled from the bed. He found his trousers and slipped into them, then pulled on his boots, his head up, listening. He moved to stand between the two French doors, his back to the wall. Turning his head, he pressed back until he could see out the left door.

The footsteps came nearer, almost creeping. Ramon's tall form merged with the still darkness. The breeze from the sea moved into the room, causing the mosquito netting to sway. It brought with it the night coolness and the soft rustle of the palms in the garden, which sounded a little like falling rain. With wide and burning eyes, Lorna stared at the door opening, her hands clenched on the pillow that had somehow worked its way down beside her.

The slow creak came again, just outside. A shadow moved, looming large, then crossed the threshold into the room. Ramon lunged, grabbing an arm, twisting it behind the man's back. At the same time, he locked his other arm around the man's neck. There was a savage grunt and a curse; then all was still.

"The light," Ramon said.

Lorna scrambled erect, finding her nightgown, pulling it on without thought of whether it was right side out, snatching at her wrapper as she leaped from the bed and went toward the gas fixture. With fingers that trembled, she found matches and struck one, then removed the globe and held the flame to the burner before turning the key. Only then did she turn toward the two men at the French doors.

"Nate," she said. There was no surprise in the sound, only angry disgust.

In the glow of the gaslight, his face was contorted with rage, darkened by the blood that suffused his face from the strength of Ramon's grip on his throat. "Who did you expect, another of your precious blockade captains to bed you? I should have known one had preceded me when I found the rope and saw the outside guard missing."

The words ended in a shallow wheeze as Ramon's grip constricted his breathing still further. "Keep a civil tongue in your head, if you care about living," he advised in harsh tones.

Nathaniel Bacon was forced up onto his toes by Ramon's hold on him. His arrogance was scarcely troubled, however. "You won't harm me, not here. You may as well let me go before I decide to make trouble for you."

"You make trouble for me?" Ramon asked in grim amusement. "I wonder how Her Majesty's police would feel about a sneak thief creeping up and down the verandas of the Royal Victoria? Don't you think they might find that a bit suspect?"

"You would have to explain to them why you were here with our dear Lorna. You won't go to the officials." Nate raised a hand to the arm clamped at his throat, clawing at it.

"She isn't our Lorna," Ramon corrected with deadly softness. "She is mine."

"And who else's?"

Nate had lowered his hand. Even as he coughed, choking at the relentless increase of the pressure on his windpipe, his fingers went groping to the pocket of his waistcoat of grass green brocade.

Lorna guessed his purpose before she saw the glint of dark metal. She started forward, crying, "Look out, he has a gun!"

Ramon released his hold, throwing himself to the right even as Lorna's former father-in-law twisted around, pulling the trigger. The snub-nosed derringer went off with a shattering roar in the night's stillness. A pane of glass fell tinkling to the floor.

Hard on the sound, Ramon cannoned into Nate, driving him backward. They hit the floor with a resounding crash. The derringer flew from Nate's hand, skidding across the floor. Lorna dashed forward in a flurry of white batiste to scoop it up, then whirled out of the way as the two men wrestled on the floor.

From outside the room came the sound of running feet, the cries of awakened hotel guests. "Douse the light," Ramon snapped.

As she swung to obey, she saw the tight fury that darkened his face, the vicious strength that went into the blow he drove at Nate in the last rays of the fading light. The older man gave a groan; then all was quiet. She heard the thud plainly as he fell back against the floorboards.

Ramon sprang up, looking, groping for his shirt. He slung it around his neck, then spun back toward Nate. At that moment, a hard knocking began on the corridor door.

"Miss? Miss Forrester? Are you all right?"

Ramon leaned to grasp the lapels of Nate's jacket, heaving him up and over his shoulder. He swung toward the French doors, then pivoted back. His voice low, he said, "Answer them. Stall as long as you can, but don't take any chances."

"What shall I tell them?" she asked in dismay.

"Anything. Make up something, and don't forget the gunshot." He leaned to kiss her, a brief, hard salute on her lips parted in protest. Then he was gone.

"Miss Forrester?" As the call came again, the doorknob rattled.

"Yes, just a moment," she answered. "I . . . I'm not dressed."

She could not resist following Ramon to the French doors, watching as he moved like a burdened wraith along the veranda, merging with the darkness. Even as she whirled to go back inside, however, a woman screamed several doors down. A man in a nightshirt to his ankles and a tasseled cap appeared in a doorway. He stared fixedly at the dim movement where Ramon, with Nate on his shoulder, was straddling the railing, beginning his descent on the rope. As the hotel guest started along the veranda toward Ramon, Lorna cried out, running toward him, clutching his arm and babbling hysterically of intruders, prowlers, everything she could bring to mind. From the corner of her eye, she saw Ramon swing out, then disappear from sight.

"Here, I think I saw your intruder just there," the man said, trying to shake off Lorna's grasp. "He's getting away. Hey! You there!"

He was about to set the chase hard on Ramon's trail. There was only one thing she could do, and, without hesitation, she did it. She gave a low cry and swooned with boneless elegance into the man's arms. He held her for a stunned moment, his hold slowly tightening; then carefully, as if she were made of finest porcelain, he lowered her to the floor just inside the room from which he had come.

"Well!"

The man's wife, a woman of large girth made larger by a yoked nightgown with layers of ruffles and sleeves to the wrists, appeared in the doorway. With her fists on ample hips, she stared at Lorna, at her creamy shoulders sweetly curved above the rounded neckline of her nightgown with her wrapper falling open, and at her hair lying in shining splendor across her husband's arm as he held her.

"She fainted, pet," he said helplessly.

"Did she indeed?" Lorna, watching the woman through slitted eyes, saw her swell with indignation.

"She had a fright, I think. A man outside her room. Perhaps if you could bring your smelling salts?"

"A few drops of water in the face sometimes suffices," the woman declared with a voice of grim authority.

Lorna, seeing her step ponderously to the bedside carafe, pour a full glass, and start back, thought from the look of bland malice on the woman's face that it would be prudent if she revived by herself. Accordingly, she let her lashes flutter upward, sighing artistically. She looked around her, began to raise a hand to her face only to realize she still held the derringer and lowered it hastily again. She assumed an air of delightful confusion, frowned, then gave a realistic shudder, her gaze going to the woman now standing over her.

"Oh, Madam," she said. "It was a prowler, a murderer at the least, come to smother us in our beds and steal our jewelry.

I saw him outside my window and fired my little gun, but he got away.''

"So that was you who made that infernal racket?" the woman said, her small mouth pinched as if she tasted something sour.

"I saw the man, too, Martha," her husband said placatingly. "Looked like he was carrying something to me. What did you think, my de—uh, young lady?"

"I couldn't say, I'm sure. I just closed my eyes and pulled the trigger of my pistol as my dear uncle taught me. I don't think I even hit him, for there is a great hole in the glass of my door, and I don't know what the owners of the hotel will say about the damage." She gave a worried shake of her head, then brightened. "But perhaps I scared him away, which is the important thing, or so my uncle always says."

"Yes. Yes, indeed," the man agreed. "I expect we may all owe the safety of our valuables, if not our lives, to you, young lady."

"Humph," his wife said, her gimlet gaze on Lorna's shoulders where her husband still held her.

By that time, the veranda was filled with people, all talking at the same time. Lorna, shivering now with reaction, was happy to have the man she had accosted take over the task of explaining. Gaining her feet with his solicitous help, she turned from them all to the veranda railing, staring with anxiety as a group of men emerged from the hotel entrance down below and began to look around. Among them was the desk clerk, the night watchman, and, ironically, Lorna's own guard. They turned, shouting up, wanting to know if anyone had seen which way the prowler had gone. A man, down from where Lorna stood, pointed toward the harbor. Immediately she contradicted him, declaring that she had seen a definite movement on the carriage drive to the right. She turned to the man in the nightshirt, urging him to corroborate her observation. To her delight, he did so, though she was well aware that he had not so much as looked in that direction since she had latched hold of him. Her only worry was that Ramon, instead of striking for the harbor and the *Lorelei*, had actually gone in the direction she indicated.

By the next morning, it was plain that he had not, for though police constables had been called in and the streets combed until daylight, no sign of the prowler had been found. They had discovered Nate Bacon lying behind a grogshop on the lower end of Bay Street. He had smelled of cheap whiskey and his pockets were empty; not surprising, considering the locality in which he had been found. The questions put to him by the constables had been met with surly answers. He had no memory of how he had come to be where he was, he said, and did not consider the matter anybody's business except his own. Making his way to the docks after he was released, he was seen to stare in rage and chagrin at the place where the *Lorelei* had been tied up the night before.

It was Lorna who saw him. Unable to sleep after the turmoil, she had risen early, put on her clothes, and left the hotel. She had walked for a time but turned, finally, as if drawn, toward the harbor. Seeing Nate, she had hung back out of sight, coming out only after he had stalked away uphill toward the Royal Victoria. She stood for a long while, resting against a piling, gazing out at the blue-hazed North West Channel, where Ramon's ship had steamed away during the night. She watched the fishing boats going out, followed by clouds of gulls with the light of the rising sun on their wings. The shifting colors of the water were still a wonder as the sun grew stronger, filtering through its clear depths. As the haze on the water cleared, Hog Island loomed sharp and clear, so close a strong swimmer could reach it with little effort. The wind blew the smells of decaying conch shells and ripening fruit down the shoreline to vie with the smell of coffee and baking bread from somewhere nearby. It rustled the palms and sighed through the sea grape trees. Men woke and stretched where they had been sleeping rolled up in the lee of the warehouses. They shouted at each other with rough oaths and obscenities. When one, down the dock from where she stood, unbuttoned his trousers and began to attend to a necessary morning function against the trunk of a palm tree, she turned away. Gaining Bay Street, she swung west, walking aimlessly, leaving behind the hammering and sawing of construction just beginning.

Ramon was gone. He could not have delayed, not and been able to make the run with a chance of success. She had not expected him to stay behind after the fiasco of the night before; still, she felt numb, bereft, as if a part of her had been severed. Would it have been so terrible if he had elected not to make another run? Would it?

What was she going to do? Her lack of control when near Ramon was degrading, a bitter blow to her pride. He had only to touch her, anywhere, and she became weak and pliant in his hands. The sensuality that he brought forth within her was an affront. She did not want to be so aware of her body and its responses, to crave the feel of his under her hands. She wanted peace and order and self-respect. She wanted an end to this peculiar suspended feeling in her life. She wanted stability. She wanted love.

Ramon did not love her. He was obsessed with his need for her body, with the passion she evoked in him. He cared nothing for her as a person, had only contempt for the processes of her mind. It did not matter to him what she felt, whether she was abased by the strength of the desire he aroused in her, or whether his every act of possession drew tighter the bonds of love that held her. But if he did come to feel some more tender emotion toward her, what then? He had made it plain he had no place for a woman in his life—other than as a release, a convenience separate from the job that he was doing.

What would happen if she had ceased fighting him, if she succumbed to the lure of his desire for her and lived only to be with him when he wanted her? Could she bear such a life in the shadows, or would the sweetness of the times they shared change slowly to the bitterness of shame? She was certain, given her own strong sense of herself as a person of value, that what she feared most would happen but, oh, how tempting it was to throw caution into the sea and take the risk.

"Lorna!"

She turned at the sound of her name and saw Peter hastening after her. His smile was wry as he neared, removing his hat to sketch her a quick bow.

Her mouth curved in gentle mockery. "Looking for me again?"

"Conceited wench," he said, "Of course I was. I called to you three times just now, but you were so preoccupied you didn't hear."

"I'm sorry," she murmured. She took his arm, and they strolled, leaving the warehouses and shops behind, coming into the open road with only a straggling house or two on the left and the wide expanse of the sparkling turquoise ocean on their right. They spoke of the captains who had left on a second run, and of the engine repairs that had kept him from being among them—thus leaving him able, to his delight, to serve as her escort. He mentioned the opera, and so full had been the time since she had said good-bye to him the night before that it was a moment before she could recall it and enter into a discussion of its merits. In a few minutes, they came to a clump of sea grape trees growing beside the sea wall that had been erected just there. He stopped and dusted the top of the wall with his handkerchief before seating her and dropping down beside her.

Peter hesitated, as if choosing his words with care. "I understand there was some disturbance at the hotel last night."

"You are a master of understatement. Your British heritage, no doubt," she said, sending him a smiling glance. "The disturbance was a prowler. I shot at him."

"I take it you didn't hit him."

"Unfortunately, no." It was difficult to tell if he accepted her explanation at face value. She almost wished he would not, for she did not like abusing his trust.

"I didn't realize you kept a gun about your person. I would have been more careful how I conducted myself!"

She managed a smile for his sally. "It was a . . . recent acquisition, but I don't take it everywhere."

That much was certainly so. She still had the small weapon secreted in the drawer of the washstand. It gave her confidence to have it there; why, she could not have said. She had watched her uncle fire a much larger pistol once, watched him load and unload it, but had never handled one herself until the previous night.

"Did you get a look at the man?" he asked, the expression in his dark blue eyes serious.

She had been over this with the very correct police constable who had been called in the night before. It had been unpleasant, that crisp interrogation, and she was not certain the man had believed her tale, but he had had no choice but to accept it. Similar questions now could not surprise her.

"I'm afraid not. It was a dark night."

"Yes," he said thoughtfully. "Sometimes, if you know a person well, a great deal can be told from a mere outline."

"It was not anyone I knew well."

He nodded. After a moment he said, "Does this . . . incident have anything to do with your sudden need for other lodgings?"

"My what?"

"I had meant to wait until I had plied you with food and wine at dinner this evening to do my prying, but I'm a great believer in grasping opportunities. You have been making inquiries about town for another place to stay. I wondered if you . . . if there was someone who has been annoying you at the Royal Victoria."

There was, of course, but she had no wish to have him feel responsible for remedying the situation. She had a vague feeling that there might have been something more he had wished to ask of her. Had he considered making her some kind of proposal? She was relieved that he had apparently thought better of it, but could spare little thought for the form it might have taken. "No, no. It's just that the expense—"

There was no need to say more. "Ah, yes, money. Everything is becoming hellishly high as the money pours in from Nassau's newest form of piracy. I'm sure your uncle didn't expect it when he handed over funds for your stay. Who could?"

"Yes," she echoed stiffly, "who could?" How distasteful was all this subterfuge, these lies.

"I don't see the problem, however. Surely Ramon will stand as your banker; Lord knows he has enough of the ready. You need not feel in his debt; your uncle will certainly want to repay him."

She sent him a sharp glance, afraid of the whip end of sarcasm in his light words. It was not there. "Possibly," she agreed, "but I dislike being indebted in any way. And there is no need to pay the toll for the most luxurious accommodation in the city."

"It's where a woman like you belongs," he said simply.

"You don't stay there," she pointed out.

"I'm thinking of moving."

The smile he gave her was warm, leaving little doubt as to his reasons for contemplating the change. She said sharply, "Not for my sake."

"There you go again," he complained. "Was there ever a more self-centered female? Have you had breakfast?"

"No, but—"

"I have a notion to try out the service and cuisine of this hostelry before I give them my custom. Come along."

"I'm not hungry."

"But I am. You may have the great felicity of watching me gorge myself."

She went with him because he would have it no other way. In the same manner, in the next few days, he coaxed and bullied her into taking not only dinner with him every night, but the midday meal as well. She was dragged up and down the Queen's

Staircase, the great flight of stairs cut from solid limestone by slaves some seventy-odd years before as a means of access between Fort Fincastle and the town. They had explored the fort also, laughing over its walls constructed in the form, though not deliberately of course, of a blockade steamer; the fort's flagstaff was even in the shape of a mast. Because Fort Fincastle was built on the highest point on the island, it was possible to see far out over the sea, to the North West Channel and the reefs and islands that lined it. For this reason, it was used these days as the location for a signal tower.

Another day, they visited Fort Charlotte, too, on the west end of town, strolling around its massive walls and staring at its obelisk while a carriage waited. Nothing would do then, except that they also see Fort Montagu on the east end of the island, though it was something of a disappointment after the other two, being little more than a massive ruin. The main pleasure of the outing was that they were able to hire horses and ride a part of the distance along the beach, with the hooves of their mounts kicking up sand and spattering sea spray, and the trade wind in their faces.

Not all of her time was spent with Peter. She managed finally to speak to Mrs. Carstairs. The woman seemed as doubtful of her need of employment as Peter had been of her need to economize on her place of lodging. She had flatly refused to allow Lorna to work in the shop and wait on customers but was persuaded, finally, that the men crowding the city had need of shirts. If Lorna would make up a few samples, she would supply the material and arrange to sell them through a tailor she knew. It was plain to see, however, that the dressmaker expected her desire for employment to end when Ramon returned.

The sewing did not prove difficult. It scarcely occupied half Lorna's attention, though many of her free hours. She acquired the habit of taking a basket filled with cut-out pieces up to the belvedere on the roof of the hotel, where the light was good and the view of the sea exceptional. Because of the height, she was seldom disturbed, and then not for any length of time. She looked up often from setting stitches to stare out over the ever-changing waters of the ocean, straining her eyes down the North West Channel in the direction from which Ramon must return.

She heard nothing from the Lansings. It was as if she were no longer alive, so completely did they drop her from their guest list. She had thought at first it was because Ramon had not insisted upon her inclusion, but as the days passed she began to wonder if it were not more than that. Once, as she crossed the lobby of the hotel, she saw the large woman in the arms of whose husband she had fainted on the night of the excitement speaking behind her hand to another lady, her eyes malevolent as they followed her. Another time, she was aware of women whispering behind her as she left the dining room. More than once she glanced at a man to find him watching her, a speculative gleam in his eyes as he inspected her with obnoxious familiarity.

She no longer had time for the gatherings on the piazza; it was too difficult to concentrate on her sewing while being plied with offers of drinks and, also, invitations. The peculiar thing was that most of the requests for her company seemed to be for events that would occur in the late evening. More than one night, in the late hours between midnight and dawn, she had awakened to the sound of raised voices remonstrating with her guard in the hall outside her room. They were always male. Still, she did not spend much time worrying over it. She had no desire to go out, except now and then with Peter; no need for other company or the gaiety of the social whirl. Mrs. Carstairs had approved the work she had done and given her more, and that was all that mattered.

Her main source of news of the war at this time came from the English papers brought in on the transport ships. Peter shared his supply of them when a new bundle arrived. The things she read concerning New Orleans filled her with pity and impotent rage.

Farragut had turned the city over to the army commander, General Benjamin Butler. The general's first act had been to hang a boy still in his teens who, in the flush of anger and frustrated patriotism immediately after the fall of the city, before its official surrender, had torn down the federal flag. His second had been to require the signing of an oath of loyalty to the Union. The property of those who would not sign had been confiscated. They themselves had been loaded into wagons and herded across the state line into Confederate Mississippi.

The threat of search and seizure was constant, with much wanton destruction attending it. The belongings of Rebel sympathizers, the silver and china, books, bric-a-brac, jewelry, clothing of lace, silk, and velvet, the carriages and horses, all were impounded and sold at auction, often for less than a tenth of their value.

No one was immune to arrest. More than sixty men had been rounded up and arbitrarily sentenced to hard labor at various federal forts. Clergymen were dragged from their pulpits and brought before Butler for refusing to pray for the defeat of the South; editors faced him for daring to print news of southern victories, druggists for selling medicines to the men being smuggled out to join the Confederate army, storekeepers for refusing to open their stores, and even a bookseller for displaying a skeleton tagged with the name of a well-known northern defeat.

A woman was taken up for laughing as a federal funeral procession passed her home, another for refusing to walk under the federal flag, and yet another for having Confederate literature in her armoire. Several young girls were hustled before the military commander under guard for daring to sing "Dixie" and "The Bonnie Blue Flag."

But in the British press the greatest outrage was expressed for Butler's Order Number 28, which stated simply that any female who insulted a member of the federal army by word or deed would be treated as a woman of the streets plying her trade.

Lorna thought often of New Orleans and of what her situation might now be in that city if Ramon had not taken her from it. Would it have been better or worse? There was, of course, no way to tell.

Late one evening as she descended the rather steep stairs that led from the belvedere, she looked up to see Nate Bacon blocking her way. She had not seen him alone since that night in her room; he had merely bowed to her, his mouth twisted sardonically, across the width of the dining room several times, but had made no attempt to come close to her again. There had been a rumor circulating about the docks that he had bought a ship, a former merchantman, and was fitting her out, with no expense spared, as a blockade runner. Lorna had hardly been able to credit such a rumor. Now he stood with his hands behind his back and his feet spread, a cold smile in his blue eyes.

She made as if to step around him, and he shifted to prevent it. Her voice sharp, she said, "Let me pass."

"After finding you alone for once? Don't be foolish, my dear."

That superior, patronizing tone grated on her nerves, though she refused to allow him to see it, or the apprehension he roused in her. "I have nothing to say to you."

"But I have a great deal to say to you. There will be no one to interrupt us this time, I think. This is not a popular spot, and most of the other guests are dressing for dinner."

"After the last time, I would think you would be embarrassed to face me."

If she had hoped to disconcert him by her plainspeaking, she was forced to accept disappointment. "I will admit the meeting gave me no . . . satisfaction, but I don't hold it against you."

"Don't you?"

"Oh no. You see, I know that you will come crawling to me in the end. I intend to see to that."

Lorna gave him a look of purest contempt. "I can think of nothing more unlikely."

"Oh, but you will. When you haven't a shred of reputation left, when your friends desert you and your lovers are driven away, then I will be there, waiting. I will take you in and dress you in silk and lace and diamonds when we go out in public. But at home, I will keep you naked, at my mercy. I will teach you every whore's trick and you will perform them at my command. Your body will be mine, every inch, every curve and orifice, and I will use you until I tire of the pleasure."

A shred of reputation. She should have known it was Nate who had started the whispered innuendos, the echoes of which she had caught around her. She gave him a cold look.

"What of you? Does it make no difference that I am the woman who killed your son?"

"My son, and also his invalid mother, my wife, who did not live five days after I gave her the terrible news of Franklin's death. But no matter. I care nothing for what people here think of my predilection for you. It will be a fitting punishment, I think. You will hate it more than anything I could do. And if thoughts of Franklin intrude, I can always beat you—at least until the urge passes and others take its place."

"Aren't you forgetting something?" The ugliness of what he was saying made her feel unclean. She had to stop him somehow.

"Cazenave? I have plans for him."

"You had plans once before, if memory serves, but they never came to pass."

"Next time there will be no mistake; that's *if* he makes it back, of course."

"He will!" she cried.

"Who can say? It's a dangerous business he's in, mighty dangerous. When he's gone there'll be no one to protect you. No one to keep me from doing . . . this."

He reached for her as she stood on the step above him. His beefy arm circled her waist and the sewing basket she held fell, tumbling downward. But she had been afraid he would try some assault and the piece of shirt collar she had been stitching was clasped in her stiff fingers.

His thick, formless lips were wet and hot as they sought her mouth. She turned her head, feeling them smearing over her cheek, while his stubby fingers with their wiry black hairs fumbled for and found the curves of her breasts. He squeezed one so hard she gasped with the bruising pain, and he lifted her against him, her upper hoop pressing into his groin. Blindly she sought a place on his body not padded by material. There was a small space between his waistcoat and the top of his trousers at his side that she could reach with the hand that was clamped to her side. Making certain of it, she grasped the needle that was woven into the collar and thrust it into him with all her strength.

He bellowed, releasing her, thrusting her from him so that she fell backward on the stairs. Twisting, he found the cloth and embedded needle. He grabbed them and, cursing, pulled the sharp instrument from his flesh. He stared at it, then looked down at her. Flinging it away over the stair rail, he reached to grab her by the material of her gown between her breasts. Jerking her toward him, he slapped her viciously.

"Stick a needle in me, will you, you bitch," he said, and brought his hand back again, catching her on the other cheek.

"Lorna!" Someone called out.

Nate yanked her to her feet, then pulled down his waistcoat and straightened his cuffs. He was bending to pick up her basket, all solicitousness, when Peter rounded the turn of the stairs.

"I knew you were up here when I saw this floating down," he began as he caught sight of her. In his hand was the collar piece, still holding its bloodstained needle. It dropped to his side as his gaze fell on her face where the livid prints of Nate's fingers stood out against the paleness of her skin. His tone entirely different, he said, "Is something wrong?"

"Now, now, don't get in a pelter," Nate said, at his most unctuous. "We had a little run-in here on the stairs. I'm afraid, me being the heftier of the two, that Lorna got the worst of it."

"Is that right, Lorna?"

What she would not have given to be able to say no, to loose the rage and horror she felt for Nate Bacon. But to do so might well involve Peter in a problem that had nothing to do with him. She nodded, reaching for the collar, taking the basket Nate proffered. "If you gentlemen will excuse me, I feel a little shaken. I think I will go to my room."

"Why, Lorna, I'm so sorry," Nate said. "I never meant to do so much damage, I swear. But I don't know what this gentleman must be thinking about your manners. Permit me to introduce myself, sir. I'm Nate Bacon, this young lady's father-in-law."

The Englishman's aplomb was perfect. Not a muscle in his face moved as he inclined his head in a bow so shallow as to be an affront, ignoring the hand Nate offered. "How odd that you should be here," he said. "You must be the father of the man she killed." Turning to Lorna, he said, "I came to tell you, love, that a message has come from Fort Fincastle. There are steamships in the channel, heading toward Nassau. The runners are back."

Chapter 17

The *Lorelei* was not among the ships that steamed slowly up the channel and dropped anchor in the harbor during the night, nor was she one of the two that arrived just before daybreak. She had left Wilmington on the same night, but had not been sighted since. It had been a rough trip, with a gale encountered just before they reached the Gulf Stream. The federal cruisers had been out in force, as thick as fleas on a dog.

The salient fact that Ramon had not returned had been evident as soon as the ships hove-to in the harbor. The remainder of the information came the following morning as the captains gathered on the piazza, throwing themselves into chairs with the bonelessness of exhaustion and shouting for drinks with the vigor of men who had met danger and given it a nod before sailing past. The money and liquor flowed, the boombay music played, and the trade winds blew. None wanted to think of Ramon for long. Instead, they proposed a party.

The plans were drawn up then and there. There would be a ball held in the hotel dining room as soon after dinner as the place could be cleared. A cold collation could be set up somewhere, perhaps in the ladies' parlor, for supper. Musicians would be rounded up. Everyone would ride in a different direction to deliver the invitations. The only question that remained was whether the champagne should be served by itself, in a cocktail, or as a punch. Where was the difficulty the ladies always complained of in the arranging of a ball? Let the hotel manager be called and given his orders.

Lorna was present because, seeing her passing by, the captains had insisted. The last thing she felt like doing was entering into the preparations for an impromptu party; still, she could not get out of it. Before she knew where she was, she had agreed to supervise the preparations; to see to it that flowers and greenery were brought in and that the fruit punch for the elder ladies was mixed and set to chill, and to inspect the food for the supper. It crossed her mind to wonder if they were trying to distract her from dwelling on Ramon's absence. But no, they could not know how disturbed she was, not even if she did get up and move to the railing, staring out over the sea, a dozen times in the hour.

It had been assumed that she would be in attendance at the party, and she did nothing to change that assumption. But she would not be there. She had no stomach for merriment, and neither was she anxious to see the moment when the gossip about her reached the runner captains. She would stay in her room, slipping out for a few minutes only to check on the supper before returning.

She reckoned without Peter. He knocked on her door five minutes after the ball had begun. As she opened the door to him, nodding to the guard at his side to indicate that it was all right, she could hear the music of a waltz coming through the French doors behind her, rising from the converted ballroom on the ground floor below.

"I've come to escort you," he said.

He was impeccably dressed in his frock coat with a crimson hibiscus flower in the lapel. As he sketched a short bow, giving her a warm smile, the gaslight gleamed on the fine blonde hair brushed back from his high forehead.

"I don't believe I'll go, Peter. Really, I don't feel well."

He studied her. "Sick with fright?"

"What can you mean?" She stared at him, her gray eyes cold. He did not look away. "Oh, I think you know."

"So you've heard," she said, her voice flat as she swung from him, moving into the center of the room.

"I heard, but you forget; I know the truth." He pushed the door wide, as convention demanded, then followed her.

"The truth? But that day in Wilmington, Ramon only said—"

"He said you had killed your husband. He told me the whole story, later."

Had he? Had Ramon told him everything? She doubted it. Somehow, she hoped he had not. Some things were too personal to tell even someone like Peter.

She shook her head. "It doesn't matter. There's no reason I should go downstairs and let them stare at me."

"Would you rather they thought you were hiding?"

"Of course not," she snapped, "but why should they notice one way or another?"

"They will notice," he said dryly, "the men because they miss you, the women because of the men."

"And if I go, they will look to see how a murderess comports herself."

"You are no murderess. What should they see but pride and beauty?"

You are no murderess. Ramon had said that once too. Where was he now?

Twenty-four hours past due. Had he and his men been chased down and captured by a cruiser, taken prisoner? Had his ship, dangerously overloaded as the runners always were, foundered in the gale? Had damage from shelling on the outward run through the blockade made the *Lorelei* unseaworthy in rough weather? Or had she been sunk with all hands, lying now on the bottom with the shifting ocean currents washing through her while sharks and barracuda feasted? Such thoughts, such images, had haunted her all day. She shook her head now to rid herself of them, raising her hands to her mouth.

"Lorna?"

"Peter," she whispered, "where is he?"

His voice hard, he asked, "Are you mourning him already? Is that why you won't come?"

She whirled on him. "No!"

He stood watching her, waiting, a brooding look in the back of his blue eyes.

"Oh, all right!" she cried, flinging out her hands. "If you will wait in the gentlemen's parlor, I will be with you as soon as I can."

She dressed quickly, taking little pains with her appearance. The music rising in the dark outside her window tore at her nerves. The gown of lavender tulle was her only choice and she put it on, then braided her hair into a coronet. She bit her lips to make them red, wishing for some lip pomade. To add color to her pale face there was the milk-glass pot of French carnelian rouge, and she used it with a liberal hand. She stepped into her slippers, searched out her fan and gloves from a drawer, snatched up her key and slipped it into the net purse that lay on the washstand, then slipped the strings over her arm. Feeling rushed and half-dressed, she whirled from the room and locked the door behind her. For all her hurry, it had been nearly three-quarters of an hour since Peter had left her.

He looked up as he caught the silken whisper of her skirts on the stairs. Rising, he came forward from the parlor to meet her in the hall. He took her arm, turning immediately back toward the stairs. Smiling down at her as they descended, he said, "Lovely, as always."

She had need of the boost of his compliment. The music had just stopped as they paused at the open double doors that gave access to the dining room-cum-ballroom that, like the eastern end of the building, was shaped in a half-oval. It seemed to her that every head in the room turned toward them as they entered, that every gaze was narrowed in sordid speculation. She ignored them as best she could, gazing around at the potted palms, ferns, and aspidistra that were banked before the ensemble of pianoforte, French horn, viola, and two violins; at the softly glowing chandeliers suspended from elegant plaster medallions down the room; at the intricate open cornice-work around the high ceiling; the walls papered in pale pink, and the fringed and swagged drapes of gold satin at the French doors, fifteen in number, that stood open to the coolness of the night.

There was need of the last, for the room was warm with the advance of the season and the number of people crowded into it. The ladies standing with their partners around the verge of the polished floor were fluttering their fans, while the faces of the men were flushed with their exertions. Lorna had just begun to open her own fan of ivory and lace when the music struck up, a reel. Peter, his arm about her waist, swept her forward, and the dancing began.

It was more of an ordeal and, at the same time, less of one, than she had expected. The formality of dance cards had been dispensed with for this affair. It was every man for himself, since the males far outnumbered the females; there were no wallflowers. The runner captains gathered around Lorna with unabated enthusiasm, so that she scarce had time to catch her breath.

She drank champagne punch and was whirled in waltzes until she was giddy. There was no opportunity to watch the reaction of the matrons ranged in the corner opposite the musicians, or to speak to any of the younger women on the floor. The Lansing sisters were there but were surrounded by admirers. Since Lorna did not expect them to notice her, she was not disappointed. Still, there was no pleasure in twirling in the arms of one perspiring man after the other. The effort to smile and make gay conversation was wearing. Her mouth was stiff, her head ached from the noise and heat, and her feet were sore. Her heart was so leaden that she felt like a china doll moving stiffly in a child's game.

The supper dance belonged to Peter. When it was over and there was a general movement toward the stairs and the meal laid out on the next floor, Lorna begged off. She was not hungry. All she wanted was quiet, solitude, and air. She urged him to eat, saying she was going to her room but would come back down later, and finally, he agreed.

At the third-floor landing, she paused, then without conscious thought continued upward through the sleeping silence of this upper section of the hotel. She passed the fourth floor and, holding her skirts high, mounted the steep stairs to the belvedere.

The glass-paned doors had been closed for the night. Lorna skirted the chairs that were set around the walls of the small, octagon-shaped eminence and turned the handle of the nearest door, swinging it wide as she stepped outside. The wind at this height was fresh, almost cold. She lifted her face to it as she stood gazing out over the dark city lit here and there by glowing windows and streetlamps. The moon had risen, riding high above the island; it was round and full, bright gold veined with gray. Its brilliant light gleamed far out on the sea, catching the crests of the waves that moved relentlessly shoreward.

Lorna thought of Ramon and his claim that he would sail under a half-moon. He must have known even then that the phase would change to full before he could return. They were mad, these men who ran the blockade. It had been dangerous enough in pitch darkness; it was sheer reckless bravado to try it with moonlight on the sea. And why did they do it? For gold, only for gold.

There was hardly room for her skirts between the glass-paned wall of the belvedere and the railing of the walk around it. She compressed them with her hands as she paced slowly in a complete circuit, gazing out over each point of the compass. There was a light at Government House and, farther along, a pale gleam at Fort Fincastle. A small sloop was coming in from the east, with the glow of moonlight on its sail. The darkness lay more dense to the north, as if there might be a storm brewing far out to sea, a possibility since the rainy season was almost upon them. There was nothing to be seen, however, in the North West Channel, nothing more than there had been the first time she looked.

At a sound behind her, she turned. It was only Peter. In his hand he balanced a tray holding two glasses of water, two of champagne, and a plate heaped with food and covered by a napkin.

"How did you—?" she began.

"A lucky guess, since you weren't in your room."

He offered the tray, and she took a glass of water. "You shouldn't have."

"Service of the house."

"You . . . you are far too kind."

"Kind enough to marry?"

The words were spoken in a tone not too unlike his usual banter. It was a moment before their meaning penetrated. She looked up quickly, her eyes wide.

His mouth curved in a wry grin only half-visible in the darkness. "It can't be that much of a surprise. I've been out of my head since I saw you."

But it was. She had been so much involved with her own problems that she had not seen it coming. For a brief instant, she considered it. If she had never met Ramon, she might have been happy, even honored, to accept Peter. He was a dear friend, such good company; she had come to depend on him more in the past few days than was wise, or good, for either of them. Still, his touch didn't set her on fire as that of Ramon did, and when he was not with her, she did not think of when she would see him again. She moistened her lips with the tip of her tongue.

"I thought you . . . just liked women, that you enjoyed light flirtation."

"It hasn't been so light lately."

"I didn't realize."

"Now that you do, what do you think?"

She put her hand on the railing behind her. The wind swayed the bell of her skirts, lifting the tulle with little fluttering motions. It tugged his cravat from his waistcoat, flapping the ends not held by his stick pin, and tore the napkin from the plate he carried, sending it sailing out over the roof where it lodged on the shingles. He hardly glanced at it.

"Why?" she asked, her voice quiet.

"Because I love you. Because I want to take care of you. Because I want the right, if a man like Bacon touches you again, to smash his face in for him."

"Are you certain it isn't because you . . . feel sorry for me?"

He swung back inside and set the tray down on a chair, then moved back to where she stood. He reached out, taking her arms. "There is nothing to feel sorry for you about," he said. "You are a beautiful woman with much to give a man; I hope you will let that man be me."

"Your family—"

"—Is in England and will not, in any case, have anything to say about the woman I marry."

There was one other objection, the most important one. She had saved it for last because it seemed so unlikely that it would be needed once she pointed out the others. She raised it now.

"And Ramon?" As he did not answer, she went on, "Oh, Peter, can't you see that I can't do it?"

He took a deep breath. "Because he's missing?"

"Because . . . oh, because—"

"You are in love with him."

"What if I am?" She broke his grasp, swinging from him as pain surged through her, staring out over the ocean. "Is that so terrible?"

His voice grave, he said, "I don't know. Is it?"

"You . . . can't begin to guess." She lifted her head, afraid the tears welling slowly into her eyes would fall, betraying her.

He moved to her side, reaching to close his warm fingers on her shoulder. His sigh was a rustle of sound. "I think I can."

She did not answer. She put up her hand, dashing the moisture from her eyes, looking again to where the channel lay under the moonlight. She stretched out a hand that trembled. "There," she said, her tone strained. "Do you see it?"

He swung to follow the direction in which she was pointing, his forehead drawn in a frown. "No—yes. Yes!"

"Is it—"

"I can't tell."

In tense silence, they watched it come closer, a soft gray blot on the sea that resolved itself into a ship. It carried no deck cargo, no masts or bulwarks, and appeared to have no housing to the wheelhouse, no superstructure over the paddle wheels. It crept in at half-speed or less, with a peculiar crab-like movement caused by a heavy list to starboard. The smoke that boiled from its stack was black and shot with sparks, as if it were burning wood instead of coal.

"My God," Peter breathed.

The tightness of fear in her throat made the words hard to get out. "The *Lorelei*?"

His face was bleak as he answered. "What's left of her."

Lightning flashed overhead and thunder growled by the time the ship dropped anchor in the harbor. That did not deter the guests from the ball, who, discovering her limping progress, descended en masse to the dock to watch her arrival, cheering as her anchor chain rattled down. Nor did it deter Lorna and Peter, who by that time had commandeered a boat and were riding the waves made by the last turn of her paddle wheels, almost at her side.

Lorna had not thought to change. She had only paused long enough to snatch a shawl from her room and fling it around her. Staring at the landing stage let over the side, and the rope ladder leading up from it, she wished devoutly that she had at least removed her hoops, if not donned her old riding habit. But what had to be done, could be, and she was used to managing the width of her skirts. At least it was night, so that Peter, steadying the ladder from the boat below, would not be treated to a display of ankles and undergarments.

Slick and Chris were there to help her aboard. The executive officer had several cuts on the right side of his face, as if from flying glass, and his right arm was in a sling. The second officer appeared unharmed, until he turned to give a hand to Peter; then he favored his right leg. Anticipating her first question, they said that Ramon was in his cabin. He had remained upright until they had passed the breakwater at the tip of Hog Island, entering the harbor; then he had lost consciousness.

"How badly is he injured?" Lorna asked, her face pale in the lantern light.

"We caught grapeshot, Ma'am, from a cruiser late the second day out," Slick answered. "Ramon got a couple of pieces of scrap iron driven through him, a bolt and an old knife blade. Neither hit a vital spot, but there was no time to tend to them for quite awhile. He lost a right smart of blood. It didn't bother him much until yesterday morning, when the fever started. Might have still been all right, if he could have rested, but we got blown off course by the storm after we ran into it to escape the federals, and he had to bring us in.''

Lightning flashed overhead, showing the desecrated state of the ship. Peter spoke then. ''It looks as if that last took some doing.''

''I'd say so,'' Chris answered, turning from giving orders for the landing stage to be brought in. ''We ran out of coal yesterday afternoon. We were so far out we had to practically burn her to the waterline to make steam. 'Course, most of the planking was so torn up from the shelling that it didn't make a lot of difference, but throwing on the cotton soaked in the turpentine hurt.''

Nodding, the Englishman said, ''I think I should direct your attention to the crowd on the dock and warn you that you may be swamped with visitors at any moment.''

''Good,'' Slick said, casting a short glance toward shore. ''They can man the pumps. We're all about tuckered out from trying to stay afloat.''

Fear was a tight knot inside Lorna, but around it burned a slow anger. Why did men have to risk their lives in such dangerous undertakings? True, without such as these, the South would be forced to her knees before the year was out, but there had to be some other way of settling differences than putting human beings made of fragile flesh and bone at risk.

''I would like to see Ramon,'' she said.

''Frazier's with him now, seeing to him. Might not be a pretty sight, Ma'am.'' The two officers exchanged a look, then glanced at Peter.

She gave an impatient shake of her head. ''That doesn't matter.''

''If you say so.''

Slick indicated that she was to precede him, then stepped toward the place on the deck where the doorway to the companionway had stood. There was only a series of steps leading down now. Flattening her skirts with her hands, wishing yet again for simpler clothing, she began the descent.

Ramon lay upon the bunk, his booted feet hanging off the end. His shirt had been removed, but he still wore his trousers. The light from the lamp in the gimbals above him outlined the planes and hollows of his face, bringing out the flush of fever on the bronze of his skin and the dark shadows beneath his eyes. It glinted with blue lights on the growth of beard covering his chin that indicated plainly he had not had time for grooming in days, had not been out of his clothes. From the stains on the bandaging that wrapped his chest, it did not appear that the dressing had been changed.

Frazier had been kneeling beside the bunk. He got to his feet as Lorna entered, greeting her with every appearance of relief, nodding to Peter who entered behind Slick.

"How is he?" she asked.

Frazier threw a worried glance at the man on the bed. "About the same. I sponged him down with cold water, but it didn't seem to help much. He hasn't come to enough to take anything to drink."

"What about a doctor?" Peter asked.

"We can send for one now that you have brought us a boat," Slick answered. "Ours sort of got turned into kindling wood."

He swung, leaving the room to see to fetching a doctor. Frazier glanced after him. "I suppose it's best, but I don't think it's necessary. The captain has been through worse than this before. He'll mend just fine, now that he's able to stop for a minute."

Lorna moved closer, dropping beside the bunk in a soft rustle and billow of skirts. "Do you think so?"

"I know it, Ma'am. Takes more than this to get him down."

"He's so hot," she said, her hand on his forehead.

"That he is. It's my belief it's natural, like the swelling, but I don't know. Grape is a mean thing to catch, Ma'am. They load up the cannons with all manner of odds and ends, anything metal; rusty nuts and bolts and pieces of chain. Makes for ugly wounds, bad to fester."

"I don't like his being unconscious like this."

"I'd say he was just plain exhausted," the supercargo said with a shake of his head. "And if it's all the same to you, I'd as soon he stayed quiet. He's been hell to be around, begging your pardon, Ma'am, though I can't lay it to the holes in him. He had something on his mind on the trip up to Wilmington, and it didn't help his temper. He near wore a trench in the deck from his pacing, until we could get reloaded and on our way again."

It seemed best not to attempt an answer. Carefully avoiding Peter's gaze, she said to Frazier, "I expect you're tired, too. If you would like to rest, I'll stay with him."

"I appreciate the thought, Ma'am, but I'll wait to see what the sawbones says, just the same."

The doctor came, a bleary-eyed Englishman with a puffy face made wider by enormous, graying muttonchop whiskers. He lifted Ramon's eyelids, listened to his chest, and felt his forehead. He cut the bandages and stripped them off, tearing away the scabbing so that the wounds began bleeding again, then sprinkled them with a white powder and wrapped him up again so tightly it was a source of wonder that Ramon could breathe.

Lorna watched, nearly crying out at the callous way Ramon was being handled. The men who were gathered in the room, Peter and the ship's officers, seemed to see nothing amiss however. She had no real knowledge of medicine, other than what she had learned helping her aunt tend the slaves her uncle had worked, and no right to question the doctor's treatment. She remained silent but could not wait for the medical man to leave the ship. Her contempt knew no bounds when he did so without even suggesting that his patient be made more comfortable.

The moment he was gone, she threw off her shawl and directed Frazier to help her undress Ramon and get him under the covers. In the end, they had to cut the boots from his feet. He had worn them so long without removing them, and a large part of that time they had remained wet, that his feet had swollen and the leather shrunk, until the two had become almost inseparable.

They sponged him down again from head to toe, and it seemed that he grew a little cooler. The doctor had left powders to be given to him, but, though they tried to rouse him to take them, it was no use. Frazier left them, finally. The boat returned from taking the doctor ashore. Lorna heard voices on deck, and once or twice men came and put their heads into the room, but she hardly noticed them as she knelt beside the bunk, holding Ramon's hand in her own. It was Peter who spoke to them quietly, turning them away. After a time, quiet descended.

"Lorna?"

She turned her head at the sound, smiling a little at Peter, who was still leaning against the wall.

"It's getting late. Don't you think you ought to go back to the hotel? You can return in the morning."

"I'm not sleepy."

"You should be."

"I . . . would really rather stay."

As if disturbed by the sound of their voices, Ramon turned his head on the pillow with a soft rustling.

Lorna turned back instantly. Her voice low but insistent, she said, "Ramon?"

His lashes quivered, lifted. He stared at her for long moments, his dark eyes bright with fever; then, slowly, he smiled.

"Ramon," she whispered, tears in her voice.

He moistened his lips with his tongue. She reached at once for the glass of water sitting beside her on the floor. Raising his head, she helped him drink the medicine it contained, then gave him more water. When he lay back down, his gaze remained on her face.

"I saw you," he said, his voice a rasp of sound.

"Hush, don't try to talk."

"I did. I saw your face in the storm, with your hair blowing around you."

He was delirious. Her gray eyes troubled, she reached out, taking his hand in hers again and placing a finger on his lips.

He shook it away. "No. I did see you. And then I knew . . . knew we were going to make it."

The tears spilled from her eyes, creeping slowly down her face. Her mouth curved in a tremulous smile. Seeing it, his mouth twitched slightly in answer; then slowly, as if against his will, his eyes closed.

She bent her head, pressing her lips to the hard ridge of his knuckles. She looked up then to where Peter had been standing, her eyes shining with the joy that Ramon was going to be all right. Peter was no longer standing against the wall. He had gone.

The rain drummed overhead, lashing the ship. It poured with the splashing sound of a waterfall down the open companionway and mingled with the steady thump of the pumps that tried to rid the ship of both rainwater and seawater, keeping it afloat. Ramon's breathing became deep and natural as he slept undisturbed.

Lorna became stiff, crouching there on the floor. The stays of her corset cut into her, for she could not bend properly wearing it, and the stiffness of the tulle became scratchy. She thought of sending for a change of clothing, but knew at once it would not do. The men of the crew were as tired as their master, and those not manning the pump were probably asleep. Moreover, since Peter had gone, he had doubtless taken the boat, which was the only means of reaching shore at present.

Pulling herself to her feet, she stretched the cramp from her muscles. Her gaze moved to the trunk at the foot of the bed. She considered it, lifting a brow, glancing from it to the gown she wore. With sudden decision, she stepped to lift the lid. She set the top drawer aside, reaching for a shirt and a pair of trousers, holding them up to her. They were large, but the sleeves and trouser legs could be rolled up. She would be more comfortable until morning, until her own things could be brought.

A few moments later, her gown and petticoats and hooped crinoline lay like a giant lavender and white, many-petaled flower in the middle of the floor, while she stood trying to stuff what seemed like yards of shirt into the wide waist of the trousers. She had borrowed Ramon's belt, but her waist was so small none of the holes in it were serviceable. Finally, she stripped it out of the loops and tossed it to one side. She picked up her shawl, wrapping it around her waist and looping the soft wool in a large knot. The trousers were lying in folds around her, and she grinned at the picture she must present. It didn't matter. There was no one to see her, and no one to care.

Her smile a little strained, she moved to place her hand on Ramon's forehead. It seemed a little cooler, though not much. She swung away, her footsteps quiet in her dancing slippers as she stepped to the porthole to stand staring out at the few scattered spots of pale light where lamps glowed in the rain-lashed night. The ship rocked at anchor on the choppy waves, even in the quiet harbor. What must it have been like this last trip out on the ocean, beyond the protecting reefs and out-islands?

She was tired. She had slept so little in the nights since Ramon had gone, fearful for him, disturbed by the possibility of Nate Bacon's paying a return visit, tormented by thoughts of the uncertain future. It was odd, but she felt safe, safer than in weeks, there on the crippled ship in the storm. She placed her hands on the sill beneath the glass and leaned her forehead against them.

Peter. She supposed he cared what became of her. He must, since he had proposed to her. Remorse seeped through her as she thought of how little attention she had given his proposal, of how it had been shunted aside by the arrival of the *Lorelei*. Why couldn't she have fallen in love with Peter? It would have been so much simpler. Or would it? No matter what he said, she could not think that his aristocratic family would have welcomed a daughter-in-law of such sullied reputation. And there was little hope that her notoriety would not precede her; Nate had made certain of that. Nassau was a small community and its ties to England close.

What did it matter? She wasn't going to marry Peter. She wasn't going to marry anyone. She was going to earn her own keep and be beholden to no man.

The wood beneath her hands felt damp as the mist from the falling rain wafted into the cabin, bringing coolness with it. Raising her head, she turned toward the bunk. The lamplight cast swaying shadows around the room, its moving beams slanting across the planes of Ramon's face and chest above the sheet that covered him to the waist. As if drawn, she moved toward him, leaning to tug the sheet higher.

He came awake in a single movement, his hand swooping to pin her wrist as his eyelids flew open. His grip was like a hot vise, grinding the bones together. The expression in his eyes was that of a hunting hawk, black and predatory.

She made a small sound of distress, and his gaze cleared, focusing on her face and hair, moving over the men's clothing she wore, then back up to her gray eyes. His hold loosened. His mouth curved in a faint smile. The words little more than a whisper, he said, "You would have done better to have raided Chris's trunk; he's nearer your size."

"He might not have appreciated that."

"He would have been honored—as I am. How long have you been here?"

"Not long," she managed.

"Come, lie with me. . . ."

"I can't. Your wounds—"

He smiled again, as if her objection were foolish, increasing the pressure on her wrist.

"No, really," she protested.

"Come," he insisted, shifting, grimacing a little as he drew her to him.

"But Ramon, I should watch—"

"For what? I promise you I'm not going to die." He threw back the sheet.

"I . . . shouldn't," she said, sitting on the bed to relieve the pull he was exerting.

"But you will, to please me? Because without you I can't rest, can't think, may well cease to be?"

How could she resist such an appeal, or the light that burned fever-bright in his eyes, or the needs of her own body and heart? She lay down, moving carefully so as not to jar his injuries. He encircled her waist, drawing her nearer, fitting her to the contours of his body. Outside, the rain poured down in tropical abandon, and the lamp in the gimbals swung, playing its light over them until, near dawn, it sputtered out from lack of oil. Lorna did not know it.

Ramon kept to his bunk for four days. After the first forty-eight hours, he was restless, especially as by then Slick had arranged for, and begun to oversee, the rebuilding of the ship. Edward Lansing came during that period to discuss the loss of the cargo and cost of repairs. He had had to put his foot down, so he said, to keep Elizabeth and Charlotte from coming with him; they were that anxious about Ramon's health. They had heard, however, that he was being well taken care of by Miss Forrester.

Lorna had been irritated by the smile Mr. Lansing had given her as he spoke the last words. It was entirely too man-of-the-world and indulgent of his friend and partner's little peccadilloes. But this could not be helped. It had been inevitable that her absence from the hotel, and presence on board, would be noticed. She had not given up her room at the Royal Victoria, but had gone herself to remove her most practical clothing, her habit and two muslin gowns, in her trunk of woven straw.

To her and Cupid had fallen the task of nursing the none too cooperative patient. Together they planned meals, nourishing beef broths and chicken stews, that would tempt his appetite. While the trade winds drifted in at the portholes, along with the smells of fresh-sawn lumber and the sounds of saws and hammers, they had played chess and checkers and cards with him. Sometimes, Lorna read to him from books brought by first one and then another of the blockade captains. After the first two days, there was a constant stream of visitors in the afternoons, bringing small gifts, staying to talk until their numbers filled the cabin. That was after the ship had been towed to the dock and her parted seams patched and caulked, after it had begun to look as if the vessel might be salvaged after all.

On the morning of the fifth day, Ramon woke Lorna by taking the end of one of her long tresses and brushing it lightly over her lips as she lay beside him. When she opened her eyes, he was watching her with melting adoration in his dark eyes and a smile of utter charm on his mouth. She reached up at once to feel his forehead. It was cool.

He leaned to press a thorough but gentle kiss to her parted lips, then drew back to see the effect. She smiled, and a look of droll hopefulness came to his face. "What are the chances," he asked, "of steak and eggs for breakfast?"

They were, of course, extremely good. When he had eaten, and, running a hand over his beard, announced his intention of shaving, Lorna left the cabin and went topside. She was in time to see a carriage pull up beside the dock. She recognized it, even before Charlotte and Elizabeth descended, decked in lace and ribbon, in yellow and blue silk, holding delicate lace parasols over their heads and carved-ivory scent bottles to their noses, to ward off the smells of the wharf. They were followed by a liveried footman carrying a hamper with a napkin tucked into the top. They tripped up the gangway and sailed down to the cabin without so much as a glance at Lorna, who was standing, talking to Chris, not ten feet away.

Lorna turned to follow them, when she was halted by a hail. It was Peter, striding toward the dock. He bounded lightly up the gangway and fell in beside her. "I see Papa has relented—or been defeated—and Charlotte and Elizabeth have come to call."

It was as if he had never left without saying good-bye, had not stayed away for these past four days. She smiled, moving once more toward the companionway. "Yes."

"Ramon will be overwhelmed." His voice was dry.

"Especially," she said demurely, "since he is shaving—and has not dressed yet."

"Oh Lord. Shall we go and save him, or their modesty, whichever is in greatest need?"

But neither appeared in danger when Peter and Lorna arrived. Ramon must have heard the Lansing sisters coming, for he was in the bunk, with the sheet pulled up to his waist and a wisp of lather under his ear. He was doing his best to look the wounded hero, while at the same time eyeing the basket the footman had placed at his feet. Among the items that had been provided to refurbish the ship was a new set of chairs for the cabin. Charlotte and Elizabeth were seated in them, leaning back in elegant poses on the stiff, wooden seats.

". . . Shudder to think how close the *Lorelei* came to being lost," Elizabeth was saying. "Charlotte and I prayed for your safe return, and of course for your recovery from your injuries."

Lorna had done the same, though one would think, she told herself, that it had been the Lansing prayers that had been solely responsible for the favorable outcome.

"We were so worried when we heard you were hurt," Charlotte said, her color high, her eyes bright as they rested on Ramon's bare chest. She looked away, glancing at Lorna and Peter, then looking hastily at Ramon again.

"We were concerned, too, at the treatment you might be receiving. It is impossible to be too careful with wounds in this climate."

Ramon was frowning as he noticed the studied way the two women ignored Lorna. His voice had hardened as he said, "I had an excellent nurse."

"I'm sure," Elizabeth said dismissingly. "We would have come earlier, had Papa not forbidden it. No matter our desires, it would not have done to give rise to talk."

The words were innocent enough, but the tone of her voice, its cool distaste, was not. Ramon's eyes narrowed. "Perhaps you had better not linger then, for the sake of your . . . good names."

Elizabeth gave him an arch smile. "Yes, well, we are not quite alone; we chaperon each other, and we do have a servant in attendance. Besides, it isn't night. I think our known repute as females of unblemished character will stand us in good stead."

Lorna knew very well that this comment had been flung directly at her. Her tone honeyed, she said, "Still, a lady can't be too careful. If Ramon is joined by two other women, there is no telling what depravity people might say is taking place. Night, you know, isn't the only time men feel amorous."

"My dear Miss Forrester," Elizabeth began.

"Whatever can you mean?" Charlotte said, frowning, though with a gleam of interest hidden by her lashes. As she glanced from one to the other, she met Peter's ironic gaze and suddenly flushed fiery red. The look in Peter's eyes sharpened.

"Really, I think it would be best," Lorna said, too angry to stop herself or to remember that these were Ramon's guests and the daughters of his business partner, "if you would take your basket and run before you are contaminated."

"How dare you!" Elizabeth looked to Ramon for support, but he only stared at Lorna with a peculiar golden light in the dark depths of his eyes. The elder Lansing sister went on, gesturing at the basket they had brought. "There is nourishing food in there, food prepared under my own supervision. It cannot but be better for him than anything he might have been able to get on this ship."

Behind her, beyond the doorway that had not yet been fitted with a new panel, Lorna plainly heard Cupid's snort of disdain. It spurred her on. She moved around the chairs to the foot of the bunk, lifting the napkin that covered the basket. "Food? Let me see, what have we here? Jellied consommé, I think, and chipped beef."

She carried the basket toward the open porthole, as if to see better in the light. Passing the crock of consommé through, she let it fall. Before the splash of its hitting the water could be heard, she had consigned the bowl of chipped beef to the same watery fate. "Dear me," she said, "how clumsy."

Moving back toward the bunk, she reached for what appeared to be tea cakes wrapped in a clean dish towel and placed on a silver platter. Elizabeth sprang to her feet, snatching the basket from under Lorna's hand, holding it against her. "You shan't do it, you . . . you sailor's whore!"

Lorna tilted her head. "How distressing for you to have to lower yourself to use such a word. But then, the way it came so readily to your tongue must make a person wonder how familiar you are with the occupation."

"Oh!" Elizabeth cried. "Are you saying that I—"

"You can't talk to my sister like that," Charlotte said, jumping to her feet.

It was Peter who reached to take the arm of the younger girl. "Come, kitten, I don't think you are ready to take on a lioness."

"But she—"

"—Is quite within her rights, you know. Permit me to escort you back to your carriage. Elizabeth?"

As Peter paused, waiting, the older girl sent Lorna a venomous look, then whirled in a wide fluttering of skirts and went before him from the room. The footman, his face wooden, exchanged a look with Peter, then bowed, indicating that he would follow after him. Their footsteps echoed along the passage and up the companionway, then faded on the deck overhead.

The enormity of what she had done rushed in upon Lorna. She glanced at Ramon. Her tone stiff, she said, "I'm sorry."

"Come here," he said softly.

His face was stern, the expression in his black eyes unreadable. She swallowed on the tightness in her throat as she moved to the side of the bunk. He took her hand, turning it so that his thumb caressed the sensitive center of her palm.

"Look at me," he commanded, and she raised her lashes, holding his slumberous black eyes with her own clear gray ones only by an extreme effort of will. His voice was deep as he spoke again. "Tell me about these men who are amorous not only at night."

A pulse began a frantic beat in her throat. "There is nothing to tell. It was . . . only something to say."

"A formidable weapon, experience; you routed those poor girls with it. But I am intrigued. Why that experience? Did you, do you, enjoy love in the light of day?" He carried her hand to his mouth, pressing his lips to the palm, flicking it with the warm tip of his tongue.

How was she to answer? She could not think for the images conjured up by his words, his touch. She swallowed hard. "I . . . I suppose so."

"Lorna, *ma chère*," he said with a wry shake of his head as he drew her firmly down beside him. "If you only suppose, then there is nothing to be done except try it once more to be certain."

Chapter 18

The days slid past one after the other. The repairs to the ship continued at a furious pace as the ship's officers and crew, plus a full complement of carpenters, worked to get her ready for the next dark of the moon. Ramon, shrugging off suggestions that he rest, supervised the reconstruction and saw to it that the materials were available. The latter was no easy task. So great was the need for lumber and tools, in that fast growing town where every nail, screw, and foot of decking had to be brought in by ship, that stockpiled stores disappeared if not closely guarded. And, as Slick put it, if a feller set down a hammer and sack of gold eagles together, when he came back it would be his hammer that was gone.

In truth, Ramon seemed to recover quickly from his injuries. According to Cupid, it was thanks to *le bon Dieu*, the constitution of a lion, and the *capitaine*'s satisfaction with his nurse, and good food that had effected the cure. That Ramon was happy to have her with him could not be denied. He kept her beside him, taking notes of measurements and supplies as they were needed, discussing with her the work in progress, such as the new deck cabin that was being grafted onto the old deck, a lower silhouette almost like a turtle back; and the open position of the wheel, without the danger of splinters and flying glass from a wheelhouse. At night she slept against him, in the time he allowed her for rest. There was no mention of her returning to the hotel, though her room was still there, waiting.

Lorna was content. She did not think of the future, refused to consider it. Her position as Ramon's woman, a widow with a less than pristine past, would have troubled her if she had allowed it to gain purchase of her mind, but she did not. She could not help the things people said, could not control the direction her life had taken. Wisdom, pride, and the standard of morality in which she had been reared dictated that she leave Ramon and never see him again; she had no wish to be wise, proud, or moral. She was where she wanted to be, with the man she loved. What else could matter?

The news of the war brought by the returning runners was both gratifying and disturbing. In the last days of May, "Stonewall" Jackson had inflicted heavy casualties on the federal forces at a place called Front Royal, then chased General N. P. Banks out of Virginia, back across the Potomac. There had been rumors that he was threatening Washington yet again, with much ensuing uproar and movement of men and arms on northern railroads. The results had been the sending of forces under Generals Fremont and Shields into the Valley of Shenandoah to harry him, trying to catch his fast-moving brigades in a pincer strategy. There was no word of how successful they had been.

Another topic of conversation among the runners was the tales of ships being built specifically for the Confederate navy. There was one just off the slips at Birkenhead, near Liverpool, that had been christened the *Oreto*. It was claimed that she would be brought to Nassau to be armed as a commerce raider, then sent out against federal shipping as well as the cruisers in the Gulf Stream. Another ship was under construction by the Liverpool firm of John Laird, himself a venerable gentleman who was a member of the House of Commons. Called simply Ship Number 290, it was due to be ready by the end of July. The scuttlebutt was that Raphael Semmes, a thirty-years' veteran of the federal navy who had resigned his commission to offer his services to the South, had already left for England to take command of her.

Ramon had known Semmes, had served under him for a short while in the Mediterranean. His respect for the man was boundless. He argued that a fast steamer, well armed and under a captain who knew what he was doing, could disrupt federal shipping and strike fear into the hearts of the Yankee merchants who had, so far, been unmolested in this war. Enormous strides were being made in the design of ships. The "290" was supposed to have a screw-propeller, eliminating the clumsy paddle wheels and increasing the speed to twenty knots and more, twice as fast as some of the steamers now making the runs.

Ramon's black eyes were bright as he spoke, his gestures swift and positive. Lorna, watching him, knew a moment of unwilling fear. It would be a dangerous job, commanding a commerce raider, more dangerous than running the blockade, since it was inevitable that the wrath of the North would be aroused and a force sent out against the Confederate ships. They would, then, be so few against so many. What now of her tirades about the southern cause and the men needed to aid it? With shame she realized that she would rather have her lover, warm and vital beside her in the night, than to see him deliberately set out to risk death as a southern patriot.

Finally the *Lorelei* was finished, her new paint dried, her cargo gathered in the warehouse ready for loading. In celebration, and by way of relaxation, Ramon borrowed a small sloop, had Cupid pack a lunch, and took Lorna sailing.

It was a brilliant day. The sun was hot, the air humid, the water like broken bits of blue mirror, dazzling to the eyes. The owner of the boat was a fisherman by trade, and the lingering smell of his last catch was a vivid reminder of the fact. Ramon set the sail to take them to the east, along the coast to the tip of New Providence Island, past Fort Montagu and the spire of St. Matthew's Church, and then around the end of Hog Island toward another small, low-lying patch of land. They did not try to reach it but dropped anchor. Ramon secured the sail, then reached beneath the thwart to bring out a small wooden box. He held it up to show the open top and pane of glass that was set into the bottom.

"A water box!" Lorna said in delight. She had heard much talk of such things since she had been in Nassau, but this was her first look at one.

"Correct." He held it out to her. "Ladies first."

She took the box, saying frankly, "I'm not certain what to do with it."

"Sit in the bottom of the boat, so you can lean over and hold the box down in the water. Just keep the top clear so the water doesn't get into it."

She did as he said, hanging over the side of the boat. The

moment she let the box down in the water, it was like having a window on the sea. She could see the white coral sand of the ocean bottom, the waving of fingers of coral, and, darting here and there, the bright blue and gleaming yellow of fish. She also saw long pieces of gray planking with coral and barnacles growing on the sides.

"There's something down there. Wood. Is it—?"

"The wreck of an English merchant ship driven onto the reef during a storm twenty years ago."

It was strange to see it, the wreck lying there so plainly. She thought she could make out the round openings in the planking where portholes had been, and a piece of the keel. "I suppose the wreckers took everything of value."

"Before she sank," he agreed. "You are looking through something like fifty feet of water."

He moved to crouch beside her, watching over her shoulder as he told her the names of the fish she saw: a dark turquoise blue parrot fish, a huge gray grouper, a red snapper, and many others. He helped her to identify the low-growing, convoluted forms of brain coral, the waving lavender beauty of sea fans, and the spread fingers of starfish. It was marvelous, an unforgettable experience. Lorna could have watched for hours, if the ache in her neck and shoulders from bending over the side of the boat had not forced a halt.

Leaving the site of the wreck, they passed a man in a dinghy, cleaning fish he had caught and washing his knife over the side. He lifted a hand to them, the only human being they had seen since they had left New Providence. They then set a course for a distant island and held to it with the wind straining and snapping their sail while they narrowed their eyes against the sun's glare.

The island drew near. The surf caught them in its surge, carrying them over the reef. The boat grounded on the sand and Lorna, in sudden exuberance, leaped out with Ramon to pull it higher on the beach. When she waded ashore, her muslin skirts were sodden, flapping around her. The island was deserted, he told her; there was no one to care if she wanted to take off her gown and wear only her underclothing, or nothing, while it dried.

It was impossible to resist, and Lorna did not try. She stripped off her gown and hung it on the branches of a sea grape tree to dry, then removed her corset and slung it up beside the blowing muslin. When she looked up, Ramon had removed his shirt and boots, and flung them down on the coral rock. He took her hand, drawing her with him toward the beach.

"Have you ever bathed in the sea?" he asked, his black eyes alive with laughter and something more that left her breathless.

"No," she answered, holding back a little, though she was willing enough. The water looked so inviting, like liquid jewels, aquamarine and turquoise and amethyst, a priceless and promising elixir.

"It's time you did," he said, and took her splashing into the cool, clear, salty water.

They could see their toes on the coarse sand of the bottom, so crystalline were the depths; see the tiny fish that swam here and there, and the white crabs that scuttled from their approach. The surf, its strength broken by the reef, was gentle, caressing near the beach. Nudging, beneficient, it pushed them against each other. Ramon, his chest bronzed in the sunlight with the exception of the scars, which were still an angry red, cavorted around her. He swam away a few yards, offering to teach her the way of it, grinning when she refused in distrust. He returned, gliding past her, touching her under the surface in artless, familiar intimacy.

The thin, wet lawn of her camisole molded itself to her breasts, hugging their proud contours, lying cunningly over the contracted peaks. Her pantaloons clung to the gentle curves of her hips and thighs. Through the transparent material, the pink and cream of her skin glowed with the bloom of health and enjoyment and vibrant feminine awareness.

She was waiting, expectant, when Ramon came to his feet before her, drawing her to him. His mouth tasted of salt and the sweet mastery of desire; the surfaces of his lips were smooth, adhesive. His hands cupped and kneaded, clasping her against the hard strength of his body. She stood on tiptoe, twining her arms about his neck, pressing herself against him, moving with sinuous grace to the ebb and flow of the water that lapped about her shoulders.

He unbuttoned her camisole, easing the edges apart, his head bent as he studied the rose-pink peaks straining upward with the lift of the water, gleaming in the sun rays slanting through its limpid depths. He pushed the garment off her, slinging it toward the beach, then slipped free the knot that held her pantaloons.

Her thighs gleamed white, marbled with the refracted light

from the water's surface. His own were a deeper gold as his trousers went bobbing in the surf. They drifted together as gently and naturally as the first man and woman to couple under a pagan sky.

Lorna felt the strength and surge of him inside her, the strong support of his arms as she was lifted against him, her legs positioned around his body. Her breasts pressed against his chest, moving, ever moving, their peaks burrowing into the hair that furred its planes. Their mouths clung, while the world swung slowly, the horizon turning. The sound of the sea was in her ears, the taste of it in her mouth, the feel of it both upon her and inside her. She was a part of it, and it a part of her. It was right, an elemental pleasure that mounted so that her hands upon Ramon's shoulders tightened and she moaned, a soft sound that was lost in the flow and suction of the water.

Slowly, relentlessly, the tension increased, until her blood thundered in her ears and the water was cool against her heated skin. She was helpless in its grip, uncaring for where she was or who might see them there. With a need that bordered on desperation, she wanted to take the man who held her deep inside and hold him there, fused, inseparable, the two of them one with the sea.

The molten run of the ocean's current burst within her, flooding, flowing. She lifted her lashes and stared into the black eyes of Ramon Cazenave, her own gray gaze stark with love and wonder. His pupils widened and his indrawn breath was sharp. He bent his head and took her mouth, then holding her to him, plunged deep into the turquoise waves.

They glided, revolving in sweeping turns, their hearts near to bursting. The sea took them, caressing, cradling them in that moment of supreme ecstasy. Disembodied, caught in the ancient magic of the sea, they lingered, the emotions that held them more clamorous than the need for life. Then with a powerful thrust of his shoulders, Ramon rose to the surface. With her tucked against him, he found his feet and lifted her, gasping and laughing, in his arms. His dark eyes unshadowed, he smiled down at her, then hoisting her higher, carried her slowly toward the beach.

While Lorna's rescued underclothing and Ramon's trousers dried, they spread their lunch on a tablecloth laid over a blanket that smelled faintly of fish. Naked and splendidly unaware, they ate, though Lorna had to keep pushing back the long strands of wild silk hair that wafted around her where she had taken it down to dry in the wind. Afterward, they wrapped what was left in the cloth and put it in the straw basket they had brought it in, then shook the crumbs from the blanket. Replete, pleas-antly sated with the sea and sun and love, they stretched out to doze in the shade.

"Lorna?"

"Hmmm?"

"You know that tomorrow is the new moon."

She knew. It did not seem possible that it could be time, that the phases could have changed from full quarter, and back to the dark of the moon again. Her voice low, she answered, "Yes."

"You will have to go back to the hotel."

The words had a reluctant sound, as if he did not want to say them. That was some comfort. She moistened her lips. "Couldn't I go with you?"

"The risk is too great. Even if you weren't wanted by the federals as a courier, there are fewer women making the runs these days."

"I don't care."

"I do. I have to; should anything happen to you, the respon-sibility would be mine to bear."

"I absolve you of it," she said, her voice tight with disap-pointment.

He rolled to face her, heaving himself to one elbow. "You can't. It's not in your power."

"I wish . . . I wish you didn't have to go." She kept her lashes lowered, staring at a gray-black lizard that had scuttled out onto the rock beside the blanket to bask in the sun-dappled shade, showing his yellow throat.

"*Chérie,*" he said, his voice low, shaded with a peculiar uncertainty. He reached to touch her face with his strong brown fingertips. She looked up and was caught in the dark mirrors of his eyes, aware of a sudden breathlessness in her chest.

His attention moved beyond her, sharpened. Abruptly he lunged over her, snatching the blanket edge and pulling it across her as a covering. In the same movement, he came to his feet. "If you will stand now," he said, his tone resigned, "you may have time to duck out of sight and get dressed before he passes by here."

She swung her head to see the fisherman they had passed earlier in his dinghy. He was just rounding a point of the island, the square brown sail on his clumsy boat taking him slowly over the water just outside the reef. No daring seaman, he was keeping close to land as he navigated toward an island lying no great distance beyond the one on which they had landed.

With the blanket around her, Lorna struggled upward. For something to say to relieve the sense of heavy anticlimax she felt, she said, "Do you think he lives over there?"

"Probably. Most of the larger islands, the ones that have water available, are livable enough. Between what you can get from the sea and what you find growing wild, there's plenty to eat, providing you know what to look for, of course. But the damned old wrecker most likely came by to be sure I hadn't piled the sloop up on the reef, being so entranced with my companion. It would have been fair game then."

She laughed, shaking back her hair so that it rippled like a gold silk flag in the breeze. "He will be disappointed."

"By the grace of *le bon Dieu*," he agreed, his sidelong glance droll, "and he isn't the only one."

Her clothing was dry, flapping in the trade wind. The leaves of the sea grape trees that lined the shore rustled with an inviting sound, while bees hummed in the thick undergrowth beyond. If she dressed, it was probable that they would leave this quiet place with its somnolent peace, sailing back to the bustle and noise of Nassau. She sniffed at the blanket around her, wrinkling her nose at its aroma, which had been made riper by the heat of the sun. Tilting her head, she asked, "Do you think we could just hide until he goes on by? Another dip in the water would be lovely."

He glanced at the fisherman, then back to her, a warm smile moving into his eyes, curving his mouth so that his teeth flashed white. "Anything you say, *chérie*, anything at all."

Dusk was falling, lying purple across the opalescent blue water, when finally they sailed into the long harbor that lay between Hog Island and New Providence. The palm trees were silhouettes against the soft, dark blue of the sky. Fort Montagu loomed gray and stolid in the dimness, while the lights along Bay Street and on the ships lying at anchor were like fairy lanterns: small, scattered, and pulsing, reflecting over the water.

Lorna was sitting in the prow, facing forward, her face lifted to the soft breeze. They were no great distance from the *Lorelei* when she saw it. She was watching the ship that Nate Bacon had been fitting out these past weeks, a merchant tub, trim but with-

out the grace of Ramon's ship. They were within a few yards of
her when two men caught her attention. One was Nate himself,
unmistakable in his bulk and flowing brown hair shot with silver. The other was a man of medium height with a sharp, pointed
face, made oddly fox-like by a bushy growth of carrot-colored
side-whiskers and wearing a small, flat hat on the back of his
head. They were shaking hands, the pair of them, firmly, as if
to seal a contract; then the fox-faced man did a strange thing.
He took out a pipe and a metal box of matches from his jacket
pocket. He opened the box and extracted one, striking it in a
flare of sulphur-yellow flame. Instead of putting his pipe in his
mouth and applying it, however, he stood holding the match in
his fingers, watching it burn, laughing. Nate Bacon gave a rich
chuckle, too. Then as the man shook out the match, the two
clasped hands once more.

Lorna turned in her seat to see if Ramon had noticed. He was
staring ahead at his ship, where Chris stood waiting at the landing stage. Following his gaze, wondering what problem had
come up in their absence that made it necessary for the young
second officer to meet them, she forgot the incident she had just
witnessed.

The trouble was minor, a hitch in the loading that was soon
straightened out. By mid-afternoon the next day, the ship was
sitting low in the water and the last of the stevedores had padded
away down the gangplank. The passengers, four gentlemen, had
made their way to the dock and were waiting impatiently with
their trunks and carpetbags about their feet for the order to board.
Lorna had gathered her things, ready to depart. She and Ramon
had said their good-byes the night before, but still she lingered
for a final parting. He was busy with Edward Lansing and a port
official in his cabin, going over the bills of lading, signing documents for harbor clearance.

Lorna walked to the railing, running her fingers over the
smooth, freshly painted surface. She did not want to go. The
thought of returning to the hotel was a leaden weight inside her.
The days that lay ahead stretched endlessly. She would much
rather venture the dangers of the trip than endure the hours of
waiting, of not knowing, to say nothing of the stares and whispers she could not avoid.

Her gaze narrowed. One of the passengers below had a familiar look. It was the fox-faced man she had seen the night
before. She could not be mistaken; she would have recognized

those orange side-whiskers and wide flaring tufts of beard anywhere. A chill ran over her as she stared at him. She did not like
it, she did not like it at all.

She had tried to tell Ramon about the man and his action the
evening before. He had been indulgent, teasing her about her
feminine intuition and the lack of logical reason for her instant
suspicion simply because she had seen him with Nate Bacon.
He was inclined to discount the damage one man could do,
anyway, especially when surrounded by his officers and crew.

She thought of speaking to him again, of suggesting that the
man be denied passage. Would he listen or would he merely
smile and kiss her into silence? She stood frowning, trying to
decide.

At the sound of footsteps, she looked up. It was Chris. He
stopped for a few moments beside her, saying good-bye, promising they would return as quickly as the old girl, meaning the
ship, could bring them. As he walked on, slim and straight in
his uniform, with the sun shining on his soft brown hair and
glinting on his wire-rimmed spectacles as he glanced up at its
position, a vague idea came to her. She considered it carefully
for flaws, a gleam appearing in her gray eyes that gave them a
silver sheen.

She had learned in the past few weeks that an action delayed
could become useless. In a swoop of skirts, she swung and
picked up her straw bag. With it in her hand, she moved swiftly
back toward the companionway and ducked inside.

An hour later, she stood in her room at the hotel dressed in a
pair of natty brown and green plaid trousers, a crisp white shirt,
a brown silk cravat, and a forest green jacket. Her hair was
coiled up on top of her head and covered by a soft wool cap.
The shirt was rather wide across the shoulders and long in the
sleeves, the jacket the same, but the trousers were an excellent
fit. If she waited until dark and chose her time well, no one
would notice the other deficiencies, or discern that she wore
slippers instead of boots.

While the sun sank slowly into the ocean, she reviewed her
preparations. In her straw trunk, she had food enough, ordered
from the hotel kitchen, for the three-day voyage, as well as a jar
of water, a comb, one muslin gown, and her underclothing. In
one pocket of Chris's jacket, she had the last of the money that
Ramon had left her, and in the other, Nate's derringer, loaded

with recently purchased powder and ball. There was nothing else she could think of that she would need.

She would approach the ship during the dinner hour and walk on board with her baggage in her hand, for all the world like some late-arriving passenger. Once below, she would slip into the ladies' cabin, just as she had done before. Only on this occasion, there would be no female expected, so there should be no reason for Cupid to have any interest in that cabin. All the conveniences necessary for human comfort were to be found there, and she saw no reason why she should not take advantage of them. With luck, there was no reason why she should have to emerge before they reached the passes of the Cape Fear.

On the other hand, it was possible that, through some miscalculation, she might find the ladies' cabin in use. The male passengers might well have spread their belongings into it, since it was not supposed to be occupied. In that case, she would go to the hold and expect to show herself after twenty-four hours or so, when it was too late to turn back and put her off.

It wasn't that easy. The watch on deck was Chris. The others she might have fooled, but it was unlikely that he would fail to recognize his own clothes. She loitered along the wharf, keeping to the shadows, starting at every movement and staying well away from the men who passed to and fro. As the minutes passed, she grew afraid that she was making herself conspicuous, that she would draw the attention of the second officer just by being there. At the same time, she had to stay close so she could seize any chance offered to go aboard.

This could not go on. They would be leaving soon. Already, there was light gray smoke coming from the stack as the boilers were stoked for a full head of steam.

As she stared at the ship with a frown between her eyes, a young Negro boy of perhaps ten or eleven wandered past where she stood. He was a soft brownish-black, with huge dark eyes and, as he caught her gaze, a melting smile. He was eating a sugar apple, spitting the seeds out on the ground. He had several of the knobby green tropical fruits in a sack over his shoulder.

"Buy a sugar apple, lady," he said, his voice mellow and lilting as he prepared to show his wares.

She had seen him before, playing about the wharf, peddling fruits of one kind or another, jigging to the music of the goombay players for pennies from the sailors, and swimming with several others on the beach west of town. Well known to the crew of the *Lorelei*, he was always certain of a sale to Ramon, whom he addressed simply as "the captain." For reasons best known to his mother, he was called Largo. That he had penetrated her disguise so easily was disturbing, though at any other time his immense tolerance for the odd doings of the white folks might have been amusing. She had no time to dwell on this however.

"If you will do something for me," she said slowly, "I will buy all you have."

The boy played his part well, wandering out to the end of the dock, pretending to slip, flailing about in the water and screaming for help. Chris ran to look, then stripped off his spectacles, peeled off shirt and boots, and went over the side.

Lorna did not hesitate. Taking a firm grip on her straw trunk, she ran for the gangplank, darted it up and across the deck, and flung herself down the companionway. She paused for a moment at the bottom to listen, then moved with swift care to the door of the ladies' cabin. She looked quickly both ways, then turned the knob and swung inside.

She stopped suddenly with a whispered oath that would have been a credit to Frazier, or even Ramon. The room was stacked high with crates and barrels and bundles. There was barely room for her to edge inside enough to close the door. Once it was shut, she was left in darkness, with no idea of what lay in front of her or what she was going to do for three days in a room bulging with merchandise.

She could not stand there. The best thing she could do, she decided finally, would be to find a way to one of the bunks. If she could clear a space to sit or lie down, she would be all right. Leaving her trunk beside the door where she could not lose it in the dark, she set to work.

It was a heavy job, lifting bundles of odd shapes and sizes, setting them aside, piling them one on the other until they reached the low ceiling. With the portholes closed, holding in the heat of the day, it was stifling, too. She was soon streaming with perspiration as she strained, trying to work silently, feeling her way in the blackness. Doubts about the necessity of what she was doing crowded in upon her. She paused once to wipe her face with her sleeve, wondering why she didn't just walk out the door and go to Ramon. She could take him by the collar and talk until he listened to her. But no, he would be so intent on getting her safely off that he would not need her. Setting her jaws, she went doggedly back to her task.

By the time the ship started to move, she had cleared a weaving path around the bales of cloth and barrels of what must undoubtedly be lead, which she could not move. She had found a bunk with its china toilet appointments underneath. Clearing it of boxes, she wound her way back to the door to retrieve her small trunk. She was returning when she felt the ship surge forward, picking up speed. She felt the bundles on her right move, heard a bumping, slithering sound. The cargo was shifting. She had disturbed its placement. She put up an arm to protect her head, taking a quick step forward, but it was too late. The bundles and bales slid, toppled. Something big and heavy hurtled down on her, knocking her to the floor. Her temple struck something sharp, and pain exploded in her head. The darkness rushed in upon her. The thudding, sliding sounds continued for a moment, then all was silent.

When she opened her eyes, it was daylight; she could see it in shafts and splinters of brightness coming through the crates and bundles that covered her. She groaned softly. Her head ached with a dull throb; her body felt like a solid bruise; and so stiff was she from lying in one position on the hard decking that it seemed unlikely she would ever be able to move again.

She did, however, with gritted teeth and slow care. She inched upward, pushing aside a gross of bon-bon boxes, a bale of velvet, and a wooden crate marked "field glasses." As she sat up, she saw towering above her a stack of long wooden boxes, each stenciled with the word "hardware." From their shape, she thought they could only be filled with guns, though there was one that might well hold a field cannon. If those had fallen on her, she would have felt far worse than she did.

Digging her trunk out from under, she took her water from it and drank deep. Putting it back, she dragged herself over the piled merchandise to the bunk. She dropped down on it and struggled out of her jacket. Folding it for a pillow, she lay down with her head upon it, closing her eyes. Within moments, she was asleep.

The next time she woke, she was ravenous and it was dark again. She ate cold roast chicken and bread from her trunk, plus a sugar apple, washing it all down with water. Afterward, she spared a little of her precious liquid to wet a handkerchief and wipe her face, scrubbing at the sore place on her temple to remove the dried blood she felt caked there. Pushing to her feet, she stretched, wincing at the multitude of sore places her movement made known to her. She then made her way to the porthole and unlatched it, pulling it wide.

The night wind was fresh; the sound of the gurgling sea moving past the ship and of the rush of water over the paddle wheels was familiar and welcome. The mist that drifted in at the opening, settling on her lips, had the taste of salt. She steadied herself against the plunging of the ship and breathed deep. She was here. She had not been discovered. Her needs were met. It was going to be all right. It was.

They had made good time, or so it seemed. The days passed quickly between sleeping, reading, staring out the porthole to watch the waves and the streaking silver-winged shapes of flying fish, and thinking; she spent far too much time thinking. The delicious aromas that wafted from the galley at certain hours tantalized her. Now and then, she heard the voices of the men: Ramon, Cupid, Slick, Chris, and others she did not recognize. It had been difficult, once she knew they had passed beyond the Abaco lighthouse, which marked the last island of the Bahamas, past the point of turning back, not to emerge. She did not want her presence, her safety, to influence any decision that Ramon might be forced to make, however, and she was reluctant to relinquish the advantage there might be in surprise.

It was the change in the sound of the engines that warned her they were approaching the mainland. The steady beat that had marked the miles of sea slowed. Sliding from the bunk, she moved to the porthole for the thousandth time. In the distance, through the dimness of the night, she could just make out the white line of breakers that was the North Carolina coast. The hour was near midnight, she thought. Slowly they drew closer. They must be passing through the outer squadron of the blockade, making ready to turn for the run down coast.

Soon now, if she were correct, would be the time of greatest danger from the fox-faced man. Lorna turned from the porthole. Picking up her jacket from the foot of the bunk, patting the derringer that rested in the pocket, she prepared to face it.

The *Lorelei* had swung, moving south, by the time Lorna let herself out of the ladies' cabin. She paused to listen in the passage, straining her eyes to see in the darkness. There was no one moving about in this section. She pulled her cap down closer over her hair and turned toward the companionway.

The wind was fresh, blowing a stiff breeze on the deck. The smell of burning coal and smoke wafted about the ship in the down draft. A score or more of men were on deck. Among them was strung a taut excitement. A few stood around the smoke-stack. One or two were perched on the low housing of the deck cabin, while several others were standing on the steps of the wooden paddle box over the splashing wheels, night glasses trained ahead. There on their port bow was a federal cruiser, some distance away, sailing majestically past with her lights like stars caught in her rigging.

It struck Lorna that, though there was tension and a lively recognition of danger hanging over the ship, there was also con-fidence. It came from the man in command; was fed by the measured tones of his voice, the deliberate orders he gave, his calm control. His men leaped to do his bidding as much out of respect and liking as for the sake of their lucrative berths. Paus-ing to watch as Ramon stood near the wheel, conning the ship through the dangers of the night, she felt such fullness in her heart that it brought tears welling in her throat.

She turned sharply away, searching the dimness for the fox-faced man. She identified him by his scraggly side-whiskers, which flapped about his face in the wind, and by the outline of the small, flat hat he wore. He was standing on the port paddle box, holding to the railing that arched over it. Beside him was a portly man, an Englishman, judging from his accent. He was holding forth in a garrulous whisper, waving an unlighted but well-chewed cigar for emphasis.

"I've hunted tiger in India, ridden in a cavalry charge or two, and been chased by heathen pirates in the Aegean, but never have I come across anything to beat this. What an exhilarating pastime!"

"As you say," the fox-faced man commented in sour tones.

"Who can deny it? Playing cat and mouse with a goodly portion of the federal fleet, all armed to the teeth while we are as defenseless as babes, standing over enough gunpowder to blow us to kingdom come, trying to find the mouth of a small river on a featureless coast in pitch darkness, while daylight threatens to expose us. That's if we don't run aground from keeping too close in to shore. My God, just think of the respon-sibility for the lives in the captain's keeping, to say nothing of the fortune in goods entrusted in his care, I wouldn't have the job, no sir, I would not. I'll warrant there are few who would!"

The fox-faced man grunted. As Lorna drew nearer, mounting the steps, she heard his reply plainly. "There are some," he said, "to whom money means more than life, or death."

The Englishman reared back to give him a stare. "Then I say thank God for them! A pretty pickle you would be in, my good man, if there was no one willing to run the blockade into the Confederate states! The same might be said of the South, if it comes to that."

Lorna, halting behind the pair, felt a real affection for the rather pompous Englishman. This did not change the fact, however, that the fox-faced man was correct. She glanced at him as he fidgeted, holding a cold pipe in one hand, the other clenched on the railings as he stared after the cruiser now disappearing into the darkness. He was clearly impatient of the company of the other man, and that only served to make her think she was right. She edged closer, slipping her hand into her pocket and closing her fingers around the derringer.

They heard distant firing, saw the shimmer of the flashes on the horizon. After a time, it stopped. There was much speculation as to which runner had been the target, but it died away and the night closed in again. They crept onward, with the ship's officers glancing often toward the east, watching for the first light of dawn. The sky in that direction was growing less dark by swift degrees, and still they had not sighted the Big Hill that marked the batteries of Fort Fisher and the entrance to Cape Fear.

The ship appeared like a ghost. One moment there was nothing; and the next, the flagship of the federal fleet lay directly across their path.

"Hard to port!"

The *Lorelei* answered on the instant, and they were steaming east, away from the river and back out into the blockading fleet; away, too, from the shoals. Almost at once, they saw a man-of-war moving toward them. On their present course, it would strike them amidship. The order to turn starboard came clearly, if quietly, and they swung in a slow arc, easing in dead silence on a course that would take them between the two vessels.

Beside her, Lorna saw the fox-faced man dip his hand into his pocket and out again. He put his pipe between his teeth and started to bend his head. Lorna was ready. She brought out her hand and stepped to shove the muzzle of the derringer into the side of the whiskered man.

"Strike the match you have in your hand, sir, and you are dead."

A match in the darkness. The flare of light, small though it was, would have been like a beacon, drawing the fire of the federal ships down upon them. The man cursed and swung, as if he meant to try to disarm her. From the other side came the quiet voice of the second officer. "I wouldn't advise it," Chris said, "unless you would like to give me an excuse to turn you into a sieve."

"You wouldn't risk the noise," the fox-faced man said with a sneer, though he remained still, facing Lorna, with his hands held out away from his body.

"A good point, but it can be remedied," Chris answered. Hard on the words, he raised his hand and struck the man a hard blow with his pistol butt behind the ear. The fox-faced man pitched forward, and Lorna, to prevent the sound of his falling, caught him under the arms, staggering back.

The second officer leaped forward, while the Englishman, staring with dropped jaw, collected himself and reached to grab an arm of the unconscious man. Together they lowered him to the paddle box.

Chris, staring at her across the inert figure as they crouched beside it, said softly, "Lorna?"

"Not now, if you please," she said just as quietly.

It was not Chris who answered. The voice that spoke was deeper, etched with anger for all its low tone. Standing below them on the deck with his legs spread against the rise and fall of the ship and his hands now on his hips, Ramon demanded, "What is the matter now?"

Lorna came slowly to her feet, staring down at him. "I . . . I didn't want to be a distraction."

"And that is why you decked yourself out like a pitchman at a fair?"

"Here, now," Chris protested, turning from eyeing the clothing Lorna had on with puzzled recognition, "that's my best suit."

"Remind me never to ask your advice on my wardrobe," Ramon said in a rude aside before he continued, his black gaze on Lorna. "What in bloody hell are you doing here?"

"I had to come. I didn't think you had listened when I told you about him." She indicated the red-haired man at her feet.

"You were wrong."

"I couldn't know that. You didn't seem to be paying much notice."

"I always notice," he said, his tone harsh.

"Captain, another one!" It was Slick who called, his voice soft but carrying. He had taken Ramon's place beside the helmsman, with the pilot at his side.

Ramon nodded as a blossom of fire suddenly appeared in the night and guns exploded. All around them, men scrambled for cover, falling to the deck. Chris and the Englishman caught the shoulders of the unconscious man and pulled him unceremoniously down the steps of the paddle box, his boots bumping on each, until he was flat on the deck.

Lorna drew a deep breath as Ramon turned back to her. Before he could speak, she said, "I suppose I had better go below."

"Yes."

Still he stood as shells screamed past and a sheet parted, the hemp line cracking, shipping around a spar. He made a movement toward her, and she spun abruptly running lightly down the paddle box steps, coming even with him there upon the deck before slipping past.

"Go to my cabin," he said, his voice grating. "I will join you there shortly."

There were miles of open water and the federal blockading fleet between him and the leisure of a private tête-à-tête. Still, not for a moment did Lorna doubt that he would do exactly as he said. He would come, and there would be, once more, a reckoning.

Chapter 19

The federal gunners could not find the range of the fast-moving blockade runner this time. Their firepower whined around the ship in a brilliant pyrotechnic display, heating the air and plowing the waves, but the *Lorelei* raced on unscathed. Within minutes the booming of the cannons from Fort Fisher was heard, and the federal ships fell back out of range. The surging wash of the sea was left behind as they crossed the bar into Cape Fear and steamed into calm water. A short time later, they dropped anchor opposite Smithville, and all was quiet.

Lorna expected Ramon to appear at any moment. He did not. There was a great deal of activity overhead. The sound of new arrivals, possibly the health inspectors for the quarantine. The light of dawn seeped into the cabin. An hour passed. Then, just as the sun began to rise, the pipes to the engine room squealed and, with a rumble and hiss of steam, they got under way once more.

As the light increased, Lorna looked around her. There was not a great deal more room in Ramon's quarters than there had been in the ladies' cabin. It was stacked with boxes that were wedged in place by barrels. The blue stenciling on the sides was blurred, though she made it out finally. The boxes were filled with medical supplies, with morphine, quinine, calomel, carbolic acid, and with surgical instruments. There were also bolts of white linen to be torn into strips and rolled for bandaging.

She stood frowning, her hand resting on a bolt, her fingers smoothing the sewn cover that kept the linen from being soiled. It was a responsible cargo, one sorely needed, and yet the sight of it sitting there in Ramon's cabin troubled her.

At the click of the door latch, she looked up. Ramon stood in the doorway. He paused a moment, watching her, then stepped inside and closed the door behind him. His voice hard, he said, "It isn't bonnets."

"No," she answered before she could stop herself, "something even more profitable."

"I won't deny it."

"That would be a little ridiculous, wouldn't it?"

"If it irritates you so, I don't know why you insisted on sneaking on board to see it."

His scorn was like a lash. "I didn't come for that, as you well know. I came because I was afraid of what that man was going to do, of what Nate Bacon had paid him to do."

"There was no need."

"So I saw," she snapped, goaded, "though there was nothing to indicate it before."

"You might have realized that I weigh every word you say, and some you leave unsaid." There was a hint of warning in his words, but the anger had faded from his eyes, leaving them dark.

She grew uncomfortable under his gaze. Swinging from him, she lifted a hand to her hair that was coiled around her head, shining pale gold in the dim light. Its smoothness had been disturbed by the removal of her cap, and she tucked in a loose strand. She had taken off her jacket also. The soft linen of the shirt she wore draped over the globes of her breasts, outlining them in a way that made her self-conscious. As she looked, she saw that the thin weave allowed the dark rose of her nipples to show through the cloth. A quick glance at Ramon informed her that he had noticed. His gaze moved downward to the curve of her hips and the tender line of her thighs in the close-fitting trousers. She hardly knew whether to face him or turn her back, and the dilemma brought a flush of annoyance to her cheekbones.

To distract him, she said stiffly, "If my presence is an inconvenience, I apologize."

"Ungracious, *chérie*. The truth is, you think you should be congratulated."

"Not at all." It was difficult to keep from snapping at him as she heard the rise of amused indulgence in his voice.

"Shown my most fervent gratitude then. Shall I do that, *chérie*?"

He moved toward her with controlled grace. In sudden distrust, she took a backward step. "It won't be necessary."

"Oh, but I insist," he murmured. "It's either that or beat you for risking so much for so little reason."

He stretched out his hands to catch her arms. She braced against his chest with her palms. "It seemed important enough to me."

"Why?" he asked, his voice intent. "What difference would it make to you what becomes of the *Lorelei*?"

His touch sent prickles of pleasure racing along her veins. She stared up at him, swallowing on the sudden dryness in her throat, tracing her lips with the tip of her tongue.

"Why?" he insisted, his gaze on her moist mouth.

"For . . . for you. I owe you so much."

"You owe me nothing, you maddening witch, and well you know it. Tell me why you came, or I swear I won't be responsible for what happens."

The bunk was behind her; she could feel its edge against the backs of her knees. "I . . . I was afraid."

"Of what? Did Nate—?"

"No, nothing like that. I was afraid that you—and the others—would be killed, captured."

He paid no attention to her cowardly dragging of his crew into the matter. "Why should it matter?"

As he towered over her, his hands gripping her arms, she was aware of the strength he held in leash, of the smell of the sea that clung to him and his own distinctive male scent. That assault on her senses, as well as his physical coercion, snapped the last of her tenuous control.

"Oh, all right!" she cried, flinging up her arms, trying to break his grasp. "I came because I love you, because I wanted to share whatever happened to you."

He held her easily, staring at her an instant with light flooding into the darkness of his eyes. He drew her into his arms, folding her against him with aching tightness. "Lorna," he whispered, "*Dieu*, but how I have longed to hear you say it."

He made love to her then, slowly and exquisitely, and if she had ever doubted her welcome, there was, when he was done, no possible reason to doubt it longer. It was only later, when she lay drowsy and content, naked in the bunk where he had left her while he tended to the business of docking in Wilmington, that she realized that he had not spoken of his own feelings for her. She had committed herself and she did not regret it. Still, it would have been a thing of wonder if she could have known herself loved in return, instead of being merely the object of his passionate obsession.

The days in port were hectic as Ramon worked like a demon to force the unloading of his cargo and the loading of hogsheads of tobacco and over seven hundred bales of cotton in time to take advantage of the last days of the new moon. He found time, however, to replenish Lorna's wardrobe once more, dispatching the new underclothing, a gown of gray-blue crêpe de chine figured in pink, and a bonnet and shawl to the ship while he was still in town. She half expected to find that he had left out the pantaloons, but, no, he had been most thorough. Discovering this, she did not know whether to be glad or sorry.

The problem of the disposition of the fox-faced man had been easily solved. He had regained consciousness by the time they reached port, had risen from his bed in sick bay, where he had been taken, and vanished down the gangplank. No effort was made to find him. They knew who had paid him for his failed task, and why, but under the circumstances it would be nearly impossible to prove the charge, even if Nate Bacon could be brought up before a magistrate. They had to be satisfied with having foiled his design. Sometimes, however, Lorna caught the flicker of an expression so forbidding on Ramon's features as he spoke of Nate that she was afraid.

By accident or design, she was not certain which, they saw little of the other blockade runners. Peter had gone to Charleston on his run, or so Chris told her, and the others did not intrude. Ramon seemed satisfied to remain in the cabin during the evening, glancing up from the accounts he pored over now and then to smile at her where she lay reading in his bunk.

The medical supplies disappeared from the cabin on the second day. Late that afternoon, Lorna entered to find Ramon on one knee before his trunk, fitting bags of gold from a stack at his feet into it. He hesitated a moment as he saw her in the doorway, then went on with what he was doing. She said nothing, but stepped inside, moving to pick up his jacket from where he had left it on the back of a chair. Smoothing out the collar, she hung it on a peg beside the door where he usually kept it.

He spoke behind her. "Another trip, maybe two, and I'll have enough."

"Is there such a thing?" Her tone was quiet, weary.

"I'm not greedy," he said sharply. "I only want to regain what is mine."

"What if Nate won't sell?"

"Didn't you know? He already has. He liquidated his holdings in Louisiana and turned the Confederate paper into gold. Part of it he used for the blockade steamer he's been fitting out; the rest he intends to bank until the war is over. He thinks he can pick up places like Beau Repose for a few pennies then."

"He's right, isn't he?"

His brows drew together over his eyes. "What are you suggesting?"

"You said the same once, if I remember. I don't think you intend to go back to Beau Repose now, in the middle of the war. You must mean to wait until it's over, too, before you try to repossess your old home."

"Are you saying I'm no better than Nate?" he asked with irritation.

Her gray gaze was clear as she turned to him. "Not exactly, but isn't the principle the same? You will have money, while the people who own the place now will likely have none. You may be able to buy it back, but what then? If the war drags on for much longer, even if the South wins, it will be at a vast cost, one that can only be borne by the people. If we lose, then Confederate scrip will be no more than pieces of paper. The slaves will be taken from us and set free, regardless of our investment in them, and then the tracts of land that represent wealth for so many will be worthless."

"Beau Repose will be mine."

"Yes, but don't you see?" She flung out her hand in the attempt to make him understand what she saw so plainly. "The men who have beggared themselves for the cause will despise you. What good will it do to regain your heritage, if you can't live there in honor and with the respect of your neighbors? Nothing will be the same. Win or lose, nothing will ever be the same."

He placed the last bag of gold in the trunk and let down the lid, then sat back with one arm on his knee. "What am I supposed to do? Buy myself a horse and ride to Richmond to offer my sword to Lee?"

"No! That would be a terrible waste. I never suggested such a thing."

"Then the only other choice is to become an exile."

There was another choice, and they both knew it. It hovered there between them, difficult, dangerous, painfully obvious. Lorna moved with swift steps, going to her knees beside him in a billow of skirts, putting her hand on his arm. "No. I . . . perhaps I exaggerate. If General Jackson could take Washington, capture Lincoln, we might come to some kind of agreement for peace. The fortunes of the Confederacy would be so little damaged that no one would notice, or mind, the gold you have accumulated."

A faint smile touched his mouth. His dark eyes caught and held hers. "What if I said I care not a tinker's damn what people think, or how and when the war ends."

"It would be true only in part," she said with a small shake of her head.

He let out a sound between a sigh and a laugh. "How can you be so sure?"

"You did not resign your commission merely for the sake of the fortune to be made running the blockade, I think, but because you would not fight against your own countrymen. That argues some feeling for the South, and the people who live there."

"You are determined to find my redeeming qualities, aren't you?"

"Since you try to hide them."

"You may be disappointed."

"I doubt that," she said, the warmth of love making her eyes darkest gray.

"If they were not there," he said, "for you I might well pretend to them."

Her smile was tentative, a little strained as she went into his arms. "I'm not certain that isn't what we all do."

Arriving back in Nassau harbor was like coming home. From her place in the prow, Lorna watched the channel narrow between Hog Island and New Providence Island, watched the emerald green palm trees grow larger and the familiar buildings take shape, shining pale gold and pink and white in the diamond-bright light of early afternoon.

The *Lorelei* came in with panache, her few sails spread and thin gray smoke streaming backward with her speed. At a signal, her canvas came down, the engines were stopped, and she glided to a halt in a burst of steam. Lorna turned to smile at Ramon, and he gave her a triumphant grin. In both their minds was the same thought, she knew, of how different was this return from the limping progress of the last one. It occurred to her, then, as it had many times before, how much pride Ramon took in his ship, and with how much affection he used her. She was almost like a living thing, with the shudder and throb of her engines and paddle wheels moving through her timbers like a heartbeat. Lorna felt it herself; how much more must Ramon, who had been with her far longer, be attached to her?

The outward run from Wilmington had been without real incident. There had been a thick fog lying on the water. The spars and rigging of federal ships had twice been sighted above the swirling mist. Still, they made their way through the first squadron with ease, passing near the flagship whose position had been accurately given by the watch at Fort Fisher. Once only had they been seen, and that in the outer cordon of ships. It had been a slow gunboat, little more than a converted river steamer, that had opened fire. Her shells had fallen short, and the *Lorelei* had easily increased the distance between the two vessels until the gunboat had dropped out of sight. Ramon had then ordered the helm put hard over, setting them on a course at right angles to the one they had been following. After keeping to it a few minutes, they had stopped dead in the water. Looking back, they had been able to watch the progress of the next gunboat by the flashes of her guns and the soaring calcium rockets sent up to draw other blockade ships to the area. It was a wonder they had not attracted the attention of the entire fleet with their unrestrained laughter as the gunboat had plowed furiously away from them, firing into the black, fog-muffled night at nothing.

Lorna turned back to survey the ships that sat rocking on the vivid blue and green water of the harbor, bowing to their dancing reflections, which were small underneath them due to the angle of the sun. After the last few weeks, she scarcely needed their painted lettering to identify them, recognizing instead their lines and rigging. There was a new coal barque in, and Peter's *Bonny Girl* was lying alongside, refueling. He had made a swift trip, even though Charleston, where he had been bound, was closer to Nassau by some hundred miles and more than Wilmington. Still, there was shell damage to the ship's bulwarks, indicating something less than an easy run. There were other ships with worse problems in evidence, however. One appeared to have suffered damage below the waterline, for she was lying with her decks nearly awash, while another flew a quarantine flag indicating that there was yellow fever aboard. As the hot, rainy season advanced, they could expect to see more and more of this.

Nate Bacon's blockade runner looked to be ready at last. It rode heavily with its load of cargo, and there was a drift of smoke from her twin stacks, as if she were getting up steam for a run as soon as night fell. That was good; she hoped Nate intended to make the maiden voyage himself.

Her satisfaction vanished as she saw that the ship had been christened in their absence. The sight of the name swirling over the bow in crimson letters on the gray hull sent a chill running along her spine. No frivolous or dashing or grand appellation had he chosen, but one that was grim and, to Lorna, disquieting. He had called his ship *Avenger*.

They were behind the schedule of the ships that had gone to Charleston, but ahead of the others that had made the Wilmington run. They were lucky enough to find a dock waiting, and, after a quick clearance, Ramon ran the ship up to it. Unloading commenced at once, though with more leisure than dispatch in the heat of the day. Ramon was pleased, since he planned a quick turnaround for yet another run.

No matter how she pleaded, Ramon would not agree to her going with him; the danger was just too great. He had not, however, argued with her determination to remain on board while the ship was in port, returning to the hotel only just before she was due to sail again.

The ship had been met by Edward Lansing, who had been in the Bay Street office as they came in. As he and Ramon talked over coffee and brandy, poring over invoices in the cabin, Lorna decided to make a quick trip to the hotel, since she was to be allowed to remain on the ship. She had been an uncomfortably long time in the same clothing yet again, and felt the need of a change, plus sundry other articles she had left behind. More, while in port there was greater need for extra clothing.

Largo, the young black boy who had been of such help to her a few short days before, met her at the gangplank. His eyes were big and bright, his smile proud as he greeted her, took the light-weight trunk she carried, then turned to walk beside her. She congratulated him on the success of his ruse of nearly drowning, asking him what had happened after he had been pulled from the water. He had told the officer he had a cramp in his stomach from eating too many mangoes, he said. Then he had thanked the wet man and run away, leaving him dripping water on the dock. Her praise for his quick wit made him walk taller, and he was pleased to tell her that he thought her much prettier in her women's clothes than as a gentleman. She was a nice, ver' nice, lady, generous and of good judgment, and if she had more jobs to be done, he was her man.

Laughing at his blandishments, which managed to flatter them both, she invited him to come with her and carry her trunk when she returned to the ship. He was so happy to be of further service that he danced along beside her, jabbering every step of the way. It was all too obvious that he knew everything worth knowing about her and her relationship with the captain. He thought her choice of man a wise one but was in complete agreement that a woman's place was to remain on land while a man went to sea. He would own a fishing boat himself one day and come home loaded with the conch and the spiny lobster that he would sell for much, ver' much, money.

So amused by his company was she, that as she turned into Parliament Street for the uphill climb to the hotel, she nearly walked into Nate Bacon. He had been well aware of her approach, for he stood in her path with the cane he carried held across his body in both hands like a staff. Largo saw him first and put a hand on her arm. She looked up and came to an abrupt halt.

"So, you went with Cazenave again," he said, his face as he looked from her to the boy at her side a mask of sardonic contempt.

She threw out her chin. "I did, and we returned safely. Isn't that amazing?"

He did not bother to pretend ignorance of her meaning. He gave a porcine grunt. "I would have been more careful, if I had known you would be on board."

"Since your hireling failed you," she returned, "it is neither here nor there. But were I you, I would have a care for my own safety. Ramon has suffered much at your hands, but his patience is not endless."

"He can prove nothing." Nate's formless upper lip lifted in a sneer.

"Did I mention legal redress? I assure you, that wasn't my meaning at all."

A slight frown passed over his face. "He's too much the gentleman."

"That might have been so at one time, but his calling these days does not encourage the trait. Besides, few gentlemen encourage scoundrels and traitors, or fail to break the backs of the snakes that cross their paths."

"Why you little—" he began.

But she did not stay to listen. Coming down the hill toward her from the direction of the Royal Victoria, was a family group of English visitors out for an evening stroll, one of them pushing an elderly woman in a wheeled chair made of bentwood with padded velvet arms and seat. By stepping smartly, she put the party between her and Nate Bacon and, inclining her head, moved away.

"Ho," Largo said, staring up at her in admiration, "you are one ver' brave lady, too."

She smiled at him but made no answer. She did not feel brave. In truth, the way Nate had looked at her, the covetous, lascivious expression she had seen in his eyes, made her feel ill with unease.

It was later than she intended when she left the hotel for the return to the ship. Being so near the hotel's spacious bathing rooms, she had not been able to resist making use of them and changing into a fresh gown of blue-figured white calico with puff sleeves and a square neckline. Her hair, damp from having the dulling salt spray washed from it, she had coiled at the nape of her neck, meaning to let it down to dry later. With so much time wasted, her packing had been hasty. Still, she had stuffed enough into her straw trunk to make Largo puff and fall behind as she hastened toward the dock.

They had left the hotel gardens and were descending the hill along Parliament Street, where loomed the buildings of government. Lorna moved with a quick step. They had planned a late luncheon because of making port so near the noon hour, and Cupid would be holding the meal for her. She was hungry, for the first time in days. This last trip back to Nassau, she had been bothered by the motion of the vessel in a way she never had before, though the seas had been relatively calm. Doubtless Largo was hungry, too. She would insist that he share their meal; he had waited so patiently for her, and he would, she thought, consider it a treat.

Ahead of them, they could hear the faint sound of raucous music from the grogshops, barrel houses, and brothels along lower Bay Street. It sometimes seemed they never closed; even when the runners were gone, there was always the custom of the stevedores and clerks, the speculators and hangers-on. Now, of course, the runners were coming in again, and their crews would be paid off shortly.

She glanced at the carriage drawn in on the side of the street near the government buildings as she passed it, thinking some official must be working late, but paid no more heed to it than to a thousand others. At the sound of the door opening on the vehicle, she looked back, more to see that Largo did not get in the way with his cumbersome trunk than for any other reason. By the time she saw Nate Bacon jump down, landing heavily on his feet with another man behind him, it was too late.

She whirled, picking up her skirts, but they were upon her. Hard hands caught her arms, wrenching them in their sockets as they twisted them behind her. A gloved fist holding a cloth drenched in some sickening liquid was held over her nose and mouth. She twisted away as she felt herself lifted, crying out, "Largo—the captain!"

But even as she called, she heard the thud as he dropped her trunk, and the patter of his running feet. A man cursed. A groping paw found her breast, squeezed. As she drew in her breath with the excruciating pain, the cloth covered her face once more. She swung dizzily, and at the apex of the arc, fell face downward into soft and suffocating blackness.

She awoke by degrees. She heard the quiet rush of water against the hull of a fast-moving boat, the splashing of paddle wheels and the thump of the beam. She could feel the rise and fall of a ship at sea, a soothing, familiar rhythm. Her nose was assailed by the smell of sweat, however, and of bed linens long unchanged. She was lying facedown on the hard surface of a bunk, with the edge cutting into her shins where her feet dangled over the side. She opened her eyes to darkness, then realized from the slick feel of the lining and the unmistakable odor, that there was a man's jacket thrown over her head.

Remembrance returned in a sickening wave. The urge to fling off the jacket and jump to her feet was nearly overpowering, but the sound of a scuffing footstep held her immobile.

As she lay straining to hear, she discovered something else. When she was placed on the bunk, no attempt had been made to arrange her skirts. Her hoop had been tilted upward so that it collapsed upon her. Now she lay with her gown and petticoats around her waist, the steel of her hoop on a level with her head, and her lower body, clad only in pantaloons, exposed.

The footsteps moved nearer. She heard the whisper of clothing. A hand descended on her thigh, sliding to grasp the roundness of her hip, kneading the flesh with hard, digging fingers.

Lorna sprang up, slinging the jacket from her head, retaining her grasp as she brought it around, so that the sleeve struck Nate Bacon across the face. As she heard his grunt of surprise, she thrust herself to her feet and righted her hoop. Her senses whirled, and darkness rushed in upon her once more. She had to clutch at the foot support of the bunk to steady herself.

"I rather thought," Nate said in rich satisfaction, "that a hand on your backside would bring you around."

"You . . . you are as vile as your son. What have you done to me?"

"Nothing of interest—yet. Merely dosed you with chloroform. Britain's Victoria proved its usefulness in childbed, but the bawdy-house operators of England swear by it to persuade reluctant young women to part with their virtue. I am only following in their footsteps."

"You haven't—?"

"—Ravished you? The idea occurred to me, and I will admit to indulging in certain liberties while you were unconscious, but I prefer that you be awake and fully aware when I finally take you. It is a pleasure you have so long denied me that I intend to make it as painful and humiliating an experience for you as possible."

Her breasts were sore and the lace that edged the neckline of her gown hung in a strip from one shoulder. Where else he might have touched her, she could not tell, but the thought of it made her feel unclean. She turned her head slowly to send him a scathing look. "I would expect no less from you."

"My dear Lorna, you have no idea of what to expect from me, but you will learn. You will learn."

The menace of his tone, the hot look in his eyes as they moved over her, sent an alarm ringing through her brain. She straightened, turning to put her back to the bunk support, collecting her wits with an effort. Weakness threatened to overcome her, but she pushed it from her. She searched for something to say, anything that would deflect him from his purpose. "This ship we are on, I assume it's yours?"

"You assume correctly."

"Is her destination Charleston or Wilmington?"

"Neither."

"Mobile, then."

"No. Nor Galveston."

She sent him a cool stare. "Then we are simply cruising for your enjoyment. An expensive means of abduction, and a dangerous one with these waters swarming with federal frigates, but I suppose it suits your whim."

"Wrong again, my dear girl," he said, his smile expansive.

"Oh?" She lifted a brow. "Do you mean to tell me, or shall I guess again?"

"We are bound for New York."

She froze, her expression incredulous. "New York!"

"Where else should a good, loyal Union man be?"

"A loyal Union man, you? One of the biggest slave owners in the state of Louisiana? It's ludicrous."

"But I'm not a slave owner, you know, not now. I had it from most reliable sources that Lincoln is considering a proclamation freeing the slaves. It will be completely illegal, of course, the equivalent of Davis's declaring that all owners of northern railroad stock must burn their certificates. The purpose, despite the humanitarian ballyhoo, will be to create internal discord and encourage insurrections that will require the Southern armies to turn their attention to the home front. The outcome will be chaos, with men of property finding their land worthless overnight, since there will be no one to work it. Can you blame me for selling my people quickly, before I was caught in that disaster?"

"Since it is you, no."

"Take care, Lorna," he said, his tone hardening. "You will pay for every insult you utter, this I promise."

She gave him a look of cool distaste that made his jaws tighten. "You will feel ridiculous, there in New York, when the South wins."

He turned his head, and, finding a small table behind him, leaned against it with his arms crossed over his chest. He wagged his head from side to side in mock sorrow. "They won't win, you know. They will fight gallantly and die in droves, but in the end they will be defeated. And then I will come back and make the Mississippi River my garden stream, and Louisiana my outhouse."

"Even you aren't that rich," she jibed, her smile making a mockery of his pretensions.

"I will be, when I'm through."

"How? By running the blockade? This ship of yours is so old and slow compared to the *Lorelei* that it waddles; it will never get past the federals to make New York, much less stay the distance for a run."

"I could prove you wrong, but I will forego that pleasure. Once I reach the North, I may send her back to be sold, concentrating on other ways to increase my store of gold. I could sell spoiled pork to the Confederates, for instance; there's already been a fortune or two made in Yankee dollars doing that."

It was common knowledge in Nassau that much of the salt pork that was loaded for the South had come to the islands from the Midwest via Boston harbor. Some even had the stamp of the federal military inspectors still on it. "That," she said lightly, "is an occupation that should suit you admirably, your being so similar in nature to the commodity."

It was a moment before her meaning penetrated, then he came erect and reached out to slap her, a hard blow that brought the taste of blood to her mouth as her head snapped around from its force. She clenched her teeth on the pain, wishing passionately for the derringer left behind in Ramon's cabin, put away in his trunk when she had returned Chris's clothing to him. Failing that, she would have liked to flail at him with teeth and nails, except that she would give him no excuse to touch her.

She turned her head slowly, facing him once more. Her voice was soft when she spoke. "The last time you did that, if you will remember, I stuck a needle in you."

"It's you who will have something stuck in you, and it won't be a needle," he said crudely.

"Since you have been so kind as to warn me, I will do the same. I will retaliate. Believe me."

He laughed, a full-bellied sound. "When I get through with you, you will have more to worry about than some sneaking woman's revenge. I suggest you begin now, by turning your mind to what I plan on doing with you when this voyage is over."

It did not bear thinking of, and she did not intend to try. "I suspect, if I am patient, you will tell me."

He shook his head, his expression obscenely benign. "No. You will decide what will be the outcome. If you are . . . accommodating, if you show a proper eagerness to please in the next week, then I may install you as my mistress and you will discover how generous I can be. If not, then you will still perform according to my desires until I tire of the sport. Afterward, it will be entirely fitting, I think, if I turn you over to the military authorities. You are still wanted as a Confederate courier.''

"How can you know that . . . unless—?''

"Quite right, my dear. It was I who overheard your charming conversation with Sara Morgan. It was I who informed against you.''

"But why?''

"I told you once, I think. You deserved to be punished for what you had done to Franklin, and it pleased me to think of you in a northern jail. At the same time, my passing of the information served to pave my way for a return to the Union. It was a neat arrangement, but a painful decision, since I much preferred to inflict the punishment myself. Your escape was a relief, since you had served my purpose and were still available for my ends.''

His words raised echoes in her mind. Franklin, that night so many months ago, had babbled of punishment, and in his eyes had burned the same avid anticipation. What twisted thing in the minds of both men caused them to find pleasure in the prospect? Was it born in them, or had it been taught in brutal lessons?

"Your son tried to impose his will on me, and he is dead. Doesn't that trouble you?'' The implied threat was weak, but all she had as a defense. The amazing thing was that, for the first time, she could speak of it without the immediate stab of guilt.

"You mean aren't I afraid you will serve me the same? Hardly. Franklin was no match for you in anything save strength. I am.''

It might well be true. He was between her and the door, watching her, parrying her attempts to disturb his equilibrium. Even when he had struck her, he had made no move to encroach further. It was as if he toyed with her, confident of his ability to control her, in no hurry to end her mental torment by physical action. In the meantime, her resistance excited him. The more frantic she became, the more farfetched the defense she drew on, the greater his pleasure would be in subjugating her.

She sent a swift glance around the cabin. It was very like the one on the *Lorelei*, except that it was more cramped, with a single spindly chair at the small table that sat in the corner behind Nate, opposite the bunk. It was also less well kept. Dust and salt grime coated every surface, and the wood table was stained with the grease of former meals.

In an attempt to undermine his confidence, she gave him a scornful glance. "You failed once to take Ramon into account," she said, her smile scathing. "It's a pity you are making the same mistake again."

"Cazenave's ship was just in, low on coal. Even if he could get immediate access to reloading, the delay before he misses you will give me a head start he can't hope to overcome."

"Low his ship might be, but I have little doubt he will gamble on catching you before the store runs out."

"In an ocean thick with federal ships? It would be suicide."

"I doubt he will stop to count the risk. As for when he will learn I have been taken, he will hear it soon enough from Largo."

His loose mouth curled in mocking amusement. "The boy who ran away?"

"It may be he ran to find help."

"A wharf rat like him? He ran to save his skin."

She affected a shrug. "Believe it, if it makes you feel better."

"You think I'm afraid of Cazenave?" he demanded.

"I think it would be wise. I think, were I you, I would be on deck watching my wake to see if his ship was steaming after me."

He gave a short laugh. "Such a dreamer. Well, let me open your eyes."

Catching her wrist with hard, stubby fingers, he dragged her from the cabin and out onto the upper deck. Ignoring the sidelong glances of his officers and crew, he pulled her toward the stern. Lorna saw the quick grins the men exchanged, heard the ribald quips and laughter, and knew instantly what they thought of her. To change their minds, to enlist their aid, would require more time than Nate Bacon would allow her.

At the aft railing, he hauled her up beside him but directed her attention to a gray bulk there, instead of to the water. "Take a look at this," he said. "Damned if I wouldn't just as soon Cazenave did come chasing after you like a hound after a bitch. This beauty would give him a warm welcome in your place."

He reached out to thump the shining metal barrel of a gun. Lorna had never seen one, but she recognized it from descriptions she had heard. It was a long-ranged, rifled Parrott gun. Most commonly used as a bow-chaser by federal ships in pursuit, it was deadly in its accuracy and more dreaded by the blockade runners than a broadside of cannon.

"Why," she said, raising her gaze to his gloating face, "this makes you a pirate."

"By the lights of some. I looked on it as insurance, when I planned on running the ship." He lifted a massive shoulder. "I've never been one to let a little thing like legalities stand in the way when there was something I wanted. In this case, gold."

"But your men will be tarred with the same brush, will have had to pay the supreme penalty, if you are all caught."

"They didn't have to sign on. And, of course, I myself have no intention of sailing in the ship on her runs. I'm not so big a fool."

Compared to this man, Ramon was the soul of honor. She had been wrong to judge Ramon so harshly. At least he had wanted money for a purpose, to regain his heritage, to right a wrong, not just for the power of wealth. "You may have trouble getting rid of it when you sell your ship."

"I doubt that. The North is not so flush with arms that they will turn down such an effective weapon. I shouldn't wonder if I make a profit on it."

"You would sell it to be used against other blockade runners? What a revolting man you are!"

"And what a sharp-tongued bitch you are. For that I think I will have you get down on your knees and . . ." and he continued, in detail, with the punishment he thought suitable for her error. Sick to her soul, she looked away, toward the spreading wake of the ship and the broad expanse of the ocean beyond. He ceased speaking, jerking her around and waving toward where the faint, low-lying mass that was the islands already fell away behind them. "Do I make you ill? Do you long for rescue? Go ahead and look. Look good. Do you see any sign of a ship? Do you see any sign of your lover steaming to save you?"

Her eyes were, perhaps, more used to scanning the wide stretches of water than his, more used to spotting the federal frigates as cries of "Sail ho!" rang from the crow's nest. On board the *Lorelei*, the sighting of a ship was worth fifty dollars to the first man to shout a warning, and it had been a game to while away the long hours, as she tried to see if she could better the men on watch. Now her gaze roved the horizon, straining against the orange glow of the setting sun. Suddenly her vision narrowed. Her hands tightened on the railing.

"Yes," she whispered, then said louder, "Yes!"

Nate seemed to swell. He flung her from him so that she snatched for the railing to keep from falling. He slewed around. His jaws clamped and belligerent, he grabbed for the rail also and spread his legs to keep his balance while he mounted foul oaths. He ground out a final word. "Where?"

She pointed in silent triumph, then stood watching as the sails she had sighted, with the stack pouring smoke between them, came onward, resolving with amazing speed into masts set into the hull of a ship with side-wheels churning in fast pursuit. Largo, she thought in near incoherence, deserved a reward and would have it if she ever returned to Nassau.

Nate swung, shouting to his hired captain for more speed, cursing him for dawdling, before wrenching back around to glare at the chasing ship.

Then as she watched, Lorna felt uneasiness grip her. Minute by minute, she grew more uncertain. Dismay washed over her, and her shoulders sagged. The ship wasn't the *Lorelei*.

She remained resolutely standing, watching the ship rise and fall in the waves. That it was a blockade runner in its paint of gray was plain from the way it kept appearing and disappearing in the shifting light of sunset, but it was not Ramon's ship. She grew afraid that Nate would notice, fearful of what must come when he did. She stared at the fast-closing ship until her eyes burned, her mind blank with disappointment and dread. Then, abruptly, her sight cleared. She knew the ship. It was stupid of her not to have recognized it at once. It was the *Bonny Girl*.

Had Ramon commandeered Peter's ship? Or had the Englishman, perhaps, been present when Largo reached Ramon? Another possibility that occurred to her she banished at once. She refused to think that it might only be a coincidence that had set Peter on a trail behind her, that he might only be starting out on another run. Surely he would have waited for dark before leaving the protection of the island chain? And yet, darkness was so near.

From the corner of her eye, she caught a flash of orange-pink. She turned her head to stare at it. Then, as the *Avenger*'s stern rose higher on the back of a wave, she saw it more plainly: another sail with the light of the setting sun on the canvas. Nate had not seen it as he turned to berate the ship's crew again. It resolved itself into a ship, pale gray, fast, though not closing in as quickly as the *Bonny Girl* had done due to the increasing speed of the *Avenger*.

Nate flung a vicious glance at the first ship, then turned on his heel and stamped off to the wheelhouse, where he consulted with the captain. An order was given, relayed over the ship, and behind Lorna came the thud of fast-moving men. They jostled around her, carrying heavy loads. As she looked around, what she saw made gooseflesh prickle over her scalp. They were making ready to fire the Parrott gun.

The officer in charge stepped before her, executing a sketchy bow. "Could we ask you to please stand aside?"

Lorna hardly noticed his failure to use a courtesy title. She stumbled a little as she moved down the railing. The *Bonny Girl* was coming on with smoke pouring from her stack, unaware of the danger. Soon she would be in range. Peter could not guess the ship he was chasing was armed. If only there was some way she could warn him.

"Steady," she heard the gunnery officer warn. "Wait until she's too close to miss."

Lorna was trembling, the tips of her fingers white where they clutched the railing. For the first time in some minutes, she looked beyond Peter's ship to where the other was growing larger. A small cry escaped her, though it carried more despair than joy. The second ship, gaining by degrees, with black smoke pouring from her stack, indicating its use of some other fuel besides coal, perhaps cotton soaked in turpentine, was close enough to be identified. Steaming in pride and dancing grace, steering down the wake of the *Bonny Girl*, it could be none other than the *Loreilei*.

"Sail away!"

Lorna's head jerked around at the call. She saw the lookout pointing to the west. She swung in that direction, squinting against the flooding light, and saw the new ship. It came straight out of the sunset, with blood-red light behind her, making her sails glow. Huge, armed to the teeth, bearing straight down on them all, it was a federal frigate.

It was as if every man on the three steaming blockade runners were blind to their danger. None of the ships altered course to avoid this new menace. They steamed on, their smoke staining the sky, their paddle wheels spinning, leaving frothing foam on the water turning deepest blue with depth and the twilight. Lorna's heart beat with sickening strokes. She could scarcely breathe. The tension building inside her made her want to scream, to cry, anything to relieve it. She clenched one fist, holding it to the pit of her stomach.

Nate, now grim and silent, came to stand behind her. They leaned on the rail for interminable minutes, watching the racing ships. The *Bonny Girl* drew nearer, and nearer still. Finally, she heard Nate growl under his breath, "Now, damn it, now."

The Parrott gun roared. The shell burst over the other ship. Lorna screamed as she saw splinters fly from the decking and a man tossed from one rail to the other as if he weighed no more than a stuffed toy. Smoke enveloped the ship, and she saw the bow swinging as the helm was put over. The gun crew moved to the rapid fire of orders, and once more the air was blasted by the heat and concussion of the gun. The shot flew wide, skipping across the water like a stone over a mill pond. Smoke drifted, chokingly, over the ship. Again came the order. The Parrott gun, extremely accurate at that range, belched smoke and flame and spiraling shell.

The hit staggered the *Bonny Girl*, catching her nearly amidship. An enormous gash appeared in the ship's side. Smoke boiled, flames leaped, and even from where they stood could be heard the screams of the wounded. Then there came a rumbling like thunder. It grew, spreading in shock waves, rolling over the water. Suddenly the stricken ship exploded, the decks erupting, spewing splinters into the air as it broke apart. Smoke boiled black and acrid into the sky, shot with leaping, soaring flames.

Gunpowder. Peter had already reloaded for his next run, and his cargo had been barrels of gunpowder. Even as the *Avenger* pulled away, they could feel the heat of the fire, were staggered by the surge of the waves from the concussion. Stunned, too shocked to move or make a sound, Lorna watched as the ship began to list, filling with water from the gaping hole in her waist, going down. Behind the *Bonny Girl*, she saw Ramon's ship dropping behind, beginning to circle the doomed vessel even as the hands swarmed to the sides to swing out the boats.

The *Lorelei* was giving up the chase. There were men in the water now, men burned, injured, in danger of drowning. Ramon was going to their aid. In honor, he could do no less.

Chapter 20

The last orange edge of the sun sank into the sea, and the sudden tropical night descended. The burning ship grew smaller and dropped away behind them. Nate and his captain conferred, staring anxiously into the night as the *Avenger* plunged over the waves. With the last of the daylight, however, the federal cruiser had been seen making for the sinking ship and the runner delaying to pick up survivors.

Nate's fears were well-grounded, Lorna felt as she thought of it. For all his bragging about cooperation with the federals, his ship was obviously rigged out as a runner, and an armed one at that. It was probable that a conscientious northern naval commander would blast him from the sea without giving him time to argue his service to the federal cause. True, the crew members stood ready to fly the United States flag, but would the cruiser bother to look for such a thing in the dark; or, seeing it, consider it anything more than a ruse on a ship painted pale gray?

Such thoughts served to occupy her mind, to prevent her from dwelling on what might be taking place with the ships they had left in trouble. Men were dying there in the night and the surging salt waves, men she had known, with whom she had spoken, laughed, danced. Was one of them Peter? Could his quick humor and charm be extinguished so easily? She knew the answer.

It was one that had to be recognized each time a newssheet appeared with lists of casualties printed on its pages.

Above the splash and rush of their progress, she listened for the sound of renewed firing. She scanned the faint line where the ocean met the sky for the flash of guns. Each passing moment of quiet, of darkness, was a boon, one she prayed desperately would continue.

When Nate clamped his fingers on her arm, pulling her from her post at the railing, she fought him. It was blasphemy, a peculiar arrogance, but it seemed in that moment that if she failed to keep watch, to retain her concentration on the safety of the men who had followed her, that they would be left unprotected, exposed to certain death.

Nate ignored her struggles, half-carrying, half-dragging her with him to his cabin. He shoved her inside, then slammed the door upon her. She lunged back at it, beating with her fists on the thick panel, choking with rage and distress. From the other side, even above the noise of her frantic pounding, she heard the oiled snap of the key turning in the lock, shutting her in alone in the dark cabin.

That small sound brought the return of some semblance of sanity, and with it came control. She stepped back, then whirled, moving to the porthole, twisting the latch, flinging the glass open so that she could see and hear.

She was still there some time later when the key rattled once more in the door, signaling Nate's return. He paused in the doorway with a tray in one hand, his attitude wary as he surveyed her position with the help of the light from a dim lantern in the passage. Satisfied, he moved to set the tray, containing what appeared to be ham and eggs, on the small corner table. Keeping an eye on her, he reached up to light the lamp that swung in its gimbals above it, then turned to lock the door again.

Lorna did not move until he came toward her. What was the use, here on this ship out on the seas, surrounded by his men? She stepped aside, holding her skirts from him, but he only closed the porthole and drew the short, black curtains that hung on either side across it to block the light.

"Sit down and eat," he said, his tone derisive. "You're going to need your strength."

"I couldn't."

"Suit yourself."

He swung toward the table and seated himself, pulling the

tray toward him. Lorna watched him fork a bite of ham into his mouth and cut into the fried egg that lay on the single plate the tray contained. The yolk ran yellow-gold, oozing out into the ham grease, and she turned sharply away with nausea rising in her throat.

She could feel his gaze upon her in avid anticipation, whetted, she thought, by the carnage he had witnessed and the danger in which they had stood. She sent a quick glance around the cabin but could see nothing that might serve as a weapon or even as a barricade against him. She thought of Ramon, then wrenched her mind away. She could not depend on him; there was no one she could depend upon except herself.

For a brief moment, she weighed the possibility of acquiescence. It would be less dangerous. Lately, she had begun to suspect she had a special need to take care. She was so often assailed by illness, just as she had been moments before, and there were other signs. It would be natural enough under the circumstances. She had, until now, been able to push aside the idea as a complication it would be best not to face until absolutely necessary. It was necessary now.

But could she bear it? Could she lie and allow Nate Bacon to touch her as Ramon had done? His would be no gentle wooing; of this she was well aware. Could she control her aversion to his cruel caresses? Could she support his brute invasion of her body without going mad with disgust?

"Are you fretting about Cazenave? He was most likely blown to pieces. The sharks will have a feast. They infest these waters, you know, and the smell of blood attracts them like perfume does a man."

Sharks. She had not considered. An instant later, his words struck her.

"You seem to be under a misapprehension," she said, revolving slowly in her wide skirts to give him a twisted smile. "The ship you sank was not the *Lorelei*."

He gave a nod and a grunt. "Oh, I knew, my dear, since the man I hired as captain of this ship pointed it out to me, but I wasn't certain you did."

"I knew," she answered stonily.

"Yes. And you know your lover is being chased over the seas by a federal cruiser while he is burning precious coal he can ill afford, being hurried to his inevitable surrender as he steams farther and farther away from you to escape."

"That is your most fervent hope, at any rate," she returned, her tone tart as a defense against the pain of the picture he presented.

He pointed his fork at her, his voice grating as he spoke. "I've told you before, I'm not afraid of Cazenave."

"No? I'm sure I would be in your place. You cheated his father in a crooked card game in order to get your hands on Beau Repose, then hired men to set upon M'sieur Cazenave as he rode to repay his debt to you. And, when it looked as if he might still find the means to save his son's inheritance, you caused a crevasse that flooded his acres, ruining him, bringing about his death. Ramon knows this, and someday he will see that you pay."

Blood rushed purple to his face as she spoke. "Is that what he told you?"

"Yes." Ramon had made no threats, but it would not hurt if Nate thought he had.

"And you believe him?"

"Why should I not? It makes perfect sense to me, since you used a similar ploy to force my uncle's consent to my marriage to your son. I don't believe Uncle Sylvester would have agreed, if he had not been in debt to you, his wealthy benefactor, and if the warehouse holding the cotton that would have been used to pay you off had not burned."

"An unfortunate accident," Nate sneered. "I did suggest he insure his yield."

She studied him. "I'm sure you did, in such a manner that it would have seemed lacking in spirit, not equal to the proper daring of a southern gentleman, if he had complied. I heard him talking about it once to Aunt Madelyn, you see."

"You judge me harshly," he said, wiping egg from his mouth with the handkerchief he took from his jacket pocket, using it to clean his fingers with fastidious gestures, his eyes shrewd as he watched her.

"What did you expect? I know that of all the things you have done, there is none so despicable as what you did to Franklin. He thought you were bringing home a wife for him, while all the time you were intent on a mistress for yourself. Franklin, your own son, was the biggest dupe of all."

"That's not true! I let him have you."

He threw down the handkerchief, scowling as if her words had pricked him for the first time. His pale blue eyes were as hard as marbles. His silver-brown hair, greasy with pomade, had been loosened from its careful pompadour by the wind, and was falling over his ears.

She laughed, a brittle sound. "So you did, or very nearly. Was I supposed to be so grateful when you took me from him that I would fall into your arms? Your attitude toward me changed a bit when I was found with Ramon, didn't it? You were not going to be satisfied to wait quite so long. How glad I am that I went riding that day, that I met Ramon Cazenave and discovered what love between a man and a woman could be. Otherwise, I would never have known."

He pushed his half-eaten meal back, coming slowly to his feet. "I would have shown you, given you jewels, silks, anything you wanted. I was crazed with wanting you."

"As a possession, the same way you wanted Beau Repose. Like a thief, you went after both in the only way you could ever have them, without thought for the pain you would cause."

"I got them. I had Beau Repose for as long as I wanted the place, and now that I've finally laid hands on you, I'll have you the same way."

He came at her, a satisfied smile on his face, as if he expected her to be mesmerized into allowing him to do with her as he pleased. She evaded him in a whirl of skirts, backing away.

"You won't have me so easily, and even if you do manage it, you will regret it; I will see to that. I have a score to settle with you for passing on the movements of the *Lorelei*, and my own. I haven't forgotten, nor will I forget anything you may add to it."

He gave a rough laugh, moving after her. "I'm trembling."

"You may be stronger now, but you have to sleep. That's something you should remember."

"Serve me any tricks, and you'll regret it."

"Not if you are dead."

"You think I don't know Franklin's death was an accident? You couldn't do it again, not in cold blood."

She gave him a chill smile. "It's your life you are wagering on the possibility."

"But I know just how to handle bitches like you." He lunged, snatching her arm, jerking her forward so she stumbled against him. She twisted her shoulder, bending to free one hand. Immediately, she struck for his eyes, clawing at his face as he snapped his head backward. Her nails ripped down his cheek and into the skin of his neck. He slapped her, a vicious blow, and she knotted her fist, bringing it up from below her waist to slam it into his mouth. She had the pleasure of seeing his lips split against his teeth before he threw her from him. Her elbow cracked against the end of the bunk, numbing her right arm to the finger tips as she fell across the mattress.

He flung himself after her. She bounced up, dragging at the pillow with her good left hand, sending it flying into his face. He swept it aside, plunging after her. His fingers closed on the puffed sleeve of her gown, ripping it from the shoulder. She tore free, dancing away from him, massaging her arm. Brushing the wall beside the door, she set Nate's extra coat and shirts to swaying. She grabbed them, slinging them at him even as she whirled along the wall in desperate haste. He ducked under the coat and snatched a shirt from his head, diving after her. His groping hands caught at her waist, sliding along her abdomen, and he cursed the corset that kept his fingers from finding purchase on her tightly laced rib cage.

The edge of his dinner tray on the small table slid as her skirts struck it. Instantly she picked it up, hurling it at him. He snarled another oath, throwing up an arm. The plate it still held struck his wrist, flipping up, and egg yolk splattered his face. He swabbed at it in disbelief, then with a roar, he charged her.

She caught the back of the light chair, flinging it in his path. As he swerved around it, cursing as a leg scraped his shin, she tipped the table and shoved it in front of him. He leaped over it and she tried to dodge around him, but the upturned table and the bulk of his body left no room. He snaked an arm around her waist, throwing her back, and she was trapped in the corner.

She twisted and turned, writhing in his grasp. He caught her free wrist, turning it so that agony gripped her. Her hair, piled so loosely on her head, shifted, sliding from its pins that rained upon the floor. She kicked at him, and he pushed her against the wall, driving her into it with the weight of his body so that the lamp above them shuddered in its gimbals, casting swaying shadows on the cabin walls. The breath was driven from her lungs, and with a sharp, gasping cry, she was still.

Taking instant advantage of that moment of weakness, he fastened his fingers on the neckline of her gown, pulling it off her shoulders, dragging it lower to expose the full globes of her breasts. He bent his head to fasten his hot mouth on one peak, setting his teeth into the vibrant softness. Her cry of pain, the arching of her back as she tried to avoid him, seemed to excite him. He pressed closer so that the hard thrust of his desire for her could be felt through his trousers, through the layers of her skirts and hooped crinoline, which he compressed against the wall.

''I'll have you here, standing up, like the street-corner whore you are,'' he muttered.

He leaned to drag at her skirts, lifting the bottom steel band of her hoop to her waist so that her petticoats bunched upward, feeling under it for the tape of her pantaloons. She pushed at him, but his weight pinned her in place. On her breasts was a smear of blood from his cut lip, and the sight of it sent a shiver of revulsion over her. That shudder was followed by another, and another. She shoved harder, and he slammed his shoulder into her chest. Again the lamp above them trembled.

Her eyes dark with anguish, she looked up. If she stretched out her right hand, she could reach the base of the lamp. It was brass, and heavy, and she was not sure she could hold it with her numb fingers, but she had to try. He was tugging at the waist of her pantaloons, clawing at the soft skin of her abdomen as he tried to break the tapes that were cutting into her. Soon they must give, and then . . .

She reached up, touched the lamp base. It wobbled in the gimbals. She pushed upward, trying to get a grip on the smooth metal. The lamp tilted, burning brighter behind its glass globe. She pushed again, lunging a little even as she spared a glance for Nate, who was grunting, tearing at her clothing.

The lamp came free. She juggled for purchase but could not find it. It revolved, falling, pouring hot oil. She turned her head swiftly, shrinking to one side. The oil splashed down, hitting Nate's shoulder, soaking in. He jerked up with a strangled cry. His elbow struck the lamp, deflecting its course. It described an arc in the air, streaming oil, and hurtled against the edge of the bunk with a crash and the tinkling of shattered glass. Oil spewed over the bed coverings before the lamp thudded to the floor. For an instant it lay with the wick fluttering in the broken mess, long enough for Nate to slew around. Then, with a violent wafting of hot air, the room erupted in flames.

Nate staggered back, beating at the shoulder of his jacket where blue fire danced. This did no good, and he dragged it off, flinging it from him. With his eyes darting from his head, he ran to pick up the pillow from the floor and began to beat at the leaping flames that threatened to consume the cabin.

Lorna jerked up her gown to cover herself, then swooped down on the burning jacket on the floor. She coughed with the smoke that boiled around her as she slapped at the flames, pushing her hand into first one pocket and then the other. At last she came up with what she sought: the key. Scrambling to her feet, she took the long step that would bring her to the door, trying to ram the key into the lock. Her hands shook so that she could not make it work for a long instant; then it was in, turning. She snatched open the heavy panel, half-falling out into the passage.

Only then did she realize how airless the cabin had become in that short time, and how hot. Behind her, with the fresh influx of air, the fire burned brighter, higher. A man appeared down the companionway ahead of her. He took one look, then began to yell.

A large portion of the crew of the *Avenger* pounded down from above, pushing past her on the run. She huddled against the wall of the passage as they crowded inside the cabin. Then she picked up her skirts and made for the companionway.

On deck the wind was cool, the night wide and dark. She stood at the railing, breathing deep, trying to stop the trembling that shook her. She could not. Faintly the shouts of the men as they fought the fire came to her. The ship was old and the timbers dry. Apparently the flames had gotten more of a foothold than she had thought possible in so short a time. Smoke poured up out of the companionway, and there was a red glow just beyond where she stood, where the porthole of that cabin opened. As she swung to stare, she saw fire licking up toward the deck from that direction.

The captain of the ship ran past her with a frowning stare, on his way below. A short time later, Nate came staggering up, coughing, his face black and his hair singed away on one side of his head. He leaned on the rail, then with a grunted curse bent down to pull a large piece of glass from the soft leather side of his boot. By that time, smoke was puffing from the hatches of the ship, forming a haze over the deck, and the flames were leaping higher than the railing in tongues of yellow and orange and red. Lorna moved farther along, putting more distance between her and Nate, moving, too, from the heat of the fire.

There were shouts as the crew came flooding up from the cabin, choking, coughing, their eyes streaming from the smoke so that wet tracks were formed in the soot on their faces. They were followed by the captain, who flung himself on deck with a handkerchief over his face and looked around for Nate. Seeing him at the rail some distance down from Lorna, he stepped up to him.

"The fire can't be controlled. We will have to abandon ship."

Nate swung to stare at him. "You yellow-livered bastard! Why don't you try saving her?"

"It's impossible. She's an old ship, dry as tinder, with new pitch to catch like kerosene. She'll be gone in half an hour." The captain's face was stern, and it was plain he had no use for the man who paid his salary. "Of course, if *you* would like to try?"

Nate cursed again, then turned toward Lorna. Pushing from the railing, he bore down on her. "It's your fault, you bitch! You're the one who caused it."

The captain caught him by the shoulder. "There's no time for that. We have to get the boats away."

"Then do it and be damned!" Nate shrugged from the man's grasp, never taking his pale, red-rimmed eyes from Lorna.

She watched him move toward her, knowing that there was more than lust and a need to make her feel his power over her in his move toward her now. He was congealed in rage, swollen with masculine affront that she not only had dared defy him but had succeeded, that she had caused him pain and brought down on him the scorn of his captain and crew, to say nothing of his investment in gold going up with the ship. Every urge for vengeance he had felt was magnified a hundred times, and he meant her to feel it.

"You bitch, you beautiful, twice-damned bitch," he said with grating bitterness.

She would not run from him, would not retreat so much as a step. She stared at him with the red light of the fire reflecting on her pale face and the wind catching the shimmering cascade of her wild silk hair, blowing it around her. Her gray eyes were still and deep, and the trembling of her hands had died away, leaving her calm. She did not move, showed no fear, even when she saw the piece of glass he still held in his hand, a blackened shard from the broken lamp chimney.

Behind him, on the far side of the ship, there was a shout and familiar clatter of metal on wood. They were lowering the lifeboats. Time was growing short, the air that blew along the deck scorching as the fire roared. Nate did not appear to notice. He moved closer, his formless lips thinning, drawing back in a smile, his gaze fixed on the pure line of her cheek where it curved, blending over her jawbone into the tender arch of her neck. He shifted the sliver of glass in his hand, holding it with a razor-sharp corner exposed.

In the sooty darkness of his face could be seen the dark red streaks of the gouges her nails had made, the split of his lip. His shirt was charred where his jacket had burned, and through the black-edged rent could be seen the angry welts of burns. His victory was not bloodless. And if he did not kill her, she would see that he suffered more. She would not be cowed, would not take fear for a master. She would not.

She lifted her chin in silent defiance. His eyes narrowed. He raised his hand. Beyond them there were shouts and outcries. Bound in their own private drama, they did not see.

There came the whipping whir of a rope through the air, a loosened sheet from the rigging. The shadow of a man flitted over the deck, engulfed in swirls of smoke, tinged with the red of flame. The air near Lorna shifted, rushing, and Ramon released the rope that carried him, landing lightly on his feet in front of her.

But Nate had at the last moment looked up, had reached to grab Lorna around the waist, wrenching her against him. Now he stood with the glass shard held against the pulse that beat in her throat.

Ramon balanced with his hands held out, going perfectly still. He wore no shirt to hinder his movements, only his uniform trousers tucked into his boots, and his gold-fringed sash at his waist to hold the pistol thrust into it and the sword that hung at his side. His face was stern and his dark eyes steely as he gave Lorna a brief, all-encompassing glance. Then he turned his concentration on the man who held her.

"One move," Nate said, "and I'll slit her throat."

"If you so much as scratch her, you won't draw another breath," Ramon answered, his voice soft. Behind him, his crew had boarded, crossing from the *Lorelei* that was held to the side of the *Avenger* by grappling irons. They met no resistance, however, but were, rather, cheered as saviors.

"Oh, I'll do more than that, later, but first I want that pistol you have there."

"No," Lorna breathed, and felt the glass press into her neck, though it did not quite break the skin.

"Keep quiet, bitch."

Ramon's face hardened. "I don't care for your tone, or your words."

Another time, it might have been laughable. Ramon was fluently and colorfully profane on occasion, though never with Nate Bacon's considered vulgarity. It was the practice as it applied to her that he objected to at that moment. Or was it, possibly, only a play for time.

"That's too bad, isn't it?" Nate sneered, enjoying the feel of having the upper hand.

"Is it?" Ramon, his eyes intent, straightened slowly and took the pistol from his sash.

"Reverse it," Nate grated.

Ramon complied, holding the barrel of the gun in the palm of his hand.

Nate could not hold the glass and grasp the pistol both. He realized it at the same time Lorna did. He hesitated. She braced herself. He dropped the glass, snatching for the pistol, and in that moment she shoved, jostling him with her shoulder. At that exact instant, Ramon deliberately let the pistol fall.

Nate gave Lorna a hard shove, diving at the same time for the weapon. Ramon made no effort to retrieve it. Instead, there was the singing rasp of his sword as he drew it from its scabbard. At the same time, he stepped in front of Lorna, shielding her where she had stumbled to her knees against the railing.

Nate came up crouching over the pistol. His pale eyes widened, protruding as he saw the sword, but he was beyond rational thought or action. He drew back the hammer and jerked the trigger of the firearm. It went off at point-blank range, belching fire and smoke, the report deafening. Lorna screamed. Ramon flung himself to one side, dropping into a swordsman's stance. He did not pause. His face a grim mask, he stepped to drive the yard of shining steel he held deep into Nate's chest.

Nate's hands came up to clutch at the blade. He choked on a froth of red, then fell back as Ramon withdrew the sword. The ship plunged into a wave and rose as if shaking herself, with saltwater hissing against the fire that ate at her entrails. Nate rolled beneath the railing. Ramon grabbed for him, but he went over, falling limp in death into the sea.

Lorna drew a sobbing breath. Ramon thrust his blade into its sheath and swung to her, drawing her to her feet and gathering her close, pressing her face into his shoulder.

"I'm sorry," he said, his voice low, "sorry you had to see that."

She shook her head. "No," then said again more fiercely, "No!" She was glad that she had seen, glad that she could be certain, once and for all, that the thing between herself and Nate Bacon was over.

His arms tightened, a safe haven enclosing her, infinitely comforting. A moment later, he stirred. "You are all right, *chérie*?"

She straightened, giving a small nod, the smile that she summoned tremulous. "Now I am."

"We lost the federal cruiser, but the fire will be a beacon for miles, drawing it the same way it drew us, though by God's fortune and Frazier's guesswork we were closer. We have to go."

"Yes, of course."

He stared down at her an instant longer, as if assessing her strength and her well-being for himself, independent of her assurances. Then a smile curved the firm lines of his mouth, lighting the darkness of his eyes. Inclining his head in what might have been a sign of admiration, he took her hand in his strong grasp and turned toward where the *Lorelei* waited.

But he was right. Before they were a cable's length away from the doomed ship, the cruiser hove in sight out of the west, her running lights glimmering across the waves. Ramon had conferred with Frazier, and they were running south-southwest on a course that would take them back toward safety in the neutral waters of the islands. The captain of the federal ship was able to see them plainly in the flaring light of the burning hulk behind them. The vessel swung to cut them off.

Ramon and Slick, standing near the wheel, watched the cruiser maneuver. "We could swing north as soon as we're out of sight," the lanky north Louisianian said.

"How is the coal holding out?"

It was Chris, who stood with Lorna and Frazier on the other side of the helmsman, who spoke. "The stokers are scraping the bottom and there's maybe a few hundred cotton bales left. They are standing by with the axes to start on the woodwork again."

Two hundred bales of cotton left out of over seven hundred

fifty, figured at a little over one hundred fifty dollars each, meant that they had sent nearly a hundred thousand dollars' worth of cotton up in smoke out the stack and would be forced to send the rest. If Ramon had counted the cost, or even considered it, there was no sign.

Ramon shook his head, his eyes dark with swift and cogent calculation. "We can't risk it."

"We can outrun 'em, head for one of the harbors of the northeast cays," Frazier suggested.

"It will be not quite dawn when we reach there," Ramon said, his comment an indication that the alternative had been in his mind already. "Can you find your way in over the reef?"

"I can find a place to drop anchor in a hurricane at midnight, if you can get her that far."

Ramon nodded. "Full speed ahead, then."

As the order was whistled down the pipe to the engine room, Lorna heard Slick say under his breath, "And the devil take the hindmost."

Nothing impeded the progress of the cruiser, however. It inched closer and closer. There came the moment when the captain thought it possible to intercept, so near did their courses run. The federal ship yawed to fire a broadside. The cannonade boomed, blossoming in lurid colors along the side of the great ship, creating a vast, rolling explosion of sound that struck them even as the shells fell in their wake. The time the cruiser lost in coming about again gave them an advantage, one they did not fail to take. They sped on with a short lead, racing into the darkness of the night.

The chase was enjoined. It was as if the captain of the federal ship divined their intent, for though he could not see them as they ran with all lights extinguished, he hung behind them like a terrier after a rat. The winking glow of his own lamps, seen as they bobbed up and down on the waves, now vanishing, now appearing again, was a mocking threat. More threatening still was the firefly gleam of sparks that flew from the cruiser's stack, indicating a plentiful supply of rough but adequate coal.

It was the shortest night ever seen in the world, and the clearest dawn. Not even a smudge of cloud hung in the sky, and the face of the water sparkled, so free of mist or fog that visibility extended unimpaired to the distant horizon. What could not be seen was the island.

Lorna stood on the crowded deck, staring ahead in the limpid light of early morning, feeling its freshness on her face. Around them, some of the men from the other ships sat or lay rolled in blankets, though most stood watching, waiting. That the freedom of every man—and woman—on board was at stake was something well understood. Moreover, if they received heavy fire from the cruiser, with so many packed onto their ship, there were bound to be severe losses.

During the night, Lorna had worked in the sick bay with Chris, treating burns and cuts, removing splinters, helping to bandage more difficult wounds. As she worked, she asked again and again for news of Peter from the survivors from the *Bonny Girl*, but no one had seen him, none could remember where he had been when the gunpowder had ignited. Most of those who had been physically able to make their presence in the water known had been picked up, she discovered, but there had been little time to spend searching. The safety of Ramon's own men had decreed that he abandon the area before the threat of the cruiser. There was only one thing that was certain. Peter was not aboard the *Lorelei*.

She tried not to dwell on it but could not prevent her mind from returning again and again to the image of the *Bonny Girl* being blown apart, of men being tossed about on her decks like rag dolls. Death in these times was not an awesome thing, but mean and ugly and quickly over.

"Land! Land, three points on the port bow!"

Lorna jerked from her reverie at the railing, moving toward the wheel. Ramon had donned a shirt during the night and removed his sword, so that he looked more like a captain again, instead of a pirate. He and Slick were talking in low tones, throwing a glance now and then at the cruiser still trailing them. Following their example, she frowned. The federal ship seemed closer than when last she had noticed. On closer inspection, she saw that the great vessel had more sail set, to catch the freshening breeze of dawn. With her quarry now in sight, she was straining to close the gap between them, and she was gaining.

Lorna turned as Chris, his movements quick, came up, sketching a quick salute as he stopped before Ramon.

"What did you find?"

"They have picked up the last bits of the coal with a tweezer and used a pan for the dust. The cotton is gone, also the tobacco, right up in smoke. The same for the chairs, the tables, the paddle boxes, and most of the deck cabin. The question is, do you want to cut down the masts or hang sails on them?''

If they burned the masts, they might steam a little longer; if they set sails, they could move a knot or so faster as the power of the wind was added to that of the engines. The canvas they could carry on their shortened masts could not equal that of the cruiser, however. It was a difficult decision.

''Frazier,'' Ramon said, swinging to face the islander. ''How far?''

''An hour to the reef, two hours to a harbor,'' came the laconic reply.

He glanced at Slick. ''Speed?''

''At the last cast of the line, eleven knots. Not bad, considering what we're burning. I figure theirs at maybe thirteen. And I'd say she was six, maybe seven miles off.''

''If we could lighten—'' Frazier began, then stopped abruptly. The cotton and turpentine and tobacco they had carried had been turned to fuel, and they were fast ridding themselves of the bulk of the ship itself. The only thing left to jettison was the human cargo, the extra men they had picked up from the two other ships, and that was clearly impossible. The islander made a face. ''If we had just a little more coal, we could turn west, make the cruiser come about and lose the wind.''

''If,'' Slick said. ''Anyway, she'd dog our track all the way to the Florida coast.''

Chris cleared his throat. ''If we stay close in to shore for that last hour, they won't be able to follow.''

It made sense, Lorna thought; the cruiser was a deeper-draft vessel and would not be able to follow into the shallows where they could go. But even before Chris finished speaking, Slick was shaking his head. ''If she catches up, she can stand out and pound the hell out of us.''

That Ramon had taken these factors into account on the instant was obvious, for he seemed hardly to be listening. The bronze planes of his face were set in grim lines as he stared out at the federal cruiser. Finally he turned. With a brief glance at Slick, he said, ''Set sails.''

The executive officer looked at Chris, then exchanged a glance with Frazier. The man at the helm stared at Ramon in surprise. It was not the order they had expected. It would be a close race, but at the rate they were traveling, it would take the cruiser some three hours to overtake them, and they had to try to reach port.

If, on the other hand, they ran out of fuel before they could make harbor, the federal vessel would have all eternity to overhaul them.

Chris saw it first. ''I get it; we gain an extra knot or two for time, because the cruiser doesn't have to be right on our stern to start firing.''

None of it mattered, neither their calculations and browfurrowing worries nor the haste with which a pair of flying jibs, a main sail, foresail, and an aft spanker were hauled up and set to catch the wind. A half hour after they were in place, a call came up from the engine room. The boilers were overheating from flues full of soot and cotton lint. If they didn't blow off steam for a little cleaning, they would explode.

The hiss of the steam escaping, the white cloud of it boiling into the sky while the federal ship bore down upon them, was enough to make the strongest heart quail. There was, at least, no reason to wince now at the noise. By the time the gauges showed a safe margin and they were able to get under way again, the cruiser was so close they could see without glasses the preparations for firing.

They ran on. The spume flew from the uncovered paddle wheels, wetting the decks. The deck cabin structure was chopped away and carried below. The crew with their axes set to work on the bulwarks, and it was a toss-up among the men on deck whether they were glad to be rid of the potential for splinters or felt exposed without the protection from grapeshot. The relative merits would be tested, it seemed, for the cruiser was slowly gaining.

Ahead of them, the water turned aquamarine, shading with the swirls of cream that was the living reef beneath the surface, deepening to turquoise, lightening to jade. They bore down on the land, coming close enough to see the outlines of the palms, the stunted pines, and the sharp formations of coral along the shore. There was an island close at hand now on their left, neutral territory, safety, and yet because there was no channel to reach it, no harbor, it was of no more protection than if it had been a thousand miles away.

With narrowed eyes, Ramon watched the cruiser, swung to stare ahead, ran his gaze along the sand beaches that stretched beyond the reef. He stood straight, his feet slightly apart and his hands on his hips, balancing easily with the ship's movement. The wind ruffled the dark waves of his hair and flapped the fullness of his shirt. He glanced back at the cruiser again, then looked away to where the sun was just breaking above the horizon. It was a long time before he moved; then he turned to the helmsman.

"I'll take her," he said.

The seaman stepped aside, relinquishing his post. Ramon wrapped his strong hands around the spokes, holding them with care, as he might the hands of a woman. His chest filled, then he relaxed, letting his breath out slowly. He turned his head then, releasing his left hand, holding it out to Lorna where she stood watching him. She smiled, a puzzled expression in her gray eyes, but she went to him. Then, setting his jaw, he spun the wheel hard over, turning the bow of the *Lorelei* straight in toward the beach shining in the light of the rising sun, and toward the jagged teeth of the reef. Above them, her canvas spilled the wind and flapped dismally as the crew jumped to furl it.

"Captain!" Slick called, his voice sharp. "What are you doing?"

"Prepare to lower the boats," was his answer.

The first officer tried again. "Captain—"

"The risk is too great. That isn't a gunboat out there, it's a man-of-war, two thousand tons, armed to the teeth, and manned by the best gunnery officers in the United States Navy. She'll blast us to bits if we don't surrender when the order comes, and there's every reason to think it will do just that in the next half hour. Surrender would mean prison, maybe hanging, for all of us, but most of all for Lorna. Taking their fire would be suicide. The only safe place is on Bahamas soil, and that is over the reef."

"It'll tear the bottom out of her."

Ramon's tone was quiet, final, as he answered, "Don't you think I know that?"

Lorna stood in the circle of his arm, her body stiff with dismay as understanding of the sacrifice he was making struck deep into her mind. She swung, staring up at him. "Ramon, no! Not for me."

His eyes were dark, unfathomable, as he replied, "For none other, ever."

"You can't," she whispered.

"It's all I can do."

This was why women should not go to sea; not because they were useless or got in the way, or even because they were unlucky, but because their very presence, without their will or desire, affected the judgments men were forced to make. If she had not been there, she knew beyond doubting, Ramon would have taken his chances, wagering his life and that of every other man aboard against the prospect of finding a safe harbor for his ship. If she had not been there, the *Bonny Girl* would be floating still and Peter and all the others still alive. If she had not been there, Ramon and the *Lorelei* would be in Nassau. Or would they? It was difficult to find an end to this line of thought. She could not blame herself for her presence; she had been brought to sea this time against her will. Still, it was, perhaps, something within herself that had caused Nate Bacon to want her so desperately that he had abducted her.

Now they could hear the sound of the surf, see its boiling wash ahead of them. Around them men yelled and shouted and worked to free the boats from their davits, making ready to lower them the moment the ship grounded. Unconsciously, Lorna braced, felt Ramon's arm tightened at her waist. Behind them came the boom of a single salvo from the cruiser. It passed harmlessly behind them, as if in warning.

The *Lorelei* plunged on, dipping her bow into the waves so that the salt mist sprayed upward and caught the sun rays, forming a rainbow in the droplets. Mutilated but buoyant, valiant in her pride, she rode with Ramon's firm hands on the wheel holding her steady. The shouting stopped. The men fell silent. The engine beat as regularly as a giant heart, and the rushing slap of the paddle wheels was her pulse. The water ahead turned from blue to green to palest aquamarine. They saw the reef, like ancient bones, under the waves.

She struck with a ragged scream of rending iron plates and tearing timbers. She jarred to a bumping, grinding halt. Lorna was set, expecting it, still, she was thrown forward against the wheel that spun crazily as Ramon released it to catch her. The hard strength of his arms cushioned her for a moment. Then she was swept from him, pushed into a boat that was being lowered into the sea. As it pulled away from the ship, she looked back, dragging the hair out of her eyes to watch as the ship settled, listing.

The next few moments were a confusion of events. The boat she was on landed and started back to the ship to bring more of the men to shore. The federal cruiser bore down on them, opening fire on the ship as if it meant to batter the crippled vessel to pieces. Then as another boat loaded with men started toward shore, the man-of-war peppered it with grape. Seeing the men fall, the gunsmoke on the water; hearing the cries and groans, the explosions, the whining shot; knowing that Ramon was still on the *Lorelei* and would not leave until every man was gone, Lorna went mad. She stood on the beach with the bright sun of morning glittering on the wild silk of her hair that whipped around her. Her skirts billowing, she shook her fist at the cruiser, screaming her outrage.

The cruiser ceased firing, drawing in closer still until the officers could be seen standing at the railing, talking among themselves, pointing at and watching the dying ship as if in a theater box. All except the captain, who stood alone with the sun touching his epaulettes and the insignia on his cap. He removed the latter to bare his head, waving it above his brown hair, which had the sheen of mahogany.

It was Lieutenant Donavan—or perhaps it was Captain Donavan now?—the naval officer who had searched her aboard the *Lorelei* so many weeks before, the man she had persuaded Ramon to allow to escape. How strange were the fortunes of war, to bring him there in a position of command at just this moment. She had saved him from a war prison, and now he was returning the favor by holding his fire. He had not forgotten.

Lorna put up her hand slowly, hesitantly, to return his salute. He turned to rap out an order, the sound of his voice traveling clearly across the water. The federal cruiser began to sheer away. He looked back, waved again, then turned away with a great show of discipline.

Before the cruiser was a half mile out to sea, a sailing sloop appeared, ghosting from around a headland as if out of nowhere. Moving silently but with purpose, it headed toward the ship on the reef.

"Wreckers," a man said in tones of disgust from somewhere behind her.

"Wreckers," Frazier said, moving to her side, his voice filled with interest and curiosity.

They were right, both of them, and Lorna had reason to be grateful for it within the hour. It was the wreckers who brought the last load of men from the ship before going back to see what could be salvaged. Among them was Ramon, standing tall and straight, laughing with an equally tall blonde-haired man with a rakish white bandage around his head as they jumped into the crystal water at the edge of the beach and waded onto the sand. She started forward with tears rising to her eyes. When she had dashed them away, the two were still there. Ramon and Peter, striding toward her with their arms over each other's shoulders.

The Englishman caught her in a bear hug, whirling her around as she laughed and cried and tried to ask him when? How? The wreckers had made it a habit of late to stay near the entrance to the North West Channel, since it was there that the cruisers liked to lie in wait for the ships that had to take that route toward the east coast of the United States. They had seen the fire of the *Bonny Girl* and, when the excitement died away, slipped out to investigate. They had found him unconscious, lashed to a hatch cover by his belt. He could just remember taking care of that last detail before he passed out, but had no memory at all of the rescue. His bump on the head was nothing; he would live to watch a certain young Lansing sister grow up, and do his bit in the process. He was looking forward to the results, and even the proceedings, though as things were at the present, he didn't intend to rush it.

Safe.

Before, endless ages ago before she had left New Orleans, it had been a word; now it was a concept rich with meaning. Lorna sat on a rock beneath the shade of a sea grape tree and let the peace of it seep into her. From her vantage point, she could watch as the sunburned islanders stripped the ship and ferried the salvage to the shore. They worked fast, for, bit by bit, what was left of the beautiful blockade vessel was settling. Like dying gasps, the air was driven from her shattered portholes. Water reached her hot boilers, her fireboxes, bringing forth a hissing and bubbling as steam rose into the air. Men yelled, diving for the water as the hulk shifted and sank below the decks in the warm turquoise sea. Lorna closed her eyes tightly then, not wanting to see the last of the drowning masts and crosstrees as the waves lapped around them. When she opened them again, the water was smooth and empty. The *Lorelei* was gone, but they were all safe.

Peter came to sit with her awhile, lounging on the rock shelf beside her with his forearm propped on his thigh. He had been there when the ship went down, a silent companion. They had watched without speaking as Ramon, standing on the shore, had turned and walked away then, the angles and hollows of his face prominent as he disappeared among the pines and sea grapes of the limestone cay.

"What will you do now?" Lorna asked, for something to say to distract them both.

"The same, I suppose."

"You will find another ship?"

"The firm will supply one."

"What of . . . Ramon?"

He shook his head. "Who can say? You'll have to ask him, but he has been dissatisfied with running lately, I think."

She did not comment, picking up a twig and brushing at the sand that had lodged in a crevice of the rock. "Has it been decided how we are going to get back to Nassau?"

"The wreckers have agreed to take a few of us to the big town, for a price. I'll be going to see about transport for my crew. I expect Ramon will do the same, and you, of course. There's food and water for the men, enough to last a day or two, and that's all the time it should take to send after them."

There was a long pause. He looked from the beach where the wreckers were stowing goods to where she sat beside him. His gaze rested on the pure oval of her face, and, as she turned her head to face him, his dark blue gaze was clouded.

"Are you happy, Lorna?"

Surprisingly, considering the unsettled state of things around her and of her future, she was. She told him so.

"I'm glad. It helps."

"But . . . what of Charlotte?" She could not forebear to ask. It wasn't vulgar curiosity that moved her, or a probing into his feelings, but rather the need of reassurance that she had not hurt him.

"She's spoiled and willful, but there's something worthwhile underneath. I like the way she says what she thinks, and the way she is developing in looks, and . . . I'm trying."

"I'm sorry."

"Save your sympathy," he said, his smile twisted as he squinted out over the bright water. "I've broken a few hearts in my time, and I suppose I deserve to know how it feels. No doubt it will be the making of me. I'm sure Charlotte would say so, if she knew."

"Do you think she doesn't?"

He gave a light shrug. "Probably. If not, I think I'll tell her, see what she says, see if she's capable of compassion, or maybe even jealousy. Should be interesting.''

"You are not to experiment with her," she said severely. "She's too young for that."

He sent her a glance that brimmed with amusement, though it faded slowly as he looked at her. "Dear Lorna, you would tell me if you weren't really happy, wouldn't you?" He frowned, saying quickly, "No. Don't answer."

He left her soon after that. She saw him talking to the captain of the wrecker's sloop. Within an hour, he had boarded her and was gone.

Ramon did not go. Charging Peter with a message to Edward Lansing concerning arrangements for their deliverance, he stayed behind with his crew, and Lorna with him. He spent the remainder of the day organizing the men into parties to erect shelters of poles and palm thatch, dig a latrine, gather wood for fires, and to scout for fresh water, ripe fruit, and the possibility of wild boar from swine whose ancestors might have been left on the cay by buccaneers a hundred and fifty years before. His time away from the beach, in the wooded interior of the cay, or small island, had been used to good purpose, for he knew the size of it and the most likely locations for the things they would find useful.

He had also discovered a cave well away from the others. Dry, clean, not large, it had a tiny spring just below it where the limestone formation jutted out over the sloping shelf of the beach, much like the caves on New Providence, except on a smaller scale. He showed his find to Lorna early in the afternoon. She was delighted at his thoughtfulness, and the prospect of a measure of privacy away from the watching eyes of over three score of men. Toward evening, she returned with a pair of blankets from the store left behind, a tin cup to drink from, and a length of cloth for sketchy bathing. She spent a domestic hour seeing as best she could to their comfort.

The day came to an end. They feasted on roast pork, beans, hard tack, mangoes, and to drink, lemonade improved by the addition of a goodly portion of rum. It was served up by Cupid and eaten in the rose-pink glow of sunset. Lorna and Ramon ate with the others, but as the talk grew louder and more raucous, he picked up his guitar that had been brought ashore from his cabin, and led her away to their blanket-lined bower.

The trade winds blew gently over the island. The waves sighed onto the sand. A gibbous moon rose, shining over the moving sea, gleaming on their faces so they seemed pale. There wasn't room to stand in the low cave; they sat in the entrance, leaning against the sides of the opening. Ramon's guitar lay across his lap and he brushed his thumb over the strings, picking out a soft melody as they stared out over the water.

It was the first time they had been alone to talk since she had been taken from Nassau. There was so much Lorna wanted to know, to say, but she could not find a place to start. She shifted, glancing at him.

"Are you comfortable?" he asked, his voice warm in the growing darkness.

"Yes. Very. I . . . was just wondering, since you managed to save your guitar, if you also salvaged your gold."

"Part of it. It was in my trunk, and I was there to protect it with pistol in hand; otherwise the wreckers would have claimed it. As it was, because I couldn't get to shore without their help, I divided it with them for carting it in for me."

"I suppose Nate's hoard is at the bottom of the sea."

A quirk of a brow indicated that it was the first time he had considered the matter. "I guess so."

She took a deep breath. "I'm sorry about the *Lorelei*."

He sent her a brief smile across the space that separated them. "According to the ancient legends, Lorelei was a siren singing on a rock who lured sailors to shipwreck on the reef. Maybe she is where she was meant to to be."

His tone was fanciful, not meant to be taken seriously, a cover, she thought, for his loss. "You can replace her."

"There is no need. I won't be running the blockade again."

She turned her head sharply, trying to see his expression. "What?"

"I've been thinking of applying for rank in the Confederate navy. There's this urge I've had for some time to shoot at Yankees, instead of being shot at. This has helped make up my mind."

"You . . . you mean to sign on to command a commerce raider." Her tone was flat. It was not a question.

"I thought you would be pleased," he said, his tone pensive.

"It will be so dangerous." She turned again to look out over the sea, the sea that would take him away from her.

"It's something worth doing."

"You will be leaving Nassau."

"But I will be able to make the port often, as such things go."

"I would almost rather you replaced your ship."

"Why, *chérie*? You are my Lorelei." As she swung to stare at him, he went on hurriedly, "No, no, don't look so. I speak not of destruction but of living. I meant only that you are a part of me, the echo of my heartbeat, the sweet breath I draw, the quiet song that haunts my dreams, my companion I love immeasurably more than any soulless ship that ever came under my hands."

For a moment she could not speak, then she whispered, "You love me?"

He put the guitar aside and came to kneel beside her in a single fluid movement, taking her forearms in his strong grasp. "How could you doubt it, when I have told you so a hundred times, in a hundred ways."

"You said I was an obsession; you never spoke of love."

"Then let me speak of it now. You are the compass that directs me and the lodestar that will draw me home. I see your face in the storm and hear your voice in the wind. The love I feel for you defies the puny disputes of men and will endure to make an endless future. I want you as my wife, to know you are waiting for me, to know that I can find sweet solace in your arms, to feel that the blessed joy I find in you I can return, and the love, always."

"Oh, Ramon," she whispered.

She was in his arms then, and their lips were clinging as they strained together, seeking blindly the human closeness that banishes the visions of horror wars bring; attempting, in full knowledge of the impossibility, to stave off the 'morrow; finding an affirmation of life in the warmth of the desire that raced in their veins. She said again, with passion and laughing surrender in her voice, "Oh, Ramon."

"You will, won't you, marry me, that is?"

He did love her. Hadn't he proven it by following after her in the teeth of the northern navy, by destroying his ship for the sake of her safety? "If you want me."

"I want you," he said, a throbbing note in his deep tones. "And will you stay in the house I will build for you in Nassau, and wait for me?"

"Until the war is over?"

"Until the war is over," he agreed. "There will be gold

enough to maintain the household, and as for the rest, it will be put in your name, in case—''

She touched her fingers to his lips quickly. ''No, don't say it.''

''No. I will leave the gold for you then, to do with as you will, to aid the South or not.''

''I will keep it for you. For Beau Repose. Afterward.''

His hold tightened. ''We will return there. No matter what happens. With Bacon gone, there is no one to press the murder charge. Your tale of an accident will be readily believed, when witnesses to Franklin's character are brought forward. That's if there is anyone who will remember the incident or, remembering, care to see it opened again after the passage of a year, or even two, and everything that may have happened in that time.''

''You think that's possible?'' she asked, her voice low.

''I know it. We will live at Beau Repose, in the old house, and I will see you at the foot of my table dressed in silk, with camellias in your hair, and with our children lining the board between us. Later we will retire to the back bedchamber, and I will make love to you before the fire, on a cotton bale we have grown—''

She bit her lip, wrenching her mind from the enthralling picture he painted, saying quietly, ''You may see a child of ours sooner than that, while we are in Nassau.''

''What? *Chérie!*''

She heard the shock, and then the glad triumph in his voice, and she sighed, resting her forehead against his chin, aware of the release of a deeply held terror.

''Lorna?'' he said anxiously. ''Are you all right? You took no injury last night? I could murder Bacon with my bare hands for the peril to which he exposed you!''

''You did that—almost.''

''Yes,'' he answered, satisfaction rich and hard in his tone. ''Yes. Come now and lie down. You must be weary. You should rest.''

She allowed him to draw her down on the blankets beside him with her head resting on his broad shoulder. Quietly they lay. She could feel the steady and strong beat of his heart, the gentle touch of his fingers as he smoothed the hair back from her face.

It was going to be all right. They would share their lives, she and Ramon. He would care for her, and she for him. She would depend on him, and he on her. She would not give up her sewing of shirts, and might well expand the undertaking in his absences. He would not mind that, she thought, and it would be independence enough. In all other things, she wanted to be a part of him, to have him become a part of her. Loving would be a puny thing if such closeness were not a part of it.

In the sweet silence of her contentment, a thought came to her.

"Ramon?"

"Yes, *mon coeur*?"

"It was you in the garden, playing for me, wasn't it?"

"Was it?"

There was a sound of teasing amusement in his voice that sent peculiar vibrations along her spine, radiating to the center of her body. "I know it was."

"Do you?" He played with a satin strand of her hair, letting it drift from his fingers over her breast, following its length along the soft contour as he smoothed it again.

"I think it was," she answered, the words catching in her throat.

"Shall I play for you, *chérie*, so that you can see?"

"No," she whispered, lifting her hand to his face, turning, drawing his lips down to her softly parted mouth. "Not . . . not now."

Author's Note

The problems, dangers, and thrills of running the blockade during the early years of the Civil War are depicted as accurately in *Surrender in Moonlight* as the research materials available a hundred and twenty years later will allow. The attitudes and atmospheres described are as true to the times as I can make them. All characters in the book are fictional, with the exception of those famous figures mentioned in passing that will be obvious to all: Captain, later Admiral, David Farragut, the conqueror of New Orleans; the Confederate spy Elizabeth Greenhow; Confederate General Jackson; and Union Generals Butler, Banks, Fremont, and Shields. However, many of the fictional characters are partially based on fact. There was, for instance, no small number of naval officers from the South, with academy backgrounds and service records similar to Ramon's, who resigned their commissions to command blockade runners and, later, commerce raiders for the Confederate navy. Several English naval officers on furlough, like Peter, ran the blockade for the sake of experience under battle conditions, afterward gaining fame and rank in the service of England. The "conchs" of the Bahama Islands, on whom Frazier was based, were superlative seamen with intimate knowledge of the channels and reefs, and served the Confederacy well during this period. Elizabeth Greenhow, on her release from prison, made a highly successful diplomatic journey to London and Paris in 1863, much

like that ascribed to Sara Morgan, though, while returning
through the blockade with dispatches for President Davis, she
lost her life when the runner she was on ran aground.

The Royal Victoria Hotel was an actual hostelry and served
its allotted part. A magnificent building in its day, it is now
falling into ruin, with the verandas gone, the stucco disintegrating, the windows boarded up, and a strong smell of stray cats
in the rooms that are littered with falling plaster. Because of its
place in the history of Nassau, it deserves restoration before it's
too late. But its gardens are still there to be enjoyed, the old
trees grown enormous, with houseplant ivies such as *scindapsus
aureus* and *syngonium* strangling their trunks and branches, and
tropical fruits lying ripe on the ground. There, also, is the balcony in the ancient silk cotton tree, though rebuilt with a
wrought-iron railing.

I wish to acknowledge my great indebtedness in the prepa-
ration of this book to Faye Hood, Jane Stone, and the staff of
the Jackson Paris Library in Jonesboro, Louisiana, for their aid
in finding, ordering, and photocopying material from far-flung
sources for me, and for their infinite patience with my requests,
phone calls, and laxity in returning books. Thanks also to John
MacPherson of J. B. Armstrong News Agency, Winston-Salem,
North Carolina, for providing maps and information on the port
of Wilmington and the Cape Fear River; and to Joy Dean of the
Nassau Public Library, Nassau, Bahamas, for her cheerful and
competent aid in finding and photocopying information for me
on a sultry August afternoon.

Many sources were consulted for background, foremost
among them being *Running the Blockade, A Personal Narrative
of Adventures, Risks, and Escapes During the American Civil
War* by Thomas E. Taylor, and also *Blockade Runners of the
Confederacy* by Hamilton Cochran, *The Blockade Runners* by
Dave Horner, *Harper's Pictorial History of the Civil War*, and
Louisiana, A Narrative History by Edwin Adams Davis, plus
other general histories, social histories, fashion tomes, flora and
fauna guides, and atlases too numerous to mention. For the
section of the book set in Nassau, *Historic Nassau* by Gail Saunders and Donald Cartwright was invaluable in setting the scene,
interpreting the history, and understanding the architectural
make-up of the city. I am extremely grateful for further research
by Gail Saunders, archivist for the Bahamas archives, to clear
up several troublesome points; and to Donald Cartwright for

taking the time from his busy architectural practice to give me his informed opinion on a number of questions. To him, too, I would like to express my appreciation for his part in saving the old Royal Victoria Hotel, without which it would not have been still standing for my inspection. Also consulted for this section were *The Story of the Bahamas* by Paul Albury and the *Bahamas Handbook*, edited by S. P. Dupuch and Benson McDermott.

Among the many articles in periodicals that provided special knowledge and insight were "Cotton, Cotton, Everywhere: Running the Blockade Through Nassau" by John and Linda Pelzer, from *Civil War Times Illustrated*, and "The Royal Victoria of Long Ago" from *Nassau Magazine*, the issue of March 1939.

Finally, a word of loving appreciation to my husband, Jerry, for bearing me company on my journeys, for holding my handbag, guidebooks, and packages while I took pictures and scribbled notes, for sitting protective and patient in the hot sun while I tried to summon old shades in the garden of a derelict hotel, for accepting scant meals and distracted conversation, for helping decipher the terminology of steamships and sailing, and unravel such "knotty" problems as whether one ship steaming a certain distance behind another would be able to overtake the first that was within a given distance of port—and most of all for the encouragement and understanding that marks him as that epitome of romance, a southern gentleman.

Jennifer Blake
Sweet Brier
Quitman, Louisiana

About the Author

Jennifer Blake was born near Goldonna, Louisiana, in her grandparents' 120-year-old hand-built cottage. It was her grandmother, a local midwife, who delivered her. She grew up on an eighty-acre farm in the rolling hills of north Louisiana and got married at the age of fifteen. Five years and three children later, she had become a voracious reader, consuming seven or eight books a week. Disillusioned with the book she was reading, she set out to write one of her own. It was a Gothic—SECRET OF MIRROR HOUSE—and Fawcett was the publisher. Since that time she has written thirty-two books, with more than nine million copies in print, and has become one of the bestselling romance authors of our time. Her recent Fawcett books are ROYAL PASSION, PRISONER OF DESIRE, SOUTHERN RAPTURE, and LOUISIANA DAWN. The author and her husband live in their house in Quitman, Louisiana—styled after old Southern planters' cottages.